Bloom's Major Literary Characters

King Arthur
George F. Babbitt
Elizabeth Bennet
Leopold Bloom
Sir John Falstaff
Jay Gatsby
Hamlet
Raskolnikov and Svidrigailov

Bloom's Major Literary Characters

King Arthur

Edited and with an introduction by
Harold Bloom
Sterling Professor of the Humanities
Yale University

CHELSEA HOUSE
PUBLISHERS
A Haights Cross Communications ✦ Company
Philadelphia

©2004 by Chelsea House Publishers, a subsidiary of
Haights Cross Communications.

A Haights Cross Communications ⫛ Company

Introduction © 2004 by Harold Bloom.

Printed and bound in the United States of America.

10 9 8 7 6 5 4 3 2 1

Library of Congress Cataloging-in-Publication Data

King Arthur / edited and with an introduction by Harold Bloom.
        p. cm — (Bloom's Major Literary Characters)
Includes bibliographical references (p.   ) and index.
    ISBN 0-7910-7670-9 (HC)   0-7910-7980-5 (PB)
    1. Arthurian romances—Adaptations—History and criticism. 2.
Tennyson, Alfred Tennyson, Baron, 1809–1892. Idylls of the king. 3.
Malory, Thomas, Sir, 15th cent. Morte d'Arthur. 4. Arthurian romances-
-History and criticism. 5. English literature—History and criticism.
6. Knights and knighthood in literature. 7. Kings and rulers in
literature. 8. Britons in literature. 9. Arthur, King. I. Bloom,
Harold. II. Title. III. Series: Major literature characters.
    PR149.A79K56 2003
    820.9'351—dc21

                                                          2003014155

Contributing editor: David Rasnake

Cover design by Keith Trego

Cover: © SETBOUN/CORBIS

Layout by EJB Publishing Services

Chelsea House Publishers
1974 Sproul Road, Suite 400
Broomall, PA 19008-0914

www.chelseahouse.com

Contents

HAROLD BLOOM

The Analysis of Character

"Character," according to our dictionaries, still has as a primary meaning a graphic symbol, such as a letter of the alphabet. This meaning reflects the word's apparent origin in the ancient Greek character, a sharp stylus. *Character* also meant the mark of the stylus' incisions. Recent fashions in literary criticism have reduced "character" in literature to a matter of marks upon a page. But our word "character" also has a very different meaning, matching that of the ancient Greek *ēthos*, "habitual way of life." Shall we say then that literary character is an imitation of human character, or is it just a grouping of marks? The issue is between a critic like Dr. Samuel Johnson, for whom words were as much like people as like things, and a critic like the late Roland Barthes, who told us that "the fact can only exist linguistically, as a term of discourse." Who is closer to our experience of reading literature, Johnson or Barthes? What difference does it make, if we side with one critic rather than the other?

Barthes is famous, like Foucault and other recent French theorists, for having added to Nietzsche's proclamation of the death of God a subsidiary demise, that of the literary author. If there are no authors, then there are no fictional personages, presumably because literature does not refer to a world outside language. Words indeed necessarily refer to other words in the first place, but the impact of words ultimately is drawn from a universe of fact. Stories, poems, and plays are recognizable as such because they are human utterances within traditions of utterances, and traditions, by achieving authority, become a kind of fact, or at least the sense of a fact. Our sense that literary characters, within the context of a fictive cosmos, indeed are fictional personages is also a kind of fact. The meaning and value of every character in a successful work of literary representation depend upon our ideas of persons in the factual reality of our lives.

Literary character is always an invention, and inventions generally are indebted to prior inventions. Shakespeare is the inventor of literary character as we know it; he reformed the universal human expectations for the verbal imitation of personality, and the reformation appears now to be permanent and uncannily inevitable. Remarkable as the Bible and Homer are at representing personages, their characters are relatively unchanging. They age within their stories, but their habitual modes of being do not develop. Jacob and Achilles unfold before us, but without metamorphoses. Lear and Macbeth, Hamlet and Othello severely modify themselves not only by their actions, but by their utterances, and most of all through *overhearing themselves*, whether they speak to themselves or to others. Pondering what they themselves have said, they will to change, and actually do change, sometimes extravagantly yet always persuasively. Or else they suffer change, without willing it, but in reaction not so much to their language as to their relation to that language.

I do not think it useful to say that Shakespeare successfully imitated elements in our characters. Rather, it could be argued that he compelled aspects of character to appear that previously were concealed, or not available to representation. This is not to say that Shakespeare is God, but to remind us that language is not God either. The mimesis of character in Shakespeare's dramas now seems to us normative, and indeed became the accepted mode almost immediately, as Ben Jonson shrewdly and somewhat grudgingly implied. And yet, Shakespearean representation has surprisingly little in common with the imitation of reality in Jonson or in Christopher Marlowe. The origins of Shakespeare's originality in the portrayal of men and women are to be found in the *Canterbury Tales* of Geoffrey Chaucer, insofar as they can be located anywhere before Shakespeare himself, Chaucer's savage and superb Pardoner overhears his own tale-telling, as well as his mocking rehearsal of his own spiel, and through this overhearing he is emboldened to forget himself, and enthusiastically urges all his fellow-pilgrims to come forward to be fleeced by him. His self-awareness, and apocalyptically rancid sense of spiritual fall, are preludes to the even grander abysses of the perverted will in Iago and in Edmund. What might be called the character trait of a negative charisma may be Chaucer's invention, but came to its perfection in Shakespearean mimesis.

The analysis of character is as much Shakespeare's invention as the representation of character is, since Iago and Edmund are adepts at analyzing both themselves and their victims. Hamlet, whose overwhelming charisma has many negative components, is certainly the most comprehensive of all literary characters, and so necessarily prophesies the labyrinthine complexities of the will in Iago and Edmund. Charisma, according to Max Weber, its first codifier, is primarily a natural endowment, and implies a primordial and idiosyncratic power over nature, and so finally over death. Hamlet's uncanniness is at its most suggestive in the scene of his long dying, where the audience, through the mediation of Horatio, itself is compelled to meditate upon suicide, if only because outliving the prince of Denmark scarcely seems an option.

Shakespearean representation has usurped not only our sense of literary character, but our sense of ourselves as characters, with Hamlet playing the part of the largest of these usurpations. Insofar as we have an idea of human disinterestedness, we tend to derive it from the Hamlet of Act V, whose quietism has about it a ghostly authority. Oscar Wilde, in his profound and profoundly witty dialogue, "The Decay of Lying," expressed a permanent insight when he insisted that art shaped every era, far more than any age formed art. Life imitates art, we imitate Shakespeare, because without Shakespeare we would perish for lack of images. Wilde's grandest audacity demystifies Shakespearean mimesis with a Shakespearean vivaciousness: "This unfortunate aphorism about art holding the mirror up to Nature is deliberately said by Hamlet in order to convince the bystanders of his absolute insanity in all art-matters." Of *Hamlet*'s influence upon the ages Wilde remarked that: "The world has grown sad because a puppet was once melancholy." "Puppet" is Wilde's own deconstruction, a brilliant reminder that Shakespeare's artistry of illusion has so mastered reality as to have changed reality, evidently forever.

The analysis of character, as a critical pursuit, seems to me as much a Shakespearean invention as literary character was, since much of what we know about how to analyze character necessarily follows Shakespearean procedures. His hero-villains, from Richard III through Iago, Edmund, and Macbeth, are shrewd and endless questers into their own self-motivations. If we could bear to see Hamlet, in his unwearied negations, as another hero-villain, then we would judge him the supreme analyst of the darker recalcitrances in the selfhood. Freud followed the pre-Socratic Empedocles, in arguing that character is fate, a frightening doctrine that maintains the fear that there are no accidents, that overdetermination rules us all of our lives. Hamlet assumes the same, yet adds to this argument the terrible passivity he manifests in Act V. Throughout Shakespeare's tragedies, the most interesting personages seem doom-eager, reminding us again that a Shakespearean reading of Freud would be more illuminating than a Freudian exegesis of

Shakespeare. We learn more when we discover Hamlet in the Freudian Death Drive, than when we read *Beyond the Pleasure Principle* into *Hamlet*.

In Shakespearean comedy, character achieves its true literary apotheosis, which is the representation of the inner freedom that can be created by great wit alone. Rosalind and Falstaff, perhaps alone among Shakespeare's personages, match Hamlet in wit, though hardly in the metaphysics of consciousness. Whether in the comic or the modern mode, Shakespeare has set the standard of measurement in the balance between character and passion.

In Shakespeare the self is more dramatized than theatricalized, which is why a Shakespearean reading of Freud works out so well. Character-formation after the passing of the Oedipal stage takes the place of fetishistic fragmentings of the self. Critics who now call literary character into question, and who proclaim also the death of the author, invariably also regard all notions, literary and human, of a stable character as being mere reductions of deeper pre-Oedipal desires. It becomes clear that the fortunes of literary character rise and fall with the prestige of normative conceptions of the ego. Shakespeare's Iago, who wars against being, may be the first deconstructionist of the self, with his proclamation of "I am not what I am." This constitutes the necessary prologue to any view that would regard a fixed ego as a virtual abnormality. But deconstructions of the self are no more modern than Modernism is. Like literary modernism, the decentered ego came out of the Hellenistic culture of ancient Alexandria. The Gnostic heretics believed that the psyche, like the body, was a fallen entity, mechanically fashioned by the Demiurge or false creator. They held however that each of us possessed also a spark or pneuma, which was a fragment of the original Abyss or true, alien God. The soul or psyche within every one of us was thus at war with the self or pneuma, and only that sparklike self could be saved.

Shakespeare, following after Chaucer in this respect, was the first and remains still the greatest master of representing character both as a stable soul and a wavering self. There is a substance that endures in Shakespeare's figures, and there is also a quicksilver rendition of the unsettling sparks. Racine and Tolstoy, Balzac and Dickens, follow in Shakespeare's wake by giving us some sense of pre-Oedipal sparks or drives, and considerably more sense of post-Oedipal character and personality, stabilizations or sublimations of the fetish-seeking drives. Critics like Leo Bersani and René Girard argue eloquently against our taking this mimesis as the only proper work of literature. I would suggest that strong fictions of the self, from the Bible through Samuel Beckett, necessarily participate in both modes, the sublimation of desire, and the persistence of a primordial desire. The mystery of Hamlet or of Lear is intimately invested in the tangled mixture of the two modes of representation.

Psychic mobility is proposed by Bersani as the ideal to which deconstructions of the literary self may yet guide us. The ideal has its pathos, but the realities of literary representation seem to me very different, perhaps destructively so. When a novelist like D. H. Lawrence sought to reduce his characters to Eros and the Death Drive, he still had to persuade us of his authority at mimesis by lavishing upon the figures of *The Rainbow* and *Women in Love* all of the vivid stigmata of normative personality. Birkin and Ursula may represent antithetical and uncanny drives, but they develop and change as characters pondering their own pronouncements and reactions to self and others. The cost of a non-Shakespearean representation is enormous. Pynchon, in *The Crying of Lot 49* and *Gravity's Rainbow*, evades the burden of the normative by resorting to something like Christopher Marlowe's art of caricature in *The Jew of Malta*. Marlowe's Barabas is a marvelous rhetorician, yet he is a cartoon alongside the troublingly equivocal Shylock. Pynchon's personages are deliberate cartoons also, as flat as comic strips. Marlowe's achievement, and Pynchon's, are beyond dispute, yet they are like the prelude and the postlude to Shakespearean reality. They do not wish to engage with our hunger for the empirical world and so they enter the problematic cosmos of literary fantasy.

No writer, not even Shakespeare or Proust, alters the available stock that we agree to call reality, but Shakespeare, more than any other, does show us how much of reality we could encounter if only we retained adequate desire. The strong literary representation of character is already an analysis of character, and is part of the healing work of a literary culture, which implicitly seeks to cure violence through a normative mimesis of ego, *as if it were stable*, whether in actuality it is or is not. I do not believe that this is a social quest taken on by literary culture, but rather that we confront here the aesthetic essence of what makes a culture *literary*, rather than metaphysical or ethical or religious. A culture becomes literary when its conceptual modes have failed it, which means when religion, philosophy, and science have begun to lose their authority. If they cannot heal violence, then literature attempts to do so, which may be only a turning inside out of the critical arguments of Girard and Bersani.

I conclude by offering a particular instance or special case as a paradigm for the healing enterprise that is at once the representation and the analysis of literary character. Let us call it the aesthetics of being outraged, or rather of successfully representing the state of being outraged. W. C. Fields was one modern master of such representation, and Nathanael West was another, as was Faulkner before him. Here also the greatest master remains Shakespeare, whose Macbeth, himself a bloody outrage, yet retains our imaginative sympathy precisely because he grows increasingly outraged as he experiences the equivocation of the fiend that lies like truth. The double-natured promises and the prophecies of the weird sisters finally induce in Macbeth an apocalyptic version of the stage actor's anxiety at missing cues, the horror of a phantasmagoric stage fright of missing one's time, of always reacting too late. Macbeth, a veritable monster of solipsistic inwardness but no intellectual, counters his dilemma by fresh murders, that prolong him in time yet provoke him only to a perpetually freshened sense of being outraged, as all his expectations become still worse confounded. We are moved by Macbeth, however estrangedly, because his terrible inwardness is a paradigm for our own solipsism, but also because none of us can resist a strong and successful representation of the human in a state of being outraged.

The ultimate outrage is the necessity of dying, an outrage concealed in a multitude of masks, including the tyrannical ambitions of Macbeth. I suspect that our outrage at being outraged is the most difficult of all our affects for us to represent to ourselves, which is why we are so inclined to imaginative sympathy for a character who strongly conveys that affect to us. The Shrike of West's *Miss Lonelyhearts* or Faulkner's Joe Christmas of *Light in August* are crucial modern instances, but such figures can be located in many other works, since the ability to represent this extreme emotion is one of the tests that strong writers are driven to set for themselves.

However a reader seeks to reduce literary character to a question of marks on a page, she will come at last to the impasse constituted by the thought of death, her death, and before that to all the stations of being outraged that memorialize her own drive towards death. In reading, she quests for evidences that are strong representations, whether of her desire or her despair. Such questings constitute the necessary basis for the analysis of literary character, an enterprise that always will survive every vagary of critical fashion.

Editor's Note

My Introduction, while touching upon Malory and T.H. White, primarily interprets and admires Alfred Lord Tennyson's early and magnificent *Morte d'Arthur* (1833–34).

Celia Morris, tracking from Malory to Tennyson, finds a descending music in Tennyson's *Idylls of the King*, while Stephen F. Lappert discovers a hint of Arthurian survival in the ambiguous narrative of the king's death.

Malory's *Le Morte Darthur*, for John Michael Walsh, centers upon Agravain's Iago-like plot, after which Elliot L. Gilbert brilliantly judges the Arthur of Tennyson's *Idylls* as evolving into a kind of "female king."

John D. Rosenberg selects the death of Arthur in the *Idylls* as the poem's "generative moment," while Mark Allen carries us from Malory through T.H. White so as to identify Arthur's image with the idea of kingship.

E. Kay Harris finds in Malory a labyrinth of legal interpretation, employed by Arthur and his knights in order to sentence Guinevere and Lancelot for their supposed treason by adultery.

The Arthurian legend is expounded by Geoffrey Ashe, who returns us to its origins, after which Joseph D. Parry looks more closely at the "textual life" of Malory's book.

Tennyson's *Idylls* return in Clinton Machann's exploration of the poem's manliness while Alan Lupack concludes this volume with a useful overview of T.H. White's *The Once and Future King*.

HAROLD BLOOM

Introduction

1

Sir Thomas Malory (1410–1474) wrote the larger portion of his superb romance, which we call *Morte Darthur*, in prison. However Malory died, out of prison or in durance, it seems remarkable he lived so long as he did. He fought upon both sides, Yorkists and Lancastrians, in the Wars of the Roses, and was at various times accused of rape and pillage. Evidently, Malory was one of those great writers who are bad news, akin to Villon, Marlowe, and Rimbaud.

His extraordinary book is both a visionary lament for the legendary King Arthur, and also a cunning revision of the French romances of Arthur, which had emphasized the virtues of divine over earthly love. Malory, a secularist, gives us Arthur and his Round Table of knights as the highest of values, in themselves.

In his *History of the Kings of Britain* (1136), the chronicler Geoffrey of Monmouth compiled much of the material about Arthur, who *may* have been an actual British king who led the fight against the Anglo-Saxon invaders of the sixth century. But literary splendor, in English, is first conferred upon Arthurian myth by Malory, whose strong prose has the dignity and austerity that his story requires.

2

Arthur's greatest poet, surpassing even the French Chrétien de Troyes, remains Alfred Lord Tennyson, whose *Idylls of the King* (1842), though an uneven work, is now absurdly neglected. Embedded in its final section is Tennyson's superb early *Morte d'Arthur* (1833–34) which, like his great dramatic monologue, *Ulysses*, is actually a lament for the closest of the poet's friends, Arthur Henry Hallam, who had died, quite suddenly, at the age of twenty-two. *In Memoriam* is also an elegy for Hallam, as indeed much of Tennyson's poetry continued to be.

Though Tennyson closely follows Malory, his tonality is altogether different, since this later *Morte d'Arthur* actually is a mythic prelude to *In Memoriam*, another sublime lament. After the sword Excalibur at last returns to the mystical lake, three crowned Queens appear in a barge to convey the dying Arthur to the island of the Blessed, Avilion (Avalon). When the last Knight of the Round Table, Sir Bedivere, cries out to his departing King, saying that "the true old times are dead," Arthur's reply reverberates with Tennysonian resonances of elegy:

> And slowly answered Arthur from the barge:
> 'The old order changeth, yielding place to new,
> And God fulfils Himself in many ways,
> Lest one good custom should corrupt the world.
> Comfort thyself: what comfort is in me?
> I have lived my life, and that which I have done
> May He within Himself make pure! but thou,
> If thou shouldst never see my face again,
> Pray for my soul. More things are wrought by prayer
> Than this world dreams of. Wherefore, let thy voice
> Rise like a fountain for me night and day.
> For what are men better than sheep or goats
> That nourish a blind life within the brain,
>
> If, knowing God, they lift not hands of prayer
> Both for themselves and those who call them friend?
> For so the whole round earth is every way
> Bound by gold chains about the feet of God.
> But now farewell. I am going a long way
> With these thou seest—if indeed I go—
> (For all my mind is clouded with a doubt)
> To the island-valley of Avilion;
> Where falls not hail, or rain, or any snow,

Nor ever wind blows loudly; but it lies
Deep-meadowed, happy, fair with orchard-lawns
And bowery hollows crowned with summer sea,
Where I will heal me of my grievous wound.'

Going on seventy-three, I find myself, all too often, murmuring out loud the crucial passage here:

The old order changeth, yielding place to new,
And God fulfils Himself in many ways,
Lest one good custom should corrupt the world.

Those still seem to me the final words on King Arthur as a literary character. Mark Twain, in his *A Connecticut Yankee in King Arthur's Court*, was not at his best. In the twentieth century, we had the rather better-humored vision of Arthur as "the once and future King" in T.H. White's series of Arthurian narratives. Good reading as these remain, King Arthur in English continues to mean either Malory or Tennyson.

CELIA MORRIS

From Malory to Tennyson:
Spiritual Triumph to Spiritual Defeat

When we compare Tennyson's "The Holy Grail" with its source in Sir Thomas Malory's *Le Morte d'Arthur*, we see not only the erosion of Christian belief in the 19th century but also the spiritual crisis that erosion fostered. Because there has been a virtually total breakdown in the relationship between moral and spiritual experience, both have become seriously impoverished. Spiritual experience no longer serves as a guide to moral obligations, nor does it strengthen a man in his attempt to fulfill them. Consequently, it becomes a dangerous threat—of uncertain provenience and divisive, even anarchic tendencies. The moral life becomes all-important, but when a man in his inevitable weakness fails to be morally perfect, he finds no help for his struggle with sin. Tennyson accepts the basic Christian analysis of man's nature but no longer believes in Christian hope. The world of the *Idylls of the King* is one that believes in sin but not in salvation; and it is therefore a world of despair.

Not that one man fully describes or speaks for an era. But Tennyson—as Poet Laureate, as the respected friend of men intimately involved in the religious controversies of their age, as serious and dedicated idealist, as a man that many Victorians came to worship—Tennyson is not merely an individual. His words were, unfairly to be sure, taken as gospel, and his thoughts and experiences have often and rightly been considered characteristic for his times. We can, then, read a poem as important as "The

From *Mosaic* 7, no. 3 (Spring 1974). © 1974 by *Mosaic*.

Holy Grail" as a personal expression, as biographically revealing—and as a
document in the varied history of Victorian England.

Lancelot is the only major figure in both the Grail section and the bulk
of the Arthurian tales, and three things in his experience in the *Idylls* deserve
our special attention. First, he goes to seek the Grail in the hope that it will
give him moral insight and strength to purge himself of a sin he never clearly
names. He tells Arthur that he is different from those who "welter in their
sin" and describes his dilemma in terms of intertwined flowers:

> in me lived a sin
> So strange, of such a kind, that all of pure,
> Noble, and knightly in me twined and clung
> Round that one sin, until the wholesome flower
> And poisonous grew together, each as each,
> Not to be pluck'd asunder.[1]

He has vowed to seek the Grail only in the hope that the vision might cause
the good and evil in him to be "pluck'd asunder."

In Malory's *Le Morte d'Arthur*, on the other hand, Launcelot seeks the
Grail in order to participate in Holiness, and he confesses to a hermit:

> For this fourteen year I never discovered one thing that I have
> used, and that may I wyte my shame and my misadventure.
> And then he told there that good man all his life. And how he
> had loved a queen unmeasurably and out of all measure long.
> And all my great deeds of arms that I have done, I did for the
> most part for the queen's sake, and for her sake would I do
> battle were it right or wrong: and never did I battle all only for
> God's sake, but for to win worship and to cause me to be the
> better beloved, and little or nought I thanked God for it. Then
> Sir Launcelot said: I pray you counsel me. I will counsel you,
> said the hermit, if ye will ensure me that ye will never come in
> that queen's fellowship as much as ye may forbear. And then
> Sir Launcelot promised him he nold, by the faith of his body.[2]

His sin, which he lucidly describes, is excessive love for an earthly creature,
whom he has honored more than he has honored God. He has not merely
violated a social arrangement or even a sacred trust but rather has
confounded the proper relations between man and his Creator. The holy

man commands him to wear a hair shirt, deny himself wine and meat, and hear mass daily.

It may seem disingenuous to stress the fact that Tennyson's Lancelot never says exactly how he is guilty, since Tennyson could assume we know that Lancelot is an adulterer. But that is not his chief sin in Malory, and the contrast is revealing. Lancelot's purpose in Tennyson's Quest is moral rather than spiritual. But a man who cannot or does not clearly describe his guilt is seriously crippled in being able to deal with it.

Obsessed with his own unworthiness, Lancelot has no adequate means for moral struggle. He "spake" (not "confessed") to a hermit, "to whom I vow'd / That I would work according as he will'd" (780–781). He claims that he follows the hermit's advice but never says what it is. He knows the "flowers" must be "pluck'd asunder," but how this might be done remains a mystery. Because the rituals, institutions, and penances so crucial in Malory are no longer accessible, his sense of guilt is exacerbated.

Second, Tennyson imagines that Lancelot's madness recurs while he is on the quest as a direct result of an ill-defined struggle with his guilt:

> And forth I went, and while I yearn'd and strove
> To tear the twain asunder in my heart,
> My madness came upon me as of old,
> And whips me into waste fields far away.
>
> (782–785)

In the *Morte*, Launcelot's madness precedes his experiences on the Quest; he is cured before he vows to pursue the Grail, and his madness never recurs. It is inspired by Guenever's jealousy of Elaine—the other Elaine in the *Morte* whose story Tennyson chose not to tell. Launcelot makes love to the girl, whom he mistakes for Guenever because he has been "enchanted"; the Queen, whose room is next door, hears him and furiously banishes him from the court. Because of her anger he goes mad and stays so for two years.

Interjecting Lancelot's madness into "The Holy Grail," Tennyson adds to the ambiguities already surrounding the Quest by wondering, in effect, if spiritual experience is tantamount to madness: he temporizes by using the suggestion of madness to deprecate the Quest. At the same time, he cannot offer Lancelot a better way to resolve the conflicts in his moral experience; that is, the world he imagines in the *Idylls* condemns Lancelot's problem without offering any way to deal with it.

Finally, the Launcelot of the *Morte* succeeds in great part in participating in Holiness. The Lancelot of the *Idylls* fails. In "The Holy Grail" Lancelot describes what happened to him at Carbonek:

> Then in my madness I essay'd the door;
> It gave, and thro' a stormy glare, a heat
> As from a seven-times-heated furnace, I,
> Blasted and burnt, and blinded as I was.
> With such a fierceness that I swoon'd away—
> O, yet methought I saw the Holy Grail.
> All pall'd in crimson samite, and around
> Great angels, awful shapes, and wings and eyes!
> And but for all my madness and my sin,
> And then my swooning, I had sworn I saw
> That which I saw; but what I saw was veil'd
> And cover'd, and this quest was not for me.
>
> (838–849)

We may slightly paraphrase the lines: had I not been mad, sinful, and in a faint I might have been able to commit myself to my vision. As it was I saw only through a glass darkly, "and this quest was not for me." Malory's Launcelot is fully as humble, but he does not despair; he is made unconscious for twenty-four days in punishment for twenty-four years of willing sin. Tennyson's Lancelot is overcome with a sense of guilt and unworthiness, about which he can do nothing but suspect the experience he has.

The largest part of "The Holy Grail" describes the adventures of Percivale, and to compare what Tennyson and Malory do with him is to discover how readily in the *Idylls* one succumbs to doubt and despair once one has left the safe world of duty to others. To a monk long after the event, Percivale describes how his initial elation at the beginning of the quest gave way to a sense of guilt:

> Then every evil word I had spoken once,
> And every evil thought I had thought of old,
> And every evil deed I ever did,
> Awoke and cried, "This quest is not for thee."
>
> (371–374)

The experiences that follow are clearly symbolic.[3] He stops to rest, drink from a stream, and eat "the goodly apples" he finds on the bank; but everything turns to dust, and "I was left alone / And thirsting in a land of sand and thorns" (389–390). Subsequently he sees a motherly woman before a modest home, and a brilliantly armored knight—both of whom also turn to dust at his approach. Next he is attracted by a splendid city at the top of a hill, where a throng of people cheer and praise him. When he reaches it, it too is ruined, and he can find only one old man who, before turning to dust, gasps "Whence and what art thou?" (435) All this understandably leaves Percivale feeling morbid and poisonous: "Lo, if I find the Holy Grail itself / And touch it, it will crumble into dust!" (438–439). And a hermit then says Percivale lacks humility, which he calls "The highest virtue, mother of them all" (446). Apparently Tennyson wants us to understand that Percivale's turning away from public responsibility shows that he is insufficiently humble, and consequently he cannot even enjoy the various earthly delights symbolized by the Quest experiences. Damned by his particular nature to escape and to fail, he discovers no certain goal but becomes, rather, passive and despairing.

We realize more fully how quickly he despairs—and how quickly Tennyson had despaired for him—when we compare him to his prototype, who leads an active and resilient life while on the Quest; a glance at the *Morte* shows us how aggressive and eager he is. He first encounters an aunt who is a holy recluse and from her discovers how to make his way to Galahad. After hearing mass, he battles twenty armed men who try to kill him and succeed in killing his horse before Galahad "by adventure" rescues him, driving the attackers into the forest and following them. Percivale, horseless and angry, can do nothing until later, when a woman appears and says:

> Sir Percivale, what dost thou here? He answered, I do neither good nor great ill. If thou wilt ensure me. said she, that thou wilt fulfil my will when I summon thee, I shall lend thee mine own horse which shall bear thee whither thou wilt. Sir Percivale was glad of her proffer, and ensured her to fulfil all her desire. (II, 197–198)

The horse "within an hour and less ... bare him four days' journey thence" (II, 198), and carries him to the edge of a body of roaring water. When Percivale realizes that the horse is going to plunge into the water, he makes the sign of the cross on his forehead:

> When the fiend felt him so charged he shook off Sir Percivale, and he went into the water crying and roaring, making great sorrow, and it seemed unto him that the water brent. Then Sir Percivale perceived it was a fiend, the which would have

brought him unto his perdition. Then he commended himself
unto God, and prayed Our Lord to keep him from all such
temptations.   (II, 198)

After battling on the side of a lion against a serpent, he has a dream in which
a young woman sitting on a lion tells him he soon will fight for his eternal
life. She is followed by an old woman riding a serpent, who complains that
he has killed her beast and warns that she will be after him: "I ensure you in
what place I may find you without keeping I shall take you as he that
sometimes was my man" (II, 200). The dream is interpreted by an old man
who suddenly appears on board a ship covered with white samite. According
to him the young woman "betokeneth the new law of holy church, that is to
understand, faith, good hope, belief, and baptism." The old woman is of
course the old law, "and that serpent betokeneth a fiend" (II, 201).

Malory's Percivale, then, lives in a populous and *significant* world, and
confrontation is of its essence. There are forces at work which are definitely
external ones. There is a power actively trying to deceive and ruin him, and
there is also a power working for his salvation. There is a constant interplay
between him and these powers of the otherworld; and though it occasionally
seems that his salvation is due to chance, or more accurately to Grace, still
he acts, and his actions have decisive significance. He must choose, and he is
held accountable for his choices. He fights and he takes chances. For
something he thinks he needs, he makes promises by which he apparently
does not feel bound. There are dreams he must interpret because they give
valuable information about what has happened or what threatens. He seeks
counsel, but finally he must be able to choose between conflicting advice and
interpretations. Hitherto earthly, palpable figures may suddenly prove
deceptive, and he may realize they have been fiends in human disguise.[4] But
his trials always take the form of having to act in an apparently human or
actual situation.

The major temptation Percivale faces in Malory is that of succumbing
to lust. After various lively encounters, he is approached by a richly dressed
and beautiful woman, who tells him she will bring him to Galahad if he
promises to do her will, and he so promises. Claiming to have been
disinherited, she pleads for his help in regaining her rights and gives him
lavish food and drink:

> Also he drank there the strongest wine that ever he drank, him
> thought, and therewith he was a little chafed more than he ought
> to be; with that he beheld the gentlewoman, and him thought
> she was the fairest creature that ever he saw.   (II, 203)

She arouses him so that he asks her to make love with him—and then makes him promise in return "to do nothing but that I shall command you" (II, 203). He promises but before he commits the act chances to see the cross on his sword. This reminds him to cross himself, and the power of the sign makes her vanish.

Nor are the discordant demands of flesh and spirit to be reconciled by means of social arrangements: marriage is not at issue. The full life of the spirit demands the mortification of the flesh. When Percivale realizes how nearly he had given in to lust and lost his chance for the highest spiritual experience, he stabs himself in the thigh in outrage at his weakness. The Quest in Malory is, precisely, a quest for participation with God, and for the sake of that participation the things of the earth—all the things of the earth: good and bad, respectable and odious, decent and indecent—must be rejected.

In Tennyson's version of Percivale's experience, any sense of urgency and immediacy is technically distanced by the fact that Percivale tells the story considerably after the event to a monk in the cloister to which he has retired. Before the tale begins, we are twice told that the speaker has died. For the reader's vivid experience of watching, as it were, an unresolved series of important encounters and temptations, Tennyson substitutes an informal, relaxed conversation recalling events concluded and emotions long since dissipated.

Percivale's experiences have very little relation to a world outside his own consciousness. The first experience he relates in "The Holy Grail" is in fact a recollection: that of Arthur warning "That most of us would follow wandering fires" (369). This, I assume, is an experience of doubt, and the doubt victimizes Percivale; it turns into an oppressive sense of guilt: "Then every evil word ... every evil thought ..." and so on. Guilt then leads to a conviction of inadequacy, impotence, and perhaps despair: "This quest is not for thee." Percivale's apparent action is only restlessness and forward motion. He wants to stop: "'I will rest here.' / I said, 'I am not worthy of the quest'" (385–386), but he cannot. He is not denied some activity; he is only denied *meaningful* activity.

In Tennyson's Quest, moreover, one is never sure what precisely constitutes temptation. Neither Tennyson's Percivale nor the reader ever knows unequivocally what he *can* seek, and therefore neither knows what— outside his own nature—threatens his success. The attractive things that turn to dust because Percivale lacks humility symbolize earthly pleasures one would hardly expect to find honored on a spiritual quest. That is, his spiritual pride apparently prevents him from realizing pleasures that are not spiritual at all but are instead thoroughly mundane.

In Malory the beautiful young woman is a temptation to lust, to give in to which is to damn the soul. Tennyson's Percivale also meets a young woman. To Ambrosius he confesses with shame how nearly he had abandoned the search because of an experience he neglects to relate to the sequence of experiences previously recounted. He talks of coming upon a castle and his first love:

> The princess of that castle was the one.
> Brother, and that one only, who had ever
> Made my heart leap: for when I moved of old
> A slender page about her father's hall,
> And she a slender maiden, all my heart
> Went after her with longing, yet we twain
> Had never kiss'd a kiss or vow'd a vow.
> And now I came upon her once again.
> And one had wedded her, and he was dead.
> And all his land and wealth and state were hers.
>
> (577–586)

He is greatly "tempted" when she and her people solicit him to become her husband and rule over them, "but one night my vow / Burnt me within, so that I rose and fled" (606–607). Rather than offering illicit sexual delights, she represents the promise of domestic affection and social usefulness. The combination is essentially the one Tennyson exalts throughout the *Idylls*, and we cannot be sure how he wants us to judge Percivale's rejection of the lady.

Hallam Tennyson quotes his father as saying that "the key [to understanding 'The Holy Grail'] is to be found in a careful reading of Sir Percivale's vision and subsequent fall and nineteenth century temptations."[5] Surely this is not the "fall" to which he refers. On the other hand, what was Percivale's fall? With Galahad's eventual help, he succeeds in seeing the Grail at a great distance, so that in terms of the Quest itself he does not fail. Tennyson does not present Percivale's experience clearly because he does not squarely face the central question: is the Grail a message sent by God? We cannot honor Galahad for achieving a goal that is not intrinsically worthwhile. And if we honor Galahad we must honor Percivale only slightly less and feel that whatever holds him back from fully achieving the Grail is odious. Our logical conclusion—that domestic affection and social usefulness must be repudiated—makes a shambles of the moral message of Tennyson's *Idylls*.[6]

In the *Memoir* we find Tennyson saying "I doubt whether such a subject as the San Graal could be handled in these days without incurring a charge of irreverence. It would be too much like playing with sacred things" (II, 126). In the letter to the Duke of Argyll which his son quotes here, Tennyson goes on to say "The old writers *believed* in the Sangraal."[7] Deeply hostile to asceticism, he was sympathetic to F. D. Maurice's belief that the social order itself is the locus of one's spiritual life.[8] The Quest in his poem is an evasion of the knights' more serious earthly responsibilities. It violates their vows to take their spiritual direction from Arthur and to devote themselves to the righting of human wrongs:

> And in some, as faith declines, religion turns from practical goodness and holiness to superstition: "This madness has come on us for our sins." These seek relief in selfish spiritual excitement, not remembering that man's duty is to forget self in the service of others, and to let visions come and go, and that so only will they see "The Holy Thing." (II, 130)

A symptom of the collapse of Arthur's kingdom, it exemplifies the selfishness and disunity that spell the end.

Most of us would readily agree with such a description of the uses to which Tennyson puts the Quest, though he is ambivalent about it; but the Quest is simply not amenable to such an interpretation *unless* it is completely removed from the Christian world in which it was originally conceived. One might perhaps create a powerful and fascinating study in which the Grail was a fantasy sent by the Devil to tempt man away from the serious obligations of ordinary life, though such a study would still depend on basic theological assumptions. On the other hand, the idea of a quest can signify, as it has in a certain amount of twentieth century literature, a vague though persistent longing for a purity or fulfilment not to be satisfied by the mundane possibilities of ordinary experience.

Tennyson accepts neither of these very real, if contradictory, possibilities and evades rather than solves the problem. Anyone who treats *specifically* of the Grail must address himself to the central fact that it was imagined as a vision sent by God. Tennyson's Percivale speaks to the point when he says to the monk Ambrosius that the vision was not a phantom but was indeed "the cup, the cup itself, from which our Lord / Drank at the last sad supper with his own" (46–47). If this is true—and Tennyson gives us no sure reason to doubt it—he cannot hold a man self-indulgent when he tries to receive a message his Creator has sent.

A hermit tells Percivale he lacks humility, but since Percivale shows no untoward pride or self-importance, the accusation makes sense only if we insist that Percivale's dilemmas are self-created, that he is preoccupied with his own weaknesses and imperfections. He feels morbid about himself, not because of any specific failure in a real human situation, but because of some inexplicit sense of guilt. It is wholly subjective, and it is not, it seems to me, what we properly call a moral sin at all. He is a man who cannot love himself: his dilemma is a matter for a psychiatrist rather than a moralist. Further, in Tennyson's scheme the only thing Percivale can do to *avoid* this preoccupation is to do good works for the sake of the public weal—to eschew spiritual or subjective experience entirely.

Humility, then, is all-important but the path to it unclear. Galahad does indeed help Percivale in the end to get a distant glimpse of the Grail, but not by helping him face his demons and best them—not by helping him become a stronger and better person. Percivale apparently sees the Grail only because he is in the company of Galahad: his partial success is a function of *noblesse oblige*.

Because the Grail poem is a part of the *Idylls of the King*, we must know what Tennyson was about in the work as a whole before we can judge it finally. He speaks of spiritual experience as central to the *Idylls*:

> I have expressed there [in "The Holy Grail"] my strong feeling as to the Reality of the Unseen. The end, when the king speaks of his work and of his visions, is intended to be the summing up of all in the highest note by the highest of human men. These three lines in Arthur's speech are the spiritually central lines of the *Idylls*:
>
> > In moments when he feels he cannot die,
> > And knows himself no vision to himself,
> > Nor the High God a vision.
> >
> > (II, 90)

Because Tennyson's assumptions about the values he espouses in these poems are so crucial, I want to quote this speech of Arthur's at some length. He is speaking ruefully to the remnant of his knights who have come back to Camelot from their Quest for the Holy Grail:

> And some among you held that if the King
> Had seen the sight he would have sworn the vow.
> Not easily, seeing that the King must guard
> That which he rules, and is but as the hind
> To whom a space of land is given to plow,
> Who may not wander from the allotted field

Before his work be done, but, being done,
Let visions of the night or of the day
Come as they will: and many a time they come,
Until this earth he walks on seems not earth,
This light that strikes his eyeball is not light,
This air that smites his forehead is not air
But vision—yea, his very hand and foot—
In moments when he feels he cannot die.
And knows himself no vision to himself,
Nor the high God a vision, nor that One
Who rose again.

(899–915)

Here Arthur alludes to two major kinds of human experience. One is the imperative Tennyson exalts in the *Idylls*—the imperative to work for the good of the social order. The other is the private experience of a more profound and ultimate reality. By means of a simple rhetorical inversion, Tennyson asserts that things are not what they seem, that the palpable world is not real—that the Christian belief is true that imagines the Heavenly Kingdom as the real one. But undetected by the poet, a deep contradiction finds its way into the very conception of the poem. According to Arthur's speech, morality is the first order of business: the knights' primary duty is to battle evil. But the "highest note by the highest of human men" apparently recognizes something not only more important but ultimately subversive of the other: in relation to this spiritual reality, the world we experience through our senses is an illusion and therefore, logically, not worth our concern.

Christianity had its way—or perhaps ways—of reconciling such a contradiction or making it seem only an apparent one, and a fair amount of explicit, if vague, Christianity remains in the *Idylls*. Arthur is a surrogate for Christ. Tennyson equates the cause of the Round Table with that of the Church: "The King will follow Christ and we the King," ("The Coming of Arthur," 499) and in the *Idylls* he always refers to the enemy as heathen.[9] He acknowledges that of those who saw the Grail, they saw it most fully whose Christianity was most flawless:

He pointed out the difference between the five visions of the Grail, as seen by the Holy Nun, Sir Galahad, Sir Percivale, Sir Lancelot, Sir Bors, according to their different, their own peculiar natures and circumstances, and the perfection or imperfection of their Christianity.

(II, 3)

More important, he believes profoundly in the Christian concepts of obligation and accountability, of guilt and sin.

What is missing in the *Idylls* is faith in spiritual guidance; and help—in the possibilities of repentance, followed by Divine forgiveness and grace. The only connection Tennyson can honor between moral and spiritual experience is that revelation may be a reward for moral industry. King Arthur claims he has no right to indulge in spiritual excursions until he has fulfilled his ethical responsibilities; the visions in no way guide his life. Nor are his own visions accessible or valuable to his knights, despite the fact that Tennyson calls him their spiritual leader. In "The Holy Grail," when his knights feel they too have experienced "the Reality of the Unseen," he is deeply sceptical; when they resolve to pursue further the hints they feel they have received, he denounces them, with Tennyson's obvious approval, for self-indulgence.

Tennyson imagines that to seek the Grail is to turn away from the security of public commitment to explore the self in isolation. "Spiritual" in the *Idylls of the King* means "subjective." And it is at least implicit in the poems that to know oneself is potentially destructive, that once inside the lonely self, there may be no returning.[10] In the *Idylls*, spiritual experience is most unlikely to lead to holiness and God (even of Galahad, who is clearly "called," Arthur is vaguely disapproving); nor does it give renewed strength and perspective for the life of ordinary obligation.

The central contradiction in the *Idylls of the King* comes paradoxically from Tennyson's unwillingness to forego the description of human nature and experience that Christianity offered him. Any hedonistic or pagan ethic is remote from the imagination that inspired the *Idylls*. But how remote Tennyson is from the world of the great Christian, St. Augustine, who complained to God that He had counselled better than He had permitted. Such a plea assumes a world of vigorous conflict and moral struggle, while the story of Augustine's life testified that triumph was possible. Hallam Tennyson writes that "Throughout the poem runs my father's belief in one strong argument of hope, the marvellously transmuting power of repentance in all men, however great their sin" (II, 131). Contrary to such an extraordinary claim, the major burdens and themes of the *Idylls* are of inevitable defeat and inexorable corruption.

The well-known langour of Tennyson's verse may lead us to suspect that the deep passivity we find in "The Holy Grail" is merely a reflection of his personal temperament. However, the devotion to work that Arthur preaches unquestionably finds its counterpart in the world of Macauley, Dickens, Gladstone, and the Prince Albert whom Tennyson eulogizes in the "Dedication" to the poems. Similarly, Victorian writers and critics have frequently attested to the spiritual crisis the *Idylls* inadvertently reveal.[11] The despair at the heart of the *Idylls* reflects a cultural fact at least as much as a personal one.

NOTES

1. Alfred Lord Tennyson, "The Holy Grail," *The Poems of Tennyson* (London, 1969), pp. 769–74. References by poem and line number to this edition are hereafter included in the text.

2. Sir Thomas Malory, *Le Morte d'Arthur* (London, 1961), II, pp. 190–1. References by volume and page number to this edition are hereafter included in the text.

3. Stopford Brooke interprets the symbolism of Percivale's experience as follows: "A burning thirst consumes him: it is the symbol of the thirst for union with God ... he was left alone, thirsting still, and in a land of sand and thorns. It is the symbol of the thirsting soul trying to find in the beauty of Nature its true home, and failing ... a woman spinning ... is the symbol of the soul trying to find rest in domestic love, and failing ... One, in golden armour ... is the symbol of the soul seeking to be satisfied with the glory of the earth, chiefly to be attained in war ... the city ... a ruined heap ... is the soul seeking to slake its thirst by popular applause, and especially in the fame of ruler of men." *Tennyson: His Art and Relation to Modern Life* (London, 1929), pp. 320–1.

4. We can understand Malory here in either of two ways—or perhaps in both. He may have believed that angels and devils took human form in order to tempt men. Or he may have used the technique of allegory, in which case some at least of the tempters would embody warring impulses in Percivale's own soul. In either case, we realize that in Malory people acutely experience and struggle with temptation.

5. Hallam Tennyson, *Alfred Lord Tennyson: A Memoir by His Son*, 2 vols. (New York, 1897), II, p. 63. References by volume and page number to this edition are hereafter included in the text.

6. In *From the Great Deep* (Columbus, Ohio, 1967), pp. 146–179, *passim.*, Clyde Ryals devotes a chapter to "The Holy Grail" and argues that it is the only one of the idylls that is essentially a dramatic monologue. He claims that Tennyson saw the Grail Quest through the eyes of a person who is morally and spiritually flawed so as not to admit that he himself did not share the religious belief that inspired the medieval version of the Quest. Such an interpretation is ingenious rather than convincing. Tennyson cannot solve his problem by shifting from ordinary narrative to dramatic monologue because the basic conflicts of value remain untouched, the context unchanged. He cannot at one and the same time use a Christian framework, acknowledge with his source that the knights whose Christianity is most perfect experience the Grail most fully—and call the Quest a dangerous pursuit of self-fulfillment. He cannot at one and the same time present Percivale as a "sensation-seeking visionary" and a man whose moral and spiritual nature is so nearly perfect that he is second only to Galahad and to his sister in the fullness of revelation he experiences. Ryal's description of what happens in the idyll is valuable and insightful. But he greatly exaggerates Percivale's unattractive qualities. Percivale is almost identical to the figure in Malory, where he appears only in the Grail portions of the narrative—which is doubtless why Tennyson does not speak of him as one of Arthur's foremost knights in the secular world of tournament and joust. Further, Ryals analyzes Percivale as though he were the complex "realistic" figure of a novel—or indeed suggested by a dramatic monologue—rather than the type of figure more characteristic of Tennyson's technique in the *Idylls*.

7. Paull Baum, *Tennyson Sixty Years After* (London, 1963), p. 191.

8. Valerie Pitt describes Maurice's thought as follows: "Because men are born into a

created order which exists in the mind of God, and into a relationship with Him, they are born into a network of relationships, for God is a God of many not of one. These are bonds between men which subsist independently of the individual's recognition of them, and which lay on him a whole series of duties. The awareness of these bonds leads Maurice to conceive of the social order itself as 'the Kingdom of Christ,' and it is this which is the foundation of that theology of society which is his peculiar legacy to Anglicanism." *Tennyson Laureate* (London, 1962), pp. 177–8.

   9. In Malory, on the other hand, there is an explicit distinction between the Christian portion of his tale and the political and worldly reality of the Round Table: "for by the Round Table is the world signified by right, for all the world, Christian and heathen, repair unto the Round Table" (II, 193).

   10. T. S. Eliot makes a most perceptive observation: Tennyson's poetry gives "plenty of evidence of emotional intensity and violence—but of emotion so deeply suppressed, even from himself, as to tend rather towards the blackest melancholia than towards dramatic action. And it is emotion which, so far as my reading of the poems can discover. attained no ultimate clear purgation. I should reproach Tennyson not for mildness. or tepidity, but rather for lack of serenity." "Tennyson's 'In Memoriam,'" *Selected Prose*, ed. John Hayward (London, 1958), p. 179.

   11. Harold Nicolson quotes the *British Review* for October, 1864, as follows: "Tennyson's exaltation of doubt above dogma betrays the temper of modern criticism." *Tennyson* (New York, 1962), p. 226.

STEPHEN F. LAPPERT

Malory's Treatment of the
Legend of Arthur's Survival

Although much critical analysis has focused in recent years on the conclusion of *Le Morte Darthur* in regard to Malory's conception of tragedy and how the destruction of the Round Table should be interpreted in the light of political structures and individual salvation,[1] seemingly little work has been devoted to what Malory actually intended by his ending. Malory's own explanation of the passing of Arthur, in whose fate the eschatological hopes of the Round Table are figured, is ambiguous:

> Yet sour men say in many p[art]ys of Inglonde that kynge Arthure ys nat dede, but h[ad] by the wyll of oure Lorde Jesu into another place; and men say that he shall com agayne, and he shall wynne the Holy Crosse. Yet I woll nat say that hit shall be so, but rather I wolde sey: here in thys worlde he chaunged hys lyff. (III, 1242)[2]

Since Malory is very clear about death, and his terms for it, with respect to his other characters, it seems unlikely that the phrase "in thys worlde he chaunged hys lyff" is merely euphemistic. Only one similar phrase occurs in Malory's book; in the conversation which Perceval has with his aunt, the Queen of the Waste Lands, he exclaims, upon hearing of his mother's death: "Now God have mercy on hir soule! ... Hit sore forthynkith me; but all we muste change

From *Modern Language Quarterly* 36, no. 4 (1975). © 1976 University of Washington.

the lyff" (II, 906). The phrase here is not exactly that applied to Arthur's passing and could be understood simply as a reference to the death of a good Christian. However, that Perceval, who experienced a sort of translation to heaven rather than death, should speak of the "changing" of life suggests that there may be in that phrase something more than ordinary dying.

Thus the text, at least overtly, does not offer much help in an attempt to explicate Malory's wording. The sentence has been consistently understood to be essentially negative; that is, Malory actually intended to imply a normal death for Arthur. In this regard, Eugène Vinaver states that Malory's "speculations about the identity of the man buried in the hermit's chapel ... and about the way in which Arthur chaunged hys lyff ... are good examples of the author's sceptical turn of mind" (III, 1655). Discussing Malory's conception of tragedy, Charles Moorman says of Arthur's passing:

> And Arthur, whose vision and energy and whose sins had framed the new chivalry, dies disillusioned and haunted by failure. "Comforte thyselff, ... and do as well as thou mayste, for in me ys no truste for to truste in," ... he says at the last to Bedivere, and though in Tennyson he goes on to prophesy a new and letter world, in Malory he sees only the total destruction of his own order. (p. 124)

Elizabeth Pochoda offers a particularly original exegesis of Malory's phrase in reference to her theory about the notion of the king's two natures. In her view, Malory indicates that Arthur, its mortal ruler, has been severed from the immortality of his office. Like Moorman, she is definite in her negative interpretation of Arthur's end:

> Malory gives no credence to the myth of Arthur's return. He records the various versions of Arthur's passing with the impartial toile of the chronicler. To these he adds the only personal statement he is willing to make on the mysterious passing of the king: "rather I wolde sey *here in thys worlde he chaunged hys lyff.*" ... We are to understand by this that in death Arthur has shed the immortal part of his twinned being which was inviolable in "thys worlde." This is the meaning Malory places on Arthur's passing. (pp. 138–39)

Although Pochoda's argument that Malory possessed a social or political consciousness is indeed convincing, she perhaps overemphasizes a rather oblique explanation of Malory's obscure statement.

In general, most critical opinion has regarded Malory's ambiguity as an equivocation of disbelief to avoid angering an audience which believed in the myth. Pochoda states this assumption explicitly: "People coveted the notion of Arthur's return, courts seriously imitated the Round Table, and the aristocracy saw the salvation of the country in the rituals of chivalric perfection as they were embodied in Arthur's reign" (p. 34). Such an assumption would attribute to Malory an audience prone to the sort of behavior which Hermann of Laon describes in his *De Miraculis S. Mariae Laudunensis*:

> But just as the Britons are accustomed to quarrel with the French in defense of King Arthur, so this man began to brawl with one member of our party, who was named Haganello and of the household of Master Guido, archdeacon of Laon, saying that Arthur still lives. Whence, no little tumult having arisen, an armed multitude rushed into the church, and if a cleric, the aforesaid Algardus, had not intervened, it would almost have ended in the shedding of blood.[3]

Notwithstanding the fact that even in the late fifteenth century Henry VII took care to name his eldest son Arthur in the hopes of reconciling the factious Welsh, Malory's audience was not composed of readers who would start a riot in defense of Arthur's immortality. Indeed, as Loomis asserts, the legend of Arthur's survival was largely an oral, not a written, tradition, and this distinction is indicative of the public which subscribed to the myth.[4]

If one traces the references to Arthur's survival or to the Arthurian story in general throughout medieval literature, one finds that the great majority of allusions are either skeptical or flatly negative regarding Arthur's immortality.[5] Geoffrey of Monmouth, in the *Liber Merlini*, provides one of the few positive statements about Arthur's survival, and that is merely, "and his ending is doubtful."[6] But Geoffrey's contemporaries—William of Malmesbury, Henry of Huntington, and William of Newburgh—take great pains to deny the "Breton hope." In his *Gesta Regum Anglorum* (completed in 1125), William of Malmesbury is careful to distinguish between historical truth regarding Arthur and the fables which had grown up around his name: "This is Arthur about whom the fables of the Britons rave even today, a man so worthy that false fables should not be imagined about him, but rather true histories should proclaim him, since he so long sustained his tottering fatherland."[7] Included in the "fables" which William condemns is the survival legend. Although Henry of Huntington had completed his *Historia Anglorum* before the appearance of Geoffrey's *Historia*, he later felt it necessary to supplement his work with the "Epistola ad Warinum" (1139), which pointedly denies Geoffrey's remarks about Arthur's survival. Using Geoffrey as his source for the history of Arthur, Henry deletes the statement "for the healing of his wounds he sailed to the island of Avalon."[8] Instead, Henry describes Arthur's death, provides him with a death speech, and then alludes to the foolish Britons who believe the "lie" about Arthur's survival and return: "However, in the same attack he received so many wounds that he perished, even though his British subjects deny that he died and still solemnly look forward to his return."[9] Finally, William of Newburgh, writing at the close of the twelfth century, is yet more critical of Geoffrey, terming his remarks inventions and fictions and stating that he "yielded to the Briton Superstition" in his narrative of the passing of Arthur to Avalon:

> It is clear that everything which that man [Geoffrey] took care to write about Arthur and either his successors or his predecessors after Vortigern was invented in part by himself, in part by others, either because of an unbridled love of lying or even a desire to please the Britons, most of whom are reputed to be so stupid that even now they are said to be awaiting Arthur's return and will not bear to hear that he is dead.[10]

Later in the text he comments:

> And it is to be noted that he relates that afterward Arthur, who was mortally wounded in the battle, having settled the succession, departed for the healing of his wounds to that island called Avalon which the British tales invent. Because of his fear of the Britons he does not dare to say that he [Arthur] is dead whom the truly stupid Britons still expect to return. (p. 18)[11]

In the thirteenth century the chronicle tradition continues to mock the Briton superstition. In Robert of Gloucester's *Metrical Chronicle*, not only does he specify the delusion as being particularly Briton and Cornish, he supports his denial with an eyewitness account of Arthur's tomb at Glastonbury, "before the high altar, amid the choir":

> & naþeles þe brutons · & þe cornwalisse of is kunde ·
> Weneþ he be aliuezut · & abbeþ him in munde ·
> þat he be to comenezut · to winne azen þis lond ·
> & naþeles at glastinbury · his bones suþþe me fond ·

& þere at uore þe heye weued · amydde þe quer ywis ·
As is bones liggeþ · is toumbe wel vair is ·
In þe vif hundred ȝer of grace · & vourty & tuo ·
In þis manere in cornwaile · to dþe he was ydo.

(4589–96)[12]

Since each of these men was associated in some capacity with the
Church, it could be argued that their refutation of Arthur's immortality
represents merely the clerical opposition to an essentially pagan superstition.
However, an examination of the appearance of the legend in later medieval
literature reveals that such skepticism is found ill patently secular works. A
mocking tone is present in the allusions to the Arthurian hope which appear
in the love complaints of the French trouvères. Gautier de Soignies, a
thirteenth-century poet, lamenting his unrequited love, exclaims:

Amor m'occit et tormente
Je fats, je crois, tele atente
Come li Breton font d'arthur.[13]

And in the opening of the *Wife of Bath's Tale* there is similar mockery, a
relegating of Arthurian matter to mere fairy tale:

In th'olde dayes of the Kyng Arthour,
Of which that Britons speken greet honour,
Al was this land fulfild of fayerye.
The elf-queene, with hir joly compaignye,
Daunced ful ofte in many a grene mede. (857–61)[14]

In the fifteenth century, exclusive of Malory, there are three notable
references to the legend of Arthur's survival. In an expanded fifteenth-
century version of the fourteenth-century Franciscan collection of sermon
material entitled the *Fasciculus Morum*, the following passage, associating
Arthur and his knights with elves, appears:

They say that they have seen beautiful queens with mistress
Diana, the goddess of the pagans, leading them in dances,
ladies who, in our vernacular, are called elves. And they believe
that such ones are able to transform both men and women into
other natures and lead them into elvenland, where now dwell
those very valorous champions such as King Arthur and his
knights.[15]

A second fifteenth-century reference to Arthur's survival is found in John Lydgate's *Fall of Princes*. Lydgate includes the tradition that Arthur journeyed to Avalon, where

> He as a king is crowned in fairie,
> with scepter & sweord and with hys regaly
> Shal resort as lord and soveraigne,
> Out of fayrie and reigne in Britaine.

However, Lydgate also includes a second explanation of Arthur's departure from this life, which equates Arthur with classical myth:

> Thus of Bretayn translated was the sonne,
> Up to the rich sterry bright dongeon,
> Astronomers wel rehearse konne,
> Called Arthur's constellacion,
> Where he set crowned in the heuenly mancion
> Amid the paleys of stones christalline,
> Told among Christen first of the worthy nine.[16]

A final reference to the doubtful belief in Arthur's survival can be found in Caxton's "Preface" to Malory's book. Caxton notes that "dyvers men holde oppynyon that there was no suche Arthur and that alle suche bookes as been maad of hym ben but fayned and fables, bycause that somme cronycles make of hym no mencyon ne remembre hym noothynge, he of his knyghtes" (I, cxliv). Caxton argues against such disbelief, but his main argument for Arthur's historicity is the tomb at Glastonbury, which, in effect, argues against Arthur's survival.

The conclusion that would seem apparent from this survey of the literary treatments of the legend of Arthur's survival is that, superstitions of the common people notwithstanding, the literary audience of the fifteenth century did not cling to the hope of Arthur's return; indeed, the reading public would probably have scoffed at a sincere presentation of Arthur's immortality. Therefore, the assumption that Malory's ambiguity is simply all equivocation of disbelief should be seriously questioned; if Malory had wished to deny the possibility of Arthur's survival, he need not have feared the anger of his public. We must look elsewhere to discover the motivation for his obscurity.

To arrive at a more defensible interpretation of Malory's intentional ambiguity, let us examine his manipulation of his sources for the passage that deals with Arthur's passing. These are the Old French prose *Mort Artu*, the stanzaic *Le Morte Arthur*, and the alliterative *Morte Arthure*.[17] Wilfred L. Guerin has established the primacy of the stanzaic *Morte* in the composition of this passage. He asserts that Malory used the stanzaic *Morte* as a narrative guide and invented or borrowed from his other sources only where he desired elaboration or alteration of the basic narrative.[18] Guerin's identification of the primacy of one of the sources is important for this investigation, for by proving that Malory viewed one text as primary, Guerin also establishes Malory's departures from his primary text as intentional alterations. In the following discussion a descriptive collation of Malory's text and sources will be presented in an attempt to identify the purpose guiding Malory's selection of material and, thereby, the purpose for his ambiguity.

The narrative of the passing of Arthur begins with the futile attempts of Sir Lucan and Sir Bedivere to aid the wounded king (III, 1240 ff.) Malory's text corresponds closely to the order of events presented in the stanzaic *Morte*. Malory does alter Lucan's death slightly in order to clarify the muddled presentation he found in his sources. In the French piece, Lucan dies as a result of Arthur's overmighty embrace as he is lifted up (p. 378); in the English poem it is unclear whether it is the lifting or Arthur's grasp that results in Lucan's death (3430–37). Malory clarifies the situation, stating that "in the lyfftynge sir Lucan felle in a sowne ..." (III, 1238). Malory's presentation of Bedivere in the final scenes demands a more detailed examination. Bedivere's actions correspond to the narrative in the stanzaic *Morte* (3446–93): he is commissioned to cast Excalibur into the water; he fails twice (though in the English poem he does throw the scabbard into the water on the second attempt); and finally, after Arthur threatens him with physical harm, he completes the task. However, although the events correspond to the source, Malory's preparation throughout the book for the inclusion of Bedivere in the final scenes colors his presentation and suggests a possible focus for his manipulation of his material.

In the stanzaic *Morte*, Bedivere is not mentioned until line 3400, which begins the passage presenting the passing of Arthur. Thus, no previous insight into the character of the knight is offered; the reader knows only that this is one of Arthur's two remaining knights. In Malory's book, however, Bedivere appears throughout the course of the narrative, with the exception of Tale 5. Malory's characterization of Bedivere has a notable consistency, a consistency not found among the several sources for his tales. Bedivere first appears in the "Tale of Arthur and Lucius," the source for which is the alliterative *Morte Arthure*. In his first appearance in the English poem, Bedivere is selected, with Sir Kay, to accompany Arthur on his expedition against the giant of Mont-Saint-Michel. Throughout this passage there is a comic comparison of the giant with Saint Michael which concludes with

Bedivere's intentionally humorous remark upon viewing the giant's carcass, that it is a marvel that God would have such a carl for a saint, and that if all the saints are thus, Bedivere did not wish to become one (1162 ff.). It is clear in the poem that Bedivere is participating in Arthur's joke and does not confuse the giant with Saint Michael. In Malory's version, however, Bedivere's remarks do not betray a recognition of Arthur's joke; rather than smiling at the wit in Bedivere's remark about God's choice of his saints as he does in the alliterative *Morte*, in Malory's text, Arthur laughs at Bedivere's words and appears to act as if the joke were at the knight's expense (I, 204). The suggestion here that Bedivere is a rather dull figure is indicative of his later characterization.

Throughout the war with Lucius, Malory consistently assigns Bedivere the tasks of guarding the horses or protecting the retreat. When Gawain delivers his challenge to Lucius, Bedivere is left behind with the horses; when Lancelot resolves to turn on the Roman forces attacking his prisoner escort, he orders Bedivere to remain behind with Sir Berell and "sir Raynolde and sir Edwarde that ar sir Roulondis chyldir" to guard the prisoners (I, 206, 214). Further, in Malory's listing of knights present on these expeditions, Bedivere's name is consistently among the last. In the alliterative *Morte*, however, Bedivere is characterized as one of the most valiant knights of the Round Table. Although designated to remain behind with the prisoners (1743–52), he does not remain behind in the expedition to deliver the challenge to Lucius, and in the listing of the knights to undertake that venture, his name is second only to Berell and precedes the mention of Gawain (1264–65).

Similarly, in the alliterative *Morte*, Bedivere distinguishes himself in the final battle against Lucius, and, although eventually he is slain, it is, in part, his murder that inspires Arthur's forces with the fierce determination that results in their victory (2238–41). Following the battle, Arthur grants Bedivere an equal share of those high honors accorded the deceased British knights. Malory's major departure from his source in the characterization of Bedivere, that the knight recovers from his wounds, is accompanied by certain demeaning suggestions. In Malory's presentation, Bedivere is the only knight to be borne to the ground and as such is implicitly compared with Sir Kay, who, although wounded, remains mounted and is able to revenge his wound upon his attacker and to deliver a grand speech to Arthur (I, 222–23).

In Malory's subsequent tales, Bedivere is consistently listed among those knights participating in the various tournaments. However, Bedivere achieves a strikingly bad record. At the joust on Assumption Day, shortly after Gareth's appearance at court (a sourceless passage), he is unhorsed by

Tristram (I, 347). In the tournament at Winchester, at which Lancelot wore Elaine's token, Lucan and Bedivere are both borne down by Sir Lavayne (II, 1070). Again, in Malory's sources, no such event occurs. In the tournament immediately following, Sir Lavayne, although previously struck down by Arthur, is again able to unhorse Lucan and Bedivere (III, 1111); once again, no parallel is found in Malory's sources.[19]

It is clear that Malory, when composing Tale 2, had already conceived of the ending of his book, in that he preserved Bedivere for his later, and most important, appearance at Arthur's passing. It would be inconsistent, then, to deny that as he developed his characterization of Bedivere, Malory was similarly preparing for his ending. Bedivere is consistently found among the least distinguished knights of the Round Table society, a characterization either absent from or in opposition to the source material. By this portrayal, Malory prepares for the weakness of character Bedivere evidences in his inability to carry out Arthur's commands. Yet, Malory also suggests the bleak hope left for Arthur and his society, of which, in Bedivere, he retains only the dregs.

In addition to his manipulation of characterization, Malory embellishes Arthur's passing with several sourceless details similarly indicative of doom. When the ladies arrive to bear Arthur away, Malory adds that they all wear black hoods. More important additions, however, are Arthur's remarks to Bedivere as he is about to embark:

> "Comforte thyselff," seyde the kynge, "and do as well as thou mayste, for in me ys no truste for to truste in. For I muste into the vale of Avylyon to hele me of my grevous wounde. And if thou here nevermore of me, pray for my soule!" (III, 1240)[20]

With the exception of Arthur's statement of his intention to journey to Avalon, these remarks are not derived from the stanzaic *Morte*. The additions have a strongly negative import: Arthur both states that he can no longer be relied upon and intimates that he and Bedivere will not meet again. Malory adds also that, as the barge departs, "the quene and the ladyes wepte and shryked, that hit was pité to hyre" (III, 1241). These several elaborations of the source material serve to intensify the sense of doom and certainty of Arthur's impending death.

Malory's presentation of Bedivere's meeting with the hermit on the next day contains only one major departure from his sources. In the stanzaic *Morte*, it is Bedivere's reading of the inscription on the tomb that convinces him that Arthur is buried there:

The knyght redde the lettres A-ryght;
For sorow he tell vn-to the folde.
"Ermyte," he sayd, "with-oute lesynge,
    here lyeth my lord that I haue lorne,
Bold arthur, the beste kynge
    That euyr was in bretayne borne."
                                    (3548–53)

In Malory's treatment, Bedivere is left to infer from the hermit's narration of the ladies arriving at midnight that the corpse interred in the chapel is Arthur's. Malory's omission of the confirming evidence of Arthur's death is puzzling. It is possibly due to his decision to specify the inscription and to adopt the "rex quondam rexque futurus" of the alliterative *Morte*.[21] The hopefulness of that inscription would not be appropriate to the expression of certain death in these lines.

There follows next in Malory's presentation the well-known passage in which the author gives his own account of Arthur's passing and the legend of his survival. The passage warrants close examination. Malory first specifies the ladies in the boat: the three queens, among whole is Morgan le Fay, and dame Nineve. In Malory's sources, only Morgan is identified. Malory follows the mention of Nineve with the seemingly irrelevant statement: "(And thys dame Nynyve woude never suffir sir Pe[ll]eas to be in no place where he shulde be its daungere of hys lyff, and so he lyved unto the uttermuste of hys dayes with her its grete reste)" (III, 1242). R. M. Lumiansky explains Malory's intent in identifying the occupants of the barge.[22] He notes that the four women constitute two pairs: one pair Favorable to Arthur, one inimical. Nineve and the Queen of the Waste Lands are benevolent figures; Nineve constantly foils Morgan's plots against Arthur, and the Queen of the Waste Lands, in her one appearance, counsels Perceval about his parentage and his role in the Grail quest. Morgan and the Queen of North Wales are patently evil. Morgan is responsible for repeated attempts on Arthur's life, and the Queen of North Wales participates in Morgan's schemes on various occasions: for example, she helps imprison Lancelot after he refuses to accept one of the four queens as his paramour. Lumiansky notes here the balance of beneficent and antagonistic forces. Malory's remark regarding Nineve's protection of Pelleas is similarly double-edged. It could be interpreted as emphasizing Nineve's benevolent role, and, as such, further the positive possibility in Arthur's departure. It could, however, stand in contrast to Arthur's situation; that is, had someone been watching over Arthur, he would not have come to his destruction.

Malory follows the identification of the four ladies with a passage that seems to discount much of the negativity of the narrative of Bedivere at the tomb:

> Now more of the deth of kynge Arthur coude I never fynde, but that thes ladyes brought hym to hys grave, and such one was entyred there whych [the] ermyte bare wytnes that sometyme was Bysshop of Caunturbyry. But yet the ermyte knew nat in sertayne that he was veryly the body of [kyn]ge Arthur; for thys tale sir Bedwere, a knyght of the Table Ro[un]de, made hit to be wrytten.   (III, 1242)

Here Malory ascribes the account of Arthur's death not to himself or to an eyewitness, but to Bedivere, who has only inferred that it is Arthur who is buried there. The absence of the confirming proof in the reading of the inscription, which, as previously noted, is included in the stanzaic *Morte*, is significant here. By not providing Bedivere with irrefutable proof of Arthur's interment, and by not accepting responsibility for that story, Malory suggests his disavowal of it.

From this point of doubt regarding the narrative of Arthur's death, Malory moves to a hopeful statement: "Yet som men say in many p[art]ys of Inglonde that kynge Arthure ys nat dede, but h[ad] by the wyll of oure Lorde Jesu into another place; and men say that he shall com agayne, and he shall wynne the Holy Crosse" (III, 1242). Next follow the puzzling statement about Arthur's change of life and, finally, the inscription on the tomb. The stanzaic *Morte* does not specify the inscription on Arthur's tomb; the French *Mort Artu* identifies the inscription as "Chi gist li rois artus qui par sa ualor mist en subiection .xij. roialmes" (p. 382). Malory takes his inscription "HIC IACET ARTHURUS, REX QUONDAM REXQUE FUTURUS" from the alliterative *Morte*, and that borrowing is the only line in the section directly attributable to the alliterative poem. That Malory would depart from his two major sources for this single detail indicates the importance of the addition. In the inscription is figured the tension present throughout Malory's presentation of Arthur's passing. The inscription states that the body lies in the grave, but that Arthur is king to be. This dual assertion lies behind the whole of Malory's treatment of the legend of Arthur's survival. In the narrative of Arthur's passing, he embellishes his text with ominous details indicative of certain doom. In the restatement, he undercuts the narrative and, while not personally asserting Arthur's immortality, suggests hope.

If we now view the narrative of Arthur's passing in the context of the whole work, the purpose of Malory's intended ambiguity may be discerned.

In the first major section, "The Tale of King Arthur," there are frequent references to Arthur's fate and the fate of the Round Table society. The prophecies of Arthur's end are commonly associated with the begetting of Mordred, the instrument through which the destruction is effected. Immediately after Mordred is conceived. Arthur dreams that "there was com into hys londe gryffens and serpentes, and hym thought they brente and slowghe all the people in the londe; and than he thought he fought with them and they dud hyln grete harme and wounded hym full sore, but at the laste he slew hem" (I, 41). Later, Merlin, in the guise of an old man, tells Arthur: "ye have done a thynge late that God ys displesed with you, for ye have lyene by youre syster and on hir ye have gotyn a childe that shall destroy you and all the knyghtes of youre realme" (I, 44). Similarly, the loss of the magic scabbard, which would have protected Arthur from deadly wounds, is also accompanied by intimations of death. Throughout these early sections the prophecies and foreshadowing constantly tell of Arthur's death; there is no mention of the possibility of his survival and return.

But the brief section of Malory's book which follows Arthur's passing is characterized by a solerm yet certain hopefulness, suggested by the reformation of the surviving members of the Arthurian society. Guenevere takes upon herself "grete penaunce ... as ever ded synfull woman in thys londe" and holds so fast to her vows that she is able to tell Lancelot that they must never meet again and to deny him even a parting kiss (III, 1243, 1252–53). Inspired first by the force of her rejection and later by her example, Lancelot undertakes similar penance and observes it so strictly that he is a model for his kindred knights. On the night of his death, the Archbishop of Canterbury sees in a dream "the angellys heve up syr Launcelot unto heven, and the yates of heven opened ayenst hyrn" (III, 1258). Malory's closing passage tells that the remnant of the Round Table society—Sir Bors, Sir Hector, Sir Blamour, and Sir Bleoberis—depart for the Holy Land, where they fight the pagan Turks and die "upon a Good Fryday for Goddes sake" (III, 1260).

It should be noted that there is, in these final pages of the book, a retelling of Arthur's passing. When Lancelot leaves Guenevere, he wanders sorrowfully through the woods and eventually comes upon the hermit's chapel at Glastonbury. There after mass, Bedivere tells him the tale. In Malory's source for this passage, the stanzaic *Morte*, Lancelot, upon the conclusion of Bedivere's narrative,

> To Arthur-is tombe he caste,
>   Hys carefull corage wexid All cold;
> He threw hys armys to the walle,

That Ryche were and bryght of blee;
By-fore the ermyte he gan downe falle,
And comely knelyd vpon hys knee.
(3776–81)

Malory omits from his presentation only the mention of the tomb, the symbol of destruction and loss of hope (III, 1254).

The passing of Arthur stands as the pivotal point between the movement toward destruction and the reassertion of hope. The eight tales have brought Arthur and the Round Table inexorably to their ruin. The terminus of the ideal society is figuratively represented in the passing of its king. Thus, prophecies throughout the decline must perforce be negative; as part of a narrative of destruction, they must constantly point to that defeat which is inevitable. To include ambiguously hopeful suggestions of Arthur's immortality in this part of the book would work against the downward focus of the narrative.

The passing of Arthur, however, while terminating this downward movement, is not wholly a part of it, for in addition to marking the end of the Arthurian society, the passage also links the final chapter of the story to the preceding narrative of destruction. If there is in Malory's conclusion an indication of an abiding hope, then the ambiguity of the narrative of the passing of Arthur can be seen to have a purposefully dual focus. The passing marks the fulfillment of the destruction, but points also to that parting hope that the ideals of the Arthurian society, though like Arthur changed, may yet continue.

NOTES

1. Discussion of these topics can be found in Charles Moorman, "Malory's Tragic Knights;" *MS*, 27 (1965), 117–27; and Elizabeth T. Pochoda, *Arthurian Propaganda: "Le Morte Darthur" as an Historical Ideal of Life* (Chapel Hill, 1971).

2. Quotations from Malory are from *The Works of Thomas Malory*, ed. Eugène Vinaver, 2nd ed., 3 vols. (Oxford, 1967).

3. Migne, *PL*, 156.983: "Sect sicut Britones solent jurgari cum Francis pro rege Arturo, idem vir coepit rixari cum uno ex famulis nostris, nomine Haganello, qui erat ex familia domini Guidonis Landunensis archidiaconi, dicens adhuc Arturum vivere. Unde non parvo tumultu exorto, cum armis ecclesiam irruunt plurimi, et nisi praefatus Algardus clericus obstitisset, paene usque ad sanguinis effusionem ventum fuisset." The situation is described fully in H. Zimmer, "Ein Laoner Zeugnis für die Arthursage ams dem Jahre 1113," *ZFSL*, 13 (1891), 106–12. I am indebted to Professors William C. McDermott and Grace E. Geohegan for their help in preparing the Latin translations included in this discussion.

4. R. S. Loomis, "The Legend of Arthur's Survival," in *Arthurian Literature in Late Middle Ages*, ed. R. S. Loomis (Oxford, 1959), p. 71.

5. Professor David C. Fowler has brought to my attention John E. Housman, "Higden, Trevisa, Caxton, and the Beginnings of Arthurian Criticism," *RES*, 23 (1947), 209–17. Housman notes a skepticism regarding Arthur's survival similar to that observed here. Even Trevisa, who in translating Higden's *Polychronicon* defends Arthur's historicity, terms the stories of his survival mere "magel tales." The most complete study of the survival legend is M. H. Scanlan, "The Legend of Arthur's Survival" (Ph.D. diss., Columbia University, 1950).

6. *Historia Regum Britanniae*, ed. A. Griscom (New York, 1929), p. 385: "& exitus eius dubius erit."

7. Ed. William Stubbs, Rolls Series, 90, pt. 1 (1887). 11: "Hic est Artur de quo Britonum nugae hodieque delirant: dignus plane quem non fallaces somniarent fabulae, sed veraces praedicarent historiae, quippe qui labentem patriam diu sustinuerit."

8. *Historia Regum Britanniae*, p. 501: "ad sananda uulnera sua in insulam auallonis euectus."

9. "Epistola Henrici Archidiaconi ad Warinum," included in the prefatory sections of Robert of Torigni's *Chronicle*, ed. Richard Howlett, Rolls Series, 82, pt. 4 (1889), 74: "Inter eundum tamen et in ipso actu tot vulnera recepit, quod et ipse procubuit, licet parentes sui Britones mortuum fore denegent, et venturum adhuc sollenniter expectent."

10. *Historia Rerum Anglicarum*, ed. Richard Howlett, Rolls Series, 82, pt. 1 (1884), 14: "cuncta, quae homo ille de Arturo et ejus vel successoribus vel, post Vortigirnum, praedecessoribus scribere curavit, partim ab ipso, partim et ab aliis constat esse conficta; sive effrenata mentiendi libidine, sive etiam gratia placendi Britonibus, quorum plurimi tam bruti esse feruntur, ut adhuc Arturum tanquam venturum exspectare dicantur, eumque mortuum nec audire patiantur."

11. "Et notandum, quod eundem Arturum postea refert in bello letaliter vulneratum, regno disposito, ad curanda vulnera sua abiisse in illam, quam Britannicae fingunt fabulae, insulam Avallonis: propter metum Britonum non audens eum dicere mortuum, quem adhuc vere bruti Britones exspectant venturum."

12. Ed. William Aldis Wright, Rolls Series, 86, pt. 1 (1887), 324.

13. Gervais de La Rue, *Essais historiques sur les bardes, les jongleurs et les trouvères normands et anglo-normands* (Caen, 1834), I, 75; quoted in Scanlan, p. 34.

14. *The Works of Geoffrey Chaucer*, ed. F. N. Robinson, 2nd ed. (Boston, 1957). John Trevisa, Chaucer's contemporary, also disparages the belief in Arthur's return; for the relevant passages of his translation of Higden's *Polychronicon*, see David C. Fowler, "John Trevisa: Scholar and Translator," *Transactions of the Bristol and Gloucestershire Archaeological Society for 1970*, 89 (1971), 106, n. 10.

15. F. A. Foster, "Some English Words from the *Fasciculus Morum*," in *Essays and Studies in Honor of Carleton Brown* (New York, 1940), p. 151: "dicunt se videre reginas pulcherimas ... cum domina Diana choreas ducente, dea paganorum, que in nostro vulgari dicuntur *elues*. Et credunt quod tales possunt tam homines quant mulieres in alias transformare naturas et secum ducere in *eluenlonde*, vbi iam, vt dicunt, manent illi athlete fortissimi, sicut Rex Arturus cum suis militibus."

16. *A treatise excellent and compendious shewing the falles of sondry and most notable princes* (London, 1554), fol. 193v (*STC* 3177).

17. The editions of these works used in this analysis are H. O. Sommer, ed., *The Vulgate Version of the Arthurian Romances*, VI: *La mort le roi Artus* (Washington, 1913); Samuel B. Hemingway, ed., *Le Morte Arthur: A Middle English Metrical Romance* (Boston, 1912); and Stephen B. Spangehl, "A Critical Edition of the Alliterative *Morte Arthure*, with Introduction, Notes, and Glossary-Concordance" (Ph.D. diss., University of Pennsylvania, 1972).

18. "'The Tale of the Death of Arthur': Catastrophe and Resolution," in *Malory's Originality*, ed. R. M. Lumiansky (Baltimore, 1964), p. 240.

19. In the stanzaic *Morte*, when it is discovered that Lancelot (still in disguise) is wounded, the tournament is not held (414–17); in the *Mort Artu*, the tournament is held, but Lancelot follows his physician's advice and does not attend (pp. 228–30).

20. See Hemingway, *Le Morte Arthur*, 3512–17; the latter phrase comes from the *Mort Artu*: "Mais por dieu itant me dices sil vous plaist se vous quidies cute iou vous reuoie iamais" (p. 381).

21. Spangehl, p. 215. Spangehl notes that the inscription should not he considered part of the text: "This line is in an obviously different hand from the text of the poem, and in a much lighter ink. A wider pen was used. It is likely that the line was added by a later scribe" (p. 310). In that the manuscript is slated 1430–40, it is likely that the line had become part of the manuscript tradition prior to Malory's composition. However, Spangehl does not indicate how much later the addition might be, and, since the Thornton *MS* was not Malory's text for the alliterative *Morte*, it is possible that the inscription originated with Malory and was subsequently added to the manuscript of the poem by a scribe who knew both works.

22. "Arthur's Final Companions in Malory's *Morte Darthur*," *TSE*, 11 (1961): 5–19.

JOHN MICHAEL WALSH

Malory's Arthur and the Plot of Agravain

By common consent the most gripping part of Sir Thomas Malory's *Le Morte Darthur* is the concluding sequence, designated by Eugène Vinaver in his edition as the seventh and eighth tales.[1] Malory's chief sources for this part of his work are the Old French prose *La Mort le Roi Artu*[2] and the English stanzaic poem *Le Morte Arthur*.[3] Elsewhere in his book Malory appears to have alternated sources, interpolating details from some source other than his primary one, but it is only in the seventh and eighth tales that he draws concurrently on two different sources for an extended part of his work. The two sources are similar in narrative content (the English poem is in fact drawn from the much longer French romance), but they are very different in form, scope, and depth of characterization. Yet Malory handles them with remarkable skill. He confidently revises the sequence of events in the early part of the seventh tale, disentangling the stories of the poisoned apple and of the Maid of Astolat, which are interwoven in the sources. His next major innovation is to suspend his adaptation of the stanzaic *Morte* and the *Mort Artu* in order to interpolate the famous episode of the Knight of the Cart, taken from the *Lancelot* proper (an earlier part of the Vulgate Cycle or Prose *Lancelot*,[4] the massive collection to which the *Mort Artu* also belongs). Malory's version of the Cart story is heavily revised and is followed by an episode that appears to be entirely original, that of Lancelot's miraculous

From *Texas Studies in Literature and Language* 23, no. 4 (Winter 1981). © 1981 by the University of Texas Press.

healing of Sir Urry. These structural changes have far-reaching effects on Malory's characterization of the major figures, not only for the seventh tale but for the eighth as well, even though the eighth shows less revision in the narrative sequence. Thus, it is hardly possible to discuss Malory's characterization without reference to his structure.

For the last two tales, critical discussion of Malory's originality in characterization has tended to focus on Lancelot, Gawain, and Guinevere, mostly in that order. For the long middle section of *Le Morte Darthur*, as commentators have often pointed out, Arthur is a passive figure. From the end of the Roman war in the second tale (or perhaps even slightly earlier), it is not the king but his knights who carry the action forward. And in the last two tales, although he is once again often on stage, so to speak, he seldom appears to take initiatives. It is Agravain who forces him to face the issue of the adultery, and Gawain seems almost immediately to succeed Agravain as the instigator of trouble, driving the king to pursue Lancelot to France. However, in the brief period between Agravain's raid on the queen's room and Lancelot's accidental slaying of Gareth, which provokes Gawain to vengeance, Arthur becomes the main character and the focus of all attention, both ours and the other characters'. Even Lancelot can only wait to see what the king will do. Moreover, even before the raid on the queen's room, Arthur, though apparently passive, in fact exerts a considerable degree of control over the action, and his motivations and responses make for a great deal of dramatic interest. These elements in the character of Arthur are largely Malory's contribution. They are the subject of this study.

The first changes of importance for the character of the king are modifications of the structure of the *Mort Artu*. Malory, following a precedent set by the English poet, omits two of the French author's major scenes. Very early in the *Mort Artu*, Agravain becomes aware of the adultery of Lancelot and Guinevere. When a tournament is announced, Lancelot, intending to go disguised, announces that he is ill and will stay behind at court. Agravain suspects that he merely wants to be alone with the queen and informs Arthur, suggesting that the two be spied upon. The device comes to nothing, for Lancelot does in fact go to Winchester. Later the king spends several days at the castle of his sister Morgan, and she shows him certain paintings executed by Lancelot during one of the periods when she had kept him prisoner. They depict the main events of his career and of his relationship with Guinevere. Morgan explains the paintings, and Arthur declares that he will never rest until he is certain of the truth and that should he take the lovers together he will punish them cruelly.

Malory's reason for omitting the second of these scenes might have been simply that he had not recounted the story of Lancelot's doing the paintings in the first place. Yet elsewhere in the seventh tale he permits himself an important reference back to a major episode of the *Lancelot* proper that he had cut.[5] Alternatively, he might have felt that the hostility between Arthur and Morgan would make it appear inconsistent that he should trust his sister about the paintings.[6] Yet he trusts himself to her at the very end of his life (p. 1240), and in any case it hardly seems necessary that he love her in order to be disturbed by what she shows him. However, the fact that Malory also dropped the early warning by Agravain suggests that his objection was to the warnings themselves and not merely to certain details about them.

It seems then that the question of whether and to what extent Arthur is conscious of the adultery is one that Malory does not wish to answer just yet, principally perhaps for the sake of suspense. Now although Malory is following the lead of the stanzaic *Morte* in cutting these scenes, it must be noted that the effect of their absence is not at all the same as it is in the poem. There the omissions result not in suspense but in a relative thinness in the characterization, for the poet raises no questions at all about what Arthur may be thinking. Indeed the poet seldom has the time or the insight to look beneath the surface of his characters. In Malory's version, by contrast, it is clear from the evidence of earlier tales that the king knows something, even though we cannot say how much.[7] When Arthur first told Merlin of his interest in Guinevere, "Merlyon warned the kyng covertly that Gwenyver was nat holsom for hym to take to wyff. For he warned hym that Launcelot scholde love hir, and sche hym agayne" (p. 97). Now there is admittedly an ambiguity here. In the French, Merlin's warning is too equivocal for Arthur to understand it. Though the glossary in Vinaver's edition defines *covertly* as "secretly," which might mean that Merlin made the revelation in private, the *OED* gives, in addition to the above, "In a veiled or hidden manner; with the sense implied, not expressed; indirectly, by implication." And so Malory's indirect discourse and his use of the adverb *covertly* may be meant to indicate an obscurity in Merlin's communication that corresponds to the obscurity in the French.[8] However, there is another and much less problematic passage. In *The Book of Sir Tristram*, Morgan sends that knight to a tournament with a shield bearing the device of a king and queen and a knight with one foot on the head of each of them. One of her women is present to explain to the king: "Sir kynge, wyte you well thys shylde was ordayned for you, to warn you of youre shame and dishonoure that longith to you and youre quene" (p. 557). It is noteworthy that although Lancelot is not named, Arthur makes the right identification when he recalls the shield later. Having written to Mark chiding him about his harrying of Tristram, he receives a saucy reply in which Mark "spake wondirly shorte unto kynge Arthur, and bade hym entermete with hymself and wyth hys wyff, and of his knyghtes, for he [i.e., Mark] was able to rule his [own] wyff and his knyghtes" (p. 617). At this, Arthur "mused of many thynges, and thought of his systyrs wordys, quene Morgan le Fay, that she had seyde betwyxte quene Gwenyver and sir Launcelot, and in this thought he studyed a grete whyle." Considering their source, he puts these suggestions aside at the moment, but the attentive reader is not likely to assume in the opening scenes of the seventh tale that Arthur suspects nothing of the adultery. In contrast to the poem, which deals only with the story's last phase, there is in Malory's version enough in what has gone before to establish the right degree of suspense about what the king is thinking. Furthermore, in the seventh tale Malory has interpolated the episode of the Knight of the Cart, in which the queen is accused of infidelity when Lancelot accidentally leaves bloodstains on her bed. Though Lancelot acquits the queen by slaying her accuser in a judicial combat, the reader can hardly fail to notice that the king never receives an explanation of the bloodstains. Until matters come to a head at the beginning of the eighth tale, with the accusation by Agravain that results in Lancelot's being found in the queen's room (which in the French is the second time Agravain speaks out), Malory apparently wants to avoid dealing directly with Arthur. Hence, the omission of the scenes of Agravain's first warning and of Morgan's showing the paintings.

The omission of these early revelations profoundly affects our view of Arthur in the seventh tale. In the French the revelations do not thoroughly convince the king that Lancelot and Guinevere are betraying him, and this is certainly as it should be. Agravain's is an unsupported assertion. Morgan's evidence, though rather arresting, is of an extraordinary kind and Arthur's uncertainty is understandable. On the one hand is the security of a lifetime, on the other certain incriminating pictures on a wall which Morgan says are the work of Lancelot. In fact all he has now that he did not have before is her word added to Agravain's. He oscillates between belief and unbelief, and Jean Frappier is right in defending his hesitancy as psychologically credible.[9] But one should note the effect that the French author's way of dramatizing that hesitancy exerts on the stature of Arthur. After the tournament at Winchester, the king tells Gawain what Agravain had said and adds, "si me tenisse ore bien a honni, se ge l'eüsse creü de sa mençonge; car ge sei or bien que se Lancelos amast la reïne par amors, il ne se fust pas remuez de Kamaalot, tant com ge fusse hors, einz i fust remés por avoir de la reïne sa volenté" (Sec. 30). When he returns to Camelot from Morgan's castle and learns that Lancelot came back but stayed only one day,

il li estoit avis que se Lancelos amast la reïne de fole amor, si
comme l'en li metoit sus, il ne peüst pas la court tant
eslongnier ne metre ariere dos tant comme il fesoit; et c'estoit
une chose qui moult metoit le cuer le roi a aise et qui moult li
fesoit mescroire les paroles que il of ores de Morgain sa sereur.
(Sec. 62)

But in fact Lancelot has always spent extremely long periods of time away
from court. Nearly all of the *Lancelot* proper is taken up with adventures away
from Camelot, and he is separated from Guinevere for the entire duration of
the Grail quest. If mere willingness to leave the court is to be taken as
disproving the charges against Lancelot, Arthur ought to realize that he need
not have entertained them for a moment. Of course the purpose behind
these little irrationalities is clear. They are touching. There is an ironic
poignancy about the old king's clutching at straws in this way. Yet one may
well feel that such pathos is out of place here, for it inevitably diminishes its
subject. Later in the story the French author resorts to this device again.
When Lancelot has rescued Guinevere from the fire and taken her to Joyous
Gard, the pope intervenes to stop the war that has ensued. The king, on
hearing that Lancelot has agreed to surrender Guinevere, says, "Par Dieu,
s'il fust autant a Lancelot de la roïne comme on me faisoit entendant, il n'est
mie si au desous de ceste guerre qu'il la rendist des mois, se il l'amast de fole
amour" (Sec. 118). This surely makes once too often, and after all that has
happened, such credulity ceases to be touching and begins to look faintly
foolish. Through the omission of the charges of Agravain and Morgan,
Malory's Arthur escapes the diminishment in stature that the French king
suffers in our eyes as we watch his vacillating reactions to those charges.
Instead, having long since established that the king has reason to be watchful,
Malory leaves it at that and refuses to chart the pulse of his anxieties,
focusing on the lovers for the duration of the seventh tale, and not widening
that focus to show what Arthur has been thinking until the next, when the
adultery erupts into scandal.

That eruption begins in the very first scene of the eighth tale. The
corresponding passage in the French provides another instance of pathetic
irony. The king enters while Agravain and his brothers are arguing over
Agravain's intention to disclose Lancelot's treason, and he asks what they
have been talking about in such loud voices.[10] Gawain refuses to say, warning
that no good will come of it for any of them, and he and Gareth leave the
room. The king then asks Agravain, but Agravain will not answer and tells

him to ask the others. When Gaheris and Mordred also refuse to speak,
Arthur threatens Agravain with a sword, whereupon the latter drops his
apparently feigned reluctance and says that he was telling Gawain that it is
disloyal of them to have concealed for so long the shame and dishonor that
Lancelot has been doing the king. "'Conment,' fet li rois, 'me fet donc
Lancelos honte? De quoi est ce donc? Dites le moi, car de lui ne me gardasse
ge jamé que il ma honte porchaçast; car ge l'ai touzdis tant ennoré et chier
tenu que il ne deüst en nule maniere a moi honte fere'" (Sec. 86). Agravain
replies that Lancelot has been sleeping with the queen. "Quant li rois entent
ceste parole, si mue couleur et devint pales, et dist: 'Ce sort merveilles.'"
When after a long pause the king speaks again, it is to exhort the brothers to
prove their charge. He swears to wreak vengeance on the lovers.

The irony of the king's determination to make Agravain speak the
words that will precipitate the ruin of the fellowship which he has so long
held together sorts well with the presentation of Arthur's responses to the
earlier charges, but once again the pathos results in a certain loss of dignity.
The French Arthur is no Othello. The English poet, probably simply for the
sake of compression, eliminates Agravain's reluctance to speak out, and
Malory has not seen fit to restore it. So here also Malory's Arthur gains in
stature by comparison with his French prototype.

A more important question about the scene in the *Mort Artu* is the
puzzling inconsistency of Arthur's shock and wonderment at Agravain's
statement. The king reacts as if the possibility of Lancelot and Guinevere's
deceiving him were a wholly new one, when in fact, as we have seen, the
accusation has already been made to him twice. The poet changes Arthur's
surprised response to one of sadness:

> "Allas!" than sayd the kynge thore,
>   "Certes, that were grete pyte,
> So As man nad neuyr yit more
>   Off biaute ne of bounte
> Ne man in worlde was neuyr yit ore
>   Off so mykylle noblyte.
> Allas! full grete duelle it were
>   In hym shulde Any treson be."
>   (ll. 1736–43)

This too is curious in its own way. It is as if the poet had noticed the
inconsistency between Arthur's reaction and the fact that the charge is not a
new one, and sought to remove it. Yet the precaution is in fact unnecessary

in his version, since he has already omitted the earlier charges. An alternative explanation is that the poet is simply skipping a page and translating not the lines quoted above but an exclamation the king makes a bit later: "Ha! Dex, quel douleur et quel domage quant en si preudome se herberja onques traïson!" (Sec. 87). This is the more likely because the French king speaks these words just before he sends for the brothers to ask their counsel on how to take Lancelot in the act, and it is this request for counsel that immediately follows in the poem (ll. 1744–47).[11] It is also possible that the poet's substitution of a saddened reaction for the surprise in the French source is merely a fortuitous change, made by the poet without specifically intending revision in the course of freely adapting, rather than conscientiously translating and abridging, the French. It is probably true that even an alert reader would not be struck by Arthur's failure to express surprise at Agravain's disclosure, especially given the hit-or-miss psychology of the poem in general, if the reader did not compare it with the French.

By way of contrast, I think it is impossible for any attentive reader of Malory's version not to notice that there the king expresses neither surprise nor sadness. When Agravain has spoken, Arthur replies without hesitation,

"Gyff hit be so ... wyte you well, he ys non othir [than a traitor]. But I woude be lothe to begyn such a thynge but I myght have prevys of hit, for sir Launcelot ys an hardy knyght, and all ye know that he ys the beste knyght amonge us all, and but if he be takyn with the dede he woll fyght with hym that bryngith up the noyse, and I know no knyght that ys able to macch hym. Therefore, and hit be sothe as ye say, I woude that he were takyn with the dede."   (p. 1163)

There are no oaths of vengeance. The tone is calm and businesslike. It seems shockingly cold-blooded of Arthur to proceed so directly to the practical necessity of taking his best knight and his queen "with the dede." Malory follows this statement of Arthur's with a comment that appears to be a strange non sequitur:

For, as the Freynshe booke seyth, the kynge was full lothe that such a noyse shulde be uppon sir Launcelot and his quene; for the kynge had a demyng of hit, but he wold nat here thereoff, for sir Launcelot had done so much for hym and for the quene so many tymes that wyte you well the kynge loved hym passyngly well.

That "the kynge had a demyng of hit" of course explains the absence of surprise in his reaction, but his love for Lancelot and his wish to avoid scandal are odd reasons for licensing Agravain and the others to attempt to trap the lovers. Yet that is what Malory says; the paragraph opens with the conjunction *for*. Now this might be an instance of what P. J. C. Field sees as a tendency of Malory's, the use of *for* to "connect things which have no natural connection."[12] But still the juxtaposition of these two paragraphs is striking and demands attention, especially in a scene where so many other details are obviously so carefully wrought. To make sense of the sequence of thought, it is necessary to attempt to get behind the king's words and into his mind, the mind that we noticed was so conspicuously closed to us in the seventh tale.

We can begin by considering what we are specifically told about the king's thoughts here, putting aside for the moment the question of the connection between them and the words he speaks just previously. The king, Malory tells us, has been willing to live with the possibility that Lancelot is cuckolding him in order to avoid a disruptive scandal and to keep Lancelot, the chief glory of the Table and his closest friend, in the fellowship. As E. Talbot Donaldson has put it, "Arthur's previous silence suddenly appears as the result neither of ignorance nor of complacency, but of a deep desire not to have the conflict of loyalties come to the surface, where he would—with what disastrous consequences he well knew—have to face it."[13] This alone sets him poles apart from the French author's characterization. Faced on two previous occasions with a situation now before Malory's Arthur for the first time, the French king had exploded into oaths of vengeance only to allow his mind to be set at rest shortly afterward by wholly factitious considerations. There is no indication anywhere in the French that he would be willing to blink at the affair for the sake of a higher good. After the episode of Morgan's showing him the paintings, there is a passage in which the narrator comments that Arthur did not want anyone to enter the chamber with the pictures for fear that his shame might become public knowledge: "car trop doutoit honte" (Sec. 54). It would become no man to sneer at this; yet by comparison Malory's Arthur is a stronger and nobler person. He has been able to sink his masculine pride in the concern for the unity of the fellowship. One need not amass quotations to prove that the Round Table is of primary importance to him. To establish his priorities, it is enough merely to cite what he says after Lancelot has decimated his company to rescue the queen from the fire: "And much more I am soryar for my good knyghtes losse than for the losse of my fayre quene; for quenys I myght have inow, but such a felyship of good knyghtes shall never be togydirs in no company" (p. 1184). To argue that this is merely another form of vanity would surely be unfair, for the whole book has made it clear that, far from existing for Arthur's personal satisfaction or aggrandizement, the Round Table and the values it represents are synonymous with the good order of the state. On the question of the adultery, which the passage quoted above tells us has long been before him, Malory's king has chosen public over private good, and Edward D. Kennedy has amply demonstrated that this choice, as well as Arthur's love for the knight whose prowess has been so valuable to the realm, is thoroughly consistent with the medieval idea of a good king.[14]

But it is in the very nature of this modus vivendi at which Arthur has arrived that it is practicable only so long as it is private. As a public figure, the choice he has made is in fact not open to him. Once the adultery erupts into scandal, he cannot tolerate it except at the cost of the respect of his court and his kingdom. As he says after the raid on the queen's room, "I may nat with my worshyp but my quene muste suffir dethe" (p. 1174). He has, of course, always realized this, and it is his having anticipated such circumstances as those which have now arisen that accounts for the readiness of his reply to Agravain. However, his telling Agravain to take Lancelot and Guinevere "with the dede" is not prompted by any fatalistic sense that he cannot now avert the ultimate rupture and that he had better play the outraged husband his subjects will expect of him. If his interest in the question of how to prove it is just what a person like Agravain would expect, it is not prompted by Agravain's kind of reason. As Arthur sees it, the task he has set his malicious nephews is an impossible one. He is relying on the discretion of his wife and her lover, or at least on the prowess of the latter, to make it so. While he speaks calmly of the practical difficulties of proving their guilt, he is really setting Agravain, though the latter does not realize it, a challenge. It is not what he says, but why he says it, that explains the conjunction for which introduces Malory's comment about his attachment to Lancelot and his wish to scotch the rumors. He is defying Agravain, not encouraging him.

This is clearly not the sense that Arthur's addressing himself to the plan to trap the lovers bears in the French version, in which the king is intensely jealous and gives Agravain his sanction "moult volentiers" (Sec. 87), but it may yet have been the French that furnished the suggestion for this phase of Malory's characterization of Arthur. In the sequel to the above scene, the French provides considerable support for the reading I have given. When Agravain and his party find the door of the queen's chamber bolted (something which, oddly enough, they seem not to have expected), the narrator comments, "si n'i of celui qui n'en fust touz esbahiz; lors sorent il bien qu'il avoient failli a ce qu'il vouloient fere" (Sec. 90). The fact that after the escape of Lancelot the knights enter the queen's chamber and begin abusing her (a scene Malory omits for the simple reason that they are all dead) seems to me to point in the same direction. The author says that they "entrerent en la chambre et pristrent la reïne et li firent honte et laidure assez plus qu'il ne de lüssent et distrent que ore estoit la chose prouvee et qu'ele n'en puet eschaper sanz mort" (Sec. 92). The author condemns their pitilessness, and in the context, where it is clear that the knights are taking out on Guinevere their frustration at the escape of Lancelot, their assertion that the thing is proven sounds like downshouting bravado. Later on, when the pope intervenes to make Arthur desist from the siege of Joyous Gard, where Lancelot has taken Guinevere, it is because he has heard "que on ne l'avoit pas prise provee el meffait que on li metoit sus" (Sec. 117). Malory's version also contains a passage drawing attention to the inconclusive nature of the evidence. He completely rewrites the scene in which Gawain attempts to dissuade Arthur from executing Guinevere. When Gawain learns in the French of the sentence which has been passed, he determines not to witness her death and threatens to renounce his fealty to the king: "Sire, ge vos rent quanque ge tieng de vos, ne jamés jor de ma vie ne vos servirai, se vos ceste desloiauté soufrez" (Sec. 93). Malory develops this moment into the occasion for a detailed critique of the verdict which underscores the fact that the king was justified in his belief that Agravain would never be able to provide positive evidence. Gawain advises against hasty judgment "for many causis. One ys thys, thoughe hyt were so that sir Launcelot were founde in the quenys chambir, yet hit myght be so that he cam thydir for none evyll" (pp. 1174–75). He cites Lancelot's numerous services to the queen and suggests that she may have summoned him to reward him. Gawain even defends the secrecy of the interview:

> "And peraventure my lady the quene sente for hym to that entente, that sir Launcelot sholde a com prevaly to her, wenyng that hyt had be beste in eschewyng and dredyng of slaundir; for oftyntymys we do many thynges that we wene for the beste be, and yet peradventure hit turnyth to the warste."

I suggest further that a concern to reproduce the French source's emphasis on the absence of positive proof may be the explanation for a passage that has drawn attention from nearly all of Malory's critics. When Lancelot goes to Guinevere's room on the night of the ambush, Malory writes, "For, as the Freynshhe booke seyth, the quene and sir Launcelot were togydirs. And whether they were abed other at other maner of disportis, me lyste nat thereof make no mention, for love that tyme was nat as love ys nowadayes" (p. 1165). Both the French book and the English poem say rather more than that they were "togydirs": "Si se deschauça et despoilla et se coucha avec la reïne" (Sec. 90); and "To bede he gothe with the quene" (l. 1806). It seems to me very likely that Malory's statement is meant as yet another point against the conclusiveness of Agravain's case. In the scene in which Lancelot surrenders the queen to Arthur, he says, "I was sente unto my lady, youre quyne, I wote nat for what cause, but I was nat so sone within the chambir dore but anone sir Aggravayne and sir Mordred called me traytoure and false recrayed knyght" (p. 1197). I believe it is possible to take Lancelot at his word when he says that he had hardly entered the queen's room when the cry was raised. Malory is carefully planting a doubt about the actual guilt of the lovers *in the present instance*.[15] The point of it all is that Arthur was right in believing that Agravain could not succeed in meeting the stipulation he had set.

However, after the raid on Guinevere's chamber, Malory's Arthur is just as angry as his prototype. In the French the king is presented after the springing of the trap as being fiercely determined that the queen shall die. He says to his counselors,

> "Je bé ... que por ce mesfet qu'ele a fet l'en en face grant justise. Et ge vos commant ... que vos esgardoiz entre vos de quel mort ele doit morir; que sanz mort n'en puet ele eschaper, se vos meïsmes vos teniez devers lui, en tel maniere que, se vos disiez qu'ele ne deiist pas morir, si moria ele."
>
> (Sec. 92)

He asks his counselors not whether Guinevere should be executed but only how, and whatever their reservations, the author tells us, "A ceste chose s'acordent li un et li autre a fine force, car il voient bien que li rois le velt" (Sec. 93). At this point Malory portrays his king as likewise moved mainly by anger. Lancelot says,

> "For thes knyghtes were sente by kynge Arthur to betray me, and therefore the kyng woll in thys hete and malice jouge the quene unto brennyng, and that may nat I suffir that she shulde be brente for my sake. For and I may be harde and suffirde and so takyn, I woll feyght for the quene, that she ys a trew lady untyll her lorde. But the kynge in hys hete, I drede, woll nat take me as I ought to be takyn." (p. 1171)

Though Lancelot is mistaken in his view of the king's attitude toward Agravain's trap, the narrative voice bears him out in his assessment of

Arthur's later mood: "So than there was made grete ordynaunce in thys ire, and the quene muste nedis be jouged to the deth" (p. 1174). The obvious question now is this: If I am correct in attributing to Malory's king, in contrast to his French counterpart, not just the expectation but the positive hope that Agravain will not succeed in the task he sets him, and if it is true that that hope is justified by the event, is it not then inconsistent for Arthur to pass up the loophole he has so cannily provided for? The answer will appear from a comparison of the grounds of the king's anger in Malory's version with those in the French. The French Arthur regards the device of Agravain as having proven the queen's guilt, in spite of the reservations implied by the narrator in the passages quoted above. Guinevere is to die for adultery, and Lancelot too if that can be managed. But for Malory's Arthur the adultery is, as I have said, a secondary consideration. It is certainly a factor, since the king's "worshyp" forbids his publicly submitting to cuckoldry. Yet if that were all, the loophole would still exist, as indeed Gawain says it does. However, it is not all. The sources disagree on the number of knights killed in the struggle outside Guinevere's door. In the French version Lancelot slays only one of the party.[16] It is significant that Malory chooses to follow the poem, having Lancelot kill all of them except Mordred.[17] In connection with the change wrought in the situation by the springing of Agravain's trap, it is the high death toll that is cited as necessitating the punishment of the treasonous adultery. Lancelot says to his allies, "And for cause I have slayne thys nyght sir Aggravayne, sir Gawaynes brothir, and at the leste twelve of hys felowis, for thys cause now am I sure of mortall warre" (p. 1171). The narrator tells us that "bycause sir Mordred was ascaped sore wounded, and the dethe of thirtene knyghtes of the Rounde Table, thes previs and experyenses caused kynge Arthure to commaunde the quene to the fyre and there to be brente" (p. 1174). In Malory's version it is not the adultery but the slaughter to which it has led that angers Arthur. Now that the love of Lancelot and Guinevere has damaged the Table, the very motive that had led Arthur to tolerate it makes him wish to punish it. This is a powerful irony, and it is wholly Malory's contribution.

It may be objected that Malory's king seems to have foreseen the bloodshed to which Agravain's plot leads, for he said to him, "I counceyle you to take with you sure felyshyp" (p. 1163), and "beware ... for I warne you, ye shall fynde hym wyght" (p. 1164). If he has expected it all, then the reversal of his attitude when it actually happens is unconvincing. But the tone of the lines seems to indicate that he is cautioning them rather than urging them to do the job thoroughly. By contrast the only counsel given by the French king, who is genuinely concerned that they should succeed, is that they be sure to keep the plan a secret. It is precisely because Malory's Arthur takes

Lancelot's resistance for granted that he advises them to go in force. It is a precaution urged for the sake of their safety rather than their efficiency. It backfires. Malory once again displays a sharp sense of irony in arranging events so that what had been meant to restrain Lancelot only gives him occasion to do that much more damage.

This anger in Malory's Arthur at the damage to his fellowship is a vital dramatic detail. If his attitude toward the covert adultery makes him a nobler figure than his French counterpart, it is also possible to feel that it makes him colder and less sympathetic too, something of a moralist's construct held up to view for our edification. The very human anger that enters the characterization at this point enriches it, and Malory is careful to keep it before us. We have already noticed two references to the king's "hete" and "ire." When Gawain, in the passage quoted earlier, suggests that the interview between Lancelot and the queen may have been innocent and concludes by saying that Lancelot will "make hit good" against anyone who says otherwise, Arthur replies,

> "That I beleve well ... but I woll nat that way worke with sir Launcelot, for he trustyth so much uppon hys hondis and hys myght that he doutyth no man. And therefore for my quene he shall nevermore fyght, for she shall have the law. And if I may gete sir Launcelot, wyte you well he shall have as shamefull a dethe."   (p. 1175)

The tone here is clearly vindictive. When Gawain replies that he hopes he will never see it, Arthur goes so far as to attempt to win him to share his wish for vengeance by reminding him that in escaping from the queen's room Lancelot slew his brother Agravain and two of his sons as well. Clearly this attempt to rouse Gawain to anger is the tactic of a prejudiced advocate and not of an objective judge. Later, after Lancelot has wreaked further havoc among the fellowship in rescuing the queen from death, slaying Gareth in the process, Arthur and not Gawain is the first to broach the issue of revenge. Though he subsequently loses all stomach for the war and it is Gawain who is responsible for its continuation, Arthur needs no encouragement to initiate it. The wrath that flashes out in the characterization after the night of Agravain's raid prevents our regarding Arthur as an inhumanly idealized ruler.

Yet Malory is careful to make clear that though Arthur acts in anger he acts no less than justly. Lancelot and Guinevere are, after all, guilty of treason. Having stated that the queen was sentenced to death in "ire," Malory goes on to explain that death was the only punishment for treason, and "othir the menour other the takynge wyth the dede shulde be causer of their hasty jougement" (p. 1174). With the alternative grounds, we are reminded on the one hand of the sense in which Agravain failed in not taking the lovers in the act, while on the other hand we are assured that the conviction is still legal. *Menour* is glossed in Vinaver's edition as "behaviour," and Lancelot's behavior in killing thirteen knights while resisting arrest is certainly incriminating.[18] The loophole was, finally, only a loophole. Moreover, in spite of the wrathful tone in which Arthur rejects Gawain's suggestion that Lancelot be tried by combat, the refusal itself is surely justified. The king knows all too well where the truth lies in the present case, and he also knows that Lancelot's prowess would ensure its being contradicted. He is after all the embodiment of the law. He cannot countenance a complete travesty of justice. The legal explanation of the "menour" being sufficient grounds for conviction and the reason for Arthur's refusing to try the case by combat are not in the sources. The French version gives us an Arthur who acts simply in haste and anger, forcing his counselors to return the verdict he wants; and the poem tells us nothing at all of Arthur's state of mind between his sorrow at Agravain's accusation and his sorrow at the death of Gareth, except what is implied in his referring to Lancelot as "that treitour" (l. 1908). Malory, however, is at pains to explain that, though the king is motivated by anger, from a legal and moral standpoint his decision is just.

It is noteworthy that the pattern of reversal in the king's attitude toward Lancelot is remarkably similar to that of Gawain, which so many critics have deplored. From the advocate of peace who dissociates himself from Agravain's plot and defends Lancelot's presence in Guinevere's room, Gawain changes to an implacable warmonger when Lancelot inadvertently kills Gareth. The cause of Gawain's reversal, as of Arthur's, is an act forced upon Lancelot by circumstances. Reduplicative patterns in Malory's book have been noticed by all of his readers and examined by many of his critics. Two of the more recent full-length studies show that there are still things to be said about this aspect of Malory's art. Larry D. Benson's thematic analysis devotes considerable space to patterns in sequences of episodes,[19] and Mark Lambert has a valuable account of "the great number of phrases, situations, and motifs which occur in the seventh tale and then echo, either loudly or faintly, in the eighth."[20] This is not the place to reopen the debate about the credibility of Malory's Gawain. Let it suffice to suggest that the parallel courses of Arthur's and Gawain's relations with Lancelot should affect our assessment of Malory's picture of Gawain. The reversal in Arthur's attitude to Lancelot (which seems entirely credible) serves to prepare the reader for the more problematic change in Gawain, which follows so closely upon it.

It appears, then, that the French sequel to Agravain's plot suggested to Malory a radical change in the character of Arthur as he draws it prior to the night of the fatal assignation between Lancelot and Guinevere. Malory indicates that the king's endorsement of his nephew's plan is only apparent. Taking his cue from the French author's attention to the sense in which Agravain fails, Malory attributes to Arthur a foresight of and reliance on this failure. The result is that instead of the vacillating French king, who swings back and forth between angry suspicion and easy reassurance, we get a figure who has not been duped at all by Lancelot and Guinevere, but rather one who has been strong enough to forego revenge for as long as the actual practice of the adultery poses less of a threat to the unity of the court than his exposing and punishing the lovers would do. Ironically, however, the circumstances of Agravain's failure are such as to turn Arthur against Lancelot. Thus, after the raid the resemblance between Malory's king and his irascible French prototype is closer than before it, though Malory motivates Arthur's anger differently—the thirteen dead knights are the issue—and insists that the anger is justified. The canny and noble king of *Le Morte Darthur* is the product of an insight into character much sharper than the French author's, and the symmetry between Arthur's and Gawain's relations with Lancelot is an important instance of the shaping power at work in the masterful last part of Malory's book.

NOTES

1. *The Works of Sir Thomas Malory*, ed. Eugène Vinaver, 2nd ed., rev., 3 vols. (Oxford: Clarendon, 1967). Quotations of Malory are from this edition, and page references are given in the text.

2. *La Morte le Roi Artu: Roman du XIIIe Siècle*, ed. Jean Frappier, 3rd ed. (Geneva: Droz, and Paris: Minard, 1964). Quotations of the *Mort Artu* are from this edition and are identified by section numbers in the text.

3. *Le Mort Arthur: A Romance in Stanzas of Eight Lines*, ed. J. Douglas Bruce, Early English Text Society, Extra Series, No. 88 (London: Kegan Paul, Trench, Trübner, 1903). Quotations of the poem are from this edition, with line numbers given in the text.

4. Published as *The Vulgate Version of the Arthurian Romances*, ed. H. Oskar Sommer, Carnegie Institution Publication No. 74, 7 Vols. and Index (Washington: Carnegie Institution, 1908–16). The *Lancelot* proper (which recounts the hero's life from birth to the eve of the Grail quest) occupies Volumes III–V.

5. See *Works*, p. 1058, where Lancelot recalls how Guinevere provided him with a sword at the beginning of his career.

6. The hostility between Arthur and Morgan goes back to the first tale, to the episodes of Morgan's theft of Excalibur, the combat she arranged between her brother and her lover Accolon, and the magic mantle in which she intended to burn Arthur alive. This material derives not from the Vulgate Cycle but from the *Suite du Merlin*. As for such evidences of Morgan's treachery as do occur in the Vulgate, they are apparently concealed from Arthur (hence his trust of her in the *Mort Artu*). They consist mainly of several

occasions on which Morgan imprisons Lancelot, either because she hates him (*Vulgate Version*, V, 166), loves him (V, 218), or wishes to take revenge on the queen through her lover because the queen had earlier broken up an affair between a cousin of hers and Morgan (IV, 124). I can find no indication in the Lancelot proper that Lancelot in recounting his adventures ever tells Arthur of his sister's harassments. On two important occasions when the hero returns to court, he waits to be alone with Guinevere before mentioning Morgan by name (V, 190–93, 322), and on another occasion the author states explicitly that, in recounting his adventures to Arthur, Lancelot conceals a great part of them (IV, 227). It seems that he wishes to spare the king's feelings, for after one of his escapes he leaves Morgan a message saying that only his consideration for Arthur has prevented his killing her (V, 223).

7. That Malory's omission of the earlier charges is effective in a way the poet's is not is also the position of E. Talbot Donaldson, "Malory and the Stanzaic *Le Morte Arthur*," *Studies in Philology*, 47 (1950), 460–72. But he does not cite the indications in earlier tales of Arthur's grounds for suspicion: "The reader never knows whether or not [the king] is aware of Guinevere's infidelity. The result is a curious and subtle sort of suspense" (pp. 469–70).

8. This possibility seems to have gone unnoticed. Malory's version of Merlin's warning is usually regarded as explicit and perfectly clear to Arthur. See, for example, R. M. Lumiansky, "'The Tale of Lancelot and Guinevere': Suspense," in *Malory's Originality: A Critical Study of Le Morte Darthur*, ed. R. M. Lumiansky (Baltimore: Johns Hopkins Univ. Press, 1964), p. 207; and Edward D. Kennedy, "The Arthur–Guenevere Relationship in Malory's *Morte Darthur*," *Studies in the Literary Imagination*, 4, No. 2 (1971), 29–30. Though the glossing of covertly as "secretly" would seem to place Vinaver in the company of Lumiansky and Kennedy, it should be noted that the glossary was prepared not by Vinaver but by G. L. Brook, and that Vinaver's note on the passage may imply an interpretation of *covertly* that is close to the meaning cited above from the *OED*. The note calls the passage "an attempt to clarify and expand Merlin's obscure ('covert') remarks in [the French] which even Arthur fails to understand" (p. 97 n., ll. 29–31). Possibly Vinaver means that Malory wanted to make Merlin's meaning clear to the reader but not to Arthur.

9. Jean Frappier, *Etude sur La Mort le Roi Artu*, 2nd ed., rev., Publications Romanes et Françaises, No. 70 (Geneva: Droz, and Paris: Minard, 1961), pp. 302–07.

10. Both the French and Malory's versions of the scene proper make it clear that the Orkney brothers are alone; but at the beginning of the scene, Malory suggests that others are present: "and than sir Aggravayne seyde thus opynly, and nat in no counceyle, that manye knyghtis myght here ..." (p. 1161). This is not borne out by what follows, and the poet must have been responsible for the momentary confusion. He says, "A tyme be-felle, sothe to sayne, / the knyghtis stode in chambyr and spake" (ll. 1672-73), and a few stanzas later he refers to "Gawayne and All that other pres" (l. 1713).

11. In the French version, the disclosure of Agravain and the planning of the trap are divided between two different scenes; Malory and the poet telescope them into one.

12. P. J. C. Field, *Romance and Chronicle: A Study of Malory's Prose Style* (London: Barrie & Jenkins, 1971), p. 41. (Field does not specifically refer to the passage in question.)

13. Donaldson, p. 470.

14. Edward D. Kennedy, "Malory's King Mark and King Arthur," *Mediaeval Studies*, 37 (1975), 190–234. My view of Arthur's psychology in some ways resembles Kennedy's (though it was developed independently). However, I believe that in this article and in his "The Arthur–Guinevere Relationship in Malory's *Morte Darthur*," Kennedy overstates Arthur's indifference to his queen, thereby diminishing our sense of the complexity of the king's dilemma and the difficulty of the noble choice he made.

15. Vida D. Scudder, *Le Morte Darthur of Sir Thomas Malory and Its Sources* (New York: Dutton, 1921), pp. 320, 327, points out a very similar technical reservation connected with Meleagant's formulation of the charge against Guinevere in "The Knight of the Cart." See also Charles Moorman, *The Book of Kyng Arthur: The Unity of Malory's Morte Darthur* (Lexington: Univ. of Kentucky Press, 1965), pp. 16–17.

16. Possibly he slays two. Having put on his first victim's armor, he goes out "et fiert si le premier qu'il encontre qu'il le porte a terre tout estendu en tel maniere qu'il n'a povoir de soi relever" (Sec. 90). The last clause may or may not be a periphrasis meaning the knight was dead.

17. Vinaver's note on the death count in the poem is inaccurate. He says, "There is no mention of any of them [except Agravain] being killed or wounded" (p. 1168 n., ll. 19–20). But lines 1858–59 and 1910–11 make it clear that all but Mordred are killed.

18. Some such meaning as the one Vinaver suggests would seem to be exactly what the context requires, a "distinction ... similar to that between direct and circumstantial evidence" (p. 1174 n., ll. 23–24). Yet the *OED* does not seem to bear this out. It gives "The stolen thing which is found in a thief's possession when he is arrested," and for *with the mainour*, "in the act of doing something unlawful, 'in flagrante delicto'" (s.v. Mainour, manner). The second meaning eliminates the distinction that Malory is clearly trying to make between "menour" and "takynge with the dede." The first meaning seems to fit the dramatic situation only if we assume that Malory is thinking of Guinevere figuratively as a stolen thing. But Malory may have associated or confused the idea of possessing incriminating evidence with that of being taken in incriminating circumstances. *Ballentine's Law Dictionary*, 3rd ed., says, "A thief was said to be taken with the mainour when taken with the stolen goods upon him, in manu, in his hand. When so taken, the thief could be arraigned and tried without being first indicted. This practice was discontinued under Edward the Third, in England, but in Scotland it was followed in Blackstone's time" (s.v. with the mainour). Malory may have known vaguely of a time or place in which incriminating circumstances—of one kind or another—were cause for arraignment and trial without previous indictment, or, as he puts it, "hasty jougement." Certainly a degree of imprecision in his use of the legal terminology here is of a piece with the vagueness of his description of the process by which the queen is condemned. The French version gives more specific detail.

19. Larry D. Benson, *Malory's Morte Darthur* (Cambridge: Harvard Univ. Press, 1976). See especially Chapters 4, 5, and 6. By "thematic" Benson means "the conformance of a narrative to some external, preexisting pattern" (p. 73). He isolates several patterns that Malory uses repeatedly.

20. Mark Lambert, *Malory: Style and Vision in Le Morte Darthur* (New Haven: Yale Univ. Press, 1975), p. 143.

ELLIOT L. GILBERT

The Female King:
Tennyson's Arthurian Apocalypse

Yet in the long years liker must they grow
The man be more of woman, she of man.
            —Tennyson, *The Princess*

Dr. Schreber believed that he had a mission to redeem the world and to
restore it to its lost state of bliss. This, however, he could only bring
about if he were first transformed from a man into a woman.
            —Freud, "A Case of Paranoia"

The happiest women, like the happiest nations, have no history.
            —George Eliot, *The Mill on the Floss*

Queen Victoria, there's a woman ... when one encounters a toothed
vagina of such exceptional size....
            —Lacan, "Seminar, 11 February 1975"

La femme est naturelle, c'est-à-dire abominable.
            —Baudelaire, *Mon Cœur mis à nu*

I

Sooner or later, most readers of the *Idylls of the King* find themselves
wondering by what remarkable transformative process the traditionally virile
and manly King Arthur of legend and romance evolved, during the

---

From *PMLA* 98, no. 5 (1983). © 1983 by the Modern Language Association of America.

nineteenth century, into the restrained, almost maidenly Victorian monarch of Alfred Lord Tennyson's most ambitious work. Many of the earliest of these readers of the *Idylls* deplored the change, noting in it disquieting evidence of the growing domestication and even feminization of the age.[1] And more recent critics, though they may have moderated the emotionalism of that first response, continue to see in Arthur's striking metamorphosis a key element in any analysis of the poem. I will argue here, however, that such a metamorphosis was inevitable, given the nineteenth-century confluence of what Michel Foucault has called "the history of sexuality" with what we may call the history of history, and that Tennyson's Arthurian retelling, far from being weakened by its revisionary premise, is in fact all the stronger and more resonant for depicting its hero as a species of female king. Tennyson was attracted to the legend of King Arthur as a prospective subject for literary treatment almost from the beginning of his career; "the vision of Arthur had come upon me," Hallam Tennyson quotes his father in the *Memoir*, "when, little more than a boy, I first lighted upon Malory" (2:128). *Poems, Chiefly Lyrical*, published in 1830, when Tennyson was just twenty-one, contains the picturesque fragment "Sir Lancelot and Queen Guinevere," and by 1833, when his next volume appeared, the poet had already written, or was in the process of writing, two of his best-known Arthurian works, "The Lady of Shalott" (1832) and the ambitious rendering of King Arthur's death that, at its first publication ten years later, he called "Morte d'Arthur."

By this time, however, Tennyson had come to question the propriety of a nineteenth-century artist devoting his energies to the reworking of medieval materials. That is, he came to feel that only some contemporary significance in the Arthurian retellings, only "some modern touches here and there" (as he puts it in "The Epic"), could redeem his poetry "from the charge of nothingness," from Thomas Carlyle's characterization of it as "a refuge from life ... a medieval arras" behind which the poet was hiding "from the horrors of the Industrial Revolution" (quoted in Priestley 35) or from John Sterling's judgment that "the miraculous legend of 'Excalibur' ... reproduced by any modern writer must be a mere ingenious exercise of fancy" (119).[2]

The idea that nineteenth-century artists ought to concern themselves with nineteenth-century subjects was a pervasive one (see Gent). When, for example, Matthew Arnold omitted *Empedocles on Etna* from a collection of his poetic works, he found it necessary to explain that he had not done so "because the subject of it was a Sicilian Greek born between two and three thousand years ago, *although many persons would think this a sufficient reason*" (italics mine). In the *Preface to Poems* (1853), Arnold goes on to quote "an intelligent critic" as stating that "the poet who would really fix the public attention must leave the exhausted past, and draw his subjects from matters of present import, and therefore both of interest and novelty" (1, 3). Four years later, in a long discourse on poetics in *Aurora Leigh*, Elizabeth Barrett Browning takes a similar position. "If there's room for poets in this world," Barrett Browning declares in book 5 of her blank-verse novel,

> Their sole work is to represent the age,
> Their age, not Charlemagne's
>
> . . . .
>
> To flinch from modern varnish, coat or flounce,
> Cry out for togas and the picturesque,
> Is fatal—foolish too. King Arthur's self
> Was commonplace to Lady Guenevere:
> And Camelot to minstrels seemed as flat
> As Fleet Street to our poets.   (200–13)

That Tennyson himself was influenced by such attitudes is plain from the fact that when he published "Morte d'Arthur" in 1842, he set his medieval story in a modern framing poem, "The Epic," whose only partly ironic theme is the irrelevance of such a historical subject to the contemporary world. Edward Fitzgerald asserts that Tennyson invented this setting "to give a reason for telling an old-world tale" (quoted in H. Tennyson 1:194). Otherwise, as poet Everard Hall remarks in "The Epic," explaining why he has burned his own long Arthurian poem,

> "Why take the style of those heroic times:
> For nature brings not back the mastodon,
> Nor we those times; and why should any man
> Remodel models?"

The lapse of fifty-five years between the writing of the "Morte d'Arthur" in 1833 and the publication of the complete *Idylls of the King* in 1888 suggests how difficult a time Tennyson had finding the contemporary significance he was looking for in his medieval material. Nevertheless, nearly all readers agree with the poet that "there is an allegorical or perhaps rather a parabolic drift in the poem" that permits the work to be read as "a discussion of problems which are both contemporary and perennial" (H. Tennyson 2:126–27).

The exact nature of that discussion remains an open question, though a few facts about the allegory do seem clear. The book, proceeding seasonally as it does from spring in "The Coming of Arthur" to winter in "The Passing of Arthur," is certainly about the decline of a community from an original ideal state, about the corruption and nihilism that overtake a once whole and healthy social order. Just as surely, an important agency of this decline is identified by the story as human sexuality and, in particular, female passion. The four idylls published by Tennyson in 1859—"Vivien," "Guinevere," "Enid," and "Elaine"—under the general title *The True and the False* focus on the polar extremes of feminine purity and carnality, and however the author may have altered his plans for the book in the following years, his emphasis on the corrosiveness of female sexuality never changed. "Thou has spoilt the purpose of my life," Arthur declares grimly in "Guinevere," about to part forever from the queen and plainly placing the whole blame for the decay of the Round Table and the fall of Camelot on his wife's unfaithfulness.

The association of marital fidelity with the health of the state did not please all the first readers of the *Idylls*. Swinburne, for one, condemned what he felt was the reduction of Sir Thomas Malory's virile tales of chivalry to a sordid domestic quarrel. To him, Victorian King Arthur was a "wittol," or willing cuckold, Guinevere "a woman of intrigue," Lancelot "a co-respondent," and the whole story "rather a case for the divorce court than for poetry" (57). In the same essay, Swinburne refers to the *Idylls* as "the Morte d'Albert" (56), alluding to Tennyson's 1862 dedication of his poem to the recently deceased prince consort but, even more than that, to the royal family's celebrated bourgeois domesticity.

Swinburne was right to see that Tennyson's idylls turn on the issue of domestic relations and specifically on the willingness or unwillingness of men and women to play their traditional social and sexual roles in these relations. He was wrong, however, to think such a subject contemptible. Indeed, his sardonic reference to "the Morte d'Albert" inadvertently calls attention to a major theme in the poem as well as to one of the central problems of Victorian society: the growing assertion of female authority.

In his Dedication of the *Idylls of the King* to Prince Albert, Tennyson describes a relationship between husband and wife that on the surface is entirely conventional. Albert is presented as an active force in national life, as "laborious" for England's poor, as a "summoner of War and Waste to rivalries of peace," as "modest, kindly, all-accomplished, wise," and, most important, as the ultimate pater familias, "noble father" of the country's "kings to be." Victoria, by contrast, appears in the Dedication principally in the role of bereaved and passive wife, whose "woman's heart" is exhorted to "break not but endure" and who is to be "comforted," "encompassed," and "o'ershadowed" by love until God chooses to restore her to her husband's side.

What lies behind this traditional domestic relationship is, of course, a very different reality. In that reality, Victoria is the true holder and wielder of power, the repository of enormous inherited authority, while Albert possesses what influence and significance he does almost solely through his marriage. This reversal of the usual male–female roles, superimposed on the more conventional relationship depicted in Tennyson's Dedication, produces a curious dissonance, much like one that came to sound more and more insistently in the culture as a whole as the nineteenth century progressed and that received powerful expression in the *Idylls of the King*. Indeed, Tennyson's very contemporary poem can be read as an elaborate examination of the advantages and dangers of sexual role reversal, with King Arthur himself playing, in a number of significant ways, the part usually assigned by culture to the woman.

II

Such revision of the female role in the nineteenth century is closely associated with the period's ambivalent attitude toward history. It was during the nineteenth century that the modern discipline of history first came fully into its own as a truly rigorous inquiry into the past, demanding, as Frederic Harrison puts it, "belief in contemporary documents, exact testing of authorities, scrupulous verification of citations, minute attention to chronology, geography, paleography, and inscriptions" (121). Defined in this new way, history had a distinctly male bias. This was true for a number of reasons. To begin with, its "disavowal of impressionism" (Douglas 174) in favor of a preoccupation with hard facts permitted it for the first time to rival the natural sciences as a "respectable" career for intellectual young men. Francis Parkman, American student of the Indian Wars, "defiantly chose history," one commentator tells us, "as a protest against what he considered the effeminacy of the liberal church" (Douglas 173). In addition, as a record of great public events, history had always tended to dwell almost exclusively on the activities of men. "It should not be forgotten," writes Arthur Schlesinger, "that all of our great historians have been men and were likely therefore to be influenced by a sex interpretation of history all the more potent because unconscious" (126). In *Northanger Abbey*, Jane Austen alludes sardonically to this fact when her heroine dismisses history books for being full of "the quarrels of popes and kings, with wars and pestilences in every page; the men all so good for nothing, and hardly any women at all" (108).

But nineteenth-century history was male-oriented in an even deeper and more all-pervasive sense than this; for to the extent that historians were principally concerned with recording the passage of power and authority through the generations, their work necessarily preserved the patrilineal forms and structures of the societies they investigated. "The centuries too are all lineal children of one another," writes Carlyle in *Past and Present*, emphasizing the intimate connection that has always existed between history and genealogy (45). In *The Elementary Structures of Kinship*, Lévi-Strauss argues that culture, and by extension history, can only come into existence after the concept of kinship has been established. But this means that in those societies where family structure is patrilineal, women must inevitably play a secondary role in history, since they do not have names of their own and therefore do not visibly participate in the passing on of authority from one generation to the next. The rise of "scientific" history in the nineteenth century, then, might have been expected to confirm, among other things, the validity of the traditional male-dominant and female-subordinate roles.

But in fact, those roles came more and more frequently to be questioned during the period, as did the new history itself. Ironically, it was the very success of scientific history at reconstituting the past that provoked this resistance. For what soon became clear was that, seen in too much detail and known too well, the past was growing burdensome and intimidating, was revealing—in Tennyson's metaphor—all the models that could not be remodeled. John Stuart Mill's celebrated dismay, reported in his *Autobiography*, that all the best combinations of musical notes "must already have been discovered" was one contemporary example of this anxiety. Another was George Eliot's declaration, in *Middlemarch*, that "a new Theresa will hardly have the opportunity of reforming a conventual life ... the medium in which [her] ardent deeds took shape is for ever gone." For a nineteenth-century woman like Dorothea Brooke, George Eliot tells us, it is often better that life be obscure since "the growing good of the world is partly dependent on *un*-historic acts" (612; italics mine).[3] Such a conclusion follows inevitably from the idea that history, simply by existing, exhausts possibilities, leaving its readers with a despairing sense of their own belatedness and impotence. And this despair in turn leads to anxious quests for novelty, to a hectic avant-gardism, and in the end to an inescapable fin de siècle ennui. "The world is weary of the past, / Oh, might it die or rest at last," Shelley declares in *Hellas*, expressing a desire for oblivion, a longing for the end of history. Only through such an apocalypse, the poet suggests, can life be made new and vital again.

The great apocalyptic event for the nineteenth century was the French Revolution, at its most authentic a massive and very deliberate assault on history. To be sure, regicide is the ultimate attack on the authority of the past, but if it is dealt with merely on a political level, its deeper significance is likely to be missed. To be fully understood, it must, rather, be placed in the context of the many other revolutionary acts whose collective intent was to overthrow not only the old historical regime but history itself. Among these acts were laws that abolished the right to make wills and that declared natural children absolutely equal with legitimate offspring. Both struck directly at the power of the past to control the present and, just as important, at the right of patrilineal authority to extend itself indefinitely into the future. Revolutionary calendar reforms were an even more literal attack on history. By decree, official chronology, for example, began at the autumn equinox of 1792; the first day of the new republic thus became the first day of the new world. Even the names of the months were changed in the revolutionary calendar, with the seasons replacing the Caesars—nature replacing history— as the source of the new nomenclature.

From these revolutionary activities two important principles emerged. The first is that wherever intolerable social abuses are the consequence of history, reform is only possible outside of history.[4] The French Revolution sought to incorporate this idea, at least symbolically, into an actual working community, a community for which not history but nature would provide the model. In that new dispensation, each person would be self-authorized, independent of genealogy, and each day would have the freshness of the first day or, rather, of the only day, of *illo tempore*, a moment in the eternal present unqualified and undiminished by an "exhausted past." Such an ambition has never been entirely fanciful. Mircea Eliade, for one, reminds us of "the very considerable period" during which

> humanity opposed history by all possible means.... The primitive desired to have no "memory," not to record time, to content himself with tolerating it simply as a dimension of his existence, but without interiorizing it, without transforming it into consciousness.... That desire felt by the man of traditional societies to refuse history, and to confine himself to an indefinite repetition of archetypes, testifies to his thirst for the real and his terror of losing himself by letting himself be overwhelmed by the meaninglessness of profane existence.
>
> (*Cosmos* 90–91)

The Revolution's famous exchange of "fraternity" for "paternity" makes the same point. The father–child relationship is generational and thus principally a product of history. Brothers, on the other hand, are by their nature contemporaries, and their relationships are therefore more "spatial" than temporal. In *Parsifal*, Wagner describes the realm of the Grail knight brotherhood in just these terms. "Zum Raum," Gurnemanz explains to the at-first uncomprehending Parsifal, "wird hier die Zeit" 'Time changes here to space.' Significantly, James R. Kincaid finds this same idea built into the very structure of Tennyson's *Idylls*. "The overlaid seasonal progress in the [poem]," he writes, "suggests not so much objective, physical time as the spatial representations of time in medieval tapestry or triptychs. This emphasis on space seems to imply the absence of time, the conquest of time" (151–52). It is a conquest that Ann Douglas believes was, for the nineteenth century, inescapably gender-identified; distinguishing between "scientific" historians and feminine and clerical historians, she remarks that the latter, "in their well-founded fear of historicity ... substituted space for time as the fundamental dimension of human experience" (199).

As the Douglas comment shows, the second principle established by the Revolution is closely related to the first, asserting that the apocalyptic end of history signals the end of a system in which women are instruments of, and subordinate to, patrilineal continuity. In particular, the revolutionary law making natural children the absolute equals of so-called legitimate offspring had the effect of taking from men their familiar right to direct and subdue female sexuality. In the saturnalia of sexual "misrule" that followed, with its release of aboriginal energy and its invitation to self-discovery and self-assertion, traditional gender roles were radically reexamined. Eliade's study of ceremonial transvestism describes this symbolic sex role reversal as

> a coming out of one's self, a transcending of one's own historically controlled situation, a recovering of an original situation ... which it is important to reconstitute periodically in order to restore, if only for a brief moment, the initial completeness, the intact source of holiness and power ... that preceded the creation.
>
> ("Mephistopheles" 113)

Interestingly, 1792, the first year of the new French Republic, was also the year in which Mary Wollstonecraft published her *Vindication of the Rights of Woman*, inaugurating the modern era of feminism. Wollstonecraft would later include in her own study of the French Revolution descriptions of the part women played in overturning the monarchy. "Early ... on the fifth of October," she reports, "a multitude of women by some impulse were collected together; and hastening to the *hôtel de ville*, obliged every female they met to accompany them, even entering many houses to force others to follow in their train." The women are only temporarily delayed by national guardsmen with bayonets. "Uttering a loud and general cry, they hurled a volley of stones at the soldiers, who, unwilling, or ashamed, to fire on women, *though with the appearance of furies*, retreated into the hall and left the passage free" (133; italics mine).[5]

One can perhaps find in these latter-day Eumenides the originals of Dickens' Madame Defarge and her ferocious female companions of the guillotine. The same image seems to have occurred independently to Edmund Burke, who equated the insurrection on the Continent with the dismemberment of King Peleas of Thessaly by his daughters, an act contrived by the vengeful Medea (109).[6] Clearly, the nineteenth century perceived the French Revolution as juxtaposing two key contemporary themes, the attack on history and the assertion of female authority. The reading of Tennyson's *Idylls of the King* proposed here focuses precisely on this juxtaposition: on the rich potential for a new society that emerges from the original association of these two themes and on the disaster Tennyson says overtakes such a society once all the implications of the Arthurian apocalypse are revealed.

III

The coming of Arthur at the beginning of the *Idylls* is plainly an apocalyptic event, recognized as such by the whole society.[7] The advent of a king who proposes to reign without the authorization of patrilineal descent is an extraordinary and threatening phenomenon. "Who is he / That he should rule us?" the great lords and barons of the realm demand. "Who hath proven him King Uther's son?" The community first attempts to see if the situation can be regularized, to see, that is, if some evidence can be found that Arthur is, after all, the legitimate heir of an established line of kings. Leodogran, the king of Cameliard, is particularly anxious for such confirmation since Arthur has asked to marry his daughter, Guinevere. "How should I that am a king," Leodogran asks, "Give my one daughter saving to a king, / And king's son?" In seeking evidence of Arthur's legitimacy, Leodogran, parodying the methodical inquiries of a historian, tracks down one source of information after another: an ancient chamberlain, some of Arthur's own closest friends, a putative stepsister. None can supply the absolute assurance the king wants, and over against their only partly convincing stories stands the undoubted truth that, while Arthur's supposed parents, Uther and Ygerne, were dark-haired and dark-eyed, the new monarch is himself "fair / Beyond the race of Britons and of men."

What emerges from all this investigation is the fact that Arthur represents not a continuation and fulfillment of history but rather a decisive break with it. Indeed, the failure of Leodogran's conventional historical research to establish some connection with the past suggests that in Arthur's new dispensation even the traditional methods for acquiring knowledge have become ineffectual. "Sir and my Liege," cries a favorite warrior after one of Arthur's victories, "the fire of God / Descends upon thee in the battlefield. / I know thee for my King!" Here is a way of recognizing authority very different from one requiring the confirmation of genealogy. Arthur's fair coloring also confounds genealogy. Not only does it set him apart from the people most likely to have been his parents, it isolates him as well from all other Britons and even, we are told, from all other men. Radically discontinuous with the past in every one of its aspects, Arthur is like some dramatic mutation in nature, threatening the integrity of the genetic line as the only means of infusing new life into it.

In fact, nature does replace history as the sponsor of the new king. Tennyson affirms this idea both in what he chooses to drop from the traditional account of the coming of Arthur and in what he invents to replace the omission. Perhaps the best known of all legends associated with the identification of Arthur as England's rightful king is the story of the sword in the stone. In Malory, for example, young Arthur wins acceptance as lawful ruler because he is the only person in England capable of removing a magic sword from a marble block on which have been inscribed the words "Whoso pulleth out this sword of his stone and anvil is rightwise king born of all England."

In nearly every retelling of the Arthurian stories down to our own time, this dramatic incident plays a prominent part. Tennyson's omission of the anecdote from his own rendering of the Arthurian material, then, is at least noteworthy and may even be a significant due to one of the poet's principal intentions in the *Idylls*. For what the phallic incident of the sword in the stone emphasizes is that Arthur, though not as incontrovertibly a descendant of the previous king as the people of England might like, is nevertheless the inheritor of some kind of lawful authority, the recipient of legitimate power legitimately transferred. And the participation in this ritual of the church, with its traditional stake in an orderly, apostolic succession, further ensures that such a transfer is, at least symbolically, patrilineal. Tennyson's rejection of this famous story, therefore, may well suggest that the poet was trying to direct attention away from conventional continuity in the passing of power to Arthur and toward some alternative source of authority for the new king.

What that alternative source of authority might be is hinted at in "Guinevere," the eleventh of the twelve idylls, an unusual work in that, as Jerome Buckley points out in his edition of the poetry, it draws on little "apart from Tennyson's own imagination" (536). This "self-authorized" and so-to-speak "unhistorical" idyll contains a striking description of the early days of Arthur's reign—the account of a magical initiatory journey, invented by Tennyson, we may conjecture, as a substitute for the omitted episode of the sword in the stone. We hear this story from a young novice, who repeats the tale her father had told her of his first trip to Camelot to serve the newly installed king. "The land was full of signs / And wonders," the girl quotes her father's narrative of that trip. By the light of the many beacon fires on the headlands along the coast

>   the white mermaiden swam,
> And strong man-breasted things stood from the sea,
> And sent a deep sea-voice thro' all the land,
> To which the little elves of chasm and cleft
> Made answer, sounding like a distant horn.
> So said my father—yea, and furthermore,
> Next morning, while he past the dim-lit woods
> Himself beheld three spirits mad with joy
>
> . . . .
>
> And still at evenings on before his horse
> The flickering fairy-circle wheel'd and broke
> Flying, and link'd again, and wheel'd and broke
> Flying, for all the land was full of life.
> And when at last he came to Camelot,
> A wreath of airy dancers hand-in-hand
> Swung round the lighted lantern of the hall;
> And in the hall itself was such a feast
> As never man had dream'd; for every knight
> Had whatsoever meat he long'd for served
> By hands unseen; and even as he said
> Down in the cellars merry bloated things
> Shoulder'd the spigot, straddling on the butts
> While the wine ran.

This visionary scene both celebrates and ratifies the coming of Arthur, affirming that the young king's authority over the land proceeds directly from the land itself, from the deepest resources of nature, and that "all genealogies founder," as J. M. Gray puts it, "in that 'great deep'" (11). Metaphors of depth and interiority are everywhere: seas, woods, chasms, clefts, cellars. All the spirits of nature rejoice in Arthur, seeing in him their rightful heir, the repository of their power. In Tennyson's remarkable vision, radically departing as it does from historical sources, Arthur's coming fulfills that revolutionary law of the French National Convention which declared "natural children absolutely equal with legitimate."

This Romantic idea that the true source of kingly power is natural and internal rather than historical and external is more fully developed in the first of the idylls. There, Arthur's legitimacy is shown to derive from two sources: an inner strength, of which his successful military adventures are symbols, and the depths of nature, themselves metaphors for the young king's potent inwardness. When we first meet Arthur in the *Idylls*, he is a newly fledged warrior, driving the patriarchal Roman Caesars from his land as determinedly as the French would later drive them from the calendar.[8] Later, we see the young monarch receiving the sword Excalibur from the Lady of the Lake, a mystic wielder of subtle magic who "dwells down in a deep" and from whose hand, rising "out of the bosom of the lake," the new king takes the emblem of his authority.

To the extent that such derivation of power from the deep symbolizes access to one's own interior energy, Arthur's kingly mission is ultimately self-authorized; and in particular, it is authorized by that part of himself which, associated with creative, ahistorical nature, is most distinctly female. Tennyson emphasizes this idea not only by assigning the Lady of the Lake a prominent role in the establishment of Arthur's legitimacy but also by introducing the mysterious muselike figures of the "three fair queens" who attend the young king at his coronation: "the friends / Of Arthur, gazing on him, tall, with bright / Sweet faces, who will help him at his need."[9] In his Preface to *The Great Mother*, Erich Neumann declares that the "problem of the Feminine [is important] for the psychologist of culture, who realizes that the peril of present-day mankind springs in large part from the one-sidedly patriarchal development of the male intellectual consciousness, which is no longer kept in balance by the matriarchal world of the psyche" (xlii). Clearly, the new dispensation promised by the coming of Tennyson's nineteenth-century Arthur will involve, as an important part of its program, the freeing of that matriarchal psyche, of feminine energy, from its long subservience to male authority and consciousness. Everything we know about the new king makes this certain. The very manner of his accession directly challenges such authority and consciousness, and his establishment of the community of the Round Table can best be understood as an attempt to assert the wholeness of the human spirit in the face of that sexual fragmentation described by Neumann.

What the dominance of male consciousness over female psyche can lead to in society is made plain in the *Idylls* through Tennyson's description of the all-male community of King Pellam in "Balin and Balan," the last of the books to be written. Pellam, a rival of King Arthur's, determines to outdo the court of Camelot in piety, and as a first step he pushes "aside his faithful wife, nor lets / Or dame or damsel enter at his gates / Lest he should be polluted." As a manifestation of abstract male reason and will, such suppression of the feminine renders the society moribund. The aging Pellam, described by Tennyson as "this gray king," has "quite foregone / All matters of this world" and spends his listless days in a hall "bushed about ... with gloom," where "cankered boughs ... whine in the wood." Nature here, rejected as a source of energy and replenishment, takes suitable revenge on its sullen oppressor.

King Pellam is the guardian of a most appropriate relic. The old monarch, who "finds himself descended from the Saint / Arimathaean Joseph," is the proud possessor of "that same spear / Wherewith the Roman pierced the side of Christ" as he hung on the cross. Death-dealing, Roman, phallic, linear, the spear—its ghostly shadow haunting the countryside—symbolizes the dessicated male society of Pellam's court; indeed, it is very literally the male "line" through which Pellam—who, unlike Arthur, is deeply interested in genealogy—traces the source of his authority back to Joseph of Arimathaea. Significantly, as a symbol of the linear and the historical, the spear belies the cyclical promise of the resurrection represented by the Grail, the companion relic from which, in the sexually fragmented culture described both by Neumann and by Tennyson, it has long been separated.[10]

As the country of King Pellam is the land of the spear, so Arthur's Camelot is the court of the Grail. At least, it is from Camelot that the knights of the Round Table, tutored in Arthur's values,[11] set out on their quest for the sacred cup, familiar symbol both of nature and of the female, a womblike emblem of fecundity associated with what, in pagan legend, is the Cauldron of Plenty, an attribute of the Goddess of Fertility.[12] Such female energy is, in traditional mythography, ahistorical, a fact to which the Grail also testifies. The vessel's circular form, like that of the Round Table itself and like the "flickering fairy circles" and "wreaths of airy dancers" associated with the coming of Arthur, mimics the timeless cycles of nature, a timelessness in which the Round Table knights themselves participate. As we noted earlier, fraternal relationships are necessarily contemporaneous ones, expressing themselves in space rather than in time. The whole of Camelot partakes of this anachronistic quality. The young knight Gareth, catching his first glimpse of the sculptured gates of the city, marvels at how intermingled—how contiguous rather than continuous—all the events depicted there seem to be: "New things and old co-twisted, as if Time / Were nothing." His intuition of the ahistorical character of Camelot is confirmed by the "old seer" at the gate, who speaks of the city as a place "never built at all, / And therefore built forever." Significantly, the principal subject of "Gareth and Lynette" is young Gareth's commitment "to fight the brotherhood of Day and Night" in "the war of Time against the soul of man," a war in which, in this early idyll, the soul signally triumphs.[13]

IV

The optimism expressed in the early idylls about the joyous and lively new society that would result from an apocalyptic release of natural and, by extension, female energy into a world heretofore dominated by history and male authority was largely a product of one form of nineteenth-century Romantic ideology. Traditionally, nature has been seen as the enemy of rational and historical human culture. Indeed, it has been argued that culture functions to permit human beings to assert their independence of—and superiority to—nature. In examining the origins of kinship, for example, Lévi-Strauss suggests that the whole elaborate and extended structure of the family can best be understood as a means by which "culture must, under pain of not existing, firmly declare 'Me first,' and tell nature, 'You go no further'" (31).[14] In this view, nature is dangerous, anarchic, indifferent to human concerns. Its frightening power may have to be placated or invoked on special occasions, but it must always be treated warily, must be controlled and even suppressed.

The Romanticism of the early nineteenth century, as one of its most striking innovations, managed momentarily to suspend the traditional enmity between nature and culture. In the benign natural world of the Wordsworthian vision, for example, breezes are "blessings," vales are "harbors," clouds are "guides," groves are "homes." Where human culture is a burden, it wearies the poet precisely because it is "unnatural." Under such circumstances, Wordsworth attempts to reconcile these traditionally polar opposites, submitting his cultivated sensibility to a sustaining and unthreatening nature in order to receive a new infusion of energy. It is nature in this ameliorative sense that underlies the scene in the *Idylls* in which the coming of Arthur is celebrated by all the mermaidens, elves, fairies, spirits, and merry bloated things we would naturally expect to find inhabiting a land that is "full of life."

The same Romantic optimism that permitted nature to be so readily domesticated in many early nineteenth-century works of art, that allowed nature's powers to be courted so fearlessly, also made possible the hopeful invocation of female energy that is such a striking feature of the *Idylls*. Historically, this benignant view of female power is unusual. Both in history and in myth women have for the most part been associated with the irrational and destructive forces of nature that threaten orderly male culture. As maenads, bacchantes, witches, they express in their frenzied dances and murderous violence an unbridled sexuality analogous to the frightening and sometimes even ruinous fecundity of nature. Indeed, the control of female sexuality is among the commonest metaphors in art for the control of nature (just as the control of nature is a metaphor for the control of women; see, e.g., Smith and Kolodny). And as Lévi-Strauss points out, the earliest evidences of culture are nearly always those rules of exchange devised by men to facilitate the ownership and sexual repression of women.

Tennyson's departure, in the early idylls, from this traditional fear of female sexuality coincides with a dramatic development in modern cultural history. "Between the seventeenth and the nineteenth centuries," Nancy F. Cott remarks about this change, "the dominant Anglo-American definition of women as especially sexual was reversed and transformed into the view that women were less carnal and lustful than men" (221). Or as Havelock Ellis put it more succinctly in his *Studies in the Psychology of Sex*, one of the most striking creations of the nineteenth century was "woman's sexual anesthesia" (3:193–94). Cott substitutes for Ellis' "anesthesia" her own term "passionlessness," linking it with Evangelical Protestantism, which "constantly reiterated the theme that Christianity had elevated women above the weakness of animal nature for the sake of purity for men, the tacit condition for that elevation being the suppression of female sexuality" (227). Plainly, Tennyson's nineteenth-century recreation of Camelot depends to a considerable extent on this contemporary theory of female passionlessness—what another critic calls woman's "more than mortal purity" (Christ 146)—and its ameliorative influence on male sensuality.[15] Unlike the society of King Pellam, which preserves the earlier view of women as sexually insatiable and which adopts a grim monasticism as the only defense against feminine corrosiveness, Arthur's court welcomes women for their ennobling and now safely denatured regenerative powers. In this respect, Camelot seems to resemble the many nineteenth-century utopian communities that attempted to experiment with a new and higher order of relationship between the sexes and that Tennyson himself had already commented on obliquely in *The Princess*.[16]

It is in his own "passionlessness" that Arthur most clearly embodies the nineteenth-century feminine ideal on which he seeks to build his new society."[17] "Arthur the blameless, pure as any maid," he is called, sardonically but accurately, in "Balin and Balan," and it is in these terms that he becomes a model for all his knights, urging them

To lead sweet lives in purest chastity,
To love one maiden only, cleave to her,
And worship her by years of noble deeds.

Such sexual restraint will, according to Arthur, win for the Round Table knights the moral authority to purify a land "Wherein the beast was ever more and more, / But man was less and less." These lines perfectly express the Evangelical Protestant belief, just noted, that "Christianity had elevated women above the weakness of animal nature for the sake of purity for men," and they confirm that it is on the female ideal of passionlessness that Arthur means to found his new community. Tennyson even goes so far as to alter his sources in order to make this point, rejecting Malory's designation of Modred as Arthur's illegitimate son and instead having the king refer to the usurper as "my sister's son—no kin of mine."

V

The scene would now appear to be set for the triumph of the Round Table experiment. With the apocalyptic overturning of history and male authority and the substitution for them of a benign nature and a safely contained female energy, Arthur's new society ought certainly to flourish. How, then, are we to account for the famous decline of this ideal community into corruption and nihilism, how explain the fall of Camelot? Tennyson's revision of the story of Modred's origins may offer one answer to these questions. As I have suggested, the point of the poet's departure from Malory is to maintain unblemished the record of Arthur's sexual purity. But the textual change has unexpected ramifications that reveal a serious flaw in the Arthurian vision. For if Modred is not Arthur's son, illegitimate or otherwise, then in the story as we receive it, Arthur has no children at all. He and Guinevere produce no offspring, and even the foundling he brings to his wife to rear as her own dies.

Such sterility, appropriate symbol of a denatured sexuality, means the end of Arthur's dream of a new society; the rejection of history and patriarchy that is the source of the young king's first strength here returns to haunt the older monarch, who now perceives that without the continuity provided by legitimate descent through the male line, his vision cannot survive him.[18] This point has already been made obliquely in the passage from "Guinevere" describing the natural magic that filled the land when Arthur first began to rule. The story, we know, is recounted by a young novice who explains that she is repeating a tale her father had told her. Thus, even this early in Arthur's reign, the dependence of the king's authority on the preservation of a historical record is recognized, a preservation that in turn—the passage reminds us—requires men capable of begetting children through whom to transmit that record.[19]

It is precisely Arthur's incapacity to propagate his line that renders his new society so vulnerable. In "The Last Tournament," for example, the Red Knight calls tauntingly from the top of a brutally phallic tower:

> Lo! art thou not that eunuch-hearted king
> Who fain had clipt free manhood from the world—
> The woman-worshipper?

The Red Knight's equation of Arthur's sterility with a worship of woman suggests how enfeebling the king's sentimentalizing of nature has become. The female ideal worshiped by Arthur (and scorned by the Red Knight) is tame, disembodied, passionless, itself the product of an abstract male rationalism and no real alternative source of strength. Lancelot, describing to Guinevere, in "Balin and Balan," a dream he has had of "a maiden saint" who carries lilies in her hand, speaks of the flowers as "perfect-pure" and continues:

> As light a flush
> As hardly tints the blossom of the quince
> Would mar their charm of stainless womanhood.

To which Guinevere replies, resenting such an imposition of the ideal on the natural,

> Sweeter to me ... this garden rose
> Deep-hued and many-folded! sweeter still
> The wild-wood hyacinth and the bloom of May!

In the end, Guinevere's reality triumphs over Arthur's and Lancelot's abstraction in the *Idylls of the King*, just as her irresistible sexual energy at last defeats her husband's passionlessness.

Given the subject and the theme of the *Idylls*, this outcome is inevitable. Indeed, Tennyson's profoundest insight in the poem may be that nature cannot be courted casually, that the id-like energy of the deep must not be invoked without a full knowledge of how devastating and ultimately uncontrollable that energy can be. Again, for the nineteenth century it was the French Revolution that most dramatically embodied this insight. We have already seen how that event, for all its celebration of myth over history, nature over culture, female over male, itself began by trying to contain the outburst of insurrectionary energy it had released within a number of easily manipulated abstractions: new laws governing the inheritance of property, new names for the months of the year. Even regicide was intended as a kind of abstract statement, the removal of a symbol as much as of a man.

But unaccountably, the blood would not stop flowing from the murdered king's decapitated body. It poured into the streets of Paris from the foot of the guillotine and ran there for years, as if newly released from some source deep in the earth. From the first, the bloodstained Terror was associated with female sexuality. The key symbol of the Revolution was the figure Liberty, later memorably depicted by Eugene Delacroix as a bare-breasted bacchante striding triumphantly over the bodies of half-naked dead men. The Dionysian guillotine haunted the imagination of Europe; a mechanical *vagina dentata*, it produced, with its endless emasculations, an unstoppable blood flow, the unhealing menstrual wound curiously like the one suffered by the maimed king in the story of the Grail. In primitive societies, such menstrual bleeding is the ultimate symbol of a polluting female nature, an unbridled sexual destructiveness that the power of patriarchal authority must at all costs contain. In nineteenth-century England, the bloody denouement of the French Revolution produced a similar reaction, a suppression of sex and a repression of women that to this day we disapprovingly call Victorian.

From the beginning of his career, Tennyson had been preoccupied with these issues—with what Gerhard Joseph has called the poet's "notion of woman as cosmic destructive principle" (127)—and in particular with the point at which the themes of nature, blood, and female sexuality converge. An early sonnet, for example, begins:

> She took the dappled partridge fleckt with blood,
>   And in her hands the drooping pheasant bare,
>   And by his feet she held the woolly hare,
> And like a master-painting where she stood,
> Lookt some new goddess of an English wood.

This powerful figure of female authority, bloody, dangerous, but curiously attractive, springs from the imagination of a young poet already moving toward a post-Wordsworthian view of nature as "red in tooth and claw." In "The Palace of Art," the protagonist, withdrawing too deeply into self, approaching too closely the dark, secret springs of nature, comes "unawares" on "corpses three-months-old ... that stood against the wall" and on "white-eyed phantasms weeping tears of blood." In the *Idylls*, the doom of the Round Table is sealed at the moment during "The Last Tournament" when, to defeat the bestial Red Knight, Arthur's men give themselves up to the almost erotic appeal of blood lust, when

swording right and left
Men, women, on their sodden faces, [they] hurl'd
Till all the rafters rang with woman-yells,
And all the pavement streamed with massacre.

But the dismantling of the brotherhood had begun even earlier, as a direct result of the Grail quest. The blood-filled holy cup, itself a menstrual symbol, first appears in the *Idylls* to Percival's sister, a young nun in whose description the vessel seems almost explicitly a living female organ:

Down the long beam stole the Holy Grail,
Rose-red with beatings in it, as if alive,
Till all the white walls of my cell were dyed
With rosy colors leaping on the wall.
("The Holy Grail")

It is when the Round Table knights abandon themselves to the visionary pursuit of this symbol of the "eternal feminine" that Camelot, literally "unmanned," begins to fall into ruin.

"Creator and destroyer," Robert M. Adams comments on the Victorian image of the femme fatale,

but more fascinating in the second capacity than the first, woman for the late nineteenth century ... is both sacred and obscene, sacred as redeeming man from culture, obscene as content with a merely appetitive existence that declines inevitably from the high fever of Eros to the low fever of dissolution and decay.   (185)

In the end, Arthur's dream of a natural community is destroyed, Tennyson suggests, by the carnality to which such a dream must necessarily lead, is spoiled by an irrepressible female libidinousness that, once released by the withdrawal of patrilineal authority, can be neither contained nor directed. The second half of the *Idylls* is one long record of licentiousness: the faithless depravity of Gawain and Ettarre, the crass sensuality of Tristram and Isolt, the open adultery of Lancelot and Guinevere. "Thou hast spoilt the purpose of my life" we have already heard Arthur declare bitterly to the queen at their last meeting, a key passage in the long-standing controversy about the psychological and moral sophistication of the *Idylls*. For if Christopher Ricks, among others, is right that in this speech Guinevere is made "too much a scapegoat, [since] the doom of the Round Table seems to antedate her adultery," he is surely wrong to find, in such an attack on her, evidence of "a root confusion in Tennyson" (272). Rather, what the poem preeminently shows is that the confusion here is Arthur's. It is Arthur's naiveté about the dynamics of the human psyche that dooms his ideal community from the start; it is his own well-intentioned but foolish binding of his knights "by vows ... the which no man can keep" that threatens his dream long before the adultery of Guinevere and Lancelot can precipitate its destruction.[20]

In his isolation from reality, the king resembles other self-authorizing post-Renaissance heroes, from Faust to Frankenstein, who begin by creating the worlds in which they live out of their own private visions and end by succumbing to the dark natural forces they have raised but fail to understand or control. The solipsistic isolation of such figures becomes their fate as well as their failing, their retribution as well as their sin. For where the historical record provides individuals with a context independent of themselves, a past and a future in which they need not participate to believe, a variety of experiences unlike their own but just as real, myth asserts the sovereignty of the eternal moment, which is forever the present, and the ubiquitousness of the representative human, who is always the same, without antecedents or heirs. It is into this reductive timelessness and silence of myth that characters like Merlin and Arthur ultimately fall in the *Idylls* for having cut their connections with patriarchal history.

Merlin, Tennyson tells us in the sixth idyll, derives his power from an ancient volume that is the paradigmatic book of history, passed down through the generations from one male magician to another. The first owner we hear of is a little, shriveled, Pellam-like wizard whose strength comes from his rejection of sensuality in favor of the intensest possible concentration on the text. (The seer's principal use of this text is to help a local king exercise absolute control over his queen.) The book then "comes down" to Merlin, who describes it as

> Writ in a language that has long gone by.
> . . . .
> And every margin scribbled, crost, and cramm'd
> With comment, densest condensation, hard
> . . . .
> And none can read the text, not even I;
> And none can read the comment but myself;
> And in the comment did I find the charm.

Here is the perfect symbol of what we have been calling patrilineal continuity, continuity dependent on a bequeathed historical record that is both the ultimate source of male power and, with its antiquity and its accumulating burden of interpretation, a constant reminder of the belatedness of the present. Shut out of history by her gender, a vengeful Vivien determines to seduce Merlin from the satisfactions of male tradition with the blandishments of female sexuality. For a long while the old magician holds out against the woman, but in the end he yields, revealing to her the secret of the ultimate charm. The next moment, Vivien has turned the spell back on him, robbing him—significantly— of "name and fame," the two best gifts that patrilineal history can bestow on a man, and casting him into the eternal isolation of myth, "Closed in the four walls of a hollow tower / From which was no escape for evermore."[21]

In his final battle, Arthur suffers a fate much like Merlin's. Because he has received authorization from no father and conveyed it to no son, the king is trapped in the reflexiveness of the prophecy that has governed him all his life: "From the great deep to the great deep he goes." That same solipsistic reflexiveness characterizes Arthur's last hallucinatory battle against his sister's son, a war, he tells us,

> against my people and my knights.
> A king who fights his people fights himself.
> . . . .
> I perish by this people that I made..
> ("The Passing of Arthur")

The war is fought in "a death-white mist" in which the solid reality of the world proves an illusion, "For friend and foe were shadows in the mist, / And friend slew friend not knowing who he slew."

Ironically, the reign that began with the whole world doubting the legitimacy of the king ends with the king himself doubting it. "On my heart," says Arthur,

> hath fallen
> Confusion, till I know not what I am,
> Nor whence I am, nor whether I be king;
> Behold, I seem but king among the dead.

In the end—Tennyson summarizes the central theme of the *Idylls*—all certainty is impossible for a man who rejects the stability of patrilineal descent and seeks instead to derive his authority from himself, to build a community on the idealization of nature and female energy.

VI

The resemblance of this scene, in which "friend slays friend," to the equally confusing struggle of "ignorant armies" on "the darkling plain" in Matthew Arnold's "Dover Beach" reminds us that, in writing the *Idylls of the King*, Tennyson was participating in an elaborate symposium with his fellow Victorians on the troubling state of their world. But where Arnold's poem focuses on a particular moment in the history of that world, Tennyson's *Idylls* provide, in John D. Rosenberg's phrase, "the chronicle ... of a whole civilization" (34) as it passes from the Romantic optimism of its first days— about which Wordsworth could exult, "Bliss was it in that dawn to be alive"— to the fin de siècle disillusionment of the last hours—which found, in Walter Pater's words, "each man keeping as a solitary prisoner, his own dream of a world." The springtime innocence and eagerness of the first idylls wonderfully convey the excitement of the Romantic rediscovery of nature, and the Arthurian credo of passionlessness embodies the early Victorian belief in the benevolence and controllability of that nature. But just as the Victorians' famous efforts to suppress female sexuality only succeeded in generating a grim and extensive sexual underground, so Arthur's naive manipulations of nature conclude in the society of the Round Table being swept away on a great wave of carnality.

Despite the failure of the Arthurian assault on history, Tennyson persists at the end of the *Idylls*, as he does elsewhere, in seeking a rapprochement with myth. Thus, against the linear and historical implications of the king's famous valedictory, "The old order changeth, yielding place to new," the poet reiterates the traditional cyclical promise of Arthur's eventual return as *rex quondam rexque futurus*. In the same way, at the end of *In Memoriam* Tennyson sets the historical and progressive "one far-off, divine event / To which the whole creation moves" within a cycle of seasons. To be sure, the hero of "Locksley Hall" seems to offer the definitive disavowal of myth when he declares, "Better fifty years of Europe than a cycle of Cathay." But it is significant that the narrator of that poem lives long enough to discover how the inevitable alternation of "chaos and cosmos" in the universe renders even the most intense vision of historical progress trivial.

Such ambivalence about history, our starting point for this consideration of the *Idylls*, marks the history of the poem itself, a history that records the poet's entrapment in a familiar nineteenth-century dilemma, one with its own broader ramifications. Like Merlin, Tennyson is committed— since "first light[ing] upon Malory"—to the authority of a historical text of which he is his generation's principal interpreter.

> And none can read the comment but myself;
> And in the comment did I find the charm.

But no belated expositor such as he, no descendant of patriarchal exegetes, can hope to make the unimaginable backward leap through commentary to the mystery of the text itself. Indeed, it is the very weight of traditional commentary—"densest condensation, hard"—that renders such a leap impossible, precisely that burden of the past that unmans where it means to empower. For in exhausted latter days, as Merlin informs us, "None can read the text, not even I." Yet Tennyson's attempt, in the face of this exhaustion, to reject traditional sources in favor of a contemporary, ahistorical representation of Arthurian materials—his refusal, that is, to "remodel models"—courts another kind of weakness, risking, in the absence of patrilineal resonances, the domesticity and effeminacy of a "Morte d'Albert."

A similar ambivalence toward history characterizes the century for which Tennyson wrote. Already during the early decades Viconian cyclical theory was becoming influential, Thomas Carlyle was denouncing scientific reconstructions of the past as "tombstone history" and time as "a grand anti-magician and wonder-hider," and the First Reform Act, Britain's bloodless version of the French Revolution, had dramatically rejected genealogy as society's sole authorizing principle. In the light of such reformist impulses, Tennyson's investigation of a natural community in the *Idylls of the King*, one in which the female energy of myth substitutes for the male energy of history, seems inevitable. Equally inevitable, however, is the failure of that community, given the growing Victorian disillusionment with the Romantic experiment.[22] For Carlyle, for instance, who in his own way shared the fate of Tennyson's Arthur, the magic creativity of *Sartor Resartus* unavoidably declined into the solipsistic self-imprisonment of the *Latter-Day Pamphlets*. Just as inescapably, the First Reform Act led to the Second and toward that "anarchy" which Matthew Arnold prophesied and deplored and of which the developing women's movement was seen by the Victorians as a powerful symbol. And, despite eager celebrations of myth, over this perceived decline brooded a sense of the enervating, irreversible historicity of things. Particularly in the *Idylls*, Tennyson depicts a disintegration of society from which there can be no reasonable expectation of a return. From his long, dark Arthurian speculation, Tennyson seems to be saying, the century can only move inexorably forward through fin de siècle hedonism into the fragmentation and alienation of a modernist waste land.

NOTES

1. See, e.g., George Meredith's description of Arthur as a "crowned curate," quoted in Martin 423–24. "Tennyson was criticized," Mark Girouard writes, "both at the time and later for turning Malory's king and knights into pattern Victorian gentlemen" (184).

2. See also John Ruskin's comment to Tennyson about the *Idylls* in a letter of Sept. 1859: "So great power ought not to be spent on visions of things past but on the living

present.... The intense, masterful and unerring transcript of an actuality ... seems to me to be the true task of the modern poet" (36:320–21).

3. The complete passage from *Middlemarch* reads: "[Dorothea's] full nature, like that river of which Cyrus broke the strength, spent itself on channels which had no great name on the earth. But the effect of her being on those around her was incalculably diffusive: for the growing good of the world is partly dependent on unhistoric acts; and that things are not so ill with you and me as they might have been, is half-owing to the number who live faithfully a hidden life, and rest in unvisited tombs" (613). In speaking of Theresa at the end of the novel, George Eliot implies that it is the girl's childish innocence, analogous to the innocence of her time, that made possible her great work. By contrast, the present is so burdened with knowledge of the past that "its strength is broken into channels," and people like Dorothea Brooke are effective precisely because they are "unhistoric." Were they to be historic—that is, memorable—they would only add to the burden of the next generation, become one more influence for the future to be anxious about. Their importance, then, derives from the fact that their lives are "hidden" and their tombs "unvisited." Note that unhistoric people are likelier to be women than men (history remembers more Cyruses than Theresas), women's "hidden" influence being "incalculably diffusive." like nature, rather than immediate and focused, like history. In this connection, consider the puns on Dorothea's "nature" and on her last name, closer in meaning to channel than to river.

4. See, e.g., National Socialism's twentieth-century exploitation of this nineteenth-century idea in support of its own revolutionary theories. "I, as a politician," Hitler is quoted by Hermann Rauschning, "need a conception that enables the order that has hitherto existed on an historic basis to be abolished and an entirely new and antihistoric order enforced" (229).

5. "The Revolution," writes Virginia Woolf of Mary Wollstonecraft, "was not merely an event that had happened outside her; it was an active agent in her own blood" (143).

6. G. P. Gooch writes that "in combating the French Revolution, Burke emphasized the continuity of historic life and the debt of every age to its predecessors" (9), just those patriarchal values under attack by the apocalyptic female energy Burke associated with the Revolution.

7. See John D. Rosenberg's discussion of Tennyson's deep interest in apocalyptic subjects, an interest evident as early as the poet's fifteenth year in the fragment "Armageddon" (14–19).

8. Indeed, the early nineteenth century found victory over Rome a particularly compelling metaphor. When Napoleon seized the crown from Pius vii at Reims and placed it on his own head, he was attacking the most venerable patriarchy in Europe, substituting for an "apostolic" descent of royal power a self-authorizing kingship that may well have influenced Tennyson's depiction of Arthur in the *Idylls*.

9. Tennyson himself refused to be tied down to a specific identification of the three queens; he responded to readers who saw them as Faith, Hope, and Charity that "they mean that and they do not.... They are much more" (H. Tennyson 2:127).

10. Some forty years earlier, Tennyson had dealt with this same fragmentation in "Tithonus." In that poem, he sets the Pellam-like figure of the aged male protagonist—unable to die, obliged to move always forward in time burdened more and more by his own past, his own history—against Aurora, the female representation of the dawn, a natural phenomenon who, existing out of time in Eliade's *illo tempore* and always circling back to her beginning, continually renews her youth. In the end, Tithonus' dearest wish is to awake from the nightmare of history, to which he had willfully consigned himself, and to reenter the restorative cycle of nature, even though that change can only be inaugurated by his own death.

11. That Arthur is himself dismayed at how the embodiment of those values in the Grail quest must necessarily destroy the Round Table brotherhood prefigures the king's later despair at the final collapse of his ideal.

12. See Jessie L. Weston's discussion of this symbol (72–76). See also Robert Stephen Hawker's contemporary "Quest of the Sangraal" (1863), where the poet writes about Joseph of Arimathaea, keeper of the Grail, that "His home was like a garner, full of corn / and wine and oil: a granary of God" (184).

13. "The timelessness of myth was one of its greatest attractions to the Victorians," writes James Kissane. "It was the realm of myths and legends that came closest to constituting an idealized past that could solace Tennyson's imagination as a kind of eternal presence" (129).

14. If Lévi-Strauss does not explicitly equate culture and history, he clearly links the two through his association of culture with genealogy.

15. See also Ward Hellstrom's comment that "if the *Idylls* fail to speak to the modern world, that failure is the result to a great degree of Tennyson's attempt to preserve a lost and perhaps ultimately indefensible ideal of womanhood" (134). As my own essay tries to establish, it is Arthur rather than Tennyson who futilely defends this ideal. I fully agree with Hellstrom, however, that "the woman question is more or less central to all the books of 'The Round Table'" and even with his more daring assertion that it is "perhaps the most significant and revolutionary question of the nineteenth century" (109).

16. "In the *Idylls*, Tennyson takes up with complete seriousness, although not without irony, the question of woman's role in private and public life—a topic that in *The Princess* he treated half seriously, half satirically" (Eggers 144).

17. Tennyson had also dealt with the issue in *The Princess*, where he dramatizes "a pattern of feminine identification in his portrayal of the Prince" (Christ 154). Such mildness would also be appropriate, of course, to the more conventional association of Arthur with Jesus. But the attack on mid-nineteenth-century Christianity for its effeminacy, already noted, suggests that the familiar image of Arthur as Christ and Tennyson's new depiction of him as female king were beginning to coincide.

18. Margaret Homans makes a similar point, speaking of Arthur as "a victim of continuity: his origins, from which he has endeavored all his life to escape, have successfully reasserted the claim that the past makes on the future" (693).

19. Interestingly, Robert B. Martin sees this issue reflected in what he calls the poet's "slackened language" in the *Idylls*, a neglect of grammatical cause and effect that "robs the characters of any appearance of '*real* man' because there is no feeling of behavior resulting from antecedents" (496; italics mine).

20. Jerome Buckley comments that Arthur is "ineffective" in dealing with Lancelot and the queen "despite his ideal manhood, or perhaps because of it" (177).

21. Henry Kozicki describes this passage as portraying "the lotos death of old historical form through its hero's withdrawal into self" (112). Kozicki's study comments usefully on Tennyson's vision of, and attitude toward, history during the course of his career.

22. "With its lesson that the world is irredeemable," writes Clyde de L. Ryals, "the *Idylls of the King* seems to reflect much of the pessimism of nineteenth-century *philosophy*" (94).

Works Cited

Adams, Robert M. "Religion of Man, Religion of Woman." In *Art, Politics, and Will: Essays in Honor of Lionel Trilling*. Ed. Quentin Anderson et al. New York: Basic, 1977, 173–90.

Arnold, Matthew. Preface to *Poems* (1853). In *On the Classical Tradition*. Ed. R. H. Super. Ann Arbor: Univ. of Michigan Press, 1961.

Austen, Jane. *Northanger Abbey*. In *The Novels of Jane Austen*. Ed. R. W. Chapman. Vol. 5. London: Oxford Univ. Press, 1923.

Browning, Elizabeth Barrett. *The Poetical Works of Elizabeth Barrett Browning*. Ed. Ruth M. Adam. Boston: Houghton, 1974.

Buckley, Jerome. *Tennyson: The Growth of a Poet*. Cambridge: Harvard Univ. Press, 1960.

Burke, Edmund. *Reflections on the Revolution in France*. Ed. Thomas H. D. Mahoney. New York: Bobbs-Merrill, 1955.

Carlyle, Thomas. *Past and Present*. Ed. Richard D. Altick. Boston: Houghton, 1965.

Christ, Carol. "Victorian Masculinity and the Angel in the House." In *A Widening Sphere*. Ed. Martha Vicinus. Bloomington: Indiana Univ. Press, 1977, 146–62.

Cott, Nancy F. "Passionlessness: An Interpretation of Victorian Sexual Ideology, 1790–1850." *Signs* 4 (1978): 219–36.

Douglas, Ann. *The Feminization of American Culture*. New York: Knopf, 1977.

Eggers, J. Philip. *King Arthur's Laureate*. New York: New York Univ. Press, 1971.

Eliade, Mircea. *Cosmos and History*. New York: Harper, 1954.

———. *Mephistopheles and the Androgyne*. Trans. J. M. Cohen. New York: Sheed & Ward, 1965, 78–124.

Eliot, George. *Middlemarch*. Ed. Gordon S. Haight. Boston: Houghton, 1956.

Ellis, Havelock. *Studies in the Psychology of Sex*. 2nd ed. Philadelphia: F. A. Davis, 1913.

Gent, Margaret. "'To Flinch from Modern Varnish': The Appeal of the Past to the Victorian Imagination." In *Victorian Poetry*. Ed. Malcolm Bradbury and David Palmer. Stratford-upon-Avon Studies 15. London: Edward Arnold, 1972, 11–35.

Girouard, Mark. *The Return to Camelot*. New Haven: Yale Univ. Press, 1981.

Gooch, G. P. *History and Historians of the Nineteenth Century*. London: Longmans, 1913.

Gray, J. M. *Man and Myth in Victorian England: Tennyson's "The Coming of Arthur."* Lincoln, Nebr.: Tennyson Society, 1969.

Harrison, Frederic. "The History Schools." In his *The Meaning of History*. 1894; rpt. New York: Macmillan, 1908, 118–38.

Hawker, Robert Stephen. "Quest of the Sangraal." In *The Cornish Ballads and Other Poems*. Oxford, 1869, 180–203.

Hellstrom, Ward. *On the Poems of Tennyson*. Gainesville: Univ. of Florida Press, 1972.

Homans, Margaret. "Tennyson and the Spaces of Life." *ELH* 46 (1979): 693–709.

Joseph, Gerhard. *Tennysonian Love: The Strange Diagonal*. Minneapolis: Univ. of Minnesota Press, 1969.

Kincaid, James R. *Tennyson's Major Poems: The Comic and Ironic Patterns*. New Haven: Yale Univ. Press, 1975.

Kissane, James. "Tennyson: The Passion of the Past and the Curse of Time." In *Tennyson*. Ed. Elizabeth A. Francis. Englewood Cliffs, N.J.: Prentice-Hall, 1980, 108–32.

Kolodny, Annette. *The Lay of the Land*. Chapel Hill: Univ. of North Carolina Press, 1975.

Kozicki, Henry. *Tennyson and Clio: History in the Major Poems*. Baltimore: Johns Hopkins Univ. Press, 1979.

Lévi-Strauss, Claude. *The Elementary Structures of Kinship*. Boston: Beacon, 1969.

Martin, Robert B. *Tennyson: The Unquiet Heart*. New York: Oxford Univ. Press, 1980.

Neumann, Erich. *The Great Mother*. Princeton: Princeton Univ. Press, 1955.

Priestley, F. E. L. "Tennyson's *Idylls*." *University of Toronto Quarterly* 19 (1949): 35–49.

Rauschning, Hermann, ed. *Hitler Speaks*. London: Butterworth, 1939.

Ricks, Christopher. *Tennyson*. New York: Macmillan, 1972.

Rosenberg, John D. *The Fall of Camelot: A Study of Tennyson's Idylls of the King*. Cambridge: Belknap-Harvard Univ. Press, 1973.

Ruskin, John. *The Works of John Ruskin*. Ed. E. T. Cook and Alexander Wedderburn. 39 vols. London: George Allen, 1909.

Ryals, Clyde. de L. *From the Great Deep: Essays on Idylls of the King*. Athens: Ohio Univ. Press, 1967.

Schlesinger, Arthur. "The Role of Women in American History." In his *New Viewpoints in American History*. New York: Macmillan, 1921, 126–59.

Smith, Henry Nash. *The Virgin Land*. Cambridge: Harvard Univ. Press, 1950.

Sterling, John. Rev. of Tennyson's *Poems* (1842). *Quarterly Review*, Sept. 1842, 385–416. Rpt. in *Tennyson: The Critical Heritage*. Ed. John D. Jump. London: Routledge & Kegan Paul, 1967, 103–25.

Swinburne, Algernon Charles. *Under the Microscope*. In *Swinburne Replies*. Ed. Clyde K. Hyder. Syracuse, N.Y.: Syracuse Univ. Press, 1966, 33–87.

Tennyson, Alfred Lord. *Poems of Tennyson*. Ed. Jerome H. Buckley. Boston: Riverside, 1958.

Tennyson, Hallam. *Alfred Lord Tennyson: A Memoir by His Son*. 2 vols. London, 1897.

Weston, Jessie L. *From Ritual to Romance*. New York: Anchor-Doubleday, 1957.

Wollstonecraft, Mary. *An Historical and Moral View of the Origin and Progress of the French Revolution and the Effect It Had Produced in Europe*. In *A Wollstonecraft Anthology*. Ed. Janet M. Todd. Bloomington: Indiana Univ. Press, 1977, 125–41.

Woolf, Virginia. *The Second Common Reader*. New York: Harcourt, 1932.

JOHN D. ROSENBERG

Tennyson and the Passing of Arthur

Every great poem springs from some generative moment that gives rise to all the rest. The generative moment of *Idylls of the King* comes at the very end of the poem as we now read it, although the lines are among the first that Tennyson drafted in his elegy to the fallen Arthur. We all recall the scene—if not from Tennyson, then from Malory—as the three Queens receive the wounded king into the barge and Bedivere, bereft of his lord, cries aloud,

> Ah! my Lord Arthur, whither shall I go?
> Where shall I hide my forehead and my eyes?
> For now I see the true old times are dead,
> ....
> Such times have been not since the light that led
> The holy Elders with the gift of myrrh.
> But now the whole Round Table is dissolved
> Which was an image of the mighty world,
> And I, the last, go forth companionless,
> And the days darken round me, and the years,
> Among new men, strange faces, other minds.
>
> (PA, ll. 396–406)[2]

From *Victorian Poetry* 25 (1987). © 1987 by West Virginia University.

I sometimes believe that the great world of Arthurian myth came into being solely to memorialize this primal scene of loss, the loss of a once-perfect fellowship in a once-perfect world. Malory tells us that Merlin "made the *Round Table* in token of the roundness of the world."[3] Circles are emblems of inclusive perfection, microcosms that, in a fallen world, are made in order to be broken. In the springtime of Arthur's realm, Tennyson's Vivien, seductress of Merlin and the femme fatale of the *Idylls*, prophesies that her ancient sun-worship "will rise again, / And beat the cross to earth, and break the King / And all his Table" (BB, ll. 451–453). Much later, in the bleak winterscape of Arthur's passing, her prophecy is fulfilled. Bedivere carries the King's shattered body to the water's edge, beside a ruined chapel topped with a broken cross (PA, ll. 174–177). In this landscape of apocalyptic desolation—"A land of old upheaven from the abyss / By fire, to sink into the abyss again" (PA, ll. 82–83)—the three Queens arrive for Arthur's uncertain embarkation to Avalon. There, the "flower of kings" may perhaps find a land of eternal spring, a heaven-haven "Where falls not hail, or rain, or any snow, / Nor ever wind blows loudly" (PA, ll. 428–429). There, healed of his grievous wound, Arthur may perhaps re-embark for his second coming to Camelot.

"*Flos Regum Arthurus*": Tennyson took the epigraph for the *Idylls* from Joseph of Exeter. But if Arthur is the very Flower and Epitome of Kings, the bright epithet conceals a dark underside, for flowers, like all flesh, wither and die. From the first line of his Coming to the last line of his Passing, whether Tennyson's Flower of Kings is an annual or a perennial remains a great open question.

More equivocal even than the question of Arthur's return is the question of whether he ever really walked among us in the first place. I raise here more than the vexed issue of Arthur's historicity, about which Tennyson read everything in print. I mean to suggest that the *idea* of Arthur as Tennyson envisioned him carries with it a strong supposition of nonbeing, of a ghostly presence made all the more vivid by virtue of its very absence. For the grand peculiarity of Tennyson's Arthur is that the shadow he casts is more real than his substance. In so penumbrating his hero, Tennyson remained true to that most memorable of epitaphs, carved on Arthur's purported tomb at Glastonbury: HIC JACET ARTHURUS, REX QUONDAM, REXQUE FUTURUS, *The Once and Future King*. The phrase haunts us less for what it says than for what it leaves out, its total elision of an Arthurian present. The quick iambic trimeter—"the once and future King"—propels us from Arthur's remote past directly to his return in an unspecified future; it is tight-lipped about Arthur here and now.

So, too, is Tennyson. At once the central and most elusive figure in the *Idylls*, Arthur exists in time and transcends time; he exists in time because we who imagine him live, move, and have our being in time; and he transcends time by virtue of inhabiting a perpetual past and art eternally promised future. Malory's Arthur is born after the normal nine-month term at an unspecified season. Tennyson's King, both a Christ figure and a solar deity is born "all before his time" (CA, l. 210)—preternaturally—on the night of the New Year, in the season of Epiphany. His Coming is a kind of Incarnation; his Passing evokes the Passion: a shadow in a field of skulls, the mortally wounded Arthur exclaims, "My God, thou has forgotten me in my death: / Nay—God my Christ—I pass but shall not die" (PA, ll. 27–28). Malory's Arthur is killed in early summer, eight weeks and a day after Easter Sunday. Tennyson's Arthur passes as he comes, in mid-winter, when "the great light of heaven / Burned at his lowest in the rolling year" (PA, ll. 90–91).

His birth, like his death, is shrouded in mystery. That mystery is deepened, not dispelled, by the genealogical riddling of Merlin: "From the great deep to the great deep he goes" (CA, l. 410). According to one account in "The Coming," Arthur's purported parents are the dark-haired, dark-eyed Uther and Ygerne; but Arthur, as befits a sun-king and the Son of God, is fair / Beyond the race of Britons and of men" (CA, ll. 329–330). Of uncertain pedigree, he is also without progeny. Arthur, that is, exists outside genealogy; outside history; perhaps also outside humanity—"Beyond the race ... of men."[4]

Tennyson more than once hints that Arthur is illusory, conjured into being by magicians like himself, just as Merlin, Arthur's architect and wizard, conjures Camelot into being. We first see Camelot through the dazzled eyes of Gareth, the spires of the dim rich city appearing and disappearing in the shifting mists. Gareth rides through city-gates that depict

> New things and old co-twisted, as if Time
> Were nothing, so inveterately, that men
> Were giddy gazing there. (Gl., ll. 222–224)

A great peal of music stops Gareth dead in his tracks, and Merlin's mystifications compound his confusion:

> For an ye heard a music [says Merlin], like enow
> They are building still, seeing the city is built
> To music, therefore never built at all,
> And therefore built forever. (GL, ll. 271–274)

Tennyson here draws on the myth, old as cities themselves, of the city as a sacred center, an *axis mundi* where heaven and hell intersect. Camelot is supernatural in origin, supertemporal in duration. Like Troy, which rose to the music of Apollo's lyre, Camelot is "built to music." But since, as Saint Paul warns, we can have "no continuing city" here on earth (Hebrews 13.14), Camelot is never finally built. Yet the ideal that animates it predates its founding and will survive its fall, and hence the city is "built forever." Camelot embodies in stone the same paradox that Arthur embodies in flesh. A Byzantium of the artist-sage's imagination, Camelot, like its king, triumphs over time by never having entered time; its fall is as purely illusory as its founding.

Arthur is the point of focus at which the idealisms of all other characters in the *Idylls* converge; as their belief in Arthur's authority and reality breaks down, the king and his fair city vanish into the mists from which they first emerged. Bedivere, the last believer, companionless on the desolate verge of the world, watches Arthur dwindle to a mere speck on an empty horizon, his death-pale, death-cold king departing for a paradise that can never be, in the faint hope of returning to a kingdom that never was.

Bedivere's lament, like much else in Tennyson's "The Passing of Arthur," finds its source in the final book of Malory's *Morte d'Arthur*. But Bedivere's last three lines, spoken as he goes forth companionless, have no source in Malory; nor could they have, for they arise from direct personal experience—the poet's own—of overwhelming loss at the death of Arthur. Not the death of the mythical king, but of Arthur the flesh-and-blood friend of Alfred Tennyson—Arthur Henry Hallam, to whom Tennyson dedicated his other great Arthur poem: *In Memoriam [To.] A.H.H.*

Arthur Hallam's death was the single most important event in Alfred Tennyson's life. In Section VII of *In Memoriam*—

> Dark house, by which once more I stand
>   Here in the long unlovely street,
>   Doors, where my heart was used to beat,
> So quickly, waiting for a hand,
>
> A hand that can be clasp'd no more—

Tennyson pictures himself as a ghost, guiltily haunting Hallam's empty, tomblike house, until the blank day breaks on the bald London street. At the end of *Idylls of the King*, Tennyson again stands alone and Arthurless, this time on the desolate verge of the world, the sole survivor of the last dim weird battle of the West, an alien compelled to

> go forth companionless,
> And the days darken round me, and the years,
> Among new men, strange faces, other minds.

Tennyson's profoundly personal quest for reunion with Hallam in *In Memoriam* becomes, in *Idylls of the King*, a profoundly impersonal despair for the passing not only of a hero, but of civilization itself.

In a moment, a word about why Arthurian myth exerted so powerful a hold on Tennyson's imagination and on Victorian culture at large, but I still can not quite let go of Bedivere. Holding on, after all, is what Arthur's story is all about. Perhaps we are all Bediveres in our need to preserve some relic of an idealized past, be it the sour shards of our infant blanket or the bejewelled hilt of Excalibur. The special pathos of Bedivere's Peter-like betrayal of his lord's command—to return the sword to the great deep—is that Arthur mistakes heroic loyalty to his memory for vulgar theft. The literal-minded Bedivere cannot see that it is the words of poets, not the hilts of swords, that memorialize the past. To Bedivere is left the burden of perpetuating the King's story after all living witness to his presence is gone. In the "white winter" of his old age, Bedivere narrates "The Passing of Arthur," serving as both actor and chronicler in the idyll in which he figures. As the poem draws to a close, its various narrators themselves seem to age, like the poet himself, who began the *Idylls* in his early twenties and made the last of his myriad additions and revisions fifty-eight years later, within months of his death. In the later idylls, the legend of Arthur becomes self-perpetuating and cannot be confined to any single teller, be it Bedivere or that nameless Bard—"he that tells the Tale," Tennyson calls him—who is at times Malory, at times Tennyson himself, at times the great chain of Arthurian chroniclers and poets who came before him.

Self-reflexive in virtually every line, the *Idylls* not only recounts Arthur's story but also recreates the process by which myths are made. We see the process at work in scenes that recall the former splendor of the Round Table even as it goes up in flames. Thus Arthur, alone with the repentant Guinevere at Almesbury Convent, recalls the glorious world he believes her sin has wrecked:

> that fair Order of my Table Round,
> A glorious company, the flower of men,
> To serve as model for the mighty world,
> And be the fair beginning of a time.
> ("Guinevere," ll. 460–463)

In the idyll that immediately follows "Guinevere"—"The Passing of Arthur"—Bedivere, as if he had overheard Arthur at Almesbury, incorporates Arthur's description of the Round Table into his own lament. You recall the words—the ones I can not let go—

> But now the whole Round Table is dissolved
> Which was an image of the mighty world,
> And I, the last, go forth companionless.

Arthur's very words—the Round Table as image of the mighty world—have now become canonical, a part of his own story, transmitted whole, like verbal relics, from character to character and place to place. Bedivere suffers a kind of anxiety of posterity, for if he discards Excalibur,

> What record, or what relic of my lord
> Should be to aftertime, but empty breath
> And rumours of a doubt? (PA, ll. 266–268)

The dying Arthur is himself preoccupied in arranging, like the folds of a shroud, his own afterhistory. He commands Bedivere to fling Excalibur into the mere; then shapes through prophecy the legend of which he is himself the subject: "And, wheresoever I am sung or told / In aftertime, this also shall be known" (PA, ll. 202–203).

Characters within the larger fiction of the *Idylls* generate lesser fictions within it—mirrors within mirrors that reflect the whole. The result is that as the realm sinks ever deeper into the abyss, it reemerges in retrospective glory. Tennyson's most daring use of retrospect for this purpose occurs in "Guinevere," the idyll least indebted to any source. Before Arthur arrives at the Convent, cruelly to denounce, then to forgive, Guinevere, a naive young novice keeps vigil with the contrite Queen. Unaware of Guinevere's identity, the novice prattles about magical signs and wonders that, years ago, accompanied the founding of the Round Table "before the coming of the sinful Queen" ("Guinevere," l. 268). The novice's father, now dead, had served as one of Arthur's first knights, and her account of his recollections, although dating back only one generation, takes on the aura of a garbled legend barely recoverable from the past. The mystery of the King's birth, invested with the highest powers of Tennyson's imagination in "The Coming of Arthur," is here lowered in key to a folktale. Divinity lapses into popular superstition; and for an instant the city built to music threatens to become a Victorian Disneyland with fairy palaces and magical spigots gushing wine. The novice's fantastical, vulgarized account of the wonders of Arthur's coming serves, by contrast, to authenticate the "original" wonders, themselves of course no less fictional than the novice's. So too her morally simplistic indictment of the "sinful Queen" and of Lancelot enlarges our sympathy for the adulterous lovers, who are "marred ... and marked" (LE, l. 246) by their sin but, uncannily, grow in grace because of it. The ruins of Camelot recall the city arising in its initial splendor, just as Arthur's passing contains the possibility of his return. The reciprocal movements of rise and fall are held in perfect poise by the seasonal cycle to which all twelve idylls are linked: the founding of the Round Table in earliest spring, its flourishing to the point of rankness in the long summer idylls, its falling into the sere and yellow leaf in the autumnal "Last Tournament," its ruin in the chill mid-winter of "The Passing" with a distant hope of renewal to come. Incorporating this cycle into its narrative structure, *Idylls of the King* is itself a kind of literary second coming of Arthur, a resurrection in Victorian England of the long sequence of Arthuriads extending back centuries before Malory and forward through Spenser, Dryden, Scott, and Tennyson. The poem takes on the quality of a self-fulfilling prophecy and validates itself, like Scripture, by foretelling in one idyll what it fulfills in the next, until at the end the nameless narrator foretells the survival of his own poem, a prophecy that our gathered presence here today triumphantly confirms.

Tennyson drafted his "Morte d'Arthur" late in 1833, under the first terrible shock of Arthur Hallam's death, at age twenty-two, of a cerebral hemorrhage. They had met four years earlier, as undergraduates at Trinity College, Cambridge, and at the time of his death Hallam was engaged to Tennyson's sister Emily. Dead too young to have shaped a life in public, the gifted Hallam lived on posthumously as a prince of friends, a king of intellects, among his remarkable circle of acquaintance. The draft of "Morte d'Arthur," which Tennyson later incorporated verbatim into the completed *Idylls* as "The Passing of Arthur," appears in the same notebook that contains the earliest sections of *In Memoriam*. This first-composed but last-in-sequence of the *Idylls* is sandwiched between Section XXX of *In Memoriam*, which commemorates the Tennyson family's first desolate Christmas at Somersby without Hallam, and Section XXXI, which depicts Lazarus rising from the dead. The physical placement of the "Morte" graphically expresses the poet's longing.[5] At the end of his life, in the autobiographical "Merlin and the Gleam," Tennyson wrote:

> Clouds and darkness
> Closed upon Camelot;
> Arthur had vanished

I knew not whither,
The king who loved me,
And cannot die. (ll. 75–80)

The "king who loved me" is the friend who died on the fifteenth of September, 1833, and whose passing left the young Tennyson stranded "among new men, strange faces, other minds."

Poets, I believe, are impelled to write the same poem over and over again, in myriad different guises, just as Dante Gabriel Rossetti painted the same face again and again. At first glance, *In Memoriam* and *Idylls of the King* could not appear more unlike: the one is a deeply personal elegy, about the death of an actual friend, set in the contemporary moment and concerned with contemporary issues like the conflict of science and faith; the other is a consciously archaic recreation of mythical figures from a world that never was. But at bottom elegy and idyll are, if not the same poem, variations on the same theme—Tennyson's single overriding theme—the theme of loss; or, as he phrased it to himself in early boyhood, the "Passion of the Past."[6] That absence was more vivid to his senses than presence is a singularity of Tennyson's nature: "it is the distance that charms me in the landscape, the picture and the past, and not the immediate to-day in which I move."[7] If poets are born, not made, then Tennyson was a born Arthurian. His eldest son, Hallam Tennyson, namesake of Arthur Hallam, writes in the *Memoir*, "What he called 'the greatest of all poetical subjects' perpetually haunted aim" (II, 125). Tennyson himself tells us that "'the vision of Arthur as I have drawn him ... had come upon me when, little more than a boy, I first lighted upon Malory'" (*Memoir*, II, 128). Malory's *Morte d'Arthur* assuredly "influenced" the *Idylls*, just as Arthur Hallam's sudden death assuredly "inspired" Tennyson to write *In Memoriam*. But causality in the psyche is quite unlike causality in external nature. What ultimately determines what we do and become are those external accidents that are in accord with out inner nature. Malory matters less than the antecedent disposition that drew Tennyson so early and powerfully to the myth of Arthur; Hallam matters less than the antecedent disposition that caused Tennyson to mourn so obsessively and so long for his absent friend, until poetry sprouted from his grave.

In Memoriam begins with a funeral and ends with a marriage-feast; the *Idylls* opens with a marriage—Arthur's to Guinevere—and ends with a funeral. Elegy and idyll are bound by a deep inner complementarity. Hallam Tennyson was the first to point out the curious sandwiching of the "Morte d'Arthur" between two of the earliest sections of the elegy to Arthur Hallam. Mourning, at which Tennyson was something of a professional, is the ritual by which we learn both to hold on and let go, to clasp the dead and to live without them. *In Memoriam* and *Idylls of the King*, each written over a period of decades and then revised for decades more after their publication, are the most exquisitely protracted holdings-on and lettings-go in our literature. Late in *In Memoriam* Tennyson compresses a lifelong trauma into a phrase

> and my regret
> Becomes an April violet,
> And buds and blossoms like the rest. (CXV.18–20)

Tennyson learned to fashion his greatest poetry out of the corpse of his friend, a process that quickened his guilt and preserved his sanity. Within months of Hallam's death in Vienna—the bad tidings reached Tennyson early in October 1833—he had begun *In Memoriam*; drafted "Morte d'Arthur"; composed the originating lyric of *Maud*—

> Oh! that 'twere possible,
>   After long grief and pain,
> To find the arms of my true-love
>   Round me once again![8]—

written "Break, Break, Break"; and drafted his two greatest dramatic monologues, "Ulysses" and "Tithonus," all centering on the experience of loss.

In the same year that Tennyson wrote his "Morte d'Arthur," Coleridge opined, "As to Arthur, you could not by any means make a poem national to Englishmen. What have *we* to do with him?"[9] With a simplicity surprising in this subtlest of English critics, Coleridge took the common position—as common in 1833 as it is today—that Arthurian literature is escapist, irrelevant to the real concerns of the modern world. To this day the prejudice persists that Tennyson's doom-laden prophecy of the fall of the West is a Victorian-Gothic fairy-tale. The majority of Tennyson's contemporaries believed that the modern poet's proper business is to portray modern life, a position whose logic would have disbarred Shakespeare from dramatizing the plight of King Arthur's ancient British neighbor and colleague, King Lear, or prevented Homer from depicting a war "far on the plains of windy Troy" that had ended centuries before Homer was born. Tennyson was urged to write an epic not about knights in armor but about Work or Sanitation. He had to create the audience by which his poem came to be appreciated. And that is precisely what he did in the long intervals between drafting the "Morte" in 1833–34, prefacing it with the embarrassingly apologetic frame-poem of 1842, and waiting another seventeen years before publishing the 1859 *Idylls of the King*. Of course, the audience was latently present— Arthurians have always been among us—but they took awhile to come out of the Victorian-Gothic closet. Arthur underwent a revival in the nineteenth century, particularly during the reign of Victoria, because England had become so quickly and radically un-Arthurian. Saint Augustine wrote *The City of God* as the barbarians were storming the gates of the earthly city; so, too, Camelot rose again as the railroads tore out the heart of ancient cities, the streets of Coketown shook with machines and the misery of exploited labor, the skies darkened with factory smoke, rivers ran foul with industrial wastes, and God most alarmingly disappeared from England's once green and pleasant land. The medieval revival, of which Arthurianism was a part, was not so much an attempt to escape the hard new world of industrial capitalism as a radical attempt to reform it. Tennyson's *Idylls*, Pugin's advocacy of Gothic architecture in *Contrasts*, Carlyle's *Past and Present*, Ruskin's "Nature of Gothic"—all recreate the medieval past in order to remake the English present. The Victorian medievalizers are not idle dreamers but social critics, zealots, prophets. Reading Malory's *Morte d'Arthur* or *The Mabinogion* helps us understand Tennyson's *Idylls*, but so too does Lyell's *Principles of Geology* or Carlyle's *On Heroes*. Perhaps the surest road to Tennyson's Camelot is via another great Victorian epic that appears in the bookshops alongside the *Idylls* in 1859, Darwin's *Origin of Species*. Evolution is an idea with two faces. One is smiling and beckons us onward and upward to ever higher forms; the other face is a death's head, bones encased in stone, a struggle ending in extinction. Tennyson's two Arthur poems, in addition to their deeply personal content, are profound meditations on the leading idea of his century: evolution. In *In Memoriam*, Hallam figures as "The herald of a higher race," a "noble type" of the perfected humanity into which we will ultimately evolve (CXVIII.14; Epilogue.138). In *Idylls of the King*, evolution undergoes a catastrophic reversal; mankind, in Arthur's anguished words, "Reel[s] back into the beast" (LT, l. 125). Evolution has been tinged by Apocalypse. That three of the more notable long poems of the later nineteenth century—"The Wreck of the Deutschland," *The City of Dreadful Night*, and *Idylls of the King*—are apocalyptic in design and imagery is no more coincidental than that Yeats, who came to maturity at this time, is the great modern poet of Apocalypse. The fin-de-siècle became a type of the fin-du-monde. "The blood-dimmed tide is loosed" might serve as epigraph for *Idylls of the King*, and Christ the Rough Beast slouching toward Bethlehem is the perfect heraldic emblem for Arthur's Last Battle, which Tennyson himself eerily glossed as "a presentment of human death"—of human extinction (*Memoir*, II, 132). The

Battle is fought in a landscape literally as old as the hills but as imminent as nuclear winter:

A land of old upheaven from the abyss
By fire, to sink into the abyss again;
Where fragments of forgotten peoples dwelt,
And the long mountains ended in a coast
Of ever-shifting sand, and far away
The phantom circle of a moaning sea.

....

Nor ever yet had Arthur fought a fight
Like this last, dim, weird battle of the west.
A deathwhite mist slept over sand and sea:
Whereof the chill, to him who breathed it, drew
Down with his blood, till all his heart was cold
With formless fear.   (PA, ll. 82–98)

The Apocalypse is an ancient idea; evolution, when Tennyson wrote, a new one. The marriage of the two he entitled *Idylls of the King*.

NOTES

1. An earlier version of this essay was read at the Conference on The Passing of Arthur at Barnard College on November 15, 1986.

2. All quotations of Tennyson's poetry are from *The Poems of Tennyson*, ed. Christopher Ricks London, 1969) and cited in the text. Titles of individual idylls will be abbreviated as follows: "The Coming of Arthur," CA; "Gareth and Lynette," GL; "Balin and Balan," BB; "Lancelot and Elaine," LE; "The Last Tournament," UT; and "The Passing of Arthur," PA.

3. See *La Mort d'Arthur*, ed. R. Wilks (London, 1816), III, chap. 50; and David Staines, *Tennyson's Camelot: The Idylls of the King and its Medieval Sources* (Waterloo, Canada, 1982), p. 173.

4. See Elliot L. Gilbert, "The Female King: Tennyson's Arthurian Apocalypse," *PMLA*, 98 (1983), 868.

5. See Hallam Tennyson, *Alfred Lord Tennyson: A Memoir*, 2 vols. (London, 1897), I, 1119.

6. See "The Ancient Sage," ll. 217–219.

7. Quoted by Sir James Knowles, "Aspects of Tennyson," *Nineteenth Century*, 33 (1893), 170.

8. See Ricks, pp. 598–599 and 1082.

9. *The Table Talk and Omniana of Samuel Taylor Coleridge* (London, 1923), p. 279.

MARK ALLEN

The Image of Arthur and the Idea of King

The literary King Arthur is not essentially a figure of strength, of guile, nor of love. He is also not a religious hero for the most part. Arthur's knights are more knightly than he, his courtiers more courteous, and his cross-bearers more Christian. Gawain is stronger; Merlin is wiser; Galahad, holier; and if Guinevere is any judge, Lancelot is lovelier.

Yet what Arthur is that they are not, is king. In a sense, Arthur is kingship, he is the representative figure of the idea of king for Anglo-American culture. No other figure in our tradition more clearly or more directly epitomizes our notion of kingship than Arthur. David or Solomon might have had a chance if they had not been supplanted by descendants who had no interest in a kingdom of this world. Charlemagne competed with Arthur as a representative king for a time in the Middle Ages, but historiography and his biography got in the way and told us too much about him. Walter Scott tried to give us Richard the Lion-Hearted as a quintessential king in *Ivanhoe*, but again, history tells us that Richard was not the king he was cracked up to be. Representatives, ideals, and symbols do very well as long as they are not encumbered with historical facts or religious convictions that invite us to judge motives and accomplishments harshly. As long as Arthur can avoid being deified or pinned down in the history books, he is likely to remain our figure of a king.

From *Arthurian Interpretations* 2, no. 2 (Spring 1988). © 1988 by *Arthuriana*.

Not surprisingly Arthur's representative value as a king is an index to his popularity in Western tradition. As the role of king changed historically, so changed the Arthur of literature, reflecting social and political developments in metaphorical, literary portraits. And like many literary reflections of history, Arthur encapsulates more than just the social and political past; he also reflects interpretations of this past, providing means both to survey historical kingship and to epitomize modern understanding of what kingship implies. The word "king," of course, operates in a huge semantic field, covering religious contexts as well as political ones, and narrowing at times to function in very specific contexts, e.g., king of the hill (a children's game), king of the road (a bum), and king of beasts (the lion). King cobra, king salmon, king penguin, kingfisher, king blossom, king cup, etc., are all so named for their impressive size or their adornment which suggests coronation. Yet these attributive uses of king, valuable for indicating the prevalence of the idea of king in our culture, do not suggest more than simplified aspects of kingship. For the complex and evocative qualities of kingship, we can—perhaps must—turn to Arthur.

The first and easiest observation to make in this respect is that the Arthur of history was no king at all. He was, the best surmises tell us, a romanized Celt of the island of Britain who led defensive raids against the invading Anglo-Saxons with some success and perhaps attempted a raid or two of his own on the Continent.[1] He probably lived in the late fifth or early sixth century and therefore looked and acted a great deal more like Beowulf than Shakespeare's Henry the Fifth or the great medieval monarch, St. Louis. There were no castles, no jousts, and no plate armor. Roman short-swords, tribal raids, and hand-to-hand combat on foot were the style of the day—a style inconsistent with our connotations of "king."

Our first literary reference to Arthur by name comes some 300 years after he flourished, in a history of the British by a monk named Nennius who clearly distinguishes between Arthur, the *dux bellorum*, or leader of battles, and the *reges Brittonum*, or rulers of the British (*British History*, section 56). Like the historical Arthur, the first literary Arthur is a warrior, not yet a king. Indeed, since Nennius wrote in Latin, he could not have referred to Arthur as king even if he had wanted to, and his word *rex* then meant something quite different from what our word "king" means today. *Rex*, especially in its genitive form *regis*, is the ancestor of our words "regal" and "royal," but our word "king" goes back to the Anglo-Saxon word contemporary with the historical Arthur—*cyning*. Neither word, however, connoted our idea of king since, in a manner of speaking, kings had not yet been invented. Regal people in Arthur's sixth and Nennius's ninth centuries were probably the same ones that the Anglo-Saxons called "cyningas," but they were unlike what we mean when we use "king." They lived in wooden halls rather than castles and ruled by consent of common election rather than royal primogeniture. Outside of war or certain legal situations, they had little function, certainly spending no time presiding over jousts or awaiting marvels in samite pavilions. These are traditions—literary and maybe even historical ones—that later accrued to the figure of Arthur, but such traditions can hardly be applied to the Arthur of history or to Nennius's Arthur.

Our image of king, it is true, was coming to a very slow awakening about the same time that Nennius was writing, but it was awakening on the Continent, and it was awakening in a nascent form almost unrecognizable. When Charlemagne was crowned Holy Roman Emperor on Christmas Day in the year 800, Nennius was probably alive. Yet the Roman imperial ideal that Charlemagne succeeded in temporarily reviving was a far cry from *cyning-scipe*, even though the idea of kingship stemmed from the roots of this ideal some 250 years later. Whether or not Nennius had ever heard of Charlemagne is a matter for speculation, but if he had, he would not have referred to the new imperator as *cyning*.

In the middle of the twelfth century, three centuries after Nennius, another monk writing in Latin cuts King Arthur almost out of whole cloth. About 1136, Geoffrey of Monmouth wrote his fanciful history of the kings of Britain, giving Arthur center stage. Unlike Nennius, Geoffrey refers to Arthur as *rex* rather than *dux*, and even more importantly, by Geoffrey's day, the word *rex* had connotations different from those it had in Nennius's earlier age—connotations that our word "king" now carries. In the years that separate Geoffrey from Nennius and from Charlemagne, Western Europe witnessed forces and events which modified the Roman imperial ideal that had flickered back into life with Charlemagne. The invasions of the Vikings, the rising political power of the Papacy, the Crusades, and many, many other factors too extensive to list here combined, first, to break Europe into independent, defensible units, and second, to reunify it in the shape of provinces and growing nations. The first stage is the age of feudal barons and the second is the age of kings.

The imperial ideal obtained in parts of eleventh- and twelfth-century feudal Europe, but in many ways, especially in France and England, it was more an ideal than a reality. French rulers held sway over England and France since Duke William the Conqueror's victory over Harold Cyning at Hastings in 1066. The subsequent struggle between the lineage of the duke and his liege lord in France neatly represents the non-imperial struggle for power within the upper echelon of the feudal pyramid. The English barons owed fealty to the English king, who as Duke of Normandy, owed fealty to France, complicating the political obligations at all levels of society, and from our point of view, confusing the meaning of kingship. What king kneels before another secular ruler? Certainly not Arthur. Eroded imperialism, complex feudal relations, and growing nationalism encouraged rulers to regard themselves as kings in the sense that we understand the term.

Geoffrey of Monmouth wrote near the dawn of the age of kings, and his representation of Arthur epitomizes many of the features of kingship developing at this time and passed on to later tradition. Some of these are older and rather obvious like the importance of heredity and the necessity of military success, but some are more abstract and more interesting. Geoffrey is the first to record, for example, the mysterious conditions of Arthur's conception and birth; he is the first to tell us of Uther's transformation by Merlin, and the secret entry into Tintagel on the night of Arthur's conception. He combined these conditions with the curious and difficult to understand *Prophecies of Merlin* that pertain to the promise of Arthur and the future of Britain. Together, the two may well be remnants of a Celtic, not English, tradition of Arthur as a demi-god—leader, hero, and semi-divine priest and victim. But whether Celtic tradition is the source or not, it is clear in Geoffrey's presentation that Arthur's kingship is defined by more than personal ability or common election; as Merlin's prophecies suggest, he is sanctioned by a force or power superior to human affairs. In the following prophecy, recited before Arthur is born, the Boar of Cornwall signifies the coming king:

> Woe unto the Red Dragon, for his extermination draweth nigh; and his caverns shall be occupied of the White Dragon that betokeneth the Saxons whom thou hast invited hither.... At the last, she that is oppressed shall prevail and resist the cruelty of them that come from without. For the Boar of Cornwall shall bring succor and shall trample their necks beneath his feet. The islands of the Ocean shall be subdued unto his power, and the forests of Gaul shall he possess. (139)

Geoffrey depicts Arthur as the savior of the British people (Red Dragon), predicting his success over the Anglo-Saxons (White Dragon) and his hegemony in the British isles (islands of the ocean) and on the Continent (forests of Gaul). He is Britain's greatest king in Geoffrey's presentation because his right and ability to rule derive from mysterious forces beyond the ken of ordinary men. Kings in the high Middle Ages held their thrones by dint of this sort of mystery—mystery that solidified only later into the tradition of the so-called divine right of kings.[2] For example, by the time Thomas Malory composes his Arthurian story in the fifteenth century,

Merlin's prophecies have disappeared and Arthur's right of rule is proved by means of the sword in the stone which stands in a churchyard where Merlin and Archbishop alike proclaim that God has made Arthur king (10). Kingship in Malory's day carried with it an articulate notion of Christian divine right, but broader idealization is evident in Malory's combination of secular and sacred signs that Arthur must rule. The idea of kingship that grew out of history and comes down to us in Geoffrey's and Malory's stories—our idea of kingship—carries with it something less specific and more pervasive than divine selection. Propriety and inevitability underlie our idea of a king, but kingship is not specifically a Christian notion. Certainly the kings of the high Middle Ages were Christian and they were anointed by the Church; yet, if Geoffrey's rendering of the story of Arthur is any indication, old and deep traditions, difficult to describe, complicate the image of king that has grown from his time to our own.

This complicated image comes down to the present in one of the successful twentieth-century versions of the Arthurian story, Mary Stewart's *The Crystal Cave*, the first volume of her Arthurian tetralogy and a work that readily acknowledges a direct debt to Geoffrey of Monmouth. Stewart presents Merlin attempting to explain the "power," as he calls it, that enforces him to manipulate conditions which will lead to the birth of Arthur. Arthur's father, Uther, even before Arthur's birth, worries whether the child will be accepted as king in the future since the child was conceived out of wedlock—a distinctly un-Christian start for our idea of king. Merlin speaks first:

> "It is God who keeps the price secret, Uther, not I."
> "God? God? What god? I have heard you speak of so many gods. If you mean Mithras—"
> "Mithras, Apollo, Arthur, Christ—call him what you will," [Merlin] said. "What does it matter what men call the light? It is the same light, and men must live by it or die." (372)

Although Merlin speaks of God, he refuses to specify any one God, including even the unborn Arthur in his list of possibilities: "Mithras, Apollo, Arthur, Christ." Stewart captures here an essential aspect of our modern idea of king: spiritual but not religious, appropriate but not selected, Arthur is kingship.

By following this line of thinking, I have rapidly traced one thread in the tapestry of Arthurian literature. Before dropping it, let me suggest that another important contribution Geoffrey makes to the Arthurian story corroborates the mysterious appropriateness of kings. Geoffrey was the first to record the ambiguous death of Arthur, suggesting paradoxically that he was "mortally dead" and that he went to the isle of Avalon for healing (236). Geoffrey leaves the paradox unresolved and later tradition blossoms with mysterious women on barges and swords caught by arms rising from lakes, extensions of Arthur's mysterious fitness as king. In no account does Arthur simply die to be rewarded in a Christian heaven. Rather, he seems to be reabsorbed into a pattern of necessity, seemingly waiting for the time that he can return: "The Once and Future King" as the translation of his epitaph reads in Malory (717) and as he is presented in later tradition.

If kingship entails the idea of mysterious appropriateness, it also entails majesty, and the literature of Arthur is rife with requisite splendor. Individual knights of his court may be splendid in their battle array, but they do not compare with the magnificence of the court at large. Splendor requires accumulation and Arthurian literature accumulated quickly after Geoffrey, as quickly as knights accumulated in Arthur's court. The great tradition of romance rose in the late twelfth and thirteenth centuries, no doubt in response to the popularity of Geoffrey's work and to the maturation of the idea of king in Western culture. These are the centuries of the great medieval kings that bridge the earlier age of feudalism and the later age of parliaments and revolutions. These are the centuries that witnessed the great reigns of England's Henry II and Edward I, France's Louis IX, and Charles of Anjou in southern Italy. This is not the place to recall the greatness of these historical kings or explore the reasons for their greatness, but it is no coincidence that the age of the great kings saw the explosion of Arthurian literature into the extravagant and glorious tradition of romance. As went the idea of king, so went the image of Arthur.

One of the curiosities of this tradition is that the romances have, in relative terms, little to do with Arthur himself, concentrating on his knights instead. We get the strong sense that the king is not one who does, but one who has others do for him. In the romance tradition, Arthur would not join a feast until someone reported or provoked high adventure, and it is in the context of such feasts that Lancelot is prompted to save Guinevere, Perceval demands his knighthood, and, with the irony of a slightly later age, Gawain faces the horrible but grand Green Knight. Arthur's court became the central clearing house for all the successful knights, disparaged damsels, or sacred cups that happened to be in the neighborhood. His court had the knight of two swords, his court met about the Table Round, his court was visited by the Lady of the Lake. Stories collected around the Arthurian Round Table in a manner never duplicated, drawing upon and adding to the magnificence of the court of King Arthur.

Importantly, the splendor of Arthur's court is not just physical or visual; it is not just conspicuous consumption. Each of his knights participates in the grandeur of his court and the court is represented in each of their individual adventures. Kay's failures no less than Lancelot's successes are part of ibis court. The ancient grace of Ector combines with the youth and energy of Gareth. Guenivere's lushness is modified by the austerity of Perceval's sister, Elaine. What I am trying to capture here is a sense of extension—a presence that embraces all of these figures and is greater than their sum, the representational value of kingship that allows, even today, monarchs to use the royal "we" form of the pronoun. Mention of Arthur evokes images of victory and defeat, hope and tragedy, purity and voluptuousness. His name connotes pain rather than ache, joy rather than mere happiness, weariness without tedium, failure without defeat. His image and the idea of king both carry with them the grandness of court life still emulated in our culture. Many cities across the United States annually select monarchs to preside over Mardi Gras, Fiesta, or May Day celebrations. Our high schools and colleges, nationwide, elect Homecoming kings and queens. When Prince Charles of England visits, Americans proud of their tradition of independence sit in record numbers to, in effect, eat at court—1600 strong at the Hemisphere Plaza in San Antonio, Texas, alone (*Express-News*, 22 Feb. 1986: A1). Apparently, we wish still to celebrate in the grand style, to be part of the splendor that goes with kingship.

Arthur is the only king we have returned to time and again. The romance tradition gave us an incredible variety of individuals and exploits, but Arthur is the name everyone knows. After the medieval histories, legends, and romances, he was taken as the hero of Spenser's Renaissance epic, *The Faerie Queene*, even though the work was published, unfinished, only fifty years before the ax fell on Charles I of England and on English political kingship. Tennyson represented in his Arthurian *Idylls of the King* all the rich, intimidating idealism of Victorian England, although, largely, the work was written while the likes of Gladstone and Disraeli directed England and Queen Victoria mourned for her dead consort, Albert. Arthur's splendor was again captured well in T. H. White's popular classic, *The Once and Future King*, source for the even more popular stage and screen musical, *Camelot*, reason that the politicos nicknamed the Kennedy administration Camelot, and inspiration for an incredible outbreak of Arthurian materials in the fifties, sixties, seventies, and eighties—works by Mary Stewart, already mentioned, as well as by Thomas Berger, Rosemary Sutcliff, Henry Treece, Marion Zimmer Bradley, Gillian Bradshaw, Vera Chapman, John Steinbeck, H. Warner Munn, Catherine Christian, Parke Godwin, and many, many more.[3]

Again, I find myself at this end of history looking backward, rather than at the other end looking forward. Yet, that is as it should be: Arthur and kingship mean mystery and majesty more so for us than for the Celtic tribesmen he led, more than for Geoffrey of Monmouth, more even than for the *trouvères* who sang or spoke before Henry II and St. Louis IX. The mystery and majesty of Arthur enforces itself upon us more than it did on our ancestors because Arthur, because the idea of kingship, is an obsolescent idea—not an obsolete one, an obsolescent one. In the days when people had great kings before them, Arthur represented what a contemporary king could be, an idealization that was both flattering to the courts and a model for emulation. Today, Arthur represents what kings should or could have been. His name and what he represents tug at us like a memory that we know is important. We cannot know the future, and the present is completely evanescent, so we look to the past, rummaging in our mental attics to find a story that offers a stable standard or ideal. Arthurian literature is and has been just such a story for our culture, a tale that we return to periodically to remind ourselves that mystery and majesty are grand memories, even though they no longer pertain to all that is "new-fangill" about us, to borrow a word popular with Malory. It is not exactly that we wish to return to the standard of the past, but that we use the standard to derive a comforting sense of presentness from our awareness of what we leave behind. We leave behind mystery in the confidence that now our beliefs are wholly correct, or the more modern conviction that we no longer need beliefs at all. We leave behind majesty, telling ourselves that its elitism is no longer necessary. But at the same time that we leave these behind, our language reinvokes them, dredges them up, reenlivens them, allowing us to treasure mystery and majesty for what they are and savor the sense that they are behind us—nearly.

"King" is a bit of language that performs such a function, one that adapts very nicely to expressing superlatives, but also maintains an aura of the past and a sense of idealization. We use the word to describe children's games and figureheads of politics and society, touching these present realities with passing ideals, conveying some of the splendor and majesty—some of the extended magnificence—that the word has accumulated through the ages. But it is when we read of Arthur that the magnificence touches us most poignantly, for in our literature of Arthur the magnificence is always obsolescent.

Indeed, Arthurian literature reflects a remarkable concern with memory and with the passing of an age, whether expressed through T. H. White's nostalgic tone, Mary Stewart's narrative layers, or C. S. Lewis's superimposition of an Arthurian character on modern society in *That Hideous Strength*. Charles Williams (*War in Heaven*) brings the Grail to a London publishing house; Sanders Anne Laubenthal (*Excalibur*) rediscovers Arthur's sword in an American archeological dig; and Susan Cooper (*The Dark Is*

Rising series) invents a son for Arthur so he can visit modern Wales. Each of these authors in his or her own way communicates the fond sense that the mystery and the majesty are going, not gone, that Arthur and the idea of king are in their last twilight. Yet this twilight has been a long one, since the dusk was already falling five hundred years ago in the works of Malory, seven hundred years ago in the great romances, eight hundred and fifty years ago in Geoffrey of Monmouth. Geoffrey's Arthur is already a king from the past, even though the very idea of kingship was just developing. The romances depict Arthur as background to the exploits of his famous and, in their own chivalric terms, more modern knights. Malory, the *sine qua non* of later presentations, wrote in an age when kingly majesty was giving way to political expediency and national rivalry. Gone were the days of the great kings who led their own battles and who, like Louis IX, bathed the feet of peasants. Gone were the glorious days of mystery and majesty since courtiers, not warriors, flattered the Tudor monarchs of Malory's day. His disdain for people who are "new-fangill" and for the slander and noise that leads to the fall of the Table Round reflects his yearning for the high nobility of the early court of Arthur and his regret for its demise. He admires the majesty of Arthur, recognizes that it is past, and, in the "King's English" of his day, yearns that it might have sustained:

> Lo ye all Englysshemen.... [Arthur] was the moste kinge and nobelyst knyght of the worlde, and moste loved the felyshyp of noble knyghts, and by hym they all were upholdyn, and yet might nat these Englyshemen holde them contente with hym. Lo thus was the olde custom and the usayges of thys londe, and men say that we of thys londe have nat yet loste that custom. (708–09)

Since Malory is the source of most later versions of the story of King Arthur, his kind of nostalgia tinges our very idea of king, a nostalgia of loss and regret. Modern versions of the Arthurian story use various techniques to convey this sense of obsolescent royalty, and combine it richly with the requisite mystery and majesty. As in Malory's day, we regret its loss, and as in Malory's version, we try to fit ourselves to it as much as we try to fit it to us. For when Excalibur is rediscovered in Mobile, Alabama (Laubenthal's *Excalibur*), it demands heroic effort of the archaeologist; when the Grail shows up in a London publishing house (Williams's *War in Heaven*), it must be saved by the unsuspecting editor from age-old evil. Modern Arthurian literature provides many examples of the revival of such Arthurian talismanic objects and ideals, as well as the return of Merlin to modern society (Lewis's

That Hideous Strength), psychological justifications for the Green Knight (Chapman's *The Green Knight*) and Modred (Treece's *The Great Captains*), even the return of a kind of Lancelot no less at odds with his ideals now than then (Percy's *Lancelot*). Leonard Wibberley brought the ghost of Arthur back to us in *Quest of Excalibur*, but no version that I know of dares to bring back— or rather, bring forward—Arthur in all his fullness. Kingship would, presumably, be too much for us.

But though Arthur himself is not brought back into modern setting, various modern works reclaim his mystery and majesty, tinged with nostalgia. Taking their tone from Malory most directly, modern authors incorporate obsolescence into the idea of king, and therefore keep Arthur at a distance, not daring to get too familiar. The best modern versions of the Arthurian story are the layered re-shapings or interpretations of earlier versions, where a narrator or a character participates both in the Arthurian context and in our world, bridging for us the distance we cannot or do not wish to break. Again, Mary Stewart's *The Crystal Cave* is a fine example, where her character Merlin of strikingly modern sensibility tells his story in flashback, recalling his past and the Arthurian court. Mark Twain used a similar bridging technique to satirize modern society in *A Connecticut Yankee in King Arthur's Court*. Parke Godwin (*The Firelord*) creates a delicate balance between the historical Arthur and his literary tradition by having a dying Arthur recount his life to his scribe. Each gives us a character who talks like us but lives in an Arthurian world, enabling us to share this world for a time.

The most influential and among the very best of the modern versions of the Arthurian story is also the one with the most fleeting kind of nostalgia for Arthur and for the idea of kingship, bridged by a narrator who stands both in our world and in Arthur's. White's *The Once and Future King* successfully captures the rich mixture of history, mystery, majesty, and nostalgia implicit in kingship and explicit in Arthurian literature by giving us a narrator who seems to care more for Arthur's world than his own. No single quotation can do the work justice, as no single work can do justice to the idea of king. Yet, several passages in White's work come close, encapsulating the Arthurian world, a world only a king could command. As White's narrator asks us to look with him out of Guinevere's window, the subjective perspective enables us to feel the kingly richness of Arthur's world, but it also reminds us that this richness is past:

> There under the window in Arthur's Gramarye, the sun's rays flamed from a hundred jewels of stained glass in monasteries or convents, or danced from the pinnacles and cathedrals and castles, which their builders had actually

loved.... Picture the insides of those ancient churches—not the grey and gutted interiors to which we are accustomed—but insides blazing with colour, plastered with frescoes in which all the figures stood on tip-toe, fluttering with tapestry or with brocades from Bagdad. Picture also the interiors of such castles as were visible from Guinevere's window.... Their walls rippled doorless with the flexible gaieties of Arras, tapestries like the Jousts of St. Denis which, although covering more than four hundred square yards, had been woven in less than three years, such was the ardour of its creation.... Remember, too, the goldsmiths of Lorraine, who made shrines in the shape of little churches, with aisles, statues, transepts, and all, like dolls' houses: remember the enamellers of Limoges, and the champlev work, and the German ivory carvers, and the garnets set in Irish metal.... It was the age of fullness, the age of wading into everything up to the neck. Perhaps Arthur imposed this idea on Christendom, because of the richness of his own schooling under Merlyn.

For the King ... was the patron saint of chivalry.... Arthur was the heart's king of a chivalry which had reached its flower.... He was the badge of everything that was good in the Middle Ages, and he had made these things himself. (562–64)

White's narrator describes a kingly world rather than an individual here, although elsewhere he gives Arthur a remarkable childhood and some tender, personal moments. But *The Once and Future King* is better than many other works of its kind because of its strength of atmosphere. The description guards its mystery in delicate personifications and images, it asserts its majesty in the proliferation of details, and it conveys nostalgia in sentence cadence and the repetition of "remember." We share the narrator's yearning for this kingly "age of fullness" because White's style bridges for us the distance between ourselves and the idea of king, between ourselves and this notion that is more literary than it is historical or political. In White's presentation, kingliness is a mood, a feeling, a desire—a function of style as much as plot and a result of White's own familiarity with Arthurian literary tradition.

In White and in other Arthurian authors, Arthur and kingship are connotations rather than denotations, extensions and expansions of the single idea that has been developing nearly as long as has European vernacular literature. The cultural importance of this idea is evident in the breadth of application of the word "king," and in the enormous popularity of

Arthurian literature from Geoffrey down to White—over eight hundred years. In this literature, the idea of kingship thrives in the image of Arthur.

NOTES

1. Geoffrey Ashe, *The Discovery of Arthur*, has attempted to identify the legendary Arthur with the historical Riothamus and trace his activities on the continent as well as in Britain. Most earlier discussions of the historical Arthur are content to assess his British battles. See, for example, Ashe's *The Quest for Arthur's Britain* and the work of Richard Barber.

2. Kingly divine right was not possible before the conflict between the Papacy and the crowns of Europe. John Wycliffe's condemnations of ecclesiastical abuses in the late fourteenth century led him to assert the primacy of secular power in his treatise *De officio regis* and gave the English kings the leverage that led, eventually, to the establishment of the Church of England and the assertion of the divine right of English monarchs. See Nicolson, 188–203, and Figgis's dated but useful work.

3. For extensive bibliographies of modern Arthurian works, see Thompson, and Taylor and Brewer.

WORKS CITED

Ashe, Geoffrey. *The Discovery of Arthur*. New York: Doubleday, 1985.
———. *The Quest for Arthur's Britain*. London: Pall Mall, 1968.
Barber, Richard. *King Arthur in Legend and History*. Totowa: Rowman & Littlefield, 1974.
———. *The Figure of Arthur*. London: Longman, 1972.
Berger, Thomas. *Arthur Rex: A Legendary Novel*. New York: Delacorte, 1978.
Bradley, Marion Zimmer. *The Mists of Avalon*. New York: Knopf, 1983.
Bradshaw, Gillian. *Hawk of May*. New York: Simon, 1980.
Chapman, Vera. *The Green Knight*. London: Collings, 1975.
Christian, Catherine. *The Pendragon*. New York: Knopf, 1979.
Cooper, Susan. *Over Sea, Under Stone*. London: Cape, 1965.
———. *The Dark Is Rising*. New York: Atheneum, 1973.
———. *Green Witch*. New York: Atheneum, 1974.
———. *The Grey King*. New York: Atheneum, 1975.
———. *Silver on the Tree*. New York: Atheneum, 1977.
Figgis, John Neville. *The Divine Right of Kings*. 1896. New York: Harper, 1965.
Geoffrey of Monmouth. *The History of the Kings of Britain*. Trans. Sebastian Evans and Charles W. Dunn. New York: Dutton, 1958.
Godwin, Parke. *The Firelord*. New York: Doubleday, 1980.
Laubenthal, Sanders Anne. *Excalibur*. New York: Ballantine, 1973.
Lewis, C. S. *That Hideous Strength*. New York: Macmillan, 1946.
Malory, Sir Thomas. *Works*. Ed. Eugène Vinaver. 2nd ed. London: Oxford UP, 1971.
Munn, H. Warner. *Merlin's Ring*. New York: Ballantine, 1974.
Nennius. *British History and the Welsh Annals*. Ed. and trans. John Morris. Totowa: Rowman, 1980.
Nicolson, Harold. *Kings, Courts and Monarchy*. New York: Simon, 1962.
Percy, Walker. *Lancelot*. New York: Farrar, 1977.
Steinbeck, John. *The Acts of King Arthur and His Noble Knights*. New York: Farrar, 1976.
Stewart, Mary. *The Crystal Cave*. London: Hodder & Stoughton, 1970.
———. *The Hollow Hills*. London: Hodder & Stoughton, 1973.

———. *The Last Enchantment*. London: Hodder & Stoughton, 1979.

———. *The Wicked Day*. London: Hodder & Stoughton, 1984.

Sutcliff, Rosemary. *Sword at Sunset*. London: Hodder & Stoughton, 1963.

Taylor, Beverly, and Elisabeth Brewer. *The Return of the King: British and American Literature since 1900. Arthurian Studies 9*. Totowa: Barnes, 1983.

Thompson, Raymond H. "Arthurian Legend and Modern Fantasy." *Survey of Modern Fantasy Literature*. Ed. Frank N. Magill. Englewood Cliffs: Salem. 5:2299–2315.

Treece, Henry. *The Great Captains*. New York: Random House, 1956.

Twain, Mark. *A Connecticut Yankee in King Arthur's Court*. New York: G. Wells, 1923.

Wibberley, Leonard. *Quest of Excalibur*. New York: Putnam, 1959.

Williams, Charles. *War in Heaven*. 1949. Grand Rapids: Eerdmans, 1980.

White, T. H. *The Once and Future King*. New York: Putnam, 1958.

E. KAY HARRIS

Evidence Against Lancelot and Guinevere in Malory's Morte Darthur: Treason by Imagination

Who, then, can live secure of himself or his own under ... a law that offers assistance to anyone hostile to him?
—Sir John Fortescue, *De laudibus legum Anglie*

One of the problems that continues to occupy Malory scholars is the difficulty of relating his *Morte Darthur* to the fifteenth century, a period of civil war. One way of realizing the historicity of Malory's text is to compare it to the French *Mort le roi Artu* (or *Mort Artu*, c. 1225), the concluding section of the Prose *Lancelot*, Malory's most important source. Most comparisons of the two texts have concentrated on stylistic and philological matters and are important for understanding the *Morte Darthur*. These studies, however, tend to overlook or dismiss as unimportant a distinctive feature of Malory's text, that is, what Derek Brewer has called its *mixture of inconsistencies*.[1] This essay focuses on two important departures Malory makes from his French source—deviations which constitute internal contradictions in his text—to show the *Morte Darthur*'s intersection with the legal and political dimensions of the crime of high treason in fifteenth-century England. The two departures are: Malory's ambiguous representation of Lancelot and Guinevere's treason, their adultery, when proof of the deed is being sought; and his creation of a law that sentences Guinevere to death.[2]

From *Exemplaria* 7, no. 1 (1995). Copyright © 1995 by Pegasus Press.

Unlike the French *Mort Artu*, which presents Lancelot and Guinevere's act of adultery in unequivocal terms, Malory tells his audience

> whether they were abed or at other maner of disportis, me
> lyste nat thereof make no mencion, for love that tyme was not
> as love ys nowadayes.[3]   1165

This peculiarity of the *Morte Darthur* has been explained in terms of a fifteenth-century morality that regarded chivalric romances as "guide[s] to conduct," so that condoning "adultery was no longer acceptable."[4] By having the adultery of Lancelot and Guinevere take place offstage, Malory complies with this moral dimension of chivalric romance. Yet if Malory in this instance chooses to be ambiguous for the sake of a moral version of chivalry, then we must ask why he describes so explicitly in earlier sections of his text the adulterous relationships of Tristram and Isode, Tristram and the wife of Segwarydes, and Lancelot and Guinevere themselves (in the Knight of the Cart story). With such precedents as these, Malory's ambiguous treatment of adultery in this latter episode seems an oddity. Moreover, depictions of vices other than adultery are plentiful in this text. Indeed, they are so numerous that Caxton, in his preface to the *Morte Darthur*, warns readers to "doo after the good and leve the evyl" (cxlvi). We are left to wonder why, if this instance of adultery must be relegated to the wings for the sake of morality, earlier incidents of adultery and other forms of vice, such as murder, do not take place offstage as well.

Caxton's admonition to readers of the *Morte Darthur* "can only be explained," Elizabeth Kirk has observed, "on the assumption that Malory's text troubled Caxton in a way no comparable text had done."[5] Even now, in the latter part of the twentieth century, the *Morte Darthur* still troubles us. In fact, a number of Malory's critics have echoed Caxton's exhortation, following their own advice by ignoring Malory's textual inconsistencies. The *Morte Darthur*, it is said, is not "an intellectual book: we are called upon to feel ... not to analyse or reason." Nor should we be too curious about Lancelot and Guinevere's adultery, since Malory expects his readers to have a "cool attitude" towards physical love. Likewise, we are told that Malory is concerned with the "public recognition of one's action" not guilt or innocence, not "the inner life."[6] One can get the sense, from these remarks, that to ask about Malory's inconsistent representations of adultery is bad manners or, worse, a violation of the text's privacy. Curiously enough, by instructing readers what to do and not to do with Malory's text, such comments as these enunciate their own form of chivalry. Rather like chivalric knights, readers are to protect the *Morte Darthur* from its inconsistencies by behaving or reading in a certain way. We are encouraged to adopt a respectable distance from the textual puzzles, what we could call the "inner life" or private spaces, of the *Morte Darthur*.

Yet the dissonance of the *Morte Darthur* signals a narrative complexity that challenges and enriches our interpretive efforts and provides a way for us to gain a fuller understanding of this Arthurian tale.[7] Malory's perplexing, ambiguous treatment of adultery when Agravain attempts to gather proof of the deed is inconsistent not only with his earlier depictions of adultery, but it is also at odds with the law on treason he creates for the sentencing of Guinevere—a law that requires for its application physical proof of the act of treason. This particular inconsistency functions to pose a legal dilemma: a law which specifies the types of proof necessary to establish the guilt of an alleged traitor is applied despite the fact that no such proof has been obtained. With this problem of evidence and legal reprisal, we can place Malory's version of the "exotic never-never land of Arthurian Britain"[8] in the chaos of the Wars of the Roses and more specifically in that era's discourse on treason.

One prominent feature of fifteenth-century legal discourse on high treason derives from a 1352 statute. In an effort to check the interpretive latitude of the Crown in the matter of high treason, Parliament sought to identify, in this law, the specific acts that constituted this crime.[9] Within the statute's "definitive" list of treasonous acts, however, Parliament included the act of imagining the death of the king. Thus the prosecution of treason did not have to be based on an overt act, one that left traces of physical evidence.[10] Through its provision for an imagined act of treason, the statute transgressed the very boundaries it had been designed to impose and posed problems regarding the type of evidence needed to establish this crime. Not until the accession of Henry IV were the potentialities of imagining the king's death fully explored: Henry and his jurists found that words spoken against the king established treason by imagination. Once its interpretive possibilities had been tapped, imagining the death of the king figured frequently in the prosecution of treason throughout the fifteenth century.[11]

As can be expected, the comings and goings of various kings during the Wars of the Roses created an atmosphere in which accusations of treason flourished, and the 1352 law assisted in that efflorescence. By equating a putative act of imagination to a physical act of treason and requiring no physical evidence to establish this crime, the statute encouraged what amounts to the spontaneous generation of treason. Rather than injecting an element of stability into the chaos of civil war, the law contributed to it. During this period, Sir John Fortescue was arguing in *De laudibus legum Anglie* that English law had brought peace and prosperity to the realm.[12] This claim is contradicted not only by the civil war but by a vociferous strain of popular sentiment that regarded law as eminently susceptible to private ambition.[13]

Malory's representation of law and legal process in the matter of Lancelot and Guinevere's treason brings into play these discordant perceptions of law in the fifteenth century. The law on treason found in the *Morte Darthur* reads as an objective statement that is binding on everyone, "whatsomever they were, of what astate or degré," caught in the circumstances it sets forth (1174). But like the 1352 law on treason in some of its fifteenth-century uses, it is applied when no conclusive proof of an overt act of treason exists. We will see that in the absence of such proof, the *Morte Darthur* accentuates the constitutive role of interpretation in what appears to be a simple application of law to the facts of the case. My analysis focuses on three issues:

(1)   Malory's law on treason and the lack of evidence;

(2)   Imaginative treason and imaginative accusations: evidence of words and reports of ill-fame; and

(3)   Gawain's alternate interpretations of the "facts": Malory's challenge to legal process.

In its peculiar representation of legal process, Malory's *Morte Darthur*, I argue, interrogates and challenges judicial and legislative interpretive practices that transform a lack of evidence or questionable evidence into unequivocal proof of crime and criminal guilt.[14]

* * *

When Guinevere is brought to trial for her adultery with Lancelot in the *Mort Artu*, Arthur asks his barons what must be done with her according to "droit jugement." In turn, the barons seek the advice of Agravain and his brothers who submit that

> "par droit qu'ele en devoit morir a honte, car trop avoit fet grant desloiauté, quant ele en leu del roi qui tant estoit preudom avoit lessié gesir un autre chevalier."[15]

> "according to justice the Queen should die a shameful death since she acted with such great disloyalty when she allowed another knight to sleep with her in the place of such a worthy man as the king."

Arthur's wanting to know what justice would be in this case and the baron's consulting others on the matter suggest that in the world of the *Mort Artu*, there is no particular law to be followed. Arthur has told his barons that the Queen will suffer death no matter what they say and this confirms the absence of any justice beyond the king's word.[16]

Rather than having to figure out what should be done in Guinevere's case, Arthur in the *Morte Darthur* consults the appropriate law:

> And the law was such in thos dayes that whatsomever they were, of what astate or degré, if they were founded gylty of treson there shuld be none other remedy but deth, and othir the menour other the takynge wyth the dede shulde be causer of their hasty jougement.   1174

Of course, by "hasty jougement" Malory could simply mean a prompt trial. But the types of proof Malory cites indicate a particular type of promptness. Both capture in the act and *mainour* were associated with an abridgement of judicial process known as summary judgment or summary justice. This association, along with the Crown's endeavors in the fifteenth century to bypass jury indictment and jury trial as a means to increase the likelihood of conviction suggests that Malory's "hasty jougement" signals summary judgment.[17] Guinevere is not tried by a jury nor given an opportunity to defend herself; rather the law is simply stated, the evidence cited for the crime of treason, and sentence pronounced—judicial process in this case takes the form of summary or "hasty jougement."

As to the types of proof, "taken with the dede" is readily understood: a person was captured in the act of crime, and, as the phrase implies, the deed was witnessed. Under such circumstances, a criminal deed was established; no other proof was necessary. The criminal captured in the act could be subjected to an abbreviated form of legal process and "summarily dispatched."[18] To ensure conviction, the thing for an accuser to establish, then, was that capture in the act of crime had occurred. But there was more than one way to accomplish this. Through various types of capture, an accuser could establish that an equivalent of capture in the act had occurred. In fact, as we will see, capture in the act could be constructed even though the act of crime had not been witnessed.

Both Malory's *Morte Darthur* and the French *Mort Artu* recognize the force which establishing Lancelot's treason by the method of capture in the act would have. Having heard Agravain's and Mordred's accusation against Lancelot, Arthur in the *Mort Artu* orders them to

"fetes tant que vous les preigniez prouvez ... mes fetes ce que
ge vos di, qu'il soient pris ensemble ... or m'enseingniez
comment on le porra seurprendre en ceste afere que vos
m'avez descouvert."[19]

"Make it so that you take them in the act.... But do this as I tell
you, they are to be taken together.... Now explain to me how,
without fail, he (Lancelot) will be taken in this deed that you
have made known to me."

Likewise, Malory's Arthur wants the proof of capture in the act, telling
Agravain that if

"hit be sothe as ye say, I wolde that he were takyn with the
dede."   1163

Since the deed must be witnessed, Agravain in both works takes with him to
the Queen's chamber a company of knights who will be able to say that they
have witnessed the deed. But, in each version, because of the noise the
knights make, Lancelot and Guinevere are alerted to their danger, and none
of the would-be capturers witnesses the deed.[20]

Malory's text takes this problem of evidence a step further by
withholding even from the reader any proof of Lancelot and Guinevere's
guilt or innocence:

For, as the Freynshhe booke seyth, the quene and sir
Launcelot were togydirs. And whether they were abed other at
other maner of disportis, me lyste nat thereof make no
mencion, for love that tyme was nat as love ys nowadayes.
1165

Although Malory pretends that such ambiguity exists in the "Freynshhe
book," it does not. The *Morte Artu* tells us that Lancelot "se deschaua et
despoilla et se coucha avec la reïne,"[21] "took off his shoes, undressed, and
went to bed with the Queen."

Malory's strategy of ambiguity, coupled with Agravain's failure to take
the lovers in the deed, contrasts strikingly with his rendering of an earlier,
successful capture in the act, the capture of Tristram by Isode's cousin Andret
(430–32). In fact, the attempt to capture Lancelot in the act is a point-by-
point inversion of the Tristram episode. Where Malory makes the adultery
of Tristram and Isode explicit both to the capturers and the reader, he

withholds such evidence from Agravain, his companions, and the reader in the latter attempt. Tristram is taken naked in the Queen's bed, while there is not even a hint that Lancelot takes his clothes off in Guinevere's chamber, a detail explicit in the *Mort Artu*. And where the capture of Tristram proceeds cautiously and quietly, a fanfare of noise accompanies the attempt to take Lancelot in the deed, enhancing Lancelot's opportunity to escape. The contrast between these two scenes underscores an absence of evidence in Guinevere and Lancelot's case—in Malory, the episode is never more than a case of suspected wrongdoing. Neither Agravain nor the reader succeed in legal "takynge in the dede."

Although the attempt to capture in the act fails in the case of Lancelot and Guinevere, Malory's law provides for one other form of proof which could also sanction summary judgment: the mainour. The OED[22] speculates that mainour, in its original sense, probably meant "the act or fact of (a crime)" and defines "with (later in) the mainour" as "in the act of doing something unlawful; 'in flagrante delicto'"—for example, as Andret takes the naked Tristram in bed with Isode. However, this definition is the second entry under mainour. The first entry defines mainour as

[t]he stolen thing which is found in a thief's possession when he is arrested: chiefly in the phrase taken, found with the mainour.

In English law, this definition seems to be earlier than that given in the OED's second entry. Capture with the mainour, a translation of the French *capta cum manuopera*, derives from an Old English concept, *aet haebbendre handa gefangen*, the hand-having thief who is caught with the stolen goods in his possession. By extension, mainour applied to other forms of circumstantial evidence, for example, a person's holding a bloody knife.[23]

Mainour, then, means two things: the physical evidence of crime and the act of crime itself. Capture with mainour could in fact function as a construction of capture in the act; as such, mainour could have the same probative weight of capture in the deed, that is, it could warrant summary judicial process and execution. The fact that witnessing the physical evidence of crime was as incriminating as witnessing the crime in process seems to have originated in the difficulty of catching people in acts of wrongdoing, since most malefactors would take precautions to ensure against such an event. The consequent interpretive supplement of mainour extended the event of capture in the act beyond the actual occurrence of the crime. Of course, although capture with the mainour is thus equated with capture in the act,[24] conflated into a single event, they represent two distinct acts which can only occur at separate moments in time. Capture in the deed requires that the act itself be witnessed—be seen and heard; while this does require the witness's interpretation, capture with the mainour is more clearly an interpretive act, requiring that objects be read as or be substituted for an act of crime.[25]

In the context of Malory's "either ... or" construction—"othir the menour other the takynge wyth the dede shulde be causer of ... hasty jougement"—mainour is not precisely the same thing as capture in the act. Still, the two terms are synonymous in the sense that either one could justify summary judgment.[26] Malory's having mainour precede capture in the act in his statement of law perhaps suggests a paramount role for it in establishing a criminal deed. Instances of such a substitution of mainour for "takyn wyth the dede" can be found in the *Morte Darthur* long before Malory offers his statement of law. I will consider two examples.

Tristram, wounded in battle, is not deterred from entering the bed of Sir Segwarydes's wife:

> So they souped lyghtly and wente to bedde with grete joy and pleasaunce. And so in hys ragynge he toke no kepe of his greve wounde ... and Sir Trystrames bledde bothe overshete and the neyther-sheete, and the pylowes and the hede-shete.   394

Warned of the husband's approach, Tristram escapes. But Segwarydes sees the bloodstained sheets, the signs of adultery, and threatens to kill his wife unless she gives him the name of her lover. She complies, and Segwarydes pursues Tristram and attempts to kill him.

Malory's "Knight of the Cart" presents a very similar situation. While Guinevere is at Melegaunt's castle, Lancelot climbs into her chamber through a window and in doing so injures his hand. Then Lancelot

> went to bedde with the quene and toke no force of hys hurte honde, but toke hys pleasuance.... And whan he saw hys tyme that he myght tary no lenger, he toke hys leve....
>
>   And therewithall [Melegaunt] opened the curtayn for to beholde her. And than was he ware where she lay, and all the hede-sheete, pylow, and overshyte was all bebled of the blood of sir Launcelot and of his hurt honde.   1131–32

Like Segwarydes, Melegaunt takes the bloodstained sheets as the sign of adultery and accuses Guinevere of treason. In these two accounts, Malory devises scenes in which the crime of adultery is established by the signs of crime, by mainour, rather than by capture in the act.

If we place these two passages alongside Andret's capture of Tristram in bed with Isode and Agravain's attempt to capture Lancelot and Guinevere in the deed, we see Malory manipulating the relation between a deed and its signs. He supplies both direct and indirect evidence of adultery in the cases that precede Agravain's scheme. But in the representation of the trap to take the Queen and Lancelot together, Malory produces no tell-tale signs—no naked lovers, no bloodstained sheets—to establish their treason. Yet Guinevere is sentenced to die by a law that calls for the proof of either capture in the act or mainour.

In light of the difficulties of actually taking someone in the act of crime, mainour offered an important means to construct capture in the act and thus to establish a crime; but, with its dependence on interpretation, the form of mainour was susceptible to change, depending on the circumstances of a case. In fifteenth-century cases of treason, the concept of mainour can be seen at times to take on the pliable form of words spoken against the king. This transformation helps us to understand Malory's peculiar representation of a legal process which is carried out despite a lack of proof that an act of treason has taken place.

* * *

As mentioned earlier, the 1352 statute on treason stipulated that it was treason

> quant home fait compasser ou ymaginer le mort nostre Seigneur le Roi.

> when one compasses or imagines the death of our lord the King.

Imagining the death of the king, of course, could not be established by capture in the deed: a thought of treason could not be seen or heard nor did it leave a trail of evidence as long as it remained in the imagination. In 1441, Sir Richard Neuton, C.J.C.P, was asked if a man could be put to death for a thing which he had never done, and he replied,

> Ouy, que on sera mort, trait et pend[u] et disclos pur chos qu'il ne jamais, en fait, ny consentat ny aidat. Come si on ou sa femme imagine le mort le Roy et ne ad fait plus, pur ce imaginacion il sera mort come devant.[27]

> Yes, because a person will die, be drawn and hanged and known for a thing which he never in fact agreed to or aided in.

This is the same as when a man or his wife imagine the death
of the King and do nothing more; by this act of imagination he
will die as already said.

Proving an act of imaginative treason was problematic to say the least, but
earlier in the century Henry IV and his jurists discovered one way to
establish this type of treason: words spoken against the king were construed
as evidence of the thought of treason. Thus words came to function as
mainour, as a sign of treason.

Although Henry IV was the first to deploy the 1352 statute in this way,
subsequent fifteenth-century monarchs followed suit, as Neuton's opinion
indicates. Additionally, chronicles of the period record this type of
construction. *The Brut or The Chronicles of England* reports that in 1444 a
woman accosted the king after Eleanor Cobham, Duchess of Gloucester, had
been convicted of treason. Speaking on behalf of the Duchess:

> the woman ... spake to hym [the king] boldly, and reviled hym
> ungoodly and unwisely for Dame Alianore Cobham.... And
> with these wordes the Kyng wexe wroth, and toke it to hert;
> and she was arested and brought into prison by the lawe, and
> so broght ... afore the Justices of the Kynges Benche. And
> there she was repreved for hir ungoodly langage, and
> folehardynesse to speake so to hir liege lorde, the Kyng.

For her words, the justices ruled that she be placed in a cart and paraded
through London "with a paupire about hir hede of hir proude and lewed
langage," and, according to the chronicler, she subsequently was pressed to
death: "Thus she ended in this world, for hir proude langage to hir Kyng and
souverayn lord."[28] In a similar case of the same year, Thomas Kerver, a
gentleman of Reading,

> untruely and ungoodly, and ayenst feith and lawe, depraued
> the Kyng; wherefore he was take and brought before the
> Kynges Consayle [which] Juged hym to deth as a traytour.[29]

In general, the deposition of a king generated the most conducive
environment for treason by word. Anyone who said anything favorable about
the deposed king flirted with treason. In fact, this type of remark sparked the
first use, under the 1352 statute, of words to establish the act of imagining
the king's death.[30]

Malory's Guinevere and Lancelot do not in fact utter hostile words against King Arthur; they have left no such track of mainour to indict themselves. What indicts them is something more subtle: the fact of being accused. Judgment rests neither on a proven, witnessed deed of treason, nor on words proceeding "ex suo proprio capite" (from his/her own head),[31] as in the fifteenth-century cases of treason by word. The mainour of this imaginative form of treason is the accusation itself—words proceeding from the accuser's head, filled with thoughts of treason, treason committed by the accused.[32] By choosing not to follow his sources and render in explicit terms Guinevere and Lancelot's treason, Malory creates the conditions for an imagined act of treason which, in this case, takes the form of Agravain's accusation against Lancelot, an accusation that relies on words, specifically the noise of ill-fame, rather than on physical evidence.

In the *Morte Darthur* as soon as Lancelot and the Queen are together

> there cam sir Aggravayne and sir Mordred wyth twelve knyghtes ... and they seyde with grete cryyng and scaryng voyce,
>
> "Thou traytoure, sir Launcelot, now ar thou takyn!"
>
> And thus they cryed with a lowde voyce, that all the courte myght here it.... But ever sir Aggravayne and sir Mordred cryed.
>
> "Traytour knyght! Come forth oute of the quenys chamber!"
>
> 1165–67

The redundant "cryyng" of Agravain and his companions underscores and punctuates a fundamental element in Malory's rendition of the attempted capture: the noise that, almost by itself alone, constitutes his representation of the attempt to take Lancelot in the deed. It is this noise of accusation that alerts Lancelot and Guinevere to their danger: "'Alas!' seyde quene Gwenyver, 'now are we myscheved bothe!'" (1165). The corresponding passage in the French *Mort Artu* renders a different sort of fracas. The noise, heard by Lancelot and Guinevere, is that of the knights who try to break down the locked door and who, in fact, never address Lancelot at all.[33]

Malory's representation, in contrast with the *Mort Artu*, ascribes to Agravain and company an intent to publicize both the crime of treason and the name of the traitor. To create such a scene, Malory turns away from his literary sources to draw upon and integrate into his text a particular custom for apprehending malefactors: raising the hue and cry, a custom common to both England and France and one that could also set in motion summary justice. To be raised when a person came upon a scene of crime, the hue and cry or clamor brought others to witness either the deed itself or its signs. If the perpetrators were not captured in the act, they were pursued by hue and cry, and if caught they were liable to summary justice.[34] The hue and cry served to bridge the temporal difference between capture in the act and mainour by making present, for a specified time, the criminal act beyond its actual occurrence.[35] Thus pursuit by hue and cry provided a way to equate capture in the mainour with capture in the act—the signs of crime were no longer signs but the event of crime itself.

Even though the hue and cry represents an old custom in French as well as English law, it is not raised by Agravain and his fellow knights in the *Mort Artu*. One explanation for this absence is the fact that no scene of crime is witnessed.[36] The French text tells us that when the knights find the door to the Queen's chamber locked,

> si n'i ot celui qui n'en fust touz esbahiz; lors sorent il bien qu'il avoient failli a ce qu'il vouloient fere.[37]

> they were confused because of this and they knew well that they had failed to do what they wished to do.

This depiction adheres to custom: that hue and cry be raised after evidence of wrongdoing has been seen. The only evidence against Guinevere and Lancelot is his presence in her chamber, as is the case in the *Morte Darthur*. But Agravain and his fellow knights in Malory's text do not admit defeat when faced with a locked door.

Although Malory's Agravain claims to Arthur that he and others know of Lancelot's treason, he mitigates his assertion by conceding that proof is yet to be obtained. But in seeking that proof, these knights, rather than sneaking noiselessly down a hallway, approach the chamber with "grete and scaryng voyce," a circumstance that does not favor capture in the deed. By having the men raise the noise before the crime is detected, Malory complicates his application of hue and cry, and such a strategy, I propose, derives from the overlap of hue and cry with concepts such as notoriety and infamy.[38]

Raising a hue and cry or clamor at the scene of crime and sustaining it during pursuit of a suspect publicized the crime. As an object of hue and cry, a suspect, caught with the signs of crime in his possession, was regarded as a common or notorious malefactor and subject to summary judgment. The noise or clamor of ill-fame could also be regarded as evidence of wrongdoing and a means to abridge judicial process. In 1341, for example, a commission of inquiry reported that the king had learned of the misconduct of Chief Justice Willoughby "by the common fame and clamour of our people." At the opening of his trial, Willoughby complained that the king had not been informed either "by indictment, or by the suit of a party." He was told that the king was "informed by the clamour of the people."[39] Thus we can see the interrelation of a number of different strategies which were devised to remedy injuries in a speedy manner: capture in the act, mainour, hue and cry, and notoriety offered proof that a crime had been committed and could instigate a summary judicial process. Agravain's hue and cry against Lancelot both operates as a clamor and reports Lancelot's common fame as a traitor.

Since Malory claims not to know whether Lancelot and Guinevere are in bed or at "othir maner of disportis" and the door to the Queen's chamber is locked, Agravain's raising a hue and cry against Lancelot's name does not proceed from an overt act of treason nor from any physical evidence beyond Lancelot's presence in the Queen's room. Malory reinforces this inversion of hue and cry, raising the clamor without a corresponding scene of crime, by having Arthur presuppose that noise is a first step in the attempt to catch Lancelot in the act:

> "but if he be takyn with the dede he woll fyght with hym that
> bryngith up the noyse."   1163

It seems to be taken for granted, then, that the clamor of ill-repute will precede the anticipated event of capture in the act.

In fact, Agravain has already tentatively taken such a step even before he outlines his scheme to take Lancelot in the deed. Speaking to all his brothers, Agravain

> seyde thus opynly and nat in no counceyle, that manye
> knyghtis myght here: "I mervale that we all be nat ashamed
> bothe to se and to know how sir Launcelot lyeth dayly and
> nyghtly by the quene. And all we know well that hit ys so."
>   1161

Thus even at this early stage, Agravain integrates common knowledge or common report into his accusation. In fact, common knowledge or report is the basis of his charge. Agravain stirs up so much contention between himself and those who will not speak ill of Lancelot that Arthur, coming into the room, "asked them what noyse they made" (1163). And it is at this point that Agravain tells Arthur that Lancelot is a traitor.

Throughout the *Morte Darthur*, Malory's use of the term "noyse" is slippery to say the least. It can be used for various purposes, such as to spread news or a rumor, to make a complaint or accusation, or to serve as proof of wrongdoing. Early in the text, for example, when Lancelot refuses the advances of a woman, she tells him that "hit is noysed that [he] love[s] quene Gwenyvere." Lancelot replies that he cannot stop people from speaking of him however "hit pleasyth them" (270). Rumor or noise can also be turned to personal advantage and enters into Andret's scheme to get Tristram's lands. Although Tristram is alive, Andret "made a lady that was hys paramour to sey and to noyse hit" that she was with Tristram when he died and "buryed hym by a well." Tristram's last wish, she claims, was that his lands be given to Andret (499). In another context, when Tristram rides into Joyous Garde, he hears "in that towne grete noyse and cry" over the death of a knight who, the people report, was wrongfully slain (690). Tristram, not having witnessed the deed, nevertheless takes up the people's cause and engages the alleged offender in battle.

Malory also uses "noyse" as a term for fame or reputation. At one point he tells us that, after Tristram had won many battles,

> all the noyse and brewte fell to sir Trystram, and the name
> ceased of sir Launcelot. And therefore sir Launcelottis
> bretherne and hys knyysmen wolde have slayne sir Trystram
> bycause of hys fame.   785

Fame or reputation, what is reported about a person, also enters into legal judgments. To settle a land dispute between two brothers, Arthur takes into consideration their reputations. Because one is "called an orgulus knyght and full of vylony" and the other is "named a good knyght and full of prouesse," Arthur awards the land to the "good knyght" (147). The use of noise or fame as a form of legal evidence appears with more frequency after Agravain has raised a hue and cry of ill-fame against Lancelot; Malory keeps the accusation of treason alive, after Agravain's death, by having others proclaim the charge again and again. At Joyous Garde, for example, after Lancelot has rescued the Queen, Arthur is the first to call Lancelot a traitor; then Gawain

> made many men to blow uppon sir Launcelot, and so all at
> onys they called hym "false recrayed knyght."   1190

Begun by Agravain, the noise of ill-fame continues to plague Lancelot, forcing him into a defensive position throughout the rest of the book.[40]

Thus noise in Malory's text comes to stand for common knowledge, rumor, complaint, fame, or a form of legal evidence. These shifting aspects parallel a legal definition of rumor and noise given by Chief Justice John Fortescue during the impeachment proceedings against the Duke of Suffolk in 1450. When the Commons asked the King's Bench for guidance on the matter of noise and infamy, Fortescue

> declared for all his Felawes and seid that in thiese generall termes, Rumoir, and noyse of sclaundre and Infamie may many thinges be understand; that is to for to sey, mesprisions or trespasses ... or elles Felonie or Tresons.[41]

The point to note here is that the veracity of rumor and noise of ill-fame is not touched upon. What matters is that the noise exists and exists as a form of evidence for various acts of wrongdoing. Agravain has made sure that the noise against Lancelot's name exists and that it signifies treason.

Although begun by Agravain, noise emerges in Malory's text as a thing in itself, detached from any specific, identifiable voice, and capable of reproducing itself, like the personified "tydyng" Chaucer describes in the *House of Fame*:

> Thus north and south Wente every tydyng fro mouth to mouth, And that encresing ever moo, As fyr ys wont to quyke and goo From a sparke spronge amys, Til al a citee brent up ys.[42]

Chaucer's "tydyng," the report, grows ever greater until it finds a point of exit from the house of fame and flies forth for the occasion. Malory renders a similar scene through Agravain's hue and cry against Lancelot. With "grete and scaryng voyce," Agravain and his cohorts shout that Lancelot is a "traytoure" so that "all the courte myght hyre hit" (1165). Their strategy provokes Lancelot himself to contribute to the general noise, until the search for evidence evolves into a cacophonous shouting match between Lancelot and the knights on the other side of the door:

> "Traytour knyght, com oute of the quenys chambir ... thou shalt nat ascape."
>
> "A, Jesu mercy!" seyd sir Launcelot, "thys shamefull cry and noyse I may nat suffir.... Now, fayre lordys ... leve youre noyse and youre russhynge...."
>
> "Traytour knyght! Come forthe oute of the quenys chambir!"   1166–67

Malory's representation of the noise of ill-repute and Fortescue's opinion on slander assign a prominent role to reputation in fifteenth-century legal process. Fortescue's opinion was given during the impeachment proceedings against Suffolk, a favorite of Henry VI, and the transformation that noise undergoes in his case is well worth noting. In 1450, Suffolk addressed Parliament in an effort to clear his name from the "rumour and noyse of sclaundre and Infamie" and to learn who his accusers were so that he could answer them directly. In addition, Suffolk sought permission to petition the king on his own behalf. The Rolls of Parliament record that he

> besought the Kynges Highness ... to admitte to his
> supplication and desire, that he myght be atte his declaration
> of the grete infamie and defamation that is seid uppon hym, by
> many of the people of this land, that he shuld be other than a
> true man to the King and his Reaume; if any man wold sey hit
> in generall or in speciall, howe, wherof and wherin, that he
> myght make his answere, in declaryng of hym self as he is.

Granted his petition, the Duke wrote to the King:

> I suppose welle that it commen to youre eeres, to my grete hevyness
> and sorowe, God knoweth, the odious and horrible language that
> renneth through your lande, almost in every Commons mouth,
> sowning to my highest charge and moost hevyest disclaundre ...
> which noise and language is to me the heaviest charge and birthen,
> that I coude in any wise receyve or bere.[43]

The Duke of Suffolk identifies the noise of slander as an unbearable offense, as does Lancelot in his exchange with Agravain:

> "A, Jesu mercy!" seyde sir Launcelot, "thys shamefull cry and
> noyse I may nat suffir, for better were death at onys than thus
> to endure thys payne."   1166

After Fortescue had given his opinion on noise, the King's Bench advised the Commons that since "there was no speciall mater of sclaundre and Infamie putte upon hym," Suffolk should not be imprisoned. Within a very short time, however, the general noise against Suffolk modulated to particularity:

> from every partie of Englond there is come among hem [the
> Commons] a greate rumour and fame, howe that this Roialme
> of England be sold to the Kynges Adversarie of Fraunce.[44]

Like Chaucer's tiding, the noise against Suffolk is shaped for the occasion. This specific charge or rumor is accompanied by many other detailed allegations. Supple enough to undergo the transformation from general to specific, "rumour and fame" in both forms originated in a general clamor disassociated from any one identifiable voice, and in this instance, the noise of ill-fame led to Suffolk's exile.

While the example of Suffolk serves to illustrate what could be done to a favorite of the king who had incurred the wrath of the Commons and certain magnates (most notably the Yorkists), the Crown had its own particular method of aligning notoriety and ill-fame with treason: attainting traitors by act of Parliament.[45] Attainder had long been a punishment for treason, but the procedure had tended to be an informal one. The proscription of the Yorkists in 1459, however, generated a formula for future acts. Enacted by Parliament, but under the close supervision of the king, attainder in the latter half of the fifteenth century was not the consequence of a trial in which an accused had been found guilty of treason. In point of fact, fifteenth-century attainder operated only in the absence of judicial process[46] and can be seen as a legislative form of summary judgment, synthesizing accusation, conviction, and punishment into one parliamentary act.

Used primarily to legalize the forfeiture of a traitor's land to the king, attainders secured such a penalty by reputing or advertising the guilt of people who had not had the opportunity to speak in their own defense. By including a provision that declared the blood of traitors to be corrupt, attainder built upon and expanded the notion of infamy. By corruption of blood, the heirs of a traitor were also attainted and dishonored and consequently were unable to inherit their patrimonial legacy.[47] Thus a person's dishonor could extend well into the future, beyond his lifetime. In effect, the traitor's memory was damned, unless the Crown saw fit to reverse the attainder.

To take a powerful example, the Duke of York was not present at the Parliament that declared that

> his fals and traiterous ymaginations [and] conspiracies [were]
> openly knowen to the [King's] liege people[48]

—a declaration that made the treason and its perpetrator a matter of notoriety and common report. The attainder also stipulated that York forfeit his lands, that his heirs be disinherited, and that he

> be reputed, taken, declared, adjugged, demed and atteynted of
> high Treson.[49]

Such stipulations disclose the synthesis of accusation, conviction, and punishment that attainder achieved. The attainder of York and his supporters was then publicized:

> by the kynges commissione in euery cyte, burghe, and toune [they were] cryed opynly and proclamed as for rebelles and traytoures.[50]

Akin to hue and cry, the publication of attainder, however, was not issued as a way to apprehend suspects so that judicial process, summary or not, could begin. This form of clamor bypassed judicial process altogether by simply declaring the treason of those named. The Yorkists, for their part, blamed their estrangement from the king on the noise that they claimed was stirred up against them by their enemies at court. In a letter to the king, they decry the way they have been "proclamed and defamed in ... name unrythefully, unlawfully."[51]

In light of the supple, legal force of noise, rumor, and slander in the fifteenth century, exemplified by the attainder of York and the impeachment of Suffolk, Lancelot's intense desire to quell the noise Agravain makes against his name is understandable. At one point during his exchange with the knights, Lancelot attempts to silence them by proposing a bargain:

> "Sires, leve youre noyse.... And therefore, and ye do be my counceyle, go ye all from thys chambir dore and make you no suche cryyng and such maner of sclaundir as ye do. For I promyse you be my knyghthode, and ye woll departe and make no more noyse, I shall as to-morne appyere afore you all and before the kynge, and than lat hit be sene whych of you all, other ellis ye all, that woll depreve me of treson."   1168

Unfortunately for Lancelot, his accusers are not to be deterred. They continue in the same vein:

> "Fye uppon the, traytour," seyde sir Aggravayne and sir Mordred, "for we woll have the magré thyne hede and sle the, and we lyste!"   1168

Fearless facing any physical battle, Lancelot does show an anxiety over this type of publicity. He is quite willing to hazard physical violence rather than endure a verbal assault on his reputation. Allowed to continue, the noise of slander can become an invisible and invincible accuser who cannot be faced on a battlefield or in a court of law.[52] As Guinevere succinctly states, "the lesse noyse the more ys my worshyp" (1128). Likewise, given the ramifications of an act of attainder which could dishonor one's reputation for generations to come, Lancelot's concern over the consequences of being banished for treason makes sense:

> for ever I feare aftir my dayes that men shall croncyle uppon
> me that I was fleamed oute of thys londe.   1202–3

The image of a clamoring Agravain and his fellow knights armed to the teeth, ready either to arrest Lancelot or kill him, suitably illustrates the actual act of violence the text assigns them: raising the hue and cry of ill-fame against Lancelot. He is not taken in the deed, and other than his presence in the Queen's chamber no sign of an actual deed is seen by his would-be capturers. But against the hue and cry, the noise of slander, Lancelot is rendered uncharacteristically vulnerable. Without offering evidence that would prove either the innocence or guilt of Lancelot, Malory consigns Agravain's accusation, the clamor of ill-fame, to the imaginative realm. Even so, that accusation which produces and publishes Lancelot's treason brings about his banishment.

* * *

In his representation of Lancelot and Guinevere's treason, Malory places before us the evidence of noise, the truth or falsity of which cannot be determined. And Guinevere is sentenced to death. But Malory does not allow such a judgment to go unchallenged. As Fortescue's statement on slander allows that rumor and noise can mean many things, Gawain's speech to Arthur on behalf of Guinevere argues that the evidence against the Queen can mean many things. One may take Lancelot's presence in Guinevere's chamber as mainour, as evidence of treason, but, as Gawain points out to Arthur, such proof is less than conclusive:

> "My lorde Arthure, I wolde counceyle you nat to be over hasty,
> but that ye wolde put hit in respite, thys jougement of my lady
> the quene, for many causis. One ys thys, thoughe hyt were so
> that sir Launcelot were founde in the quenys chambir, yet hit
> myght be so that he cam thydir for none evyll. For ye know,
> my lorde ... that my lady the quene hath oftyntymes ben
> gretely beholdyn unto sir Launcelot, more than to ony othir
> knyght; for oftyntymes he hath saved her lyff.... And
> peradventure she sente for hym for goodnes and for none

> evyll, to rewarde hym for his good dedys.... And peradventure
> my lady the quene sente for hym to that entent, that sir
> Launcelot sholde a com prevaly to her, wenyng that hyt had be
> beste in eschewyng and dredyng of slaundir; for oftyntymys we
> do many thynges that we wene for the beste be, and yet
> peradventure hit turnyth to the warste."   1174–75

From this passage we can see that Malory through Gawain offers alternate
interpretations of Lancelot's presence in the Queen's chamber. Punctuated
by the word peradventure, Gawain's speech announces its speculative,
interpretive basis of the "many causis" it cites. Thus in Gawain's counsel to
Arthur, Malory challenges what appears to be an impartial application of law
in the Queen's case by foregrounding the very thing that the applied law of
treason obscures or denies: the possibility of alternate readings, alternate
interpretations of the evidence.

Moreover, Gawain's "many causis" are incorporated into a narrative
that argues for a certain point of view. Arthur is cautioned "nat to be over
hasty," not to ignore either Lancelot's honorable or human experience, the
unforeseen, untoward consequences that "oftyntyms" beset the best of
intentions. The argumentative form of Gawain's speech accentuates the lack
of argumentation in the application of law in the Queen's case. For rather
than reasoning (as the *Mort Artu* does) that Guinevere is guilty because she
has slept with someone other than her lord, the *Morte Darthur* suppresses
altogether any connection between the Queen's judgment and the act of
adultery: Malory's Queen is sentenced to die

> bycause sir Mordred was ascaped sore wounded, and the dethe
> of thirtene knyghtes of the Rounde Table.   1174

Malory's application of law does not explain how Mordred's wounds or the
dead knights signify treason by way of adultery. It offers no reasons, no
"many causis," to construe this evidence in such a way. If Agravain's original
charge of treason, adultery, is no longer in effect, what act of treason sends
Guinevere to the stake?

It is not at all certain that Mordred's wounds and the death of Arthur's
knights can in fact substantiate an act of treason, since at this point Malory
turns away from legal terminology to offer a non-legal description of
preceding events; for "wounds" and "death" do not denote crimes. Although
legal language was certainly not standardized in the fifteenth century, we can
distinguish between terms that construe the legal significance of events,
those that do not, and those that are used in both legal and common
parlance.[53] For example, Malory through Agravain and Arthur does not

hesitate to transform the non-legal description of Lancelot's "ly[ing] daly and nyghtly by the quene" (1161), recasting it as legal fact: Lancelot is "traytoure to [the king's] person" (1163). With his facility for deploying legal terms, Malory could have easily represented Mordred's wounds and the deaths of Arthur's knights as signs of a criminal deed by inserting a phrase such as "by forecast of treson," or changing "dethe" to "murdir."[54] Had he done so, we could see some basis for construing the events as proof of treason. But "wounds" and "death" are not reinterpreted in legal terms.

In light of Malory's use of legal terminology and the questions he raises, through Gawain's commentary, about the facts of Lancelot and Guinevere's case, the switch from legal to non-legal discourse is an inconsistency but one that has important ramifications, complicating an apparently straightforward application of law. The facts of the case are represented as self-evident, as if no explanation, no interpretation, were needed. But this "just-the-facts" presentation obscures the interpretive activity that equates wounds and death with the Queen's adultery, even as the gap between treason and proof of the deed discloses the absence of sufficient evidence to establish the Queen's guilt. She may just as well have been accused and sentenced to death for imagining treason.

The discrepancy between Malory's stated law and his representation of the facts of the Queen's case places the burden of interpretation on the King. It is he who equates the "previs" of Mordred's wounds and the death of thirteen knights with an act of adultery committed by the Queen. Although Arthur has instructed Agravain to obtain the proof of treason by taking the two lovers in the deed, he now ignores that stipulation. The King's capacity to interpret inconclusive evidence as unequivocal proof of the Queen's guilt overrides any constraint the law places upon him—just as the 1352 statute's equation of imagining the king's death to an act of treason transgresses its restricted list of treasonous acts. Shown by Gawain that a presumption of the innocence of the Queen and Lancelot is as compelling as assuming their guilt, the King responds:

"I will nat that way worke ... for she shall have the law. And if
I may gete sir Launcelot, wyte you well he shall have as
shamefull a dethe."   1175

Thus, with an absolute power like God's, Arthur as king commands the freedom and authority to alter the correspondence between law and the facts of a case or the correspondence between words and things: Mordred's wounds and the death of thirteen knights signify an act of adultery. At this point in Malory's text, the law is the King's creation.[55]

The incongruity of Malory's deployment of legal and non-legal terminology in Guinevere's case also sheds light on some of the interpretive moves made by fifteenth-century justices in cases of imagining the king's death. Judgments that cite words as the signs of this type of treason also include projections of what could have happened as the result of such words. For example, in Thomas Kerver's case, the justices reasoned that his words could have incited rebellion and other crimes and could have led the king's people to withdraw their love from him.[56] Also, the justices sometimes added that by taking such unkind words to heart, the king could have become ill and died of grief.[57] The chronicler of *The Brut* may have been aware of this interpretation since he reports that "the king wexe wroth, and toke it to hert" when he heard the words of the Duchess of Gloucester's defender.[58]

Although it was possible to convict a person for an imaginative act of treason on the basis of words, such interpretations offer an internal resistance to this line of reasoning. The case of the woman who spoke on behalf of the Duchess of Gloucester patently illustrates this resistance. Writing the woman's words on a piece of paper and hanging them on her transforms them into a visible, tangible object: words become physical evidence. Similarly, projecting rebellion or the king's sickness and death as a possible effect of words spoken against the king once again brings in, through the back door, overt acts and physical evidence. Such a compensatory strategy highlights the insufficiency of existing evidence, that is, words, by disclosing a need for corroborating physical evidence which an overt physical act of treason would have rendered. Thus at some level the jurists' interpretations of imagining the king's death register the inadequacy of words alone to serve as manifest evidence. Moreover, such decisions acknowledge the interpretive acrobatics required to establish an act of imaginary treason. A remark made by Roger Bolingbroke, who was sentenced to die for predicting the death of Henry VI, succinctly captures the problem of evidence in such cases of treason. A practitioner of magic, Bolingbroke

> confessid that he was nevir gilty of eny treson ayens the kyngis persone; but he presumed to fer in his konnyng.[59]

Likewise, the gap between legal and non-legal discourse in Malory's application of law exposes and challenges the implicit contradictions in judgments that convicted people for imagining the death of the king.

* * *

Perhaps it is worth saying, here, that I do not see in Malory's text a recommendation for doing away with law and legal process. What his text ponders is the obfuscation of the the constitutive role of interpretive activity not only in statements of law, such as his own, but also in the application of law to the facts of a case. Since the law holds such power over human beings, the *Morte Darthur* shows a need for legal process to acknowledge the multiple interpretations that evidence or the facts of a case generate and to acknowledge as well the reasons for choosing one interpretation over another. In Gawain's words to Arthur, Malory advises a king or judge "nat to be over hasty" in transforming ambiguous evidence or even a lack of evidence into unequivocal proof of guilt that, in turn, sanctions judgments of imprisonment, banishment, or death. Malory, in effect, calls into question the basis of interpretive activity, and thus challenges those of us who take up the *Morte Darthur* "nat to be over hasty" in deciding not only about the innocence or guilt of Lancelot and Guinevere but also about what really matters in this Arthurian romance and what can be dismissed as insignificant inconsistencies.

Malory's textual discontinuities in fact contest a legal practice that convicted and punished persons on the basis of questionable evidence. By resorting to ambiguity, by claiming not to know what the "Freynshhe booke" means when it says the "quene and sir Launcelot were togydirs," Malory creates a voice for himself that is neutral and objective, a voice that matches or mimics the neutrality and objectivity of his statement of law; he reports only the facts given in his French source. But he misrepresents those facts, and, from another angle, his very refusal to say what the "Freynshhe booke" means highlights the necessity and possibilities of interpretation. Malory devises two alternate and conflicting opinions regarding the guilt of Lancelot and Guinevere: that of Agravain and Arthur and that of Gawain. We do not know which is true. We have to say, as Arthur does when he tells Gawain of Gareth's death, that we "wote nat how hit was ... but as hit ys sayde ..." (1185). By refusing to supply the reader with direct or indirect evidence, Malory postpones judgment of guilt or innocence. Such a tactic stands in direct opposition to the rush to judgment carried out by the legal process he creates in his text and to the historical practice of summary or hasty judgment instigated and sanctioned not on the basis of physical evidence but on the evidence of words or reports of common fame. These inconsistencies highlight the *Morte Darthur's* own interpretive activity as it refashions Arthurian legend. The case of Lancelot and Guinevere in Malory both actualizes and challenges the role of evidence and interpretation in establishing acts of treason and proving criminal guilt in the fifteenth century.

NOTES

1. Derek Brewer, "The Presentation of the Character of Lancelot: Chrétien to Malory," in *Arthurian Literature*, ed. Richard Barber (Cambridge: Brewer, 1983), 51.

2. III Edward 25, Stat. 5, c. 2, enacted in 1352, stipulated that adultery with the king's companion was an act of treason. This provision helps to explain Malory's consistent use of the term "treason" when referring to Guinevere and Lancelot's relationship rather than the feudal concept of disloyalty. *The Statutes of the Realm*, 11 vols. (London: Dawsons, 1963), 1:319–20. This law undermines Ernest York's conclusion that in equating adultery with treason, Malory is "most probably reflecting French law prior to the twelfth century" ("Legal Punishment in Malory's Morte Darthur," *ELN* 11 [1973]: 15).

3. All citations are from *The Works of Sir Thomas Malory*, 2nd ed., ed. Eugène Vinaver, rev. P. J. C. Field (Oxford: Clarendon, 1990), by page number. Malory's ambiguity also deviates from his fourteenth-century English source, the Stanzaic *Morte Arthur* (ca. 1350). See *King Arthur's Death: The Middle English Stanzaic Morte Arthur and Alliterative Morte Arthur*, ed. Larry Benson (Exeter: Short Run Press Ltd., 1986), lines 1801–7.

4. Larry D. Benson, *Malory's Morte Darthur* (Cambridge: Harvard University Press, 1976), 159. See Brewer, "Presentation of the Character of Lancelot," 45.

5. Elizabeth Kirk, "'Clerkes, Poetes and Historiographs': The *Morte Darthur* and Caxton's 'Poetics' of Fiction," in *Studies in Malory*, ed. James W. Spisak (Kalamazoo: Medieval Institute Publications, 1985), 289.

6. I oversimplify by grouping these critics together. As a group, however, their work exemplifies a certain strain of criticism that avoids the textual problematics of the *Morte Darthur* by indirectly apologizing for them. Respectively, the quotations are from Terence McCarthy, *Reading the Morte Darthur* (Cambridge: Brewer, 1988), xiv; Brewer, *Malory: The Morte Darthur* (Evanston: Northwestern University Press, 1974), 18; and Mark Lambert, *Malory: Style and Vision in Le Morte Darthur* (New Haven: Yale University Press, 1975), 179. See also Felicity Riddy, *Sir Thomas Malory* (Leiden: E. J. Brill, 1987), 13, and Brewer, "Presentation of the Character of Lancelot," 26–52. Compare the attempts made by Malory's nineteenth-century editors to remedy what they perceived as the "moral defects of the book." See Marylyn Jackson Parins, "Malory's Expurgators," in *The Arthurian Tradition: Essays in Convergence*, ed. Mary Flowers Braswell and John Bugge (Tusacaloosa: University of Alabama Press, 1988), 144–63, esp. 148.

7. A useful collection that contains several essays which analyze the dissonance in Malory's text is *Studies in Malory*, ed. James W. Spisak.

8. A. C. Spearing, *Medieval to Renaissance in English Poetry* (Cambridge: Cambridge University Press, 1985), 40.

9. III Edward 25, Stat. 5, c. 2, cited above, n2. See John G. Bellamy, *The Law of Treason in the Later Middle Ages* (Cambridge: Cambridge University Press, 1970), 63.

10. Ibid., 116–17. According to Bellamy, cases of treason by words occurred in the thirteenth century, but there were none during the fourteenth. Bracton discusses treason by imagination but also makes the point that a persons accusing others of treason had to see and hear it with their own eyes and ears. See *Bracton De legibus et consuetudinibus Angliae*, ed. George E. Woodbine, 2 vols. (Cambridge: Harvard University Press, 1968), 2:366. French custom also required the same type of proof. See Phillipe de Beaumanoir, *Coutumes de Beauvaisis*, ed. A. Salmons, 3 vols. (1900; rpt. Paris: Éditions A. et J. Picard, 1970), 2:1234. All references are to this edition, by volume and entry number. During the reign of Richard II, laws were passed that made riot and rumor (5 Richard II, Stat. 1, c. 6) and compassing the death of the king (21 Richard II, c. 3) acts of treason. These laws were repealed in 1399 by 1 Henry IV, c. 3 and c. 10; they indicate, however, that the interpretive pliability of the 1352 statute was not recognized during Richard's reign. See also I. D. Thornley, "Treason by Words in the Fifteenth Century," *EHR* 32 (1917): 556–61, and Samuel Rezneck, "Constructive Treason by Words in the Fifteenth Century," *AHR* 33 (1927–28): 544-52.

11. See Bellamy, *Law of Treason*, 136–37.

12. Sir John Fortescue, *De laudibus legum Anglie*, ed. and trans. S. B. Chrimes (Cambridge: Cambridge University Press, 1942), 41. Fortescue is speaking specifically of statutes. Compare John Alford's comments regarding the effect of statutory law on the gap between legal theory and practice in the later Middle Ages in "Literature and Law in Medieval England," *PMLA* 92 (1977): 948–49. Alford identifies "legal positivism" and "the birth of modern jurisprudence" with Thomas Hobbes's *Leviathan* (1651). For another point of view regarding the incipient forms of positivist law and modern jurisprudence in the fifteenth century, see Norman Doe, *Fundamental Authority in Late Medieval English Law* (Cambridge: Cambridge University Press, 1990).

13. See, for example, the *Paston Letters*, ed. James Gairdner (London: Archibald Constable and Co. Ltd., 1908), 1:58; *Three Fifteenth-Century Chronicles*, ed. James Gairdner, Camden Society, 3rd ser., 28 (1880), 96; *An English Chronicle*, ed. John S. Davies, Camden Society 64 (1856), 60; and *Rotuli Parliamentorum: ut et petitiones, et placita in parliamento*, ed. J. Strachey, et al., 6 vols. (London: 1767), 5:326 (where complaints are made against people who know enough about law to pose as lawyers and seek suits on a contingency basis). See also Alford, "Law and Literature," esp. 951 n34.

14. See Michel Foucault's "Nietzsche, Genealogy, History," in *Language, Counter-Memory, Practice: Selected Essays and Interviews*, ed. Donald F. Bouchard (Ithaca: Cornell University Press, 1977), 139–64. Foucault's association of law and interpretation with acts of power has been extremely useful to me in my analysis of Malory's representation of law and legal process. Jacques Derrida, in his reading of Kafka's "Before the Law," speculates that law produces the subjects it represents and that literary texts make the law ("Before the Law," in *Acts of Literature*, ed. Derek Attridge [New York: Routledge, [1992]). For a discussion of the differences between objective and subjective intepretivist arguments in critical legal studies, see Robin West, "Adjudication Is Not Interpretation: Some Reservations about the Law-as-Literature Movement," *Tennessee Law Review* 54 (1987): 203–78. While West skillfully reviews both subjectivist and objectivist positions, her attempt to distinguish between acts of power and acts of interpretation is less convincing, as is her distinction between literary and legal texts: "The legal text is a command; the literary text is a work of art. This difference implies others. Legal criticism—criticism of law—is criticism of acts of power; literary criticism—criticism of literature—is the criticism of acts of expression" (277). It is hard, if not impossible, to imagine a law or a critique of law that is not itself an act of expression. Moreover, while literary texts are not backed up by the force of the state as laws are, it does not follow that literary texts and literary criticism exist outside power and its forms. West herself cannot maintain this distinction: she interprets two literary texts to highlight what she perceives as the "irresponsibility" of both subjective and objective interpretivist views of adjudication. For a favorable opinion on the law and literature movement, see Brook Thomas, "Reflections on the Law and Literature Revival," *Critical Inquiry* 71 (1991): 510–39.

15. *La mort de roi Artu*, ed. Jean Frappier (Geneva: Droz, 1954), 121. Translations of this text are mine. In the Stanzaic *Morte Arthur*, Arthur and his knights take "their counsel.... What best do with the queen" and then sentence her to death (*King Arthur's Death*, lines 1920–25).

16. Ibid., 120–21.

17. Since Malory refers to himself as a prisoner, we can hypothesize that he had first-hand knowledge of fifteenth-century legal process. Quite apart from this, however, the attention law claimed in the fifteenth-century England exemplifies the familiar acquaintance of the non-professional with law and legal process. See the sources cited in note 13 above. For the use of the Court of Chivalry and the Court of the High Lord Steward to effect a summary form of judgment in treason cases, see Maurice Keen, "Treason Trials under the Law of Arms," *TRHS*, 5th ser., 12 (1962): 85–104; L. W. Vernon

Harcourt, *His Grace the Steward and Trial of Peers* (New York: Longmans, Green, and Co., 1907), 362–470; and Bellamy, *Law of Treason*, 143–63.

18. T. F. T. Plucknett, *A Concise History of the Common Law*, 5th ed. (London: Butterworth, 1956), 430.

19. *Mort le roi Artu*, 110–11.

20. Arthur in the Stanzaic *Morte Arthur* also wants Lancelot to be taken in the deed, and, as in the other two works, the plan fails (*King Arthur's Death*, lines 1746–77 and 1832–63).

21. *Mort le roi Artu*, 115.

22. OED 2nd ed., *sub voce* "mainour."

23. See *Britton*, ed. and trans. Francis Morgan Nichols, 2 vols. (Holmes Beach, FL: Wm. W. Gaunt, 1983), 1:36–37, and Julius Goebel, Jr., *Felony and Misdemeanor: A Study in the History of Criminal Law* (1937; reprint, Philadelphia: University of Pennsylvania Press, 1976), 75. For a recent discussion of the association of circumstantial evidence with narrativity, see Alexander Welsh, *Strong Representations: Narrative and Circumstantial Evidence in England* (Baltimore: Johns Hopkins University Press, 1992).

24. C. L. Von Bar, *History of Continental Criminal Law* (Boston: Little, Brown & Co., 1916), 14 n15, and Frederick Pollack and William Maitland, *The History of English Law before the Time of Edward I*, 2nd ed., 2 vols. (1898; reprint, Cambridge: Cambridge University Press, 1968), 2:497.

25. As Bracton remarked, "Qui suum secum portat judicium," quoted in T. F. T. Plucknett, "The Origin of Impeachment," *TRHS*, 4th ser., 24 (1942), 60. See also Pollack and Maitland, *History* 2:580; *Statutes of the Realm*, 1:81; and Britton, 1:56–57.

26. For opinions on Malory's use of *mainour*, see Vinaver, *Works of Sir Thomas Malory*, 2nd ed. (Oxford: Clarendon Press, 1967), cix and 1633, and his Malory, *Works*, 2nd ed. (Oxford: Oxford University Press, 1976), 775; John W. Walsh, "Malory's Arthur and the Plot of Agravain," *TSLL* 23 (1981): 533–34 n18; and J. A. W. Bennett, *RES* 25 (1949): at 166. The concept of mainour was not obsolete in the fifteenth century, as Walsh surmises. In *De laudibus legum Anglie*, Fortescue explains that whether or not a thief is taken in the act, the penalty is death (111–13). See also H. T. Riley, ed. *Memorials of London and London Life in the XIIIth, XIVth, and XVth Centuries, A.D. 1276–1410* (London: Longmans, Green & Co., 1868), 195 n6 and 562. Lancelot's presence in Guinevere's room could be seen as mainour, but, as we shall see, his being there can be interpreted in a number of different ways. For adultery as trespass in English law, see Thomas A. Green, *Verdict According to Conscience: Perspectives on the Criminal Trial Jury, 1200–1800* (Chicago: Chicago University Press, 1985), 41.

27. Year Books, 19 Henry VI Mich. pl. 103, quoted in Bellamy, *Law of Treason*, 123n2. The translation is mine.

28. *The Brut or the Chronicles of England*, ed. Friedrich W. D. Brie, EETS, OS, vol. 136 (1908), 483–84.

29. Ibid., 485. The chronicler identifies this person as a John Kerver, but *CPR* 1441–46 names a Thomas Kerver. He was later pardoned since he had committed the offence in "ignorance of the peril" (295). See Bellamy, *Law of Treason*, 118–19.

30. Compare *Henry IV* Part One 5.2.12–13: Worcester worries that looks will be interpreted as treason: "Look how we can, or sad or merrily, / Interpretation will misquote our looks." See also *Richard II* 4.1.8–83, where accusations of treason by words abound. References are to *The Complete Works of Shakespeare*, 3rd. ed., ed. David Bevington (Glenview: Scott, Foresman and Company, 1980).

31. A phrase that appears in a case of treason by words during the reign of Henry IV. P.R.O., K.B. 27/564 Rex m. 12, printed in Bellamy, *Law of Treason*, 117 n1.

32. A petition made in 1442 to the king on behalf of Richard Wogan, a clerk, suggests

this type of imaginative accusation. Since Wogan had "executed certain commands of the king concerning the earl of Ormond, lieutenant of Ireland, the earl *imagined* (my emphasis) him guilty of treason whereof he was indicted in a place in Ireland where none of the king's lieges dare acquit him for fear of the earl" (*CPR* 1441–46, 91).

33. *Mort le roi Artu*, 115–16. Agravain's accusations are, however, found in the Stanzaic *Morte Arthur*. Though Lancelot is called a traitor in this source, the poem does not evoke a noise that could be heard by all the court, as is the case in the *Morte Darthur*, nor does Lancelot take part in the shouting as he does in Malory's text. For an analysis that compares Malory's representation of noise and the destruction of the Round Table to the dissolution of language and faith depicted in the story of the Tower of Babel, see John F. Plummer, "'Tunc se Coeperunt non Intelligere': The Image of Language in Malory's Last Books," in *Studies in Malory*, 153–72. For a reading that relates Malory's noise to chivalric honor, see Ann Dobyns, "'Shamefull noyse': Lancelot and the Language of Deceit," *Style* 24 (1990): 89–102.

34. Plucknett, *Concise History*, 430. In cases of murder, prosecution by hue and cry was validated by reference to scripture, namely, the story of Cain and Abel. God tells Cain that "the voice of Abel thy brother's blood, whom thou has killed, crieth unto me from the ground." See *Compilatio de Usibus Andegaviae*, § 7, quoted in A. Esmein, *A History of Continental Criminal Procedure with Special Reference to France*, trans. John Simpson (Boston: Little, Brown & Co., 1913), 63.

35. Esmein, ibid., 61.

36. See Beaumanoir, *Coutumes*, 1:934 and 2:1637. See also R. Howard Bloch, *Medieval French Literature and Law* (Berkeley: University of California Press, 1977), 55–59.

37. *Mort le roi Artu*, 115.

38. Mainour was also associated with notoriety. See Plucknett, "Impeachment," 60. For examples of hue and cry as slander, see Riley, *Memorials*, 576 and 592.

39. Plucknett, "Impeachment," 61–2. Reputation figured significantly in the findings of medieval juries. See Green, *Verdict*, 8, 16–17, 20, and 26.

40. I argue elsewhere that the noise sustained against Lancelot is one of the ways Malory's text erodes Lancelot's good fame to the point that he can no longer function as a knight of the realm. In a sense the text attaints Lancelot. See "Lancelot's Vocation: Traitor Saint," in *The Lancelot-Grail: Text, Image, and Transformations*, ed. William Kibler (Austin: University of Texas Press, forthcoming).

41. *Rot. Parl.*, 5:176.

42. Geoffrey Chaucer, the *House of Fame*, 2075–80, in *The Riverside Chaucer*, 3rd. ed., gen. ed. Larry Benson (Boston: Houghton Mifflin, 1987). Compare Lydate's *Fall of Princes*, ed. Henry Bergen, EETS, e.s. 121 (1924), 2:1226–32.

43. *Rot. Parl.*, 5:176.

44. Ibid., 5:177. For Suffolk's judgment, see 5:183.

45. My discussion of attainder relies primarily on Bellamy, *Law of Treason*, 177–205. See also Michael A. Hicks, "Attainder, Resumption, and Coercion, 1461–1529," *Parliamentary History* 3 (1984): 15–31, and J. R. Lander, "Attainder and Forfeiture, 1453 to 1509," *The Historical Journal* 4 (1961): 119–51.

46. Bellamy, *Law of Treason*, 169–70. He notes one instance in which attainder was part of an actual trial in Parliament (176).

47. See *Rot. Parl.*, 5:389, for Henry Percy's attempt to restore the reputation of his father, the Earl of Northumberland, whose heirs were "unable to clayme or have by the same late Erle, any such name, estate or preeminance...." Compare *Henry VI* Part One 2.4.90–94, where Somerset challenges Richard Plantagenet by referring to the attainder of Richard's father.

48. *Rot. Parl.*, 5:346.

49. Ibid., 5:349.

50. *English Chronicle*, 83.

51. Ibid., 82.

52. Ernest York has observed that Lancelot's being called a traitor does not make him one ("Legal Punishment," 16). Fifteenth-century interpretations of imagining the king's death, which relied on words as evidence, and the role of ill-fame in prosecuting traitors challenge York's assertion. For the contagion-like quality of treason in Malory's text, see Deborah S. Ellis, "Balin, Mordred and Malory's Idea of Treachery," *English Studies: A Journal of English Language and Literature* 68 (1987): 66–74, and Stephen Knight, "The Social Functions of Middle English Romance," in *Medieval Literature: Criticism, Ideology, and History*, ed. David Aers (New York: St. Martin's, 1986), 136.

53. For a discussion of lay and legal descriptions, see Kim Lane Scheppele, "Facing Facts in Legal Interpretation: Questions of Law and Questions of Fact," *Representations* 30 (1990): 54–59. The Old French *Mort Artu* circuitously equates adultery with treason by way of disloyalty. Even then, however, the act of treason is not an act against the king but against a "preudom" (121).

54. For example, see the speech Lancelot makes to his knights after he has escaped from the Queen's chamber. Having willingly gone to Guinevere when she sends for him, Lancelot now, in this speech, imputes a treasonous motive to her summons (1171): "And thys nyght bycause my lady the quene sente for me to speke with her, I suppose hit was made by treson; howbehit I dare largely excuse her person."

55. Lancelot, of course, has killed the knights and wounded Mordred. Thus in this application of law, Guinevere must be read as a sign for Lancelot. This circumstance along with her silence at the trial suggests that Guinevere is both an extension of male identity and an object of exchange between Lancelot and Arthur.

56. Inciting the king's people to withdraw their love from him seems to have been a popular interpretation of treason by words. See Bellamy, *Law of Treason*, 118–19.

57. As in the case of the Duchess of Gloucester, Roger Bolingbroke, and Thomas Southwell. See P.R.O., K.B. 9/72/14, printed in Bellamy, *Law of Treason*, Appendix III, 237.

58. *Brut*, 483.

59. *English Chronicle*, 60.

GEOFFREY ASHE

The Origins of the Arthurian Legend

After prolonged debate, the search for the 'historical Arthur' remains inconclusive, because of the nature of the evidence which historians take into account. Possibilities arise, however, from evidence of another kind. Literary inquiry can lead towards historical insight and identify an Arthur figure who has been noticed at various times, but not adequately considered. (GA)

T o the question 'Did Arthur exist?' a straight yes-or-no answer cannot he given. More is involved here than historical doubt. With, say, Robin Hood, the straight answer is likewise excluded, but solely by insufficiency of data. A new find might some day make it possible. With Arthur the difficulty cuts deeper. For any ordinary inquirer, the answer 'yes' implies the reality of the Arthur of romance, the idealized medieval monarch, at the centre of a sort of montage that includes Guinevere and Merlin and the Knights of the Round Table. Since Arthur in that sense is a literary creation and didn't exist, the answer 'yes' is wrong. But the answer 'no' is also wrong. It implies that Arthur is fictitious as Don Quixote is fictitious, that he has no factual basis at all. The romancers themselves would never have accepted that, and it cannot be maintained as a definite statement.

Actually, of course, the literary Arthur is a shape-shifter who has taken different forms over the centuries. But all versions presumably derive from a

From *Arthuriana* 5, no. 3 (Fall 1995). © 1995 by *Arthuriana*.

source or prototype earlier than any. There have been numerous attempts to work back to this point, and, more specifically, to pin down a 'historical Arthur' as the starting-point, so that the question of existence can be affirmatively answered ... on the understanding that this is the Arthur who is meant.

I believe the 'historical Arthur' quest has, in practice, been misguided. Historians in search of him have committed themselves to a certain mode of approach. They have tried to strip away legend and isolate hard evidence. Doing so means dismissing the medieval literature (Geoffrey of Monmouth and everything later), sifting older matter of Welsh provenance, and picking out whatever may be deemed factual or, at least, arguably so. Applied with due objectivity, such a process reduces the data to two Latin documents. They refer to Arthur at no great length as a successful war-leader of Celtic Britons in the fifth or sixth century, embroiled chiefly with encroaching Saxons, ancestors of the English. One of these documents is the *Historia Brittonum*, History of the Britons, compiled early in the ninth century, and ascribed dubiously to a monk of Bangor named Nennius. In a single chapter it lists twelve Arthurian battles. The other document is a chronicle, the *Annales Cambriae*, Annals of Wales, which is somewhat later and has two Arthurian entries, also about battles. There is a penumbra of Welsh poems and traditions, and support for the Latin texts can be claimed from that quarter, especially from an allusion to Arthur's martial prowess which may be as early as 600. They alone, however, are the documents properly so called.[1]

Opinion on them has swung back and forth. One seldom-noted fact is that Edward Gibbon believed in Arthur, on the strength of the 'simple and circumstantial testimony of Nennius.' From the 1930s on, Collingwood's theory of an Arthur who revived the imperial military office of *Comes Britanniarum*, and employed Roman-type cavalry to rout pedestrian Saxons, appealed to many including novelists such as Charles Williams and C.S. Lewis. While the cavalry notion faded for lack of evidence, the image of Arthur as a post-Roman commander-in-chief, with or without civilian power as well, and as active in south and south-west Britain, flourished into the seventies. It seemed to have established itself through the work of Kenneth Jackson, Leslie Alcock and John Morris (though Alcock's review of Morris's *The Age of Arthur*, which made sweeping claims, was critical; there was never a united front). Some scholars, notably Rachel Bromwich, while accepting an Arthur who was primarily a warrior, dissented as to his homeland and made it northern.

In 1977 an onslaught by David Dumville on all such reconstructions, and on Welsh records generally, set the pendulum swinging the other way.[2] Today most historians who consider the 'historical Arthur' at all are sceptical and reluctant to discuss him. An added reason has been the partial discrediting of the topic by the appearance of further 'historical Arthur' books which are mutually contradictory, wildly unscholarly, and sometimes worse.

I would agree with the sceptics, not in giving up the procedure entirely, but in seeing it as a dead end unless it is supplemented in other ways. The Latin texts are too distant in time from Arthur's apparent floruit. The list of battles in Nennius, to use the name for convenience, is probably adapted from an earlier Welsh poem, but there is no telling how much earlier, or what exactly it said. Moreover, even taken at face value, the texts raise other chronological problems. For one thing, they spread Arthur's career over an incredible stretch of time. Two of Nennius's battles can be located with fair confidence, one at Chester and one in southern Scotland; they make sense only in the context of widespread Saxon raiding in alliance with Picts, which is attested by Gildas and Bede; and that phase can hardly have been much later than the 450s. Yet the *Annales* put the last battle of all, the 'strife of Camlann,' in 539 (or 537; there is a slight ambiguity). Was Arthur a centenarian when he fought it? This is no modern quibble. At least two medieval authors seem to have been aware of a crux.[3] We might hope at least to locate him in some part of the time-range and then treat everything outside as spurious. Apparently, however, this cannot be done, because the Welsh matter nowhere supplies a chronological fix to calibrate him with known history. We are never told that his first battle took place when X was emperor, or his last when Y was pope.

Even the stripping-away of legend doesn't really work. Reducing the evidence to what is in the *Historia Brittonum* and the *Annales* still fails to get rid of the problem. Thus, both credit Arthur with winning the battle of Badon. It was a real and important victory, mentioned by Gildas somewhere about the 530s when it was within living memory. It may have occurred near Swindon, or farther west, near Bath. But the *Historia* passage says Arthur slew 960 of the enemy single-handed in one charge. That need not invalidate the whole story of his campaigns, but it means that at least where Badon is concerned, legend-making has entered: a conclusion supported by two Arthurian fables in an appendix. The same may have happened in the *Annales* entry about this battle, which is disproportionately long because of the allusion to Arthur, itself rather curious and perhaps interpolated.

Some accept the 'strife of Camlann' entry as a plain statement, legend-free. A point in its favour is that as everyone mentioned elsewhere in the *Annales* appears to be real; a completely fictitious Arthur here, with no hint of interpolation, would be anomalous. What it says is that Arthur and Medraut, the original Modred or Mordred, fell at Camlann in 539. The trouble is that to isolate this incident as the sole fact not only upsets almost everything else because of the difficulty over dates, but also suggests that the whole vast cycle grew around a squabble of minor chiefs, otherwise unknown, at an unidentified place certainly far from the Saxon enemy whose repulse was the basis of the Arthurian glory. I, at least, cannot think my way from one to the other. The 'Camlann Arthur' who has been seriously proposed by Michael Wood, for instance, is a *reductio ad absurdum* of the method, showing that if you push it to its logical limit, the utmost it can offer is a minimal figure who explains nothing.

A more fruitful approach is to ask, not 'Did Arthur exist?' but 'How did the Arthurian Legend originate; what facts is it rooted in?' To do so is to acknowledge that this is a literary problem rather than a historical one, though with a hope that literary investigation may lead to historical insight. Such an approach casts the net wider and introduces a kind of lateral thinking. It allows, for instance, the consideration of Geoffrey of Monmouth, not in the sense of believing what he says about Arthur, but in the sense of asking what his raw materials were: sometimes, plainly, the aforesaid Welsh matter, but maybe not always. The investigation may lead to a real Arthur-figure or it may not. The first requirement is to try.

A crucial question is whether the Legend's roots are as far back as the period it professes to be about; or, to put this another way, whether the bards and story-tellers who created it were using traditions genuinely dating from that period. It is here that archaeology enters. It confirms the story of Saxon incursions into Britain and a phase when the advance more or less halted. However, it is far from confirming the Welsh-derived drama of large-scale warfare triumphantly ended by Arthur's victories. In that respect, it is of little help with the Legend as such. More promising are the results at specific sites.

Three places are outstandingly linked with Arthur. According to Geoffrey he was conceived in a ducal stronghold on the Tintagel headland, and it is generally assumed that he was born there. According to Caradoc of Llancarfan he had dealings with an abbot of Glastonbury, and the monks who exhibited a grave sixty years later said it was his and he was buried there. According to John Leland, citing Somerset lore later again, Arthur's Camelot was the ancient Cadbury hill-fort which can be seen from Glastonbury Tor. The Camelot of romance is fictitious, but a significant point about it is that it is not Britain's capital. It is Arthur's personal headquarters. The possibility of 'Camelot' having a basis in such a headquarters can fairly be entertained.

In all three instances, archaeology has proved occupancy and eminence in the period to which the Legend refers. Tintagel, formerly interpreted as a darkage monastery, has emerged in recent years as a major centre, very likely a regional seat of government, during the fifth century. At Glastonbury a

Christian community existed almost or quite as early, if perhaps on the higher ground rather than the site of the Abbey, and may have been the only one in that part of Britain. At Cadbury, excavation in 1966–70 showed that the hill-fort was reoccupied probably during the second half of the fifth century, and fortified with a new stone-and-timber rampart nearly three-quarters of a mile in perimeter, including a gatehouse. Excavation of other hill-forts has since shown reoccupation and refurbishment, but no full parallel for the great Cadbury fortification, with its gatehouse, has turned up anywhere else in post-Roman Britain. It implies a very special occupant with impressive resources of manpower: a king or chief unique (so far as present knowledge goes) in his time.[4]

These three places were picked as major locations of Arthur's story, and all three now stand revealed as important and apt in the right period. The implication is clear. At Tintagel the headland would have gone through a long phase of vacancy or near-vacancy before Geoffrey told his tale. He was not spinning a fantasy around famous ruins as he did at Caerleon, he knew some kind of tradition of the place's long-ago appropriateness. At Glastonbury the acceptance of Arthur's grave by Welshmen, against natural inclination, and the non-emergence of any rival grave, go far to establish a similar tradition irrespective of what the monks may have heard.[5] At Cadbury, uninhabited for hundreds of years, even a modern archaeologist could not have detected the new fortification by inspection alone, without digging. It is really not to be supposed that the unknown person responsible for the Camelot identification chose the most plausible hill in Britain by a mere guess.

The people who focused on these places knew something about them. A purely accidental three-out-of-three score is beyond serious credence. They drew on traditions originating in the Britain to which they assigned Arthur, the Britain of the century or two after separation from Rome. That is truly where the Legend is rooted. All three places, by the way, are in the West Country, the former Dumnonia. Advocates of a northern Arthur have produced no comparable sites. Obviously Arthur, if he existed, could have been active in that part of Britain and inspired early bardic allusions, but nothing of consequence in the north gives him a birthplace or a headquarters or a grave, and the region's archaeology nowhere links up with any story of him. While Camlann might etymologically be Camboglanna, a northern Roman fort, the versions of Arthur's last battle never point to this fort or anywhere near it. There are two Camlanns in Wales, still called so, and even the claim of the Somerset river Cam is backed by a report of a mass burial.[6]

Given the apparent body of tradition we can venture a little further and glimpse a few individuals embedded in it from whom Arthurian characters are derived. The distant original of Uther's brother Aurelius Ambrosius is a fifth-century British war-leader, Ambrosius Aurelianus; he is mentioned by Gildas and Bede, and a continuity in legend is witnessed by Nennius. The distant original of Mark in the Tristan story is seemingly a certain Marcus, likewise Roman-named, with a father Marcianus who was called after a mid-fifth-century emperor. Romancers gave Marcus a role as King Mark of Cornwall that may be fictitious, but the Marcianus connection shows that he was 'there,' so to speak, from a very early stage.[7] Was Arthur there also, perhaps as a real person, perhaps as an imaginary hero? Or was he inserted in the traditions later when they had undergone development?

His name favours the first alternative. 'Arthur' is a Welsh form of the Roman 'Artorius,' not common, but adequately attested. Arthur falls into place alongside Ambrosius, Marcus, and others in the same category, during a phase when Roman influence lingered. Furthermore, there is a sequel. In the latter part of the sixth century, when Roman names in general had faded out, this hitherto rare one began to enjoy a vogue. Several Arthurs are on record up and down Britain, including a Scottish prince. They are best explained as having been named after a hero established in song and story; and therefore alive or invented earlier, with a long enough interval to carry his bardic fame beyond his own people.[8]

As for his historicity or otherwise, two arguments can be dismissed. Critics have urged that because he is credited with fantastic feats, such as his singlehanded slaughter at Badon, he cannot have been real. But fantastic feats were ascribed in America to Davy Crockett, who was real enough. Most were tongue-in-cheek tall tales, but they were current and popular, and within a year or two of his death at the Alamo, he was seriously alleged to have killed 85 Mexicans during the siege; not 960, admittedly, but still a pretty wild number, and after a much shorter time for exaggeration. It was formerly claimed that anyone said to have slain a dragon must be fictitious. Yet several reputed dragon-slayers, in the Balkans for instance, were undoubtedly real. Far-fetched elements in a story do not discredit the entire story. Far-fetched elements in a career do not disprove its protagonist's reality. Baron Munchausen himself was real.

On the opposite side is the 'must have' argument: that someone with such an impact as Arthur must have existed. It is not negligible, but neither is it strong. Here, a cautionary instance is Sherlock Holmes. He is so vivid that countless people have taken his existence for granted. For many years the office on the site of his Baker Street lodgings (not really identifiable, but given a street number) received a steady trickle of letters addressed to him. New stories continue to be written; new films continue to be made. The impact of Holmes has been immense. Yet we know how his saga began, and it was in Conan Doyle's imagination, not in the biography of a real detective.

It is worth observing, all the same, that those who maintain Arthur's nonexistence can be asked to explain the phenomenon without him. Incantatory repetition of words like 'myth' is mere evasion. If there was no Arthur at all, what did happen, where did the idea of him come from, who launched it, and when? What propagandist feat enabled a British leader who didn't exist to blot out the fame of those who did? So far as I know, no one has offered convincing answers.

Opponents have argued that Arthur was a Celtic god, euphemerized as a human warrior. Such things did occur, if not in comparable detail, when Christianity forbade the gods to go on being divine. Belinus became Beli, mythical king of Britain and ancestor of Welsh dynasties. Maponus became Mabon, associated with Arthur himself. His mother Matrona became— probably—Morgan le Fay; at any rate Morgan has a divine origin and is even called a goddess, though with a Christian explaining-away, by Giraldus Cambrensis and the author of *Sir Gawain and the Green Knight*.[9]

However, 'Artorius' could scarcely have been the name of a Celtic god, and there is no trace of any pre-Christian divinity whose name could have evolved into 'Arthur' by another route. This deity has never been more than a speculation, concocted for the sake of the theory. A notion that Arthur began as the war-god of a fifth-century pagan revival is refuted by the silence of Gildas, who denounces his British fellow-Christians for just about every sin except apostasy. He would have denounced neo-paganism if there had been any.

One resolute foe of historicity tried to make capital out of the 'lives' of Welsh saints, and since these seldom get much attention, they may be mentioned here. Four of them, associated with the Llancarfan community, introduce Arthur as an unpleasant figure with whom the saints come in conflict. Hence, supposedly, he was a demon in the eyes of clerics and therefore a pagan god. But the clerical author of the *Historia Brittonum* makes him a Christian champion, conquering heathen Saxons by heavenly aid, and the hagiographic items never make him hellish. They are anecdotes of a stock type demonstrating a saint's superiority over a turbulent layman. Their Arthur, abashed, shows penitence by gifts and concessions, as no demon would have done.[10]

Sometimes indeed Arthur is mythified, or involved in episodes of a mythical kind. That may apply, for instance, to the recurrent abduction of his wife. But as a purely or essentially mythical character he is a product of fashions in anthropology and comparative religion. Theorists on this line have discovered facts of genuine interest. In the larger presentation, however, they have contradicted each other too much and suppressed or distorted the evidence too often. While the self-destruction of their rival conjectures doesn't prove the contrary, the image of a real person, with a solidity that confounds exorcism, may be thought to emerge dimly by default.

One motif that certainly is pre-Christian may tell in his favour. The folk belief in an Arthur who lies sleeping in a cave or underground chamber is scattered widely involving more than a dozen locations. Cadbury-Camelot is the first that can be documented, and a century or so ago, a local villager asked some archaeologists if they meant to dig up the King. As Sir John Rhys observed, the belief had its origin in a Celtic myth recorded by Plutarch, about a banished god asleep in a cave on a western island. In Christian times this belief was suitably adapted and annexed not only to Arthur but to other heroes, sometimes perhaps in imitation of him, sometimes independently. Frederick Barbarossa is a famous instance. The folklorist Jennifer Westwood has remarked on a feature of the cave-legend that is easy to overlook. "Despite its mythic ancestry, cave legends do not attach themselves to fairy-tale characters: the sleepers are, or are regarded as, human beings in a historical context. Since Arthur is one such sleeper, he is likely to have at least some sort of historical substance."[11]

So, partly through the lack of a coherent alternative, we can detect a bias towards a starting-point for the Legend in the person of a post-Roman Briton known as Artorius and then, through linguistic changes, as Arthur. The case for him does not depend on Nennius or the *Annales Cambriae*, or on arguments of the 'must have' or 'no smoke without fire' type. If he did exist, he passed into the body of tradition handed on from the fifth century, most of it fabulous but a little of it historical, and rose gradually to dominate this tradition and extend whatever linkage he had with its factual elements. His saga may soon have come to credit him with other men's exploits, that has to be considered in connection with his long time-span, but he stands alone at the point of origin. Gildas's notorious silence is only a difficulty (a slight one at that, in view of the nature of his tract) on the supposition that Arthur would have been recent or contemporary when Gildas wrote. Too much has been made of Gildas's silence because of a tendency to assume that he would have been, that his correct position in the time-span is late. But if he flourished near the beginning of it, say in the third quarter of the fifth century, the silence means nothing. Gildas knows little about anybody beyond living memory and names no fifth century Britons at all, except Ambrosius Aurelianus. He may only mention Ambrosius to blacken his descendants by contrast.

After a slow ascent through Welsh verse and story-telling, most of it now lost to view, Arthur (whoever or whatever he was) became the monarch of the Legend, quasi-historical ruler over a splendid kingdom, through the genius of one author. Geoffrey of Monmouth's *Historia Regum Britanniae*, History of the Kings of Britain, appeared in the late 1130's and supplied the framework for the literature that followed.

There is much more in his book than Arthur. It opens in the twelfth century B.C. with an expansion of a Welsh legend telling how the island, then called Albion, was settled by migrating Trojans, under the leadership of Brutus, Aeneas's great-grandson. Geoffrey goes on through a long series of fictitious reigns, including King Lear's. He maintains that the line of British kings was unbroken even in the three and a half centuries of Roman rule, which he reduces to a vague protectorate.

It is after Britain's break with the Empire that his story moves towards its Arthurian climax. He tells how a sinister noble, Vortigern, usurped the throne and invited heathen Saxons to make their homes in Britain as auxiliary troops in his service. Reinforced from overseas, they got out of hand and ravaged much of the country. Vortigern fled to Wales, where Merlin prophesied his downfall. The rightful princes returned from exile and overthrew him. The elder, Aurelius Ambrosius, was succeeded after a brief reign by his brother Uther Pendragon. Both managed to contain the Saxons; neither could bring them under control.

Arthur, Uther's son, is presented as a kind of Messiah delivering Britain from these troubles. Strangely begotten at Tintagel, Geoffrey informs us, he came to the throne while young and proved to be an able leader, subduing the Saxons, defeating the Picts and Scots who had aided them, and conquering Ireland. He married Guinevere and reigned in prosperity for twelve years, generally beloved. He founded an order of knighthood recruiting distinguished men from all nations. Then he gradually conquered large parts of Gaul, still shakily held by Rome.

During another spell of peace he held court magnificently at Caerleon. The Roman ruler Lucius demanded tribute and a restitution of conquests. Arthur took an army to Gaul again, leaving his nephew Mordred (to use the romancers spelling) in charge at home, jointly with the Queen. He won a victory over Lucius near the land of the Allobroges, *i.e.*, the Burgundians, and pushed on into their territory. Mordred, however, turned traitor, proclaimed himself king, persuaded Guinevere to live in adultery with him, and made a deal with the Saxons. Arthur returned, and defeated and slew him beside the river Camel in Cornwall, but was grievously wounded and taken away to the Isle of Avalon (*Insula Avallonis*) for his wounds to be treated. Geoffrey leaves the door open for the folk-belief in his survival without affirming it. The King simply departs in the direction of Avalon, wherever that may be, with no recorded death. He has reigned for about twenty-five years.

Geoffrey is not a historian and can never, anywhere, be trusted for facts. However, he is not a total fantasist either. Except in the early reigns he habitually uses history, or what he would like to think is history. He inflates, he transforms, he mixes up chronology, he indulges in monstrous elaborations, but he does not contrive major episodes out of nothing at all. It is futile to sift his text, however selectively, for straightforward historical data. Yet, in pursuance of the present approach, it is proper to ask what history or supposed history he is drawing on here for his literary creation and to see whether this search for sources may lead towards an original Arthur by a fresh route.

When Geoffrey writes of events in post-Roman Britain, he is plainly drawing on something valid. Saxons did enter the country from across the North Sea, with Angles and other associates, and probably some at least came as auxiliary troops long before the misleading mid-century date which historians used to copy from Bede. A Briton known as Vortigern probably did play a part in settling them. 'Vortigern' means 'over-chief' and may denote someone comparable to an Irish high king, claiming paramountcy over regional rulers. The settlers did mutiny and raid far and wide, withdrawing eventually to their permitted enclaves, where they seem to have been contained for a while. There was a British recovery, which, after years of sporadic fighting, stabilized the situation to the Britons' advantage. Ambrosius Aurelianus was a leader in this counter-attack, and so, according to Nennius, was Arthur. Geoffrey enlarges the recovery into an Arthurian golden age. Later authors turn Arthur's Britain into the chivalric Utopia of romance.

Where did Geoffrey acquire the knowledge he clearly had, however flamboyantly he played with it? He asserts in a dedicatory preface that he translated or adapted the entire *History* from 'a certain very ancient book written in the British language' given him by Walter, Archdeacon of Oxford, where he held a teaching post. The British language could be Welsh, or it could be Breton, the kindred speech of the people of Brittany, descendants of emigrants from Britain who took Arthurian lore to Armorican Gaul. There are no extant copies of the book, or even fragments of it, and Geoffrey's claim as it stands is quite inadmissible. Many things in the *History*, such as a reference to Normans in Arthur's army, could not have come from a 'very ancient book.' Nevertheless he may have had a lost source of some kind. It could even have supplied him with information, or pseudo-information, on Arthur.[12]

However that may be, we must work with the sources that survive. Geoffrey uses Gildas, Bede, Nennius, the *Annales Cambriae*. With that much said we reach an impasse. These texts account for only about one-fifth of

Arthur's story. More important, there has been a radical shift of emphasis. Arthur's quelling of the Saxons, which, for Nennius, is the whole point of his career, is merely a prelude, a necessary stage-setting for the glories that matter. When Geoffrey deals with the wicked Vortigern, he simply expands Nennius's account of him. When he deals with the heroic Arthur, he does something altogether different. Nearly half the story concerns Arthur's activities in Gaul; more than half, if we count the preliminaries to his greater war. Assessed by allocation of space, he is more a Gallic conqueror than anything else. Nor do the subsequent romancers lose sight of this. Chrétien de Troyes and Wolfram von Eschenbach both give weight to his continental domain. Malory takes him even farther along the same path.

A related departure from known precedent is the treatment of the King's passing, which is foreshadowed first in a prophecy by Merlin that seems to hint it happened in Gaul. When Geoffrey composes the actual account, he bases it on the 'strife of Camlann.' Yet he still has the disaster strike when Arthur is overseas, and he transforms Mordred into a traitorous deputy-ruler who conspires with barbarians. It may be worth mentioning that he says only one specific thing about his 'ancient book': that it touched on the circumstances of Arthur's downfall.

This is where 'historical Arthur' investigators have gone astray, or at least ignored a problem which their own approach raises. Dismissing Geoffrey's *History* and everything later, they have brushed aside Arthur's activities abroad and restricted their attention to Britain, with the inconclusive results already noted. True, Geoffrey's Gallic narrative cannot be historical, but if we treat it as totally baseless, we have to assume that he is creating a long and important quasi-historical episode, to be precise, two installments of such an episode out of nothing whatever. That is simply not his way. He does not do it anywhere else, from Julius Caesar on. Even his fantasy about the knighthood and court has at least an echo of previous Welsh fantasy, as the tale *Culhwch and Olwen* shows. The same tale has a cryptic allusion to Arthur's going to Greece. But nothing Welsh suggests involvement in the Gallic affairs of the western Empire.

On the analogy of the rest of the *History*, Geoffrey found this idea in some source. Then where? He may have taken odd hints from other wars, real or mythical. Specifically, he may have taken such a hint from the continental campaign of the pretender Maximus in 383. However, he gives his own version of Maximus's enterprise in Book V. A fictitious Arthurian rehash in Book X would be most peculiar, suggesting an uncharacteristic failure of invention. And the Gallic warfare shows signs of a more definite inspiration.

Chronology offers clues. Suppose we survey the main post-Roman events in the *History*, asking when Geoffrey represents them as happening. If we line up various parts of the narrative, we can see roughly what he intends. Britain's separation from Rome, the family relationships of the kings, a visitation by Gallic bishops in 429, the expeditions to Gaul, and scattered mentions of periods of time, combine loosely to show that in devising his structure as far as Arthur's passing, Geoffrey meant it all to lie within the fifth century. Since there is still a western emperor, the limit of date is 476, when the line of western emperors ended. In the interests of that time-scheme Geoffrey pulls back the battle of Badon, he locates it near Bath, by several decades. Second thoughts may have sown doubt in the text as we have it, but the only real confusion is caused by the date given for Arthur's demise, 542. This date is so flagrantly inconsistent with everything prior that it is likely to be an error, scribal or otherwise, and it can be corroboratively explained as such; I shall return to this point.

Within Geoffrey's fifth-century range we get a single surprising piece of exactitude. It is not explicit, and its complete realization depends on juxtaposing a number of passages.

As remarked, one shortcoming of the Welsh matter is that it nowhere gives Arthur a chronological fix to line him up with known events. He does, however, get such a fix, the only one he gets anywhere up to Geoffrey's time, and the *History of the Kings of Britain* supplies it. Geoffrey is aware that until 476 the late Roman world had two emperors, one in the west and one in the east. In fact he refers to 'the emperors' (IX.20). The eastern one during Arthur's Gallic exploits is named three times as Leo. He can only be Leo I, who reigned from 457 to 474. We can narrow down the date further. During Arthur's first Gallic war, Leo seems to have no western colleague, and there was indeed an interregnum when this was so. But the second war is provoked by an emperor in the west called Lucius. His exact status is unclear. He is introduced as Procurator of the Republic, a title of imperial deputies in minor provinces, and the Senate has power to give him orders. Both details hint at a dim awareness on Geoffrey's part of the last western emperors' limitations. There was never a Lucius. However, the Chronicle of Sigebert of Gembloux, which Geoffrey may have known, gives Leo a western colleague called Lucerius in 469–70. Sigebert is inaccurate. The last western Augusti were ephemeral and confusing. But the name would have been enough for Geoffrey, and he was quite capable of modifying 'Lucerius' into the more familiar 'Lucius.' Arguably then, he places Arthur's greater Gallic campaign during the years 469–70, at which time alone he could have found Leo and 'Lucius' reigning together.

He has also picked up the name of a pope which he gives as 'Sulpicius.' This looks like another garble. Tatlock identifies the pope as Simplicius, whom Geoffrey could also have found in Sigebert's Chronicle and remembered imperfectly.[13] His pontificate ran from 468 to 483, so that he was pope in the Leo-'Lucius' years.

These clues are of unequal weight. Leo satisfactorily defines the period 457–74: not because Geoffrey is much concerned with chronology, but because, if he is taking hints from actual events, they must be such that any account of them would have given the name of this emperor. The clues that narrow the range depend on corrections. However, all three converge to form a triple chronological fix establishing the brief time-span 469–70. They suggest that Geoffrey made use of historical material and found something in it to indicate that Arthur, or a Briton he could take to be Arthur, campaigned in Gaul at that time. Such a 'something' would furnish a basis for the Gallic parts of the *History*.

* * *

This might still signify very little, if it were not for a single and simple fact. A Briton whom Geoffrey could have taken to be Arthur did campaign in Gaul at that time.

I noticed him long ago and, after a later and better-informed study, learned that others had noticed him too. Between 1138 and 1147 the connection was almost made by a scribe at Ourscamp near Beauvais who enlarged the Sigebert Chronicle. The English historian Sharon Turner made it in 1799. The same issue was raised in 1906 by Robert Huntington Fletcher, and in 1987 by Professor Tournoy of Leuven. This is not a personal fancy but a well-grounded realization which several authors have attained; and it is senior to the modern 'historical Arthur' search, which, because of its self-imposed restrictions, has diverted attention from it.[14]

In 467 Leo I appointed a western colleague named Anthemius, who initiated a short-lived attempt to retrieve the crumbling situation in Gaul, much of it occupied by a medley of barbarians. The powerful Visigoths, already in control of Spain, were threatening to push north and take possession. Anthemius negotiated a British alliance, and, according to the Gothic historian Jordanes, the 'King of the Britons' crossed to Gaul with 12,000 troops.[15] Historians have underrated him because of an assumption that he was merely a chief of Bretons, that is, British migrants to Armorica. Gibbon, as a matter of fact, knew better. At that stage the migrants were far too few for a purely Breton force to have had any chance of stopping the Visigoths, and the British army that did arrive is plainly stated to have come over the Ocean in ships. The purely-Breton theory has been disposed of by James Campbell, who suggests that this king may have had authority on both sides of the Channel, and by Ian Wood, who accepts as a matter of course that he brought his army over from Britain itself, and remarks justifiably on his 'extraordinary career.'[16]

After a phase north of the Loire, he advanced into central Gaul. But Arvandus, Gaul's imperial prefect, had been acting treacherously, proposing to the Visigoths that they should crush the Britons and share out Gaul with the Burgundians, who held a good deal of the east and south. Arvandus was detected, but the Visigoths took up his idea. They pushed toward Bourges, which the Britons had occupied, and defeated them in a hotly contested battle near Châteauroux before Roman forces could arrive to aid them. The British king drew off with the remnant of his army into the territory of the Burgundians, who had kept aloof from Arvandus's plotting and were friendly. No more is said about him.[17]

All this is attested by sound evidence, some of it contemporary. There is even a letter to the king from Sidonius Apollinaris.[18] We have at last escaped the recurrent Arthurian difficulty over huge gaps of time. Geoffrey might have gleaned enough for his literary flight from a careful reading of the known testimony, and Sigebert's Chronicle mentions the British action close to his 'Lucerius' items. But a lost source, assembling the scattered data, is more likely: a paragraph, maybe, in a 'very ancient book'? Geoffrey's account of the Gallic warfare may glance at such a source in a throwaway phrase, unusual for him, 'so the story goes' (*ut dictum est*, X.4). At any rate this episode provides data accounting for more of his Arthur narrative than the Welsh quasi-history does.

The 'King of the Britons' is in Gaul with his sea-borne army at exactly the right time. He advances to the neighbourhood of Burgundian country. He is betrayed by a deputy-ruler who conspires with barbarians (here we have the role and conduct imposed on Mordred with no hint from Wales). He vanishes after a fatal battle, without any recorded death. His apparent line of retreat shows him moving in the direction of the real town of Avallon in Burgundy. Rachel Bromwich has pointed out that Geoffrey's *Insula Avallonis* is not a precise Latinization of the Welsh form, *Avallach*, and is clearly influenced by this same Burgundian Avallon.[19] As observed, Merlin's prophecy of the unborn Arthur not only foretells the overseas warfare but indicates that at that stage of composition, Geoffrey may have intended the King to vanish in Gaul (VII.3), though he later adopted the Welsh tradition.

If Geoffrey exploited some version of these events, he altered the nature of the war for Arthur's greater glory. That would have been in line with his practice elsewhere. Farther back, for instance, when dealing with the imperial pretender Carausius, he turns a Roman commander into a British king, and a Roman victory into a British one (V.3–4). The present suggestion would imply similar changes. Arthur acts on his own account, not as an auxiliary to someone else, and he fights and defeats the Romans, who, in the real war, were nominal if useless allies. Geoffrey makes him vanquish the mightiest of opponents, mighty in retrospect, if hardly at the time, and come close to imperial power himself. Yet the change is not as absolute as it seems. A tell-tale phrase remains in the text, isolated. At a preliminary council, one of Arthur's sub-kings speaks of going over to the continent to fight Romans *and Germans* (IX.18). The significant point about these words is, precisely, their isolation. The Germans never appear, even in Lucius's cosmopolitan host. They are not a conscious invention of Geoffrey's; they are taken, apparently, from a source and then forgotten. The original reference could have been to the real Germanic enemy, the Visigoths.

A manifest obstacle is the date given for Arthur's passing, 542, so starkly in conflict with the whole narrative which it closes. Apart from anything else, the lifetimes of Uther and his son Arthur cannot possibly stretch so far, and in 542 there had been no western emperor for decades. There are signs, moreover, that in his original plan Geoffrey envisaged a gap of much more than 54 years between Arthur's passing and the English mission of Augustine, dispatched by Pope Gregory in 596. He takes from Gildas the names of four British regional kings who, in reality, were all living at the same time, and makes them rule over Britain successively after Arthur. Four contrived reigns are still not enough. He adds a fifth, plus the break-up of British unity, plus the triumph of the Saxons with foreign aid, plus 'a long time,' before he gets to Augustine.

So the context, not only before but after, indicates that 542 is wrong. As we shall see, several chroniclers knew enough to reject it. Medieval texts are apt to be shaky on numerical dates, and this one could have crept in as a mere blunder. But I have shown that recognized processes of error, exemplified in Nennius and in Wace's French paraphrase of Geoffrey, could have conjured 542 out of 470, the probable date of the 'passing' of the King of the Britons.[20]

The main reason why this king has seldom made an impact in the Arthurian field is that the original texts refer to him not as Arthur but, with slight variations, as Riothamus. The assumption that this was his name has distracted attention from his Arthurian attributes, despite the fact that he is the only documented person who does anything Arthurian. Geoffrey, of course, would have taken the discrepancy in his stride. Earlier in the *History* he wants to make out, in defiance of Welsh tradition, that Merlin was the same person as the seer Ambrosius in Vortigern's reign, and he does it at a stroke, by speaking of him quite casually as 'Merlin who was also called Ambrosius.'

However, there need not actually be a discrepancy. Professor Fleuriot perceived some years ago that 'Riothamus' Latinizes a fifth-century British style, *Rigotamos. The first syllable meant 'king' and *tamo–* was a superlative suffix. 'Riothamus' is 'king-most' (an analogous modern word is 'generalissimo'), and it may be translated 'supreme king' or 'supremely royal.' The same elements appear in 'Vortimer,' originally *Vortamorix*, 'over-most-king,' as Vortigern's shadowy son is called.[21] In Welsh and Breton derivatives 'Riothamus' evolves into a personal name, as 'Vortigern' does, but in the fifth century it may well have been a title or honorific, leaving the question of the king's name open to conjecture. Greek supplies an exact parallel, *Basileutatos*, and this was a term of honour bestowed on Minos of Crete.[22] Various potentates are known to history in much the same way. 'Genghis Khan,' 'Very Mighty Ruler,' is an instance: the Mongol chief began his career as Temujin. Even if 'Riothamus' was the British king's name, that would not exclude his having another. In view of its meaning, 'Riothamus' is likely to have been assumed rather than baptismal, in which case he was indeed called something else as well, and there was no obstacle to the notion that this was 'Arthur.'[23]

The phrase Jordanes applies to him, 'King of the Britons,' is more significant than it looks. It would have been usable only during a generation or so around the middle of the fifth century, say from some time in the 440s to some time in the 470s. In the early post-Roman aftermath a monarch of the ex-imperial territory would have been 'King of Britain.' By the last quarter of the century, Saxon encroachment and the rise of regional overlords had carried disintegration so far that a term implying overall sovereignty would have been meaningless. Between, however, while parts of the country were already Saxon-held, there could still have been a vestigial paramountcy over a fair number of Britons, or at least a claim to it, expressible in the phrase 'King of the Britons' paralleling 'King of the Franks,' 'King of the Visigoths,' and so forth, contemporaneous titles taken from these men's subjects and not from their ill-defined domains. The style 'Riothamus' is apt and intelligible in its time as one possessed or adopted by the leader who went to Gaul.

If Geoffrey drew on this leader's career for his story of Arthur, was the identification a fancy of his own like his Merlin-Ambrosius equation, or had he any reason to think that Arthur (or Artorius) actually was the king's name even that he was *the* Arthur? The obvious thing to ask is whether anyone else made the identification, before Geoffrey or at least independently of him.

Professedly in 1019, a priest in Brittany giving his name as William composed a 'life' or 'legend' of St Gwyddno, one of the many Welsh clerics who took part in the British colonization of Armorica. 'Gwyddno' in Breton became 'Goueznou' and in the Latin of the surviving copy, 'Goeznovius.' The saint is unconnected with Arthur, but the *Legenda Sancti Goeznovii* has a prologue about the British migration, in which Arthur figures. William cites an unidentified *Ystoria Britanica*. Scholarly comment on the prologue has been scanty and variable. A. de la Borderie noted it in 1883. So did E.K. Chambers in 1927. In 1939 J.S.P Tatlock ruled it out as Arthurian evidence on the ground that its alleged date of composition was spurious and the author simply paraphrased Geoffrey. Others, including R.S. Loomis, followed Tatlock uncritically. At length, however, Fleuriot vindicated the date as correct. Careful scrutiny shows that the prologue cannot be explained in Tatlock's terms, and he admitted as much himself in the case of one episode (a gruesome story of British settlers cutting out the tongues of indigenous women), which appears in *Goeznovius* and also in the Welsh tale *The Dream of Macsen Wiedig*, but is not in Geoffrey. There had to be a prior source, a conclusion with a much wider application.[24]

William's prologue goes over familiar ground, but with some surprising divergences. It tells, as do other accounts, how Vortigern brought heathen Saxons into Britain as auxiliary troops. They turned against their employers inflicting slaughter and devastation. Arthur pushed them back, but after successful campaigns he departed, and the way was open for fresh Saxon invasions of the island. The Britons became divided, and a fluctuating warfare went on through the times of many kings, British and Saxon. Numerous churchmen were driven by Saxon persecution to leave Britain and sail over to the 'lesser Britain' which emigration had formed in Armorica.

Even as a product of 1019, this prologue is too remote in time from its subject-matter to be used directly as history. Yet the relevant part is free from palpable legend, and whatever traditions it may embody deserve respect. The sentences about Arthur are the ones that need to be quoted fully.

> Presently their pride [*i.e.* the Saxons'] was checked for a while through the great Arthur, King of the Britons. They were largely cleared from the island and reduced to subjection. But when this same Arthur, after many victories which he won gloriously in Britain and Gaul, was summoned at last from human activity, the way was open for the Saxons to go again into the island ...

And so on. William puts Arthur's campaigns after the Saxon revolt, but not long after. The word translated 'presently,' *postmodum*, implies sooner-rather-than-later. Furthermore Arthur seems to succeed Vortigern directly, without Geoffrey's other reigns between. Neither the revolt nor Vortigern's death can be dated with any accuracy, but it would be hard to put the beginning of this Arthur's activities much after the 450s. He campaigns in Gaul as well as Britain, and Saxons are the only enemies mentioned. There was one single period when a king could have gone on from fighting them in Britain to fighting them in Gaul. During the 460s Saxons were present on the lower Loire, and for some years they were in confrontation with the Britons who were settling just north of them. They were finally beaten and dispersed in a battle near Angers somewhere about 469.[25] The Britons, in their short-lived imperial alliance, appear to have taken part along with 'Romans' and Franks, and while no one says so, it is quite possible that Riothamus himself was involved. He was certainly in the right area before his march to Bourges. It is a fact that after his fading-out in 470, new Saxon incursions into Britain, 'going again into the island' began along the south coast.

Goeznovius calls Arthur 'King of the Britons,' the same rather uncommon title, justified only for a limited time, that is given to Riothamus; and he, whether or not he came to Angers, was active in Gaul at the date indicated here for Arthur. The author certainly seems to be equating the two, and not at all as did Geoffrey. An unlocated Arthurian battle in Nennius, 'Agned,' has been explained as a scribal contraction and corruption of *Andegavum*, that is, Angers.

We may skip a century or two and consider the medieval chroniclers. With some, the Arthurian matter is their chief concern, and they adapt and paraphrase Geoffrey in various ways. The majority, for whom this is only one topic among many, tend to be rather uncomfortable with it and avoid going into much detail. In England and Scotland, several incorporate accounts of Arthur that more or less follow Geoffrey's *History*, selectively, sometimes with different sympathies, but without serious dissent. Some fasten on the unworkable date 542, and make whatever can be made of the story on that basis. The *History* is commonly accepted as truth with whatever difficulty. Explicit scepticism does not begin to bite until the sixteenth century.

But while English and Scottish chroniclers, with one major exception, to be noted, fail to take us much further with the present topic, a few overseas show traces of a tradition that is consistent with *Goeznovius* and an Arthur–Riothamus equation and cannot have been derived from Geoffrey. They ignore the fatal 542; if they are aware of it, they are evidently aware that it must be wrong. The Ourscamp re-issuer of Sigebert already has his suspicions in the twelfth century. I owe the list that follows to Professor Barbara Moorman.[26]

Albericus Trium Fontium, between 1227 and 1251, tries to give exact dates for Geoffrey's fifth-century kings, but with results that do not square with him and hint at some other basis of calculation. He says Arthur reigned only sixteen years, from 459 to 475. Earlier, his reference to Vortigern points to a mis-reading which, if corrected, would pull the series back and make Arthur king from 454 to 470. With or without correction, Albericus brackets the 460s. It may be significant that most of his information is from French sources.

The *Salzburg Annals* record the accession of Pope Hilarus in 461, and here someone a little later than Albericus has inserted a sentence: 'At this time Arthur, of whom many stories are told, reigned in Britain.'

Jean des Preis (1338–1400) accepts a sixth-century Arthur but feels bound to cite and rebut a rival statement by Martinus Polonus, to the effect that Arthur reigned during Hilarus's pontificate, which ended in 468. His source is not Geoffrey, who never mentions Hilarus. Martinus has little else that is relevant, but he does associate the stories of the Round Table with the reign of the emperor Leo.

Jacques de Guise, towards the end of the fourteenth century, says in his history of Hainaut (now part of Belgium) that the country suffered oppression in the time of 'Arthur and the Goths, Huns and Vandals.' The Huns dwindled rapidly as troublers of western Europe after Attila's death in 453, so an overlapping reign of Arthur cannot have begun much later. Further on, Jacques correctly notes Geoffrey's chronological fix putting Arthur's Gallic warfare in the reign of the emperor Leo. Further on again, he speaks of Arthur as king during the rule of the Roman commander Aegidius in northern Gaul, from 461 to 464. His source is not Geoffrey, who never mentions Aegidius.

Philippe de Vigneulles, in 1525, has a passage adapted from Gregory of Tours about the reign of the Frankish king Childeric, which began in 456, and says he was temporarily banished and replaced by 'Gillon the Roman,' established at Soissons. There is ample proof that 'Gillon' is a French version of Aegidius, and Philippe not only echoes Jacques de Guise by making him contemporary with Arthur, he says he had 'many dealings' with the Briton. Once again, Geoffrey never mentions Aegidius. He is thought to have facilitated the Britons' settlement in Armorica, and enlisted their aid in coastal defence, a policy that would have required dealings with whatever chief they acknowledged.[27]

There would not be much point in quoting someone as late as Philippe if it were not for the signs that all these chroniclers are working with the same conception. Their allusions could go back to a single source, in some degree independent of Geoffrey, making Arthur reign from about 454 to 470. And to add one further chronicler, a very important and learned one, John Capgrave in England allots Arthur to just that stretch of time. As a final touch and possible sidelight, there is a Chronicle of Anjou that calls Arthur's betrayer 'Morvandus,' which looks like a conflation of 'Mordred' with 'Arvandus,' the name of the betrayer of Riothamus.[28]

It may now be judged likely that Riothamus, King of the Britons, is at least a major constituent of the figure of Arthur and perhaps the earliest. It may also appear that the signs of an identification do not point to Geoffrey exclusively. The *Goeznovius* author seems to have adopted it, as did the aforesaid chroniclers, on other grounds than the *History of the Kings of Britain*. The solution of the whole enigma may be as simple as that: the two are the same. 'Arthur,' or rather 'Artorius,' may have been the personal name of the man known to history by a title or honorific or whatever 'Riothamus' is; and he is on record as both. Similarly, the chief Spanish epic hero is sometimes Ruy Diaz de Bivar and sometimes El Cid Campeador. If we care to pursue the notion, there are further possibilities. 'Arthur' might have been a nickname or sobriquet. A previous Arthur in Britain, Lucius Artorius Castus, was a general who took an army across the Channel in 184 to suppress an Armorican revolt. A king taking another army across the Channel, and in the same direction, if for a different reason, might have been hailed by some well-informed panegyrist as a 'second Artorius.'[29]

Riothamus's stature and resources, and the fact that the western emperor sought his alliance, imply a career of some importance in Britain before he went overseas. But nothing is said about him in that phase, at least as Riothamus. Therefore attempts to link him with the insular Arthur story must be conjectural. A few points are worth making. He could have fought some of the battles in Nennius's list, and, indeed, fully half of these, so far as they are locatable, fit better in the 450s and 460s than they do later. His trans-Channel contact suggests a home territory in the West Country, and he is the only documented person who could have organized the restructuring of Cadbury-Camelot, unless we count Ambrosius Aurelianus. Also his disappearance in Gaul would explain the long mystery over Arthur's fate and his grave, attested by a Welsh poem, and the hope of his second advent. The King of the Britons could have become like Sebastian, the lost king of Portugal whose return was expected for centuries, or like the Mexican peasant leader Zapata, rumoured to be still alive even today. Of course, though, his disappearance may be illusory, a product of our own lack of information. Britons at the time may have known quite well what happened to him.

One further negative point is not wholly insignificant. If we reject the Riothamus equation, we cannot prove an Arthur in Britain at all. The historians have reduced him to a vague probability, no more, and some would challenge even that.

To revert to the insular tradition, we face the same problems but with more ways of resolving them. If we hypothesize Arthur-Riothamus as one person, it is clear that the two *Annales* battles, Badon and Camlann, are too late for him and will remain too late after any credible shift. Standing at the beginning of the Arthurian time-span, he cannot cover all the data. But no single leader could, wherever in the time-span he might be placed. Perhaps, once Arthur-Riothamus was established as a hero, other men's deeds, outside his lifetime, were ascribed to him by the bards and story-tellers.

If, however, we think in terms of two persons, blended into a composite like Merlin, we might suppose that the one called Arthur lived somewhat later. Or that Riothamus was called Arthur as *Goeznovius* and the chroniclers indicate, but that a junior Badon-Camlann Arthur, perhaps named after him, and eventually confused with him, accounts for the spread.

A further possibility is raised by a Welsh poem about yet another battle, at a place called Llongborth, probably Portchester on the Hampshire coast, the scene of a known Saxon incursion.[30] The poem is in praise of Geraint, one of several Britons so named. It includes a stanza which has been construed as saying that Arthur was present with his soldiers, but almost certainly does not.

In Llongborth I saw Arthur's
Brave men who cut with steel,
The emperor, ruler in toil of battle.

The word 'emperor' applied to Arthur is *ameraudur*, derived from the Latin *imperator*, which may correspond to 'high king' (as sometimes in Ireland) but may mean simply 'commander-in-chief.' The main point, here, is that Arthur is not present himself. A force called 'Arthur's Men,' in the Welsh the words come together, with the adjective 'brave' following, is fighting without him, probably toward the close of the fifth century. Late Roman times supply instances of military units named after individuals: Theodosiani, Honoriaci.[31] Arthur's Men might have been Artoriani. This force could have stayed in being after his death, recruited new members, played a crucial part at Badon, and collapsed through internal conflict at Camlann. Ambiguity in poems about it, like the ambiguity in the Llongborth poem itself, could have fostered the belief that Arthur was present in person on occasions when he was present only as an Inspiration or memory. Such misunderstandings would have stretched his career. This speculation has the advantage that it postulates only one Arthur who could be Riothamus, yet preserves his connection, if by proxy, with the two famous battles.

Such topics range beyond the present discussion. What I am proposing is that the King of the Britons who went to Gaul supplies a documented starting point for at least a part of the Arthurian Legend, and, conceivably, for the whole of it.

NOTES

1. For texts, see 'Nennius,' chapter 56, and Welsh Annals in the same volume. For discussion, see Alcock, *Arthur's Britain*, 45–71; Jackson in Loomis, ed., *Arthurian Literature in the Middle Ages* (hereafter cited as *ALIMA*), chapters 1 and 2; Lacy, ed., *The New Arthurian Encyclopedia* (hereafter cited as *Encyclopedia*), articles. 'Camlann,' '*Gododdin*,' 'Nennius.' Cp also Wilhelm, *Romance*, chapters 1 and 2.

2. Dumville, 'Sub-Roman Britain,' passim.

3. Ashe, *The Discovery of King Arthur*, 106.

4. *Encyclopedia*, article 'Tintagel,' and discussions by O. J. Padel; Rahtz, *Glastonbury*, 59–60; Alcock, 'Cadbury-Camelot: a Fifteen-Year Perspective,' 358, 362–8, 380–5.

5. Cp the plaintive question by an opponent of the grave: 'Why were the Welsh so keen to give Somerset the credit?' Dunning, *Arthur: the King in the West*, 58.

6. Chambers, *Arthur of Britain*, 184.

7. Ambrosius: Gildas, chapter 25; Bede, *Ecclesiastical History* I:16; Nennius, chapters 40–42. Marcus and Marcianus: Bromwich, *Trioedd Ynys Prydein*, 443–8, 456–7.

8. Jackson in *ALIMA*, 3–4.

9. Giraldus Cambrensis, *Speculum Ecclesiae*, chapter 9; text in Chambers, 272. *Sir Gawain and the Green Knight*, lines 2446–2455.

10. Jackson in *ALIMA*, 1–2; *Encyclopedia*, article 'Saints' Lives.'

11. On the myth, see Rhys, *Celtic Folklore*, II.493–4. Jennifer Westwood made her observation in a BBC broadcast 'Tuesday Call' on February 11th 1986. See Chambers, *Arthur of Britain*, 185, 188, 192–3, 221-7, for specific instances.

12. Ashe, 'A Certain Very Ancient Book,' *Speculum* 56 (1981), 301–23 (hereafter cited as *Speculum* 1981). Cp Fleuriot, *Les Origines de la Bretagne*, 236–7, 245–7, 277, and Wright's edition of Geoffrey, xvii–xviii.

13. Tatlock, *Legendary History*, 251.

14. Ashe, *Speculum* 1981, 310–19. For Tournoy and the Ourscamp scribe see Mildred Leake Day, *Quondam et Futurus*, Summer 1987, 6–8. Cp Fletcher, *The Arthurian Material in the Chronicles*, 82–3, 185.

15. Jordanes, *Gothic History*, chapter 45. Ashe, *Speculum* 1981, 310.

16. Campbell, ed., *The Anglo-Saxons*, 37; Wood, 'The Fall of the Western Empire,' 261. Cp Ashe, *Speculum* 1981, 310–13.

17. Gregory of Tours, 2.18. Ashe, *Speculum* 1981, 311.

18. Sidonius, *Letters*, 3.9. Ashe, *Speculum* 1981, 312.

19. Bromwich, *Trioedd*, 267–8.

20. Ashe, *Speculum* 1981, 317. The basic point is a recurrent confusion between Anno Domini dating and the chronology of Victorius of Aquitaine, but see the full discussion.

21. Fleuriot, *Origines*, 172–3; Bromwich, *Trioedd*, 386; *Encyclopedia*, articles. 'Riothamus,' 'Vortimer'.

22. Plutarch, *Life of Theseus*, 16.

23. Fleuriot (*Origines*, 170–8) suggested that Riothamus was Ambrosius Aurelianus, who, however, is not spoken of as campaigning abroad in any evidential text. There are other objections to the identification: Ashe, *Discovery*, 113–14. Fleuriot did accept that the career of Riothamus, whoever he was, went into the making of the story of Arthur (*Origines*, 176).

24. Chambers, *Arthur of Britain*, 92–4, 241–3 (text given here); Tatlock, 'The Dates of the Arthurian Saints' Legends,' 361–5; Loomis in *ALIMA*, 54; Fleuriot, *Origines*, 277; Ashe in *Speculum* 1981, 304–6 Cp Wright's edition of Geoffrey, xvii, and Wilhelm, *Romance*, chapter 1 (two allusions).

25. Gregory of Tours, 2.18, 19. Morris, *The Age of Arthur*, 91–2 (certainly incorrect about Riothamus, see Ashe, *Speculum* 1981, 320, n. 37).

26. Ashe, *Discovery*, 106–11.

27. Ashe, *Speculum* 1981, 307, where the principal reference is to Chadwick in n.14; *Discovery*, 49; Morris, *The Age of Arthur*, 90; *Encyclopedia*, article 'Brittany.' Curiously enough, if Philippe in the sixteenth century and Morris in the twentieth are both right, the Arthur–Riothamus equation is virtually clinched. But I don't think so, not entirely, and the conclusion would be disastrous for Morris's own view of Arthur.

28. Fleuriot, *Origines*, 118.

29. Jackson in *ALIMA*, 2; Fleuriot, *Origines*, 47–8. Lucius Artorius Castus is linked with the Arthurian Legend by advocates of the Sarmatian Connection; see article on this in *Encyclopedia*. The emperor Domitian was reviled as a 'second Nero,' and a figurative use of 'Nero' for him by Juvenal becomes, in Geoffrey of Monmouth, a literal one (IV.16). Another suggestion is admittedly somewhat frivolous. The *h* in 'Riothamus' is probably scribal, and if so, the Latin form in his time was 'Riotamus.' 'Artorius' is close to being an anagram of this. I have shown that the letters RIOTAMUS can be arranged as they might have been, say, on a medallion so as to suggest ARTORIUS, especially if we allow an added R for Rex. See my *Kings and Queens of Early Britain*, 132–3 (British edition), 152–3 (U.S. edition).

30. Jackson in *ALIMA*, 13; Morris, *The Age of Arthur*, 104–6; Ashe, *Discovery*, 121–3.

31. Morris, *The Age of Arthur*, 100.

WORKS CITED

Alcock, Leslie, (1) *Arthur's Britain*. London: Allen Lane, The Penguin Press, 1971. (2) 'Cadbury-Camelot: a Fifteen-Year Perspective.' *Proceedings of the British Academy* 68 (1982), 355–88.

Annales Cambriae. See 'Nennius.'

Ashe, Geoffrey, (1) 'A Certain Very Ancient Book.' *Speculum* 56 (1981), 301–23. (2) *The Discovery of King Arthur*. New York: Anchor Press, Doubleday, 1985, and Henry Holt, 1987.

Bromwich, Pachel, *Trioeds' Ynys Prydein. The Welsh Triads*, with translation and notes. Cardiff: University of Wales Press, 1978 (revised edition).

Campbell, James, ed., *The Anglo-Saxons*. Oxford: Phaidon, 1982; Ithaca, N.Y.: Cornell University Press, 1982.

Chambers, E.K., *Arthur of Britain*. London: Sidgwick and Jackson, 1927, re-issue, 1966; New York: Barnes and Noble, 1964.

Day, Mildred Leake, ed., *Quondam et Futurus*, Summer 1987. Gardendale, Alabama.

Dumville, David, 'Sub-Roman Britain: History and Legend.' *History* 62 (1977) 173–91.

Dunning, R.W, *Arthur: the King in the West*. Gloucester: Alan Sutton, and New York: St Martin's Press, 1988.

Fletcher, Robert Huntington, *The Arthurian Material in the Chronicles*. Boston: Ginn, 1906; 2nd edition, New York: Franklin, 1966.

Fleuriot, Leon, *Les Origines de le Bretagne*. Paris: Payot, 1980.

Geoffrey of Monmouth, (1) *Historia Regum Britanniae*. Edited by Neil Wright. Cambridge: D.S. Brewer, 1985. (2) *The History of the Kings of Britain*. Translated by Lewis Thorpe. Harmondsworth: Penguin, 1966.

Gildas. In *History from the Sources*, vol. 7, *The Ruin of Britain*. Edited and translated by Michael Winterbottom. London and Chichester: Phillimore, 1978.

Historia Brittonum. See 'Nennius.'

Lacy, Norris J., *The New Arthurian Encyclopedia*. New York: Garland, 1991.

Loomis, Roger Sherman, ed., *Arthurian Literature in the Middle Ages*. Oxford: Clarendon Press, 1959; New York: Oxford, 1959. 2nd edition, 1961.

Morris, John, *The Age of Arthur*. London: Weidenfeld and Nicolson, 1973; New York: Scribner, 1973.

'Nennius.' In *History from the Sources*, vol. 8, *British History and the Welsh Annals*. Edited and translated by John Morris. London and Chichester: Phillimore, 1980.

Rahtz, Philip, *Glastonbury*. London: Batsford/English Heritage, 1993.

Rhys, John, *Celtic Folklore*. 2 vols. Oxford: Clarendon Press, 1901.

Tatlock, J.S.P, (1) 'The Dates of the Arthurian Saints' Legends.' *Speculum* 14 (1939), 345–65. (2) *The Legendary History of Britain*. Berkeley and Los Angeles: University of California Press, 1950.

Wilhelm, James J., ed., *The Romance of Arthur*. New York: Garland, 1994. (A combined volume. References here apply also to the first volume of an earlier edition, 1984.)

Wood, Ian, 'The Fall of the Western Empire and the End of Roman Britain.' *Britannia* XVIII (1987), 251–62.

JOSEPH D. PARRY

Following Malory Out of Arthur's World

T homas Malory's reading of his sources in *Le Morte D'Arthur* leads him
to locate Arthur's final resting place, the legendary Avalon, in two different
locations. One of these—Glastonbury—continues from the "indefinite
pastness" of Malory's text into his own, fifteenth-century world.[1] There, as
William Caxton attested in his preface to the 1485 edition, one can still travel
and see Arthur's "sepulture."[2] In all probability, Glastonbury Monastery is
where Arthur was buried by a hermit who received the body from the three
ladies who, in turn, received Arthur (while yet alive) from Bedivere.[3] Yet
Malory's sources cannot make him certain where this place is, so he refrains
from asserting a connection between Glastonbury and Avalon. Malory seems
not to have visited the grave at Glastonbury; he can only report that "many
men say that there ys wrytten uppon the tumbe thys: HIC IACET ARTHURUS,
REX QUONDAM REXQUE FUTURUS" (717:33–35). This may be the text that
Bedivere "made ... to be wrytten" (717:28), but such facts can only be
surmised. Malory can only rely on what is written in his sources, on tombs—
about Arthur and on what has been reported by "many men."[4] Reports of
others, in fact, suggest another possible "location" for Avalon: "Yet som men
say in many partys of Inglonde that kynge Arthure ys nat dede, but had by
the wyll of oure Lorde Jesu into another place; and men say that he shall com
agayne, and he shall wynne the Holy Crosse. Yet I woll nat say that hit shall

---

From *Modern Philology* 95, no. 2 (1997). © 1997 by The University of Chicago.

be so, but rather I wolde sey: here in thys worlde he chaunged hys lyff"
(717:29–33). Malory himself inclines to believe that Arthur is dead and will
not return; he has found no durable chivalric empire in the pages of
Arthurian myth that he can import into his own century. Rather, Arthur has
"chaunged hys lyff" and is now irretrievably outside the temporal boundaries
of the narrative's world. While Malory wishes to locate this other "place"
somewhere "here in thys worlde" because Arthur and his empire died "here
in thys worlde," "the vale of Avilon"—the narrative's name for Arthur's final
destination—may lie outside the spatial boundaries of Malory's narrative
England and outside the boundaries of the narrative itself.

Malory's ambiguous location of Arthur's final resting place is, I would
suggest, a fitting culmination to a narrative that, after the Grail episodes,
unfolds simultaneously in two locations and, more significantly, in two kinds
of locations. The Grail itself, that tangible witness of God's grace, had a
determinable place in the narrative—the castle of Carbonek—though it also
was the Idea of an all-consuming quest that existed everywhere at once as the
object of desire that surpasses all other desires. Yet once the Grail—and with
it the possibility of durable, political empire—vanishes from Arthur's world,
Malory's narrative, I will argue, begins to pursue two different directions at
once. His text becomes permanently fractured into two concurrent but
contradictory narratives of the dissolution of Arthurian society, each of
which exercises its own narrative logic and provides its own kind of
geography. Both of Malory's post-Grail stories unfold "here in thys worlde";
both stories relate the demise of Arthur's world and Launcelot's role in this
demise. One traces Launcelot's movements, marking the places of his
wrongdoing, pride, and illicit desire along the way. In this story Malory
suggests moral causality by means of the temporal sequences of his narrative,
and he situates these sequences within geographical relationships that refer
to Malory's own fifteenth-century world—places which carry the names and
convey the relative distances familiar to his contemporary readers.[5] Through
his text's familiar, traceable principles of temporal and physical ordering,
Malory undertakes to trace the tragedy of Arthurian society, just as he wishes
to inscribe Arthur's burial place within his own known, familiar world, so that
he might follow its logic and assign culpability to those responsible for the
tragedy. In particular, this story will reveal Launcelot's and Guinevere's
secrets; Malory will have them confess their guilt and take up separate,
cloistered, penitential lives before the narrative ends.

The other story is a story of fate and misfortune (*fortuna*), of
destinations to which every path leads because destiny has decreed it. Here
is no map of human motivation as there is for the first story, only a different,
nonlinear kind of map that is unable to connect the effects of human action

with its human causes. Consequently, this story will insert into the referential geography of Malory's first story the literary places of Malory's sources, identified by names that refer readers back to the insulated, nostalgic world of Arthurian myth, which vaguely renders the specific character of place and the measurability of relative distances. The second story depicts the obscurity, rather than the clarity, of the path down which Launcelot is driven by inexorable, contradictory desires to be true to honor and to love. Malory persistently refuses to condemn and even celebrates the beauty of the fated desire Launcelot and Guinevere share, opposing their love to the unstable love of "nowadayes" (649:22, 30). Yet though these two stories with their two logics coexist in the narrative, they are antithetical and, finally, inimical to each other. Once Arthur is dead Malory's lovers renounce, though they do not deny, their desire, out of penance for the political destruction that their desire caused. In this regard the second story must be subservient to the first. Malory demands this penance, perhaps, because of his disappointment, though not his surprise, at the failure of political empire to contain the competing desires of its servants.

I wish to illustrate in two episodes chronologically linked by Malory— "The Fair Maid of Astolat" and "The Great Tournament"—how the narrative's dual logics and geographies become particularly apparent in the way Malory's characters travel in the romance world and in the way the narrative characterizes the places to and between which its characters travel. Malory's narrator constructs a world that conveys, even shapes, the confusion his characters experience as they sense the tragedy of history that his renarration of the myth of a British political golden age registers. As Joseph M. Lenz says, "Far from passively representing a character's mental state, the romance landscape takes an active role in forming character."[6] The active/passive opposition that informs Lenz's observation is too rigid, but it opens the door to our rethinking of the relations between Malory's characters and the land they inhabit. I will demonstrate that Malory describes the relationship of character and land through the kind of mobility that his characters are allowed within the text's carefully marked geographical points of reference. Their movements within the narrative's phenomenal world articulate the sense of tragedy that Malory finds when Arthurian myth is restaged for his own century.

I

Malory's first story traces how the movements of the characters in these two episodes detail the specific nature of the political violence that the lovers unleash in response to the romance world's increasing ability, after the Grail episodes, to frustrate their movements (Launcelot's injuries, Guinevere's imprisonment, Elaine's unrequited love). Sudden, unforeseeable violence and distress obtrude in the narrative's setting wherever anyone—Launcelot, Guinevere, the Fair Maid—acts out of loyalty to love or to a loved one. In these episodes Malory's narrative geography becomes a crucial way of importing the past—its possibilities along with its failures—into the present. Beginning with "The Fair Maid of Astolat," these precarious destinations of loyalty and the resulting precarious nature of travel within this world are written into the anglicized landscape of *Le Morte D'arthur*. Malory seems to have drawn a setting in his romance that, as George Stewart claims, is "more clearly defined than that of its sources," though it remains "certainly hazy."[7] Malory's romance setting can be very much the unpredictable, magical, "not here, not now" landscape of French Arthurian romance, yet English place names—Canterbury, Bath, Winchester, etc.—bring this setting into better focus, replacing many of "the vague locations of French romance."[8]

Perhaps the most significant of the English place names is Malory's unique identification of Camelot as Winchester.[9] His interest in locating "The Fair Maid of Astolat" with some exactness becomes quickly evident as the episode opens.[10] Arthur and his knights, and later Launcelot in disguise, travel from London to Camelot/Winchester via Astolat for a tournament. In the beginning of this section Malory reminds us twice that the Camelot to which Arthur and his knights ride was also called Winchester at "that tyme" (621:28, 624:11). Though Malory first mentions the identification much earlier, in the story of Balin, he mentions it infrequently and never, as here, repeats it in close proximity. Throughout this portion of the narrative Malory refers to the city almost exclusively as Winchester. He also explicitly identifies Astolat with contemporary Guildford ("a towne that was called Astolot, that ys in Englysh Gylforde" [622:8–9]). As we will see, Astolat will become a significant place both in Malory's narrative and in his narrative geography, above all, in Launcelot's dealings with the love-stricken Fair Maid, Elaine le Blank. Guildford, as Stewart points out, is "a convenient place" to locate Astolat, given the identification of Camelot with Winchester. It is twenty-eight miles down the London–Winchester road—a day's ride, in the narrative—and it had a royal castle where "naturally" a king might stay (as Arthur does) on his way to Winchester from London.[11] Moreover, the Fair Maid's funerary river trip "offers no difficulty" with Guildford as Astolat, for thirteen miles away from Guildford lies Chertsey, a perfect place on the Thames to launch her boat toward London.[12]

Within this carefully marked world, Malory's narrative will attentively follow Launcelot's movements as these expose him to frustration, discovery, and pain. In each place Launcelot visits, his attempts to be true to the code of love and also remain loyal to his knightly code of honor reveal a hitherto unseen vulnerability (to frequently bizarre injuries, at that). Catherine LaFarge cogently summarizes: "Since his return from the Quest, Launcelot increasingly slips into the arena of the other: disguise, disappearance, woundedness."[13] But what most troubles Launcelot, a man acquainted with violence, about the injuries he receives is his impaired mobility in a world he has negotiated better than anyone else. As "The Fair Maid of Astolat" episode opens, we see Launcelot simply assuming the right and the ability to move, or not move, as he chooses.[14] Arthur declares that a tournament "I be held at Camelot/Winchester, but Launcelot chooses not to participate, "for he seyde he was nat hole of the play of sir Madore" (622:4–5).[15] Guinevere, also exercising her freedom of movement by staying behind, fears that their "enemyes" might suspect their motives for remaining in London: "Sir, ye ar gretly to blame thus to holde you behynde my lorde. What woll youre enemyes and myne sey and deme?" (622:12–13). Launcelot commends her "witte" which "ys of late com syn ye were woxen so wyse!" (622:17–18); he will travel to the tournament, apparently to preserve the secrecy of their love. At this point both seem to be acting primarily out of their passion for each other, which must be masked by their public movements. Almost immediately after the Grail Quest,

> sir Launcelot began to resorte unto quene Gwenivere agayne and forgate the promyse and the perfeccion that he made in the queste; for, as the booke seyth, had not sir Launcelot bene in his prevy thoughtes and in hys myndis so sette inwardly to the quene as he was in semynge outewarde to God, there had no knyght passed hym in the queste of the Sankgreall. But ever his thoughtis prevyly were on the quene, and so they loved togydirs more hotter than they dud toforehonde, and had many such prevy draughtis togydir that many in the courte spake of hit.   (611:10–18)

The narrative appears to divide Guinevere and, especially, Launcelot into public and private figures: secret, private motives prompt the direction and character of their public movements within the romance world.

However, Launcelot's public also includes Guinevere and God. All that Launcelot does in connection with the adventures recounted in "The Fair Maid of Astolat," Bors, tells Guinevere, is for her love (637:5). Launcelot finds that he must continually prove that fact to her. He continually seeks a way of moving about that retains not only the approbation of his community but also (perhaps more so) the approval of the volatile Guinevere. When one way does not work, he finds another—when his open service to other women's causes angers Guinevere, he tries to travel incognito in the next series of adventures while still performing his courteous duties to the men and women he meets along the way. In "The Fair Maid of Astolat" he will leave Guinevere (so tongues cannot wag), but he also does not wish to be found (which is against Guinevere's advice). At the tournament he wants the glory of triumph, but he does not want the name recognition. Launcelot rightly senses that recognition will hamper his mobility because his identity, if known, will allow Arthur's world to follow his movements. As the coming episodes show, Launcelot attracts a following wherever he goes, known or in disguise. Yet all this while Launcelot is also, as he tells Guinevere, looking to "take the adventure that God woll gyff [him]" (622:27–28). It may be an idle phrase that Launcelot utters here, or the narrative's attempt at some dramatic irony. However, Launcelot never seems to suffer much from self-deception. He may simply perceive no disparity between leaving Guinevere to avoid gossip and scandal and traveling toward divinely ordained adventures.

Launcelot may hide his actions from Arthur and his colleagues, but one cannot be certain that he discerns a need to hide them from God. Launcelot's conscience never seems to impair his mobility. It is rather fellow mortals, prominently Guinevere, who comprise the audience for the plays in which he acts. But the more Launcelot tries to travel undiscovered, the more the narrative leads him into situations that will discover him. Any movement Launcelot makes in Malory's romance world creates the possibility of his discovery, because movement in Malory's world engages one with the unforeseen and the unpredictable. The romance world is interlaced with surprises for its characters—with events that thwart any consistent sense of narrative logic. The ability to deal successfully with surprises defines and perpetually reveals the hero anew.[16] Malory's narrative continually reintroduces Launcelot as the text's "flower of chivalry." After the Grail episodes, however, these reintroductions emphasize the growing disparity between Launcelot as a political ideal—Arthur's best force for good and justice, particularly (and platonically) to noble women—and his status as ideal lover.[17]

In this episode Malory is careful to mark this place, where we can see the conflicts Launcelot's life embodies, both as a place already known in the Arthurian literature Malory reads—Astolat—and as a place known to Malory's contemporaries as Guildford. He draws attention to Astolat's double location in his audience's literary and phenomenal worlds, and within this known locale Malory will carefully follow Launcelot's futile attempts at anonymity. As Launcelot arrives in disguise at Astolat/Guildford, Arthur "aspyed" him, for "he knew hym welle inow" (622:34–35). While Arthur's long association with his best knight might explain this recognition, Launcelot's irrepressible aura also radiates out to those as yet unacquainted with him. On arriving at Sir Bernard's lodging, he immediately attracts the unswerving love and loyalty of not only Sir Bernard's daughter Elaine but also his son Lavaine, who thereafter becomes one of his most loyal followers.[18] Here the conflicts of Launcelot's life become explicit. Lavaine is irresistibly drawn to him as the ideal knight who fights in tournaments, seeks out adventures, and serves his retainer; Elaine is as irresistibly drawn to Launcelot as the ideal lover. Whereas Lavaine's undying loyalty is seen as a knightly virtue, Elaine's attraction is cast as an act of immoderation. The text announces when we first see her that "she keste such a love unto sir Launcelot that she cowde never withdraw her loove, wherefore she dyed" (623:24–25). The intensity and consistency of both her desire for Launcelot and Launcelot's desire for Guinevere seem to have decreed Elaine's destruction from the moment she first sees Launcelot. The narrative must dispose of the "Fair Maid," for her straightforward, openly expressed love for Launcelot will not fit the logic of his characterization—the knight who acts "honorably" and unsexually toward women, and the secret, monogamous lover of Guinevere. The Fair Maid appears, moreover, incapable of imagining the kind of deceptive actions that Elaine, the mother of Galahad, could take to seduce Launcelot.

Yet Malory does not finally dismiss her before putting the question to Launcelot, almost disingenuously, through Sir Bors (after he unwittingly wounds the disguised, sleeve-bearing Launcelot at the tournament): "Why sholde ye put her frome you? ... For she ys a passyng fayre damesell, and well besayne and well taught. And God wolde, fayre cousyn, ... that ye cowde love her" (635:9–11). The Fair Maid's openness unwittingly challenges the secret love life of Launcelot.[19] In her own way she acts toward the things she desires with as much force as Launcelot does, and when "she was so hote in love that she besought sir Launcelot to were uppon hym at the justis a tokyn of hers," Launcelot responds, "Damesell.... and if I graunte you that, ye may sey that I do more for youre love than ever y ded for lady or jantillwoman" (623:26–32). She pursues this knight to whom she is unabashedly attracted; she asks him to take her (by means of her token) into battle with him, that she might become part of the knight as he performs his tasks. Launcelot immediately prepares to reject her request, but "than he remembird hymselff that he wolde go to the justis disgysed, and because he had never aforne borne no maner of tokyn of no damesell, he bethought hym to bere a tokyn of hers, that none of hys bloode thereby myght know hym" (623:33–36). Launcelot uses Elaine's love to his own advantage; for an even better disguise than he had originally planned, he carries her "rede sleve ... of scarlet, well embrowdred with grete perelles" (622:39–40) into the tournament and also gives her his shield to keep "untill tyme that he com agayne" (623:1).

The narrative here explicitly traces the sequence of Launcelot's deceptive behavior toward the innocent Fair Maid. Reading sequentially, we may also conclude that for this deceptive exchange of gifts—and, by extension, for the larger acts of deception represented by this encounter (including his refusal to he a publicly sexual being)—the narrative wounds Launcelot, first with Bors's spear, then through his question. On the other hand, the text clearly shows that Launcelot has no intention of using Elaine dishonorably. The courtesy he shows her, as he would show any woman of her station, added to her all-consuming passion for him, makes for a deadly love potion, but the text gives no indication that it is his courteous behavior or talk that attracts her. She falls in love by merely looking at him: "ever she behylde sir Launcelot wondirfully. And, as the booke sayth, she keste such a love unto sir Launcelot that she cowde never withdraw hir loove, wherefore she dyed" (623:22–25). He never encourages her affections, and he tells her truthfully that he has "caste [himself] never to be wedded man" (638:20), though he does not explain why. Throughout the episode Launcelot seems so distracted by tournaments, wounds, and disguises that he may fail to note fully the depth of Elaine's feelings.

Despite showing us Launcelot's typically honorable intentions, however, Malory draws our attention to a moment when Launcelot's bearing toward Elaine implicates him in social wrongdoing. The conflicts of his lives as lover and as knight do not allow him innocence ("not harmfulness"). The grounds on which he refuses to accept her request to be his paramour, since he will not marry, trap him in the hypocrisy of his relationships with Arthur and Guinevere: "'Than, fayre knyght,' seyde she, 'woll ye be my paramour?' 'Jesu deffende me!' seyde sir Launcelot, 'For than I rewarded youre fadir and youre brothir full evyll for their grete goodnesse'" (638:21–23). There will be no retribution on Launcelot for his refusal to return Elaine's love. His statement to Arthur and, more pointedly, to Guinevere after the dead Fair Maid has arrived at Westminster in her Thames funeral barge—"I love nat to be constrayned to love, for love muste only aryse of the harte selff, and nat by none constraynte" (641:35–38)—seems to present the narrative's definition of desirable love, an insight into Launcelot's sense of how he loves to love and a specific vindication of his refusal to love someone simply for loving him. Nevertheless, through his use of the Fair Maid (dead and alive), Malory exposes Launcelot's sexual hypocrisy (he will reward Arthur "full evyll for [his] grete goodnesse" when attracted to his wife).

In characterizing Launcelot, Malory is drawn in contradictory directions. While Malory seems reluctant to point too harsh a finger, he also does not ignore the political damage that results from Launcelot's sexual secrecy. As Bors said, "God wolde" that Launcelot could love someone like Elaine le Blank rather than Guinevere, because the political salvation of Arthur's empire depends on Launcelot desiring someone who helps him build the empire rather than tear it down. Yet the narrative wishes paradoxically to accept love's motions on their own, free, self-determining conditions. True to the circular reasoning of his characterization but also to the "free" nature of love that Malory sets forth, Launcelot loves as he chooses to love. Launcelot's psychology is, in a way, quite simple—he desires all desirable things connected with chivalric life as constituted in Malory's sources. The conflicts, however, that inhere in that array of desires sets the tragedy of Le Morte D'Arthur in motion, and Malory erects Launcelot as this tragedy's exemplar.

Nevertheless, as we prepare to witness the tragedy that unfolds because of those choices, the narrative seems to fantasize in "The Fair Maid of Astolat" about how it might be if he could love openly and acceptably. Launcelot will refuse to fulfill the narrative's fantasy because of his unswerving loyalty to a forbidden but fated love. The wounds he receives appear to be the narrative's vengeance on him for this refusal. He chafes against his ever-diminishing freedom of movement, given his persistent loyalty to the competing ethical demands of his combined characterizations as knight and lover. His desire to move freely in order to protect his secret love and pursue his knightly service—his incognito movements on this occasion—begins to work against him. His irrepressible attractiveness is not dimmed by disguise; he still unintentionally wins another woman's heart and breaks it with unexpectedly tragic consequences. In the tournament his disguise wards off the loyalty of relatives who would otherwise defend him. Though in this episode he gains the loyalty of Lavaine, who is of tremendous service to him, it is the more valuable loyalty of his relatives (shown especially at the end of the narrative) from which he alienates himself. Each attempt to be courteous, serviceable, and valiant produces some kind of violent consequence to himself, or others, or both.

Thus as Malory, reading from "the Frensshe booke," follows Launcelot into restraints that his own covert motions create, his narrative depicts the contradictory nature and power of Launcelot's desires in the character of his movements within and against these restraints. What Malory adds to his renarration of "the Frensshe booke," moreover, is a marked space within which to view and to measure Launcelot's movements and where his vulnerability to injury derives from his violent resistance to the judgment that the narrative decrees for him. The text names this space "Guildford" in order to show that both the judgment and the basis on which it is made continue to reverberate from the distant past into the familiar present. Yet it also names it Astolat, thus situating the judgment in an irretrievable but no less familiar textual world of tragedy.

Perhaps Malory, in centering his two stories in one place with two names and two natures, finally wishes to map the activity of reading, in all of its contradictoriness. When, for example, he describes the Fair Maid as one who "dyd never more kyndlyer for man" when she attends to Launcelot after he is wounded in the tournament (633:38–39), the text marks the source for those feelings by explicitly citing "the Freynshe booke" (633:37–38) or "the booke" (623:24). The narrator marks his map of reading for us. His reading and renarration conspicuously retrace the path of Launcelot's destruction (his own destruction and the destruction he inflicts on others); the narrative reads and rehearses to us that the history of Guildford, Winchester, Westminster, or Windsor inscribes the damages of chivalry. A twentieth-century reader like George Stewart can follow Malory following the path of Launcelot's destructiveness by reconstructing the earnest Elaine's last, dramatic journey of self-vindication from Guildford to Chertsey and down the Thames to Westminster. In her retraceable journey the narrative will gauge the tragedy of Launcelot's public refusal to love someone like her because he loves what is socially and morally forbidden.

Astolat, then, can be contemporary Guildford, to which Malory may invite his audience, not necessarily to envision the story with absolute verisimilitude but to map it according to their own, familiar geographical coordinates. One sees nothing particular to this area that could not be found in many others in the general region; Malory conspicuously situates his story in the familiar, generic topography of meadows, woods, castles, etc.—the kind of physical surroundings one would see there.[20] Yet he is interested in the specifics of place names and relative distances in "The Fair Maid of Astolat" because he is interested in our impulse to read narratives as maps. Narration as a way of mapping the world was a common medieval practice, partly because, as P. D. A. Harvey contends, what we understand as "maps were practically unknown in the middle ages."[21] Medieval society apparently did not construct and, therefore, did not rely on generally applicable pictorial representations of the world. Instead, they produced "single-purpose maps" for particular uses or, more frequently, "written descriptions" of places and routes—itineraries, of which relatively few survive.[22] The few maps there are, according to Harvey, "are scarcely maps at all. They are diagrams—diagrams of the world—and are best understood as an open framework where all kinds of information might be placed in the relevant spatial positions, not unlike a chronicle or narrative in which information would be arranged chronologically."[23]

Malory's post-Grail episodes engage the phenomenal world with the kind of narrative ordering and occasional precision that characterize a medieval itinerary or the unique Gough Map, dating from around 1360.[24] Malory's narrative geography certainly possesses neither the global nor the local rigor and precision essential to our modern sense of "geography" and its visual realization in "cartography." Yet into geographical relations familiar to his audience Malory inscribes moral landscapes that have relationships known to his contemporaries—for example, sexual immorality that produces political catastrophe. Yi-Fu Tuan, an insightful theorist of geography, argues that modern geography, too, is a study deeply invested in morality.[25]

Yet Astolat is also Astolat, a place firmly inscribed in the Arthurian landscape of surprise adventures, that is, a place not located in particular relation to other known places in fifteenth-century British topography and a place where actions are not located in known cause/effect, sin/punishment kinds of relations. In fact, Astolat lies between Westminster/Camelot and London, between the two political centers of Arthurian government and, on this occasion, between the jousting of the tournament and the secret rendezvous with Guinevere. Astolat signifies Malory's second story of *fortuna*.

Malory's narrative in "The Fair Maid of Astolat" also shows us that Launcelot's insistent mobility comes at a tremendous cost to others, particularly to figures he uses to facilitate his own freedoms. Yet once again, the narrative locates Launcelot's responsibility for this cost, as it locates the river down which the Fair Maid's funerary procession travels, in two settings. One can locate the river—the Thames—and the specific portion of the river down which Elaine's funeral barge floats, as Stewart does, in Malory's fifteenth-century world. But Elaine's final river trip is also a journey elevated to mythical status.[26] This small myth forms part of the larger myth that perpetually anticipates Arthurian society's end, the myth whose life is its death, its tragedy. Malory's narrative sends her down this known route as an icon of tragedy, packaged with the trappings of myth. As a corpse in her funeral barge, she wishes to be accompanied by a steersman, "a mysterious Charon-figure," as Earl R. Anderson argues.[27] To inscribe Launcelot in this recreated myth, Elaine wishes him to provide her mass penny for burial (641:15). She also wishes an air of mystery to surround her corpse, inciting her anticipated audience's interest in her story, then fulfilling their interest. She dresses in her noblest attire, instructing her father, "Lette me be put in a fayre bed with all the rychyst clothis that I have aboute me" (640:10–11), as if she were a specimen of her class and gender.

More important, however, Elaine's right hand clutches a letter, addressed to Launcelot and "all ladyes" that tells the story of her love. She

will make Launcelot and "all ladyes" read this story after she dies, since he
would not read it while she lived at Astolat/Guildford: "Moste noble knyght,
my lorde sir Launcelot, now hath dethe made us two at debate for youre love.
And I was youre lover, that men called the Fayre Maydyn of Astolate.
Therefore unto all ladyes I make my mone, yet for my soule ye pray and bury
me at the leste, and offir ye my massepenny: thys ys my laste requeste. And
a clene maydyn I dyed, I take God to wytnesse. And pray for my soule, sir
Launcelot, as thou arte pereles" (641:11–17). This is her last testament of her
love and her purity, along with a complaint to all "ladyes" that her true,
"clene," unrequited love killed her. Having heard this letter read, "the kynge,
the quene and all the knyghtes wepte for pite of the dolefull complayntes"
(641:18–19). They then send for Launcelot, who explains "that she was both
fayre and good, and much I was beholdyn unto her, but she loved me oute of
mesure" because "she wolde be my wyff othir ellis my paramour, and of thes
two I wolde not graunte her" (641:32–33). Launcelot is perhaps right about
Elaine's immoderate love. Whereas Launcelot seems to have the power to
pursue or hide his desires as he chooses, she complains in her last letter about
the restraints placed on her desire.

Scholars have argued that Elaine fantasizes herself into Launcelot's life
and "excessively" imagines herself as Launcelot's destined lover.[28] Yet the
narrative, through Elaine, appears to arraign Launcelot's public bearing
toward women who love him. Malory lets her represent all "ladyes" when she
exclaims, "Therefore unto all ladyes I make my mone" and this statement
repeats, somewhat cryptically, a question in her letter that she first and more
fully uttered to "hir gostly fadir." For Malory this question does not demand
that Launcelot must love her, yet it does express the wish that he could, and
could do so openly. When her priest asks her to "leve" her thoughts of
Launcelot behind her as she dies, she exclaims: "Why shoulde I leve such
thoughtes? Am I nat an erthely woman? And all the whyle the brethe ys in
my body I may complayne me, for my belyve ys that I do none offence,
though I love an erthely man, unto God, for He fourmed me thereto, and all
maner of good love comyth of God. And othir than good love loved I never
sir Launcelot du Lake. And I take God to recorde, I loved never none but
hym, nor never shall, of erthely creature" (639:29–37). She is "an erthely
woman" who loves "an erthely man" according to God's design for her, and
this love is not returned. Certainly, her complaint repeats familiar laments
about the unfairness and pain of unrequited love. Her powerful refusal fully
to accept the notion that love should be an exchange of feeling proves to be
her downfall.

Through the power of being that Elaine displays throughout the
episode bearing her name, however, the narrative gains a forceful

spokeswoman for the ruin of its dreams for Launcelot and for Arthurian society as a whole. Again, Malory avoids directly blaming Launcelot for his choices—he portrays Launcelot as the kind of lover (of Guinevere) that Elaine describes herself as being (of Launcelot). Launcelot is constitutionally the lover whom the narrative envisions as its ideal lover. More is the pity, the tragedy, the narrative insists on saying. The potentially destructive force behind the love of its ideal lover is greater than any defense political society can erect, especially when he chooses what is forbidden and hides his choice from public view. There is also the social cost of publicly denying the "truths" the Fair Maid declares. Launcelot, too, is formed to love one and only one "erthely creature." It is tragic that mortals who are formed to love only one other mortal cannot connect in socially accepted arrangements. It is also more profoundly tragic that the expressions of Launcelot's desire must be masked and publicly muted, for the "illicit" character of his desire's object "adulterates" the chivalric codes of noble, moral love. "The Fair Maid of Astolat" is a key adventure in the post-Grail portion of *Le Morte D'Arthur*. The tragedy of the text as a whole is not exactly foreshadowed here, but it is characterized through the motions and the directions that the episode's characters take. Once Launcelot squarely reaffirms his inexorable desire for Guinevere after the Fair Maid's grand exit from life, Malory's narrative moves much faster toward its tragic end. Malory seems to grow weary of the "dilation" that has characterized his quest through Arthur's world.[29]

II

In the next episode, "The Great Tournament," the reader sees in even greater detail the forcefulness and resourcefulness of Launcelot's insistent movements and, accordingly, the romance world's responses to such an exercise of will. In the encounter between Launcelot and the huntress, Malory's text registers the coexistence of two worlds and two stories as well as the contradictions and even the antagonism that exist between Malory's two narrative modes. In this episode the obscurity—the impenetrable mystery of Malory's second world and second story—obtrudes into and then withdraws from the world of the first story suddenly and strangely, with a curious mixture of comic and real violence.

The tournament will be held "besydes Westmynster" (where Arthur holds his Christmas court), but Launcelot first travels with Lavaine "unto the good ermyte that dwelled in the foreyst of Wyndesore, whos name was sir Brastias" (643:3–4) in order to rest and prepare for the encounter. The forest is a world between worlds—between the world of "The Fair Maid of Astolat" episode and the actual tournament that Launcelot engages in "The Great

Tournament." Here Launcelot does not have to be "on guard," as he does even in the private world he enjoys with Guinevere. They travel so "that no creature wyste where he was becom but the noble men of hys blood" (643:7–8), and for a few days Launcelot enjoys an idyllic existence in the forest of Windsor, reposing by a "springing" and "burbling" well in the midst of unpopulated remoteness (643:11). Yet into this restful place comes "a lady that dwelled in that foreyste, and she was a grete hunteresse, and dayly she used to hunte" (643:13–14). That the character is a "hunteresse," not a hunter, is unique to Malory; in contrast to the male figure his sources give him, he introduces "a gentlewoman" who nevertheless lives on or just outside the gendered boundaries of his world.[30] This is not a woman who rides into men's battles by means of a token, like the Fair Maid, nor is she a female knight like the Britomart later given to us by Spenser. The huntress is rather the English ancestor of Spenser's Belphoebe: "And ever she bare her bowghe with her, and no men wente never with her, but allwayes women, and they were all shooters and cowde well kylle a dere at the stalke and at the treste. And they dayly beare bowys, arowis, hornys and wood-knyves, and many good doggis they had, bothe for the strenge and for a bate" (643:14–19). LaFarge notes that she is the descendant of the Arthurian Diana of French romances, a female predator who is "spontaneously generated by the heat of the hour or season and daytime slumber."[31] Nevertheless, she is a nice, mannerly predator who is singularly unresponsive to Launcelot's aura, unlike the other women who swoon before him.

Malory seems fascinated with this company of women, their hunting accoutrements, and especially the expert huntress herself. LaFarge is right that the huntress "combines the features of feminine and masculine in an alarming fashion,"[32] but it is Launcelot, not Malory, who is alarmed by her. Even though she and her company seem to wander accidentally into his narrative, Malory describes their hunting activities in great detail: "And so the hynde, whan he came to the welle, for heete she wente to soyle, and there she lay a grete whyle. And the dogge cam aftir and unbecaste aboute, for she had lost the verray parfyte fewte of the hynde. Ryght so cam that lady, the hunteres, that knew by her dogge that the hynde was at the soyle by that well, and thyder she cam streyte and founde the hynde" (643:27–32). In fact, with the amount of descriptive detail he provides about their movements, Malory seems to suggest that the wounding of Launcelot is an accident—"and anone as she had spyed hym she put a brode arow in her bowe, and shot at the hynde, and so she overshotte the hynde, and so by myssefortune the arow smote sir Launcelot in the thycke of the buttok over the barbys" (643:32–35)—though the inconsistent pronouns, if intentional, may complicate such a reading.[33]

Malory clearly manipulates his materials to open the possibility of seeing these women who travel without men as the female avengers of Elaine and her ilk. That Malory creates a female figure for this episode, that he inserts it immediately after "The Fair Maid of Astolat," that the huntress wounds Launcelot comically but also "pointedly" in the buttocks—all these factors might dispose us to read this episode as a moment of retributive justice on Launcelot. Yet the narrative also insists, as we have seen, that Launcelot loves as he must, and one cannot necessarily read such episodic connections into the structure of the narrative. Malory may wish us to take Launcelot's encounter with the huntress and her retinue in an incidental fashion—women like these live and roam around in Malory's forests, these sorts of accidents can happen to men sitting around in these forests, and Launcelot happened to be a man who got in the way. The narrative has some fun with Launcelot by letting him get in the way, thereby revealing a kind of comic vulnerability. The comedy further depends on the contrast between Launcelot's demonstrative, frustrated reaction and the huntress's imperturbable response. It also happens that Launcelot is not seriously wounded—because he is up and jousting the next day, the narrative seems facetious in reporting that Launcelot was "so sore hurte" (644:5–6).

Launcelot is made to confront a contiguous female society which has no particular regard for his own society or its male-centered chivalric principles; the nonchalance of the huntress deflates, with mild comic effect, Launcelot's chivalric ego. This is an odd, brief glimpse into a community unaffected by the events recounted in the narrative, a community generally unconcerned with the movements and motivations of the text's characters but one lying on or just outside the boundaries of the narrative itself. Malory gazes at this community quite closely as his eyes momentarily wander away from the society he has been examining throughout the narrative. He seems to admire, maybe even envy, these females' freedom of movement. Though a reader can explain their intrusion in the logic of the narrative, and though she or he might decide that the narrator maps them onto the argument of his narrative to, for example, avenge the Fair Maid, these women retain the freedom to leave when they will with no explanation or apology. The only trace they leave is a wound in Launcelot's derriere.

Their freedom stands in marked contrast to Launcelot's restrictions. Given the gendered, social rules of chivalric society, Launcelot's only recourse in the face of his wounding, once he sees that it was performed by a woman's hand, is to complain. In this episode Launcelot is prevented from reacting with the retributive violence he characteristically displays. Since his aggressor is a "jantillwoman," he can only lament and bear the injury as well as he can. Yet the circumstances make Launcelot sound almost childish: "I may calle myselff the moste unhappy man that lyvyth, for ever whan I wolde have faynyst worshyp there befallyth me ever som unhappy thynge" (644:12–14). Though the wound proves no hindrance to Launcelot's successful participation in the "Great Tournament," his reactions to the surprises the romance world can throw at him show a new, petulant testiness. If at one level his petulance provides comic contrast, at another it seems to be his response to the frequency with which women emerge as the agents by which the narrative wounds or immobilizes him. In the narrative's view Launcelot's choices regarding women impede his exercise of free will.

Malory's treatment of women reveals, not surprisingly, the deeply ingrained sexism of the male, Arthurian romance narrator, which the Wife of Bath addresses in her tale. In Malory women characters are still the narrative tools for discussing male concerns of power and politics. However, the autonomy and freedom of movement enjoyed by the huntress and her community prevent the narrator from using these women either to embrace or to oppose male structures of behavior and thus reempower the structures the women oppose. As he lingers over the details of their movements Malory seems to want to envision this other world where women do not move in subservience to male ideologies of rivalry and reciprocal violence. He briefly imagines a society that defines itself by principles of female disinterestedness, that maps itself in ways the narrator is unable to discern. True, they escape reciprocal physical violence or injury from Launcelot because they are women— Launcelot only curses at her, "The devyll made you a shoter" (643:40). Nevertheless, they seem not to expect any special treatment from him.

There appears to be no moral force—good or evil—behind the injury the women do to Launcelot. These women occupy a location in Malory's romance world in which they are accustomed to hunting without any danger of hurting any other mortal. Once the huntress discovers her accident, she seems simply to accept that her actions resulted in accidental violence, and she expects Launcelot to accept her explanation: "'Now mercy, fayre sir!' seyde the lady, 'I am a jantillwoman that usyth here in thys foreyste huntynge, and God knowyth I saw you nat, but as here was a barayne hynde at the soyle in thys welle. And I wente I had done welle, but my hande swarved'" (643:41–44). "The lady" expects "mercy" from Launcelot because she intended no evil; she expects no reciprocal aggression or judgment, nor even the verbal aggression or judgment she receives. The actions and movements of the huntress and her retinue reveal no desire for conquest over fellow mortals; they seem uninterested in honor or "worshipfulness" as moral values or objects of individual ambition. They are driven by none of the rules of conduct and follow none of the chivalric maps that Le Morte D'Arthur celebrates.[34]

It seems unlikely that Malory would want to celebrate the qualities that define the huntress's society—its self-contained alterity and refusal to enter into the rituals of chivalric negotiation—even if he means to use its members as a stick with which to beat Launcelot. In fact, what one can say about them resides in the differences one perceives between their community and male chivalric society. They seem to come from and return to "another place" similar to that where the Grail is and where Arthur is—a place outside the bounds of our knowledge. Yet the narrative can only partially inscribe them in its world. They cannot even be fully defined as one of the surprises that romance forests can throw at readers. Even more than their self-contained alterity, their femaleness, or their refusal to enter into chivalric rituals of negotiation, it is perhaps the ease with which they disappear back into the forest, out of the range of the narrator's focalization, that most clearly indicates that they cannot or will not be contained by the structures that organize Arthurian society for our interpretation.

After the narrative's chivalric world loses Arthur and his Round Table of knights to death and dissolution and Launcelot himself to the priesthood, Launcelot dies with the superlative praises of Sir Ector—Launcelot was "the curtest knyght," "the truest frende to [his] lovar" "the trewest lover, of a sinful man, that ever loved woman," "the kyndest man," "the godelyest persone," "the mekest man and the jentyllest," and "the sternest knyght to thy mortal foo" (725:16–26). Launcelot clearly is all of the things Ector says he is; in fact, he is so much the best that the narrative briefly envisions him as the ultimate healer of Arthur's society. Yet Launcelot is a healer only when he consciously becomes an instrument of God's power and mercy: "I beseche The of thy mercy.... Thou mayste yeff me power to hele thys syke knyght by the grete vertu and grace of The, but, Good Lorde, never of myselff" (668:23–26). The narrative inscribes Launcelot within the language of Christian paradox—he is best when he is lowliest, he is strongest when he is meekest. His potential for good in Arthur's community, demonstrated in the episode where he heals Sir Urry, only emphasizes the loss this community will experience when his desire for Guinevere must finally and publicly counter his loyalty to Arthur.

Once Arthur is gone, Launcelot has no other place to go; for vague reasons the narrative can or will not trace his movements further, even though the story is at least "a twelve-monethe" (669:27–28) away from its conclusion. The narrator says he will "overlepe grete bookis of sir Launcelot ... bycause I have loste the very mater of Shevalere de Charyot" (669:22–23, 32). What he means by "loste" is difficult to say. Among the things it can mean seems to be that we lose sight of Launcelot. He will continue to perform "grete adventures" (669:23) while riding in his "chariot" but the narrative will visualize none of this. When he returns to the narrative's view, he will be seen as a catalyst of destruction for Arthur's society as the narrative finally takes up *Le Morte D'Arthur*. In this final segment Launcelot will be forced to choose between the people he loves (and the codes of behavior they represent) and the people he will hurt (680:3 ff.). The destruction unleashed by Launcelot's choice is terrible and thorough. Though he by no means bears the entire blame, after Arthur's death he is the narrative's chief focal point for the pointlessness of any further discussion about Arthurian empire. His is a "sorow [that] may never have ende" (723:23) and a life centered in penance. There is no particular good for him to do in the world anymore; he can only mourn for the evil he has done.

Once again, the narrative marks and maps Launcelot's movements, but in this world of penance it does so with a sense of finality. After hearing of Modred's treachery, Launcelot lands at Dover with a substantial host to avenge "firste" Gawain's death "and secundly" the terrible assault on Arthur and Guinevere, only to find that he is too late (718:32–35). Dover Castle, solid in its role defending Britain's border, underscores the tragedy of Arthurian society's demise by being marked in the narrative as the locale of Gawain's tomb—an emblem of the inner unravelings of an outwardly strong society. Launcelot, lying "two nyghtes upon [Gawain's] tumbe, in prayers and dolefull wepynge" (719:28–29), begins to be inscribed into this landscape of faded heroism. The narrative watches Launcelot travel not to Winchester or Windsor, but to obscure new places that commemorate the recent fragmentation of Arthur's kingdom. Searching for Guinevere, Launcelot after a week of travel finds her at "a nunry" (720:5). The narrative has previously identified this as a nunnery at Amesbury, but here it refuses to name the place. It also refuses to name the place where Launcelot, weeping after his sorrowful parting from Guinevere, arrives after a day and a night's journey—"an ermytage and a chappel [which] stode betwyxte two clyffes" (721:22). Here Launcelot finds Bedivere and the Bishop of Canterbury, the Bishop embracing an existence thoroughly withdrawn from his days in church administration, and here Launcelot, too, will live out the remainder of his days.

The narrative seems to require that Launcelot reject the kind of life that produced so much destruction in favor of the peaceful, "perfect" life of the cloister. He comes here seeking ostensibly the "perfection" which Guinevere seeks at Amesbury—she tells Launcelot that she has cloistered herself "to gete [her] soule hele" so that she might repent and be saved "on Doomesday" (720:18–22)—but they each repent differently. Guinevere styles her penance as constant attentiveness to God, shutting herself completely off from the life and more especially the love "thorow [which] ...

ys [her] moste noble lorde slayne" (720:16–17). She must be absolute about her penance because of the power Launcelot still holds over her—she swoons three times upon seeing him. She must send him away forever, refusing even to kiss him one last time as he leaves (721:12–15). This absolute break from the past means to expel Launcelot from any part of her present or her future. Yet Launcelot's penance seems to be a last and lasting act of fidelity toward Guinevere—"And therfore, lady, sythen ye have taken you to perfeccion, I must nedys take me to perfection, of ryght" (721:5–6).

Launcelot sought Guinevere here in the nunnery, hoping that she might become his "royame"; but since she is "dysposed" to the cloister, he will seek a similar life (721:7–12). In his willingness to leave the chivalric life, Launcelot may evidence some sincerity in his desire to repent of the destruction he has brought on Arthurian society. Nevertheless, the life he chooses for himself—the cloister—is, as he tells her, an act of faithfulness to her: "Nay madame, wyte you well that shall I never do [marry another, as she instructs him to do], for I shall ever be so false unto you of that I have promysed. But the selff desteny that ye have takyn you to, I woll take me to, for the pleasure of Jesu, and ever for you I caste me specially to pray" (720:35–39). His life in the cloister will be "for the pleasure of Jesu!" but he explicitly models his choice on Guinevere's and will make her, not his own sins, the chief subject of his prayers. He says little here of purifying himself in this life, though he later seems consistent in devoting himself to "prayers and fastynges" (721:35). At this moment, however, he styles his penance as an imitation of Guinevere's penance by which he remains faithful to her, not only by refusing to pursue any other woman and by staying away from her, as she requested, but also by following her into the life she chooses for herself.[35] Guinevere's manner of life becomes a substitute for Guinevere herself.

The paradoxical logics of Launcelot's life, then, bring him into a state of virtual immobility as he directs all his energies to penitential contemplation of the past, to "prayers and fastynges." The text places him where he can do no more harm, so he can remain true, after a fashion, to Guinevere, and can demonstrate extreme regret for his destructive actions of the past. The final pages of *Le Morte D'Arthur* read, on the one hand, as a conscious corrective to Launcelot's (and Guinevere's) earlier desires. As a final, supreme act of penitence, Launcelot, "in remyssyon of his synnes," will travel back to Amesbury just after Guinevere dies and will carry her to Glastonbury in order "to burye hir by her husbond" (722:22–26). The text has Launcelot reinstate Guinevere at Arthur's side, displacing himself permanently in an apparent admission of his guilt.

On the other hand, the narrative seems to illustrate a kind of aimlessness in the lives of its male figures. Even though it speaks of Launcelot's performing important religious duties, engaging in the study of "bookes," and doing "lowly al maner of servyce" (722:14–16), we see none of this. In contrast to his earlier life of chivalric service, readers do not see that the world is any better because of his "lowly" service as a cleric. Launcelot's textual life seems over. Other knights with no other places to go follow Launcelot into this life. Even Bors joins the growing community, as do Launcelot's relatives (725:36). Though the text will speak of a new age of English chivalry, the reader hears nothing of it, except that Constantine wishes Launcelot's relatives to stay. According to "the Frensshe book" Launcelot's labors may be over, though he will instruct his remaining relatives to leave Britain for the Holy Land, there to take up their chivalric battles against "the myscreantes, or Turkes" (726:44–727:8). Launcelot, like Galahad and Percival before him, approaches spiritual apotheosis by rejecting chivalry, but chivalry remains the discursive realm where the texts Malory reads return to explore the active life of Christianity.

Malory will read these texts for us no longer. With the death of Launcelot he looks back, not knowing whether to laugh with the bishop of Canterbury when he sees Launcelot in a vision entering heaven in the company of numerous angels, or whether to join in the "Wepynge and wryngyng of handes, and the grettest dole [Launcelot's fellow knights] made that ever made men" (724:17–36). If the passings of Arthur, Guinevere, and especially Launcelot are meant to evoke the eucatastrophe ("a fortunate turn that fulfills the most desired possibilities") that Lenz identifies as the typical end of the "success story"—that is, in the final analysis, the romance—it is as indistinctly and uncertainly rendered as practically everything else in Malory's concluding pages.[36] Ambivalent about his narrative world and unable (or unwilling) to talk about anything beyond the world of Arthurian chivalry, especially when it loses its most exemplary figure, Malory turns from his books to thoughts of his own death and "delyveraunce" (726:17). His authorial self-consciousness is so fully inscribed within the activity of reading and recounting the work of chivalric structures in literary images of society that death is an appropriate characterization of this narrative's end. Malory barely begins, it seems, to imagine for himself a world outside the very structures whose untenability and destructiveness weigh upon his consciousness. What characterizes this "deliverance" Malory, again, cannot say, but the much-deferred ending to Le Morte D'Arthur does not seem entirely unwelcome.

NOTES

1. P. J. C. Field, "Time and Elaine of Astolat," *Studies in Malory*, ed. James W. Spisak (Kalamazoo, Mich., 1985), p. 231.

2. William Caxton, preface, in Thomas Malory, *Malory: Works*, ed. Eugène Vinaver (London, 1971), p. xiv.

3. The hermit "knew nat in sertayne that [the body he buries] was veryly the body of kynge Arthur," brought to him by "a numbir of ladyes" there at Glastonbury Monastery. Bedivere surmises circumstantially that this body was the body of Arthur and, accordingly, "made hit to be wrytten" (Malory, p. 717, lines 26–28). I use this edition for all Malory citations, unless otherwise noted, and incorporate references for each citation by page and line number parenthetically in the text.

4. Malory sounds somewhat like Caxton's preface, which lists the "many remembraunces" of Arthur's existence (his tomb, his place in books written about him, "Gauwayn's skulle and Cradok's mantel," the Round Table in the Great Hall at Winchester) that lie scattered "in dyvers places of Englond" (Caxton, p. xiv).

5. See also W. R. J. Barron, *English Medieval Romance* (London, 1987), p. 149.

6. Joseph M. Lenz, *The Promised End: Romance Closure in the Gawain-Poet, Malory, Spenser, and Shakespeare* (Bern, 1986), p. x.

7. George Stewart, "English Geography in Malory's *Morte D'arthur*," *Modern Language Review* 30 (1935): 204.

8. Barron, p. 149.

9. See Sue Ellen Holbrook, "Malory's Identification of Camelot and Winchester," in Spisak, ed., p. 13; and Earl R. Anderson, "Camelot, Winchester, and 'The Chirche of Seynte Stevins,'" *Neuphilologische Mitteilungen* 92 (1991): 211. Beyond the historical/ideological advantages this identification offers Malory's text (because Winchester has a longer royal history than London), this link has been explained by the great Round Table that has hung in the Great Hall in Winchester since at least Malory's time; the table may date from the latter half of the thirteenth century. Holbrook argues that this identification has more to do with Malory's following John Hardying's *Chronicle* or with casual knowledge, but Anderson defends Malory's firsthand knowledge of Winchester.

10. 'Astolat' in modern English should probably be 'Ascolat'. See Toshiyuki Takamiya, "'Ascolat' in the Winchester Malory," in *Aspects of Malory*, ed. Toshiyuki Takamiya and Derek Brewer (Cambridge, 1981), pp. 125–26. I will call the town Astolat in keeping with Vinaver's spelling.

11. Stewart, p. 206.

12. Ibid.

13. Catherine LaFarge, "The Head of the Huntress: Repetition and Malory's *Morte Darthur*," in *New Feminist Discourses: Critical Essays on Theories and Texts*, ed. Isobel Armstrong (London, 1992), p. 274.

14. This opening portion, in which Launcelot and Guinevere discuss strategy, is one of Malory's invented links between the sequential episodes he inherits from his sources.

15. Mador had falsely accused Guinevere of poisoning Gawain; Launcelot in disguise (because he was in disfavor with Guinevere) consequently defeats him in a trial of arms. Before the Sir Mador episode, she had reproached and banished Launcelot for championing other women's causes, which he had done not only "for the plesure of oure

Lorde, Jesu Cryst" but also "to eschew the sclawndir and noyse" of those who suspected his relationship with Guinevere (611:22–26).

16. The text seems to treat Launcelot according to the rules of "ritual logic," as Tzvetan Todorov outlines it in *The Poetics of Prose* (Ithaca, N.Y., 1977), though I would add that there are several "logics" written into his characterization.

17. Charles Moorman argues that the "Ascolat story takes place in a larger pattern that illustrates failure in love" (*The Book of King Arthur* [Lexington, Ky., 1965], p. 25).

18. Mark Lambert argues that Lavaine and Elaine are equally infatuated with Launcelot (*Malory: Style and Vision in "Le Morte Darthur"* [New Haven, Conn., 1984], p. 104, n. 48).

19. Earl Anderson states that "compared with Elaine in the *Mort Artu*, Malory's Elayne is assertive and frank and spirited" ("Malory's Fair Maid of Astolat," *Neuphilologische Mitteilungen* 87 [1986]: 250).

20. Holbrook indicates that Malory's Winchester shares many details with the actual Winchester: "a location in the south, a forest, a meadow land for a tilting ground, a river, a major road, a royal castle, and a great minister" (n. 9 above, p. 21).

21. P. D. A. Harvey, *Medieval Maps* (Toronto, 1991), p. 7.

22. Ibid., pp. 7–9.

23. Ibid., p. 19.

24. We know nothing of the Gough Map's origins or its use; it is unlike any other map of the period, conveying, as Harvey explains, "a whole network of roads, linking towns that are correctly placed on or between the branches of a quite elaborately drawn river system.... Viewed as a collection of itineraries it is extremely accurate, and places on different routes are mostly in a correct relationship to each other, but there seems to have been no attempt to maintain a consistent scale" (p. 73). The scholarship of Stewart, discussed above, and P. J. C. Field has nicely demonstrated Malory's capacity for representing local British geography with relative accuracy; see particularly Field, "Malory's Place Names: Westminster Bridge and Virvyn," *Notes and Queries* 34 (1987): 292–95.

25. In defense of his own geographical scholarship, Yi-Fu Tuan writes that geography "is also a humane study committed to interpret the meaning of human attachments and aspirations.... As we study the human use of the earth, moral issues emerge at every point if only because, to make any change at all, force must be used and the use of force raises questions of right and wrong" (*Morality and Imagination: Paradoxes of Progress* [Madison, Wis., 1989], pp. vii–viii).

26. Malory differs from his sources in immediately following Launcelot's departure from Elaine with the funeral barge scene.

27. Anderson, "Malory's Fair Maid of Astolat," p. 241.

28. See Field, "Time and Elaine of Astolat" (n. 1 above), pp. 231–36. Field argues that her use of the word 'appele' (when she berates Lavaine and Bors for helping Launcelot try to return to his arms too early) makes specific reference to a fifteenth-century law that allowed women to appeal for redress if their husbands died in their arms. Field finds in her use of this word her "excess" with regard to her love for Launcelot, who is not her husband (pp. 233–35).

29. See Patricia Parker, *Inescapable Romance: Studies in the Poetics of a Mode* (Princeton, N.J., 1979). Borrowing from Lee Patterson, Parker introduces the notion of *dilatio* or "dilation" (deferral of the end) as the defining narrative motion of romance.

30. In his *The Medieval Imagination*, trans. Arthur Goldhammer (Chicago, 1988), Jacques Le Goff notes that the forest in the medieval West functions much as the desert in the medieval East does, as "a refuge, a hunting ground, a place of adventure, impenetrable to those who lived in cities and villages or worked in fields" (p. 110). In

England, the forest is also "a place where in a sense the hierarchy of feudal society broke down." "Broken down" hierarchies are not exactly what Launcelot finds, as we shall see, but Le Goff's sense of the English medieval forest as a place which "exists only in relation to that which is not forest" (p. 122) is a helpful starting point for my analysis.

31. LaFarge (n. 13 above), p. 267.

32. Ibid., p. 266.

33. The Winchester Manuscript has inconsistent pronouns for the "hynde," but D. S. Brewer emends "he came to the welle" to "she" and "had spyed hym" to "her" (*Malory: The Morte Darthur*, ed. and trans. D. S. Brewer, York Medieval Texts [Evanston, Ill., 1970], p. 72). I would argue that a deliberately ambiguous rendering of the gender of the hunted object here is enough of a possibility that the passage should be left as the Winchester MS has it.

34. The society Malory encounters here contrasts with Bercilak's faery community in *Sir Gawain and the Green Knight*, though in both cases Arthurian society's encounter with a foreign, mysterious community highlights its vulnerability to moral and physical injury.

35. As Geraldine Heng observes, Launcelot "subsumes his identity within [Guinevere's] own" ("Enchanted Ground: The Feminine Subtext in Malory," in *Courtly Literature Culture and Context*, ed. Keith Busby and Erik Kooper [Amsterdam, 1990], p. 288).

36. Lenz (n. 6 above), p. xi.

CLINTON MACHANN

Tennyson's King Arthur and the Violence of Manliness

Beginning with Tennyson's contemporaries, one of the targets for hostile criticism of *Idylls of the King* was his adaptation of the warrior-king protagonist portrayed in Malory's *Le Morte Darthur*. Swinburne mockingly referred to the "Morte d'Albert, or Idylls of the Prince Consort" and proclaimed that Tennyson had "lowered the note and deformed the outline of the Arthurian story, by reducing Arthur to the level of a wittol, Guenevere to the level of a woman of intrigue, and Launcelot to the level of a 'co-respondent.'" Henry Crabb Robinson thought Tennyson's Arthur was "unfit to be an epic-hero" and Henry James called him a prig. T. S. Eliot asserted that Tennyson had adapted "this great British epic material—in Malory's handling hearty, outspoken and magnificent—to suitable reading for a girls' school."[1] Clearly the gender issue is central to all these comments—contemporary readers were dissatisfied with the way Tennyson portrayed Arthur's "manhood," a problem of which Tennyson was well aware, and many modern readers either voice concerns similar to those of Swinburne and T. S. Eliot or offer readings of the *Idylls* which in my view seriously distort Tennyson's attempt to explore gender issues. Tennyson's modern editor and interpreter Christopher Ricks makes no serious attempt to defend Tennyson against the traditional critics who ridicule the Poet Laureate for making Arthur a wimp, something less than a real man.[2] On the other hand,

From *Victorian Poetry* 38, no. 2 (Summer 2000). © 2000 by West Virginia University.

more politically attuned critics taking a feminist or gender studies approach either ignore or deal inadequately with the question of Arthur's masculinity.[3]

After offering a preliminary argument for the appropriateness and value of a masculist approach to Victorian literature in general, I will discuss the issue of Arthur's masculinity and explain why I believe it is central to the meaning of Tennyson's *Idylls*. In particular, I will focus on the problem of male violence, which in various manifestations dominates the narrative from beginning to end.

1

In his widely read and influential book *The Victorian Frame of Mind, 1830–1870* (1957), Walter Houghton suggests that his study of the "general character" or temperament of the age has a special significance for his readers "because to look into the Victorian mind is to see some primary sources of the modern mind." In the mid-fifties Houghton expressed his opposition to prevailing negative and patronizing attitudes toward the Victorians, but even earlier works like Jerome H. Buckley's *The Victorian Temper: A Study in Literary Culture* (1951) and John Holloway's *The Victorian Sage: Studies in Argument* (1953) had begun to create an academic vogue for Victorian studies at least partially based on the premise that the ideas, values, and life philosophies of early-to-mid-Victorian intellectuals and artists anticipated fundamental intellectual and aesthetic problems of the mid-twentieth century. A decade later, the popularity of works like George Levine and William Madden's edition of essays *The Art of Victorian Prose* (1968) demonstrated the continuing force of this idea, at least in English literature graduate programs in American universities.[4]

By the early seventies, the now well-established tradition of the special relevance of Victorian literature was incorporating new voices that over the next two decades would profoundly transform the field of Victorian studies. Houghton, like many of the other scholars taking what now was seen as a traditionalist, humanist approach to Victorian literature, had focused on ideological and moral dilemmas associated with the sudden changes brought on by industrialization, urbanization, religious ferment, the growth of science and technology, and so on. Now, by focusing on gender issues, feminist scholars were beginning to interrogate the ways in which Victorian literature and culture had been studied. Elaine Showalter, Sandra Gilbert, Susan Gubar, Martha Vicinus, Mary Poovey, Margaret Homans, Judith Newton, and Cora Kaplan are only a few of the important writers who helped to make feminism dominant in Victorian studies by the nineties. Although feminist scholars have been associated with a variety of innovative theoretical methodologies, from Marxism to Lacanian psychoanalysis and the poststructuralism of Derrida and Foucault, it is the ideology of feminism and the methodological emphasis on gender study that have driven this transformation. Like Houghton, Victorianists are still fascinated by the prospect of finding clues to contemporary culture in literary productions of the Victorian era, but now this project is conceived in terms of understanding how gender is socially constructed and how gender issues are central to all literary and cultural discourse. Antony Harrison and Beverly Taylor's representative 1992 edition of essays entitled *Gender and Discourse in Victorian Literature and Art* is grounded in the belief that, by the nineteen-nineties, feminist critical inquiry, although far from monolithic, offered a coherent, highly developed, and, in fact, dominant approach to Victorian literature in contemporary academic discourse.

Central to the feminist program is the proposition that the supposed universal human nature postulated by Victorian poets, sages, and novelists (and by Houghton and other traditional Victorianists for that matter) is a false universal, one closely associated with the experience of white European males (but not women) of a certain class and with a patriarchal social order that embodies instabilities, contradictions, and hypocrisies of various kinds. It is generalized that "with regard to institutional modes of discourse and the power structures of Victorian society, women for the most part constituted a suppressed and marginalized underclass whose victimization was a political fact of life resisted in diverse ways or complexly exploited by artists sensitive to the relations among power, authority, and gender."[5]

However, even if one accepts the idea that feminine experience was systematically ignored or suppressed within the old paradigm of supposed universal human experience, it is by no means clear that gendered masculine experience has been adequately or authentically explored within that paradigm. In fact, even a perfunctory analysis from a masculist point of view suggests that issues of masculinity have been suppressed as fully as feminist ones in traditional humanist discourse. Men's studies focusing on homosexuality (because they too could be seen as running counter to heterosexual male traditions) were the first to be legitimated by the feminist enterprise, but recently analyses of "mainstream" masculinities have become more common. An example is Herbert Sussman's study of Victorian masculinities (1995). Even though Sussman's work is based on Eve Sedgwick's scheme of homosocial desire (1985) and, like much feminist, poststructuralist criticism, ultimately derives from the history of sexuality as formulated by Michel Foucault, Sussman rejects a monolithic, essentialist model of heterosexual male experience and attempts to analyze the conflicts and anxieties he finds in the masculinity of traditionalist writers like Thomas

Carlyle. Sussman's use of the plural masculinities "stresses the multiple possibilities of such social formations, the variability in the gendering of the biological male, and the range of such constructions over time." James Eli Adams, in another recent study of Victorian male authors, similarly analyzes "competing constructions of normative masculinity within a single historical moment."[6]

Although a few interesting studies of Victorian masculinities have begun to emerge, surprisingly little attention has been given to such seemingly obvious topics as the centrality of male violence in literary constructions of manhood. The *Idylls* have long been read as a narrative in which Tennyson traces the rise and fall of a state based on Christian ideals. F. E. L. Priestley, for example, is unequivocal in his articulation of this view: "The tragic collapse of Arthur's work in the *Idylls* is an allegory of the collapse of society, of nation, and of individual, which must follow the rejection of spiritual values." Taking a cue from Tennyson and his son Hallam, readers, have focused on the war between "Sense" and "Soul" and on Arthur as the embodiment of the "highest ideals."[7] However, Tennyson's representation of male violence, central to the narrative throughout, is complicated by tensions and contradictions that subvert the idealized code of chivalry and imply that the foundations of Western civilization are much less stable than commonly assumed. Tennyson's reputation as poet laureate and spokesman for middle-class Victorian values has obscured his insights into the fundamental instability of Victorian masculinities. If we continue to read the Victorians against our own contemporary experience, this is a particularly apt historical moment to engage this issue: the apparent transformation of Western concepts of war and male militarization— including (in the United States, at least) gender integration of the military and detachment of war from the idea of human sacrifice[8]—is one of many recent striking phenomena associated with shifting and problematic gender identities, with implications that are as yet poorly understood.

Given the proliferation of gender studies in recent years and the introduction of related terminology that is not always used consistently among literary critics, some clarification of my basic assumptions and use of key terms is in order. I use the terms "masculine," "masculinity," and "masculinities" to refer to socially constructed, historically specific definitions of gender. This does not mean that I am a "pure" constructivist, because I assume that a prior biological reality exists and that gender differences ultimately derive from an interaction of innate qualities and cultural concepts.[9] Nevertheless, if social constructions of gender are not entirely arbitrary, it seems obvious that a great deal of variability is possible. By including the plural of "masculinity" here, I want to emphasize my agreement with recent "masculist" or "masculinist" critics like Sussman that an "emphasis on the multiplicity, the plurality of male gender formations is crucial not only to counter the still pervasive essentialist view of maleness, but also to deconstruct the monolithic view of masculinity ... that, with seeming disregard to the success of feminism in exploding such essentialist and monolithic thinking about women, still pervades ... discussion of men, particularly of men in the nineteenth century" (p. 8). Even though we could probably classify Tennyson's intellectual concept of gender, like that of most Victorians, male and female, as "essentialist," Tennyson demonstrated, throughout his career, his uneasiness with dominant Victorian constructions of "manhood" or "manliness." (From my point of view, these are "masculinities"; however, in Victorian usage the term "masculinity" is more often associated with male sexuality and power.[10]) Manhood, a key term in the *Idylls*, implies virility but is not primarily an extension of biological maleness; it is rather a strategy for controlling or stifling man's natural bestiality as civilization advances. Tennyson's deeply felt fear is that manhood as he understood it—despite its positive associations with religion, moral values, and duty—is ultimately unstable and ineffective.

Houghton and other traditional Victorianists conventionally divided the larger "age," beginning with the Reform Bill of 1832 and ending with the death of Queen Victoria, into three periods: the early period or Time of Troubles (approximately 1832–48), characterized by social ferment and the Condition of England Question; the Mid-Victorian period (approximately 1848–70), a time of economic prosperity or complacency and religious controversy; and the late period (approximately 1870–1901), marked by aestheticism and decadence or the decay of Victorian values. Versions of a tripartite scheme adapted so far by literary men's studies as a branch of feminist gender studies have included the following formulations: 1) early Victorian attempts to define a masculine ideal of bourgeois respectability through ascetic discipline (Carlyle's monasticism, Evangelical and Tractarian versions of a life devoted to higher values and usefulness); 2) more aggressive mid-Victorian models of masculinity associated with British imperialism, notably Kingsley's "muscular Christianity," which celebrated animal spirits and sexual energy as well as robust physical strength and enjoyment of life, while retaining a need for self-discipline and self-denial; and, finally, 3) late Victorian eclecticism, which accommodated Pater's "aesthetic historicism" and finally saw the emergence of a previously forbidden homoeroticism. (It is assumed of all three periods, of course, that even normative masculinities are "multiple, complex, and unstable constructions" [Adams, p. 3].) While composing the *Idylls* over a period of more than fifty years, Tennyson was engaged in the search for an ideal code of masculinity that would serve to suppress the natural depravity associated with maleness through a rigorous program of social discipline and self-discipline but would also encourage the release of (properly channelled) male aggression in a manner compatible with the maintenance of military power and an expansionist state ethic. (The management of a healthy sexual energy is another matter and highly problematical for Tennyson.) Finally, in an indirect way at least, Tennyson's experiments with androgyny helped to prepare the way for the third phase cited above, although Tennyson of course remained hostile to all varieties of aestheticism that seemed to undermine social and moral order.

2

As is well known, Tennyson was fascinated by the King Arthur legend from the beginning of his poetic career. Hallam Tennyson's quotation of his father about the "vision of Arthur" that had come upon him "when, little more than a boy, I first lighted upon Malory" has been circulated by generations of critics. However, Roger Simpson has shown in detail that multiple sources of the Arthurian legend were available to Tennyson prior to his first formal use of it in his poetry in the early 1830s.[11] Clearly Tennyson was interested in Arthur primarily as a mythic, not a historical, figure. In his "Palace of Art" (1832), for example, we find "mythic Uther's deeply-wounded son / ... dozing in the vale of Avalon, / And watched by weeping queens" (ll. 105–108).[12] Many critics have seen Arthur as a Christ-figure.[13] At the same time, however, Tennyson wished to represent Arthur not as a supernatural hero but a man who had affinities with his dead friend Arthur Hallam (and with the "uncrowned king," Prince Albert, as the Dedication of 1862 makes clear). In introducing *The Holy Grail and Other Poems* (1869), Tennyson wrote that Arthur is "meant to be a man who spent himself in the cause of honour, duty and self-sacrifice, who felt and aspired with his nobler knights, though with a stronger and clearer conscience.... God had not made since Adam was, the man more perfect than Arthur." The 1891 addition of the phrase "Ideal manhood closed in real man" describing Arthur in the epilogue "To the Queen" was, according to Hallam Tennyson, the last correction to the *Idylls*, made because "my father thought that perhaps he had not made the real humanity of the King sufficiently clear" (*Memoir*, 2:129).

"Morte d'Arthur" (1842) was the first published poem that would be incorporated into the *Idylls* (although the later *Lancelot and Elaine* is to some extent a retelling of "The Lady of Shalott," originally published in 1832). However, "Morte d'Arthur" had been written during the period 1833–34, like several other key poems in Tennyson's oeuvre, "under the shock" of his friend Hallam's death, and it is easy to see a connection between the Christ-like Arthur and the Hallam of *In Memoriam*, who, like Jesus, exhibited a manhood combined with female grace.[14]

Although Tennyson wrote most of the material finally incorporated into this final version of the *Idylls* (1889) during two relatively intense phases of creativity, 1856–59 and 1868–74, it is fair to say that he was enthralled by the Arthurian subject throughout his career and that in a sense the Arthurian project dominated his whole career. Early in the process, Tennyson was interested in exploring issues of creativity and the relation of the artist to the world in the richly symbolic (but not strictly allegorical) story of the Lady of Shalott. Also very early he was drawn to the story of the adulterous Lancelot and Guinevere, and then a little later to contrasting stories of "true and false" ladies. However, the figure of Arthur was always central to the *Idylls* project: though he is in a formal sense the protagonist only in the first and last idylls, his presence dominates the entire series and gives a unified meaning to the story as a whole. As John D. Rosenberg observes, Tennyson's original "Morte d'Arthur," drafted in 1833, revised in 1835, and published in 1842, was the "germ of the whole ... instinctually right in tone and design" and, with the initial framing section added in 1869, remained in this form to the end, though Tennyson continually expanded and substantially revised the larger poem over the decades.[15] In a sense the ending is implicit in the beginning of any narrative, but Tennyson literally wrote the ending first. At the beginning of "Morte d'Arthur," the great catastrophe of the final battle already has taken place—Arthur's order of the Round Table has been definitively destroyed and nearly all of the knights are dead (an absent, repentant Lancelot apparently lives on to become a holy man, and Bedivere survives in the role of story-teller). The additional 169 lines added at the beginning when "Morte" became *The Passing of Arthur* in 1869 supply a description of the last bloody one-on-one encounter between Arthur and Modred and intensify the original effect of desolation.

In this essay I am considering the *Idylls* as a unified whole, referring to the final, complete version first published in 1889, with the exception of a few instances in which the order of composition may help to clarify a point. However, I want to point out that, beyond the intensified images of death and destruction added to the final idyll, the general tendency in Tennyson's revisions and additions through the years was to place increasing stress on patterns of violence and the issue of "manhood." The *Geraint and Enid* story, amplified and divided into two individual idylls in 1873 (part one was renamed *The Marriage of Geraint* in 1886), and *Balin and Balan*, the last-written idyll, originally published in 1885, are focused, in the first instance, on an extreme case of masculine gender identification and its relation to formulaic violence, and, in the second, on the fear of an innate male capacity for irrational violence and its relation to madness.

3

Gilbert's description of Arthur as a "female king" and his contention that Tennyson, preoccupied with the idea of "woman as cosmic destructive principle," meant to show in the *Idylls* that Arthur's ideal community is destroyed by "an irrepressible female libidinousness ... released by the withdrawal of patrilineal authority,"[16] is based on a reading of the poem that misses Tennyson's focus on the problematics of male sexuality and capacity for irrational violence. Most obviously, there is nothing in the poem to suggest that Arthur is not a male (unless he is a supernatural god-figure in the form of a man). It is his gender, not his sex, that has seemed problematical to some readers. From the beginning of his career Tennyson was sensitive to his own ambiguous social status as a male poet in the Romantic tradition, associated with the suspiciously feminized qualities of imaginative inwardness, emotive openness, isolation from the aggressive "entrepreneurial manhood" valorized by bourgeois ideals.[17] He experimented with representations of androgyny throughout his career, most notably in his long poem *The Princess* (1847), but even there, the essential difference between men and women is finally upheld: "For woman is not undevelopt man, / But diverse ... / Not like to like, but like in difference" (7.259–262). This story of a princess who founds an all-female college for the purpose of emancipating women is described by Marion Shaw as the "most comprehensive" of the literary works dealing with the "women-and-marriage question" at mid century. However, Shaw also comments on Tennyson's "acute anxiety concerning male sexual needs and definitions" and refers to Kate Millett's observation that the poem "takes fright at its own daring and turns away from the logical pursuit of its argument" for fear of the consequences of women's independence (p. 42). It seems to me that the best explanation of Tennyson's drawing back from androgyny as an ideal is not a generalized male fear of the "new woman," but a recognition of the source of the most important and finally insurmountable differences between men and women: male violence and the exclusively male role of the warrior. For Tennyson it is inconceivable that Princess Ida and her (otherwise Amazonian) followers should actually arm themselves and physically defend their College against the Prince and his warriors. (However "feminized" the cross-dressing Prince may be, he is still a warrior and is expected to submit himself to physical danger and possible death on the battlefield.) The Prince's militaristic father may be a patriarchal ogre (even to Tennyson), but he understands this essential difference.[18] The women are of course represented by male mercenaries in the staged battle of evenly matched forces. It is no accident that the Princess is overcome with sympathy for the wounded Prince and falls in love with him as she nurses him back to health.

For Tennyson, the image of a wounded warrior under the care of his lover/nurse is laden with symbolism: it is the ultimate representation of tenderness and romantic love between the sexes, and it is also the ultimate representation of gender difference. In the *Idylls* we see it most memorably in Elaine's unequivocal but hopeless love for the wounded Lancelot, who cannot fulfill his proper role as knightly lover to his loving nurse because of his improper commitment to the Queen. The noble but unfairly suspicious Geraint proudly keeps aloof from his wife Enid as he kills and mutilates one challenger after another until, after secretly bleeding under his armor, he falls from his horse and she tenderly swathes his wound with the veil of faded silk she has torn off her face. Later, after Geraint has been transported to the castle of Earl Doorm and has awakened to find "his own dear bride propping his head, / And chaffing his faint hands, and calling to him; / And felt the warm tears falling on his face" (*Geraint and Enid*, ll. 583–585), he continues to feign sleep in order to savor her display of devotion. Significantly, in *The Passing of Arthur* the (supposedly) dying Arthur is not comforted by his unfaithful wife, who is far away in a convent, but by the fantasy-queens who will accompany him on his journey to Avalon. In any case, the ultimate gender reversal that would be represented by, let us say, the image of a wounded female warrior, nursed by the man for whom she has fought and is perhaps dying, is simply unimaginable for Tennyson or any other Victorian writer.[19]

Among the most fundamental gender distinctions implicit in the *Idylls* are those associated with the "violence against women" taboo enforced by the code of chivalry. The absolute nature of this taboo is represented in the *Geraint and Enid* idyll when the wounded Geraint, whose condition has continued to deteriorate so that he is presumed to be dying or already dead, is miraculously revived by the bitter cry of Enid when the Earl, frustrated with Enid's failure to respond to his advances, "unknightly with flat hand, / *However lightly*, smote her on the cheek" (l. 717, emphasis mine):

> This heard Geraint, and grasping at this sword,
> (It lay beside him in the hollow shield),
> Made but a single bound, and with a sweep of it
> Shore through the swarthy neck, and like a ball
> The russet-bearded head rolled on the floor.
> So died Earl Doorm by him he counted dead.   (ll. 724–729)

In *Pelleas and Ettarre*, Gawain, casual about most of his knightly vows but to whom violence against women is unthinkable, advises his younger and more idealistic colleague on the way to handle the servants sent by Ettarre to restrain her persistent lover:

> "Why, let my lady bind me if she will,
> And let my lady beat me if she will:
> But an she send her delegate to thrall
> These fighting hands of mine-Christ kill me then
> But I will slice him handless by the wrist,
> And let my lady sear the stump for him,
> Howl as he may." (ll. 326–332)

Since manhood in the *Idylls* is defined primarily in terms of the warrior role, and the most fundamental duty of the knightly warrior is to protect women, a female knight is inconceivable. It is not primarily the fear of an armed "Joan of Arc" figure usurping the role of the male warrior but rather the "violence against women" taboo and the fear of the mutilation and death of women on the battlefield that accounts for the sharply defined gender boundaries here. A chivalric code emphasizing gallantry toward and protection of women along with the traditional virtues of loyalty, valor, mercy, modesty, friendship, and honor, is most basic among the "timeless" ideals readers have seen at the heart of Arthur's order of the Round Table, and this is not surprising since nineteenth-century British culture was saturated with images of medieval chivalry, images which were "absorbed into the patterns of everyday life."[20] The idea of an Arthur with the qualities of a Victorian gentleman is one which closely connects the *Idylls* with popular culture.

As John Ruskin observes in *Unto this Last*, the source of honor for the traditional soldier or warrior ultimately is self-sacrifice, not his willingness and ability to kill the enemy: "The soldier's trade, verily and essentially, is not slaying, but being slain."[21] Appropriately enough, Tennyson's Geraint, eventually restored to a healthy appreciation for his blameless wife, finally "crowned / A happy life with a fair death, and fell / Against the heathen of the Northern Sea / In battle" (*Geraint and Enid*, ll. 966–969).

Arthur himself, far from being a "female king," is a warrior-king, a powerful leader who, in spite of his gentle manner, has an enormous capacity for violence. In *Lancelot and Elaine* Lancelot describes Arthur at the Battle of Mount Baden:

> I myself beheld the King
> Charge at the head of all his Table Round,

And all his legions crying Christ and him,
And break them; and I saw him, after, stand
High on a heap of slain, from spur to plume
Red as the rising sun with heathen blood. (ll. 302–307)

Even after the final internecine bloodbath, a dying Arthur, surrounded by the corpses of his knights, when Bedivere is reluctant to follow his order to throw Excalibur into the lake, directs the following outburst to his last surviving knight:

Unknightly, traitor-hearted! Woe is
me! Authority forgets a dying king,
Laid widowed of the power in his eye
That bowed the will ....
. . . .
But, if thou spare to fling Excalibur,
I will arise and slay thee with my hands.
                    (*The Passing of Arthur*, ll. 288–300)

Arthur's relationship with his sword is the most obvious example of the fetishism concerning swords, armor, and "arms" shown by the knights throughout the *Idylls*. A great deal of Malory's warrior remains in Tennyson's Arthur—and yet readers complained about his "feminine" qualities. First, there is the implicit assumption that, in spite of his strength and courage, by his failure to challenge (and kill) Lancelot, Arthur has relinquished his manhood; this idea is, appropriately enough, articulated most succinctly by the cynical Vivien: "'Man! is he man at all, who knows and winks? / Sees what his fair bride is and does, and winks?'" (*Merlin and Vivien*, ll. 779–780). The issue of whether Arthur really knows remains unresolved in the poem, but it seems remarkable that he could not know. However, there are broader problems for Tennyson in fusing the qualities of a mythic hero with those of a Victorian gentleman. His assumptions about manhood as a repudiation of "natural" bestiality preclude his adoption of a model that would incorporate anything like Charles Kingsley's positive "animal spirits" that inform "both martial vigor and sexual potency" in men (Adams, p. 108). Swinburne, with his remark about "Morte d'Albert," was of course making a comment not only about Tennyson's obvious intention to associate Arthur with the Prince Consort but also about the values clustered around the ideal of bourgeois respectability, an ideal which had gained increased status by contemporary associations with the monarchy. In the "Dedication" Tennyson refers to Albert as "modest, kindly, all-accomplished, wise, / With what sublime repression of himself" (ll. 17–18). These qualities are consistent with the dominant image of the Victorian gentleman as well as his predecessor, the chivalrous knight. (In a famous portrait Albert himself was depicted in armor.) Mark Girouard divides mid-century attitudes toward the immensely popular Arthurian story into two groups, romantic and moral: "The romantics read Malory and were deeply moved and excited by the vividness of his stories of love, quests, fighting and marvels. The moralists saw Arthur and his knights as epitomizing (at their best) virtues which were still valid as a source of moral lessons for contemporary life."[22] In the *Idylls*, with the exception of the early romantic fantasy of *Gareth and Lynette*, Tennyson emphasized the moral approach to his subject (a fact which by itself helps to explain the unsympathetic response of Swinburne and other contemporary critics with an aestheticist bias), and for Tennyson the most fundamental problem to be dealt with was the bestial nature of men. With his emphasis on the repression of spontaneous maleness (while preserving the male capacity for violence, appropriately controlled and directed), it is no wonder that Tennyson created a restrained and thoughtful Arthur who lacked the elan of Malory's hero.

4

Sussman says of Carlyle and his works: "In seeking a psychic armor to contain the inchoate, fluid energy within, [he] presents a particularly fragile and unstable model of the male psyche always at the edge of eruption, of dissolution, of madness" (p. 19). Because Carlyle's answer to the problem of the unstable male psyche—monastic asceticism—is so far removed from Tennyson's, it may be surprising to find that Tennyson's formulation of the problem is very much the same (although, one could fairly argue, more extreme than Carlyle's). Nearly all of the knights (finally even Lancelot) exhibit at least the potential for explosive, irrational violence. Arthur's "perfection" is most evident in his ability to control his own considerable capacity for violence. However, the relation between madness and unregulated male violence is examined most closely (even schematically) in *Balin and Balan*, the fifth idyll in the final order but written last. Balin, called "the Savage," comes to Camelot in the company of his older and more sophisticated brother Balan, seeking to acquire courtesy as a cure for his frequent violent moods. Balin worships the beautiful and supposedly virtuous queen and attempts to emulate the courteous behavior of the great knight. Their example helps him to hold his violent nature in check. However, while his brother is gone on a quest to rid a forest of the demon that haunts it,

Balin inadvertently observes a compromising scene between Lancelot and Guinevere. The shock to Balin is parallel to that of Pelleas in the ninth idyll when he discovers Ettarre and Gawain asleep together in sin, the shock that triggers his descent into total disillusionment and his metamorphosis into the Red Knight. Without the steadying influence of Balan, this traumatic incident, coupled with the scandalous rumors spread by Vivien, leads to a recurrence of Balin's madness. In a violent rage, he rides into the forest where he hopes to destroy the demon, reasoning that "To lay that devil would lay the Devil in me" (l. 296). Balin comes upon King Pellam's castle, where he is taunted by the knights, who have heard of the scandal at Camelot, for displaying on his shield the crest of "The Queen we worship, Lancelot, I, and all, / As fairest, best and purest" (ll. 344–345). In particular Sir Garlon mocks the "fair wife-worship" that "cloaks a secret shame" (l. 355). Losing his precarious self-control, Balin—not in a "fair fight" but in a sudden, spontaneous move—"Hard upon helm smote him ... / Then Garlon, reeling slowly backward, fell, / And Balin by the banneret of his helm / Dragged him, and struck" (ll. 389–393). Because Garlon has been vilified in Tennyson's description (objectified, dehumanized, much like the Earl of Doorm in Geraint's story), Balin, despite his uncontrolled, murderous rage, can be seen as a sympathetic figure as he flees the unchivalrous castle of Pellam. Escaping into the forest, where he discards his shield with Guinevere's crest, Balin has fallen into bestiality like Dr. Jekyll receding into Mr. Hyde. He finally meets his brother, who mistakes him for the demon and attacks. The resulting double fratricide foreshadows the tale of the ancient unnamed king and his brother that is embedded in *Lancelot and Elaine*. In Freudian terms, this is a symbolic suicide: Balan and Balin have been consistently portrayed as a divided self, and in the end "the rational self [Balan] can control the savage, bestial self [Balin] only by destroying it."[23] Kerry McSweeney is among the critics who have interpreted Balin and Balan's story as a psychological tale about "the destructive power of sexuality," but have not explored the larger implications for Tennyson's concept of masculinity and its dependence on ideals of feminine virtue.[24]

As Rosenberg points out, "Two kinds of time ... cyclic and apocalyptic ... are built into the structure of the *Idylls*" (p. 37). Arthur himself is associated with apocalyptic time, but the "new order" he introduces by conquering the heathen, driving out the beast, and felling the forest, as described in *The Coming of Arthur* (ll. 58–62), is itself displaced by an even more barbarous one after the "last, dim, weird battle in the West." Arthur's great plan is graphically laid out in the symbols incorporated into Merlin's "four great zones of sculpture" girding the great hall at Camelot:

And in the lowest beasts are slaying men,
And in the second men are slaying beasts,
And on the third are warriors, perfect men,
And on the fourth are men with growing wings.

(The Holy Grail, ll. 234-237)

It is as though in establishing his order, instead of building on previous orders, Arthur must begin from the beginning, and Tennyson appeals to the primal human fear of beasts that recalls a prehistoric time before mankind dominated the earth, when human beings were hunted prey as well as hunters. In this sense Tennyson has Arthur's order correspond to an entire cycle of civilization. This may seem surprising because Tennyson would also have his reader think of Arthur's historical displacement of the Roman invaders and his defeat of the (Saxon) pagans. However, it is important for Tennyson to associate his mythic Arthur with the ur-story of civilization because it is symbolic of the continuing internal struggle of men with the beast within, Tennyson's principal focus in the narrative, inextricably tied to his theme of morality. And here I am referring to the internal struggle of men, not "mankind." Tennyson is surely aligned with what Sussman in his discussion of representative male Victorians such as Browning and Carlyle describes as the "hegemonic, bourgeois view" of "'manliness' as the control and discipline of an essential 'maleness' fantasized as a potent yet dangerous energy." According to this view, "manhood" or the achievement of manliness is not an innate state of being "but the result of arduous public or private ritual and ... continued demanding self-discipline ... an unstable equilibrium of barely controlled energy that may collapse back into the inchoate flood or fire that limns the innate energy of maleness, into the gender-specific mental pathology that the Victorians saw as male hysteria or male madness." I believe that Tennyson is also typical in thinking of manhood "not as an essence but a plot, a condition whose achievement and whose maintenance forms a narrative over time" (Sussman, p. 13). The fundamental problem for Arthur's order of the Round Table is to provide the ritual and teach and enforce the discipline needed to control the (natural) male bestiality and madness that Tennyson, in reaction to the legacy of his Romantic predecessors, associated with savage violence and moral anarchy. Tennyson's focus on irrational, instinctual male violence as the primary source of civilization's ills should come as no surprise to modern readers. American novelist John Updike, for example, expresses conventional contemporary views in a 1996 review essay on books dealing with the "elusive" concept of "evil" when he assumes that the spontaneous murder of women by men "overloaded with liquor and testosterone" is the sort of crime that arouses our "absolute indignation,"[25] presumably closer to pure "evil" than murders plotted with cold calculation.

In the *Idylls* Arthur's origin is shrouded in mystery—supposedly he is the son of Uther (and therefore the legitimate heir to his throne) but doubt remains. If he is Uther's son, then he is literally the product of savage male violence: Uther went to war with the "prince and warrior" Gorloïs because he lusted after Gorloïs' wife, Ygerne, and she spurned his advances. After killing Gorloïs in battle, "Uther in his wrath and heat besieged / Ygerne within [the castle] Tintagil" and, after her outnumbered defenders deserted her, forced her "to wed him in her tears, / And with a shameful swiftness" (*The Coming of Arthur*, ll. 198–204). If King Uther is not a murderer and rapist he is something very close to that, and this fact, along with Tennyson's scheme of myth-making, helps to explain why Tennyson leaves the origins of Arthur, the apotheosis of honorable manhood, shrouded in mystery. Arthur's transcendence of ordinary maleness (even as manifested in a savage king) in his supposedly perfect, Christ-like manhood is further emphasized. The most coherent explanation of Arthur's origin is given by Bedivere, the first and last of Arthur's knights, to King Leodogran, Guinevere's father: Arthur, son of Uther, was born "before his time" to Ygerne and immediately "Delivered at a secret postern-gate / To Merlin" (ll. 210–213). (And yet both Uther and Ygerne are dark-complected, while Arthur is strikingly blond.) According to Bedivere, his account is challenged by those who call him "baseborn, and since his ways are sweet, / And theirs are bestial, hold him less than man: / And there be those who deem him more than man, / And dream he dropt from heaven" (ll. 179–182). However, the only sure basis for Arthur's kingship is his charismatic, manly assertion of moral authority— binding his men by "strait vows to his own self" (l. 261) and his ability to govern effectively.[26]

Potentially destructive male energy is curbed and controlled by the rigid chivalric code instituted by Arthur, and its primary regulating instrument is woman-worship, a code which assumes the moral superiority of women and which places a premium on female life and welfare. The chivalry of the Round Table—which must be continually reaffirmed both through the ritualized court violence of the tournament and the knightly quest into the world in order to rescue women and redress their wrongs—is assumed to be consistent with the primitive, unarticulated imperative of protecting women (because of their childbearing and child-rearing functions) as the basis of tribal or national survival and also, on a more abstract, idealized and articulated level, as the basis of civilization and its triumph over barbarism. But if the *Idylls* are to incorporate a serious moral vision for his time Tennyson's version of chivalry must also conform to standards of bourgeois respectability, in particular the domestic, moral virtues of womanhood that we now routinely associate with the title of Coventry Patmore's poem "The Angel in the House" and so fully articulated by Ruskin in his essay "Of Queens' Gardens" ("It is the type of an eternal truth—that the soul's armour is never well set to the heart unless a woman's hand has braced it; and it is only when she braces it loosely that the honour of manhood fails").[27] Gender roles in the *Idylls* are in fact largely consistent with these stereotypes, whereby wives, through their innate moral superiority and freedom from the contamination of the world, have the power to ennoble their husbands, ameliorating the corrosive effects of male insensitivity and male aggression. It is obvious from the beginning of the *Idylls* that Tennyson rejects the ideal of "monastic asceticism" found by Sussman and J. E. Adams in the works of Carlyle, Pater, and the Pre-Raphaelite Brotherhood: after being smitten by the light of Guinevere's eyes, Arthur believes that

> "saving I be joined
> To her that is the fairest under heaven,
> I seem as nothing in the mighty world,
> And cannot will my will, nor work my work
> Wholly, nor make myself in mine own realm
> Victor and lord. But were I joined with her,
> Then might we live together as one life,
> And reigning with one will in everything
> Have power on this dark land to lighten it,
> And power on this dead world to make it live."
> (*The Coming of Arthur*, ll. 84–93)

Later, in *Balin and Balan*, the all-male court of King Pellam (who in his misguided desire for piety has banished all women including his own "faithful wife") is described as sterile and gloomy. And yet Arthur's idealized vision of monarchy and matrimony is doomed from the beginning. His instantaneous love for Guinevere is not reciprocated—Arthur, modestly dressed and without helm or shield, does not stand out in the parade of warriors before Leodogran's castle, and "She saw him not, or marked not, if she saw" (*The Coming of Arthur*, l. 53). Later, she falls in love with the King's lieutenant, the sexually attractive Lancelot, as he escorts her to Arthur's court. The passive and even unintentional conquest of Arthur by the beautiful Guinevere is parallel to the equally effortless conquest of the naive and idealistic Pelleas by the utterly self-centered and manipulative Ettarre in the ninth idyll. Just prior to his first sight of Ettarre, Pelleas is fantasizing about his ideal love, and, ignorant of the Queen's adultery, he imagines his lady to be "'fair ... and pure as Guinevere, / And I will make thee with my spear and sword / As famous-O my Queen, my Guinevere, / For I will be thine Arthur when we meet'" (*Pelleas and Ettarre*, ll. 42–45). When Ettarre and her entourage suddenly appear, "Pelleas gazing thought, / Is Guinevere herself so beautiful?" (ll. 64–65). Clearly this incident is a retelling of the first meeting of the King and Queen, just as the idyll as a whole is a retelling of *Gareth and Lynette*, the second idyll and the only one with the thoroughgoing fantastical quality of a fairy-tale (in which the persistence of the dedicated knightly lover pays off and the violence of combat turns out to be imaginary rather than real). But now it is feminine goodness and knightly honor that are illusory, and after being betrayed by both his lady and his fellow knight Gawain (the two of whom, he discovers, have been engaging in casual sex) and then learning of the Guinevere–Lancelot liaison, the disillusioned idealist descends into savage madness. In the next idyll, *The Last Tournament*, Pelleas re-emerges as the Red Knight, who, cynically inverting the professed values of the Round Table, mocks Arthur as a "woman-worshipper," a "Eunuch-hearted king / Who fain had clipt free manhood from the world" (*The Last Tournament*, ll. 444–445). His Round Table in the North is made up of adulterous knights and their ladies are all harlots, but since they all openly admit the truth, the embittered idealist has created a space in which professed moral values conform to reality.

Tennyson's use of the Red Knight as a kind of anti-Arthur illustrates his surprising distance from the melodramatic imagination central to much of Victorian literature, and he shows a great deal of moral ambivalence here. Of course Arthur faces his nemesis with predictable, intrepid courage, but the drunken Red Knight practically destroys himself, toppling over into the mud after an inept charge at the King, and the royal knights immediately leap on his fallen body. They "trampled out his face from being known, / And sank his head in mire, and slimed themselves" (*The Last Tournament*, ll. 469–470) before going on to massacre the entire party of rebellious knights and apparently even the women as well. Symbolically, the ostensible villain has won because the Knights of the Round Table in fact fight like wild beasts and, in spite of their professed code of honor, reveal themselves to be no better than uncivilized madmen. Most important is Arthur's consciousness of his failure: just before the fighting began, Arthur had begun to recognize the Red Knight as the once-noble Pelleas, and after the bloodbath; we are told that "all the ways were safe from shore to shore, / But in the heart of Arthur pain was lord" (ll. 485–486), a passage that parodies the description of Arthur's early triumph (also bloody but in this case, apparently glorious) over the petty feuding barons and kings in order to consolidate his power: "And in the heart of Arthur joy was lord" (*The Coming of Arthur*, l. 123).

While Arthur's men are disgracing themselves in battle, the parallel ritualistic combat of the "last tournament," presided over by a demoralized Lancelot who passively observes "the laws that ruled the tournament / Broken" (ll. 160–161) and won by the cynical Tristram, is itself a pathetic parody of bygone glory. Moral anarchy has returned, the order of the Round Table is effectively dead, and Tennyson sees no need to portray the events that lead up to the actual civil war instigated by Modred.

In the penultimate idyll, a reproachful but forgiving (and still loving) Arthur, just prior to the final, cataclysmic battle, confronts a penitent Guinevere in the convent where she has retreated. William Morris and generations of critics have defended Guinevere against "priggish" Arthur's charge that she personally is to blame for the destruction of the Round Table—"For thou hast spoilt the purpose of my life" (l. 450)—but Tennyson's narrative has shown this to be quite true. In Arthur's system, women wield enormous power: through their innately superior morality ("purity," goodness)—as symbolized by their physical beauty—women have the social function of regulating, controlling the potentially bestial, innate sexual energy of men. As Nancy F. Cott has argued, between the seventeenth and the nineteenth centuries, the "dominant Anglo-American definition of women as *especially* sexual" was reversed and transformed into the view that women were *less* carnal and lustful than men."[28] In particular, Evangelical Protestantism increasingly emphasized the idea that Christianity had elevated women above the sensuality of animal nature and made them "more pure than men." Gilbert uses this idea of the apparently unnatural suppression of female sexuality to explain the destruction of Arthur's order through an outbreak of the "irrational and destructive" natural forces associated with female sexuality. Although it is obvious that the suppression of female sexuality is central to Arthur's woman-worship, Gilbert misses the crucial point that femininity is blameworthy in the *Idylls* when it fails to control the innate, irrational, and destructive forces of the male. It is true that Guinevere is sexual, that she craves the love of man who (unlike Arthur) has "a touch of earth," and she is also self-centered and small-minded: Arthur is "A moral child without the craft to rule, / Else had he not lost me" (*Lancelot and Elaine*, ll. 145–146). In managing her adulterous affair with Lancelot, she manipulates the gullible and trusting Arthur, but she is by no means a demon lover nor does she possess extraordinary or mysterious powers beyond her charismatic physical beauty. She is a femme fatale precisely because she fails to conform to the idealized womanhood projected upon her by Arthur and the idealistic knights who worship her as a model of feminine beauty and (therefore) goodness. Although Tennyson portrays her somewhat sympathetically as having the grace and refinement befitting a queen, her feminine "powers" do not differ in kind from those of the shameless Ettarre.

If Arthur's judgment of Guinevere seems harsh it may be because the reader senses that a dysfunctional ideology rather than personal failure is the root problem in Camelot. In a sense, Guinevere, Tristram, and others who complain about the impossibly strict vows required by Arthur are right. "[C]an Arthur make me pure / As any maiden child?" asks Tristram (*The Last Tournament*, ll. 687–688), who reasons that in the beginning the vows, "the wholesome madness of an hour" (an interesting choice of words in the context of male madness) inspired each knight to reach beyond himself; doing

> mightier deeds than elsewise he had done,
> And so the realm was made; but then their vows—
> First mainly through that sullying of our Queen—
> Began to gall the knighthood (ll. 675–678)

and so began the downhill slide. As Clyde de L. Ryals puts it, "At the end Arthur learns that the world is impregnable to morality" and "Arthur does not redeem the world because the world is irredeemable." This view is consistent with the traditional interpretation of the *Idylls* as the narrative of the collapse of a society which rejects spiritual values, but it assumes that the collapse is inevitable, and indeed there is evidence even in the first idyll to suggest that this is the case.[29] Even Gilbert asserts that the poem "is certainly about the decline of a community from an original ideal state" and goes on to locate "human sexuality and, in particular, female passion" as "an important agency in this decline" (p. 864).

In my view, however, Arthur's formulation of "spiritual ideals" themselves are confused and unstable from the beginning, and, although Tennyson obviously prized spirituality and believed that the imperfections of human nature hindered mankind from achieving it, he also intuited structural problems in the dominant social ideologies of his day which were supposed to support spiritual values. In the dreamlike, mythic *Idylls* Tennyson could have it both ways, for, as Freud pointed out, dreams have a strange tendency to "disregard negation and to express contraries by identical means of representation."[30] In the list of knightly oaths given in *Guinevere*, Arthur in effect summarizes his "high ideals":

> To reverence the King, as if he were
> Their conscience, and their conscience as their King,

To break the heathen and uphold the Christ,
To ride abroad redressing human wrongs,
To speak no slander, no, nor listen to it,
To honour his own word as if his God's,
To lead sweet lives in purest chastity,
To love one maiden only, cleave to her,
And worship her by years of noble deeds,
Until they won her; for indeed I knew
Of no more subtle master under heaven
Than is the maiden passion for a maid,
Not only to keep down the base in man,
But teach high thought, and amiable words
And courtliness, and the desire of fame,
And love of truth, and all that makes a man.   (ll. 465–480)

Aside from illustrating Arthur's flaw of seeing his knights "as but the projection of himself"—which in spite of Arthur's "sweetness" would suggest a tyrant's cult of personality—this statement is very problematical in light of the narrative of "moral decline" which will soon reach its climax in the final annihilation of the Round Table and Arthur's profound self-doubts.[31]

King-worship and woman-worship are inadequate and even destructive ideals.[32] When young Pelleas sees Ettarre, "The beauty of her flesh abashed the boy, / As though it were the beauty of her soul" (ll. 74–75). Physical beauty does not correspond to spiritual goodness, which is essentially asexual, as seen in the extreme examples of Percival's sister, celibate in her convent, and Galahad, apparently translated into the New Jerusalem in *The Holy Grail*. Less extreme is the example set by Percival, who appropriately chooses the life of Ambrosius and the other good, holy men in a celibate male order that necessarily remains marginal to the larger society (as Arthur well understands). In the world of the *Idylls*, in spite of Arthur's ideology, women are not innately morally superior to men. However, they are not monsters, either: if they wield enormous destructive powers it is because of the false images that are projected upon them by the King and his knights. Even the basic value of truth-telling is immediately compromised when the "truth" about Guinevere becomes a lie and "slander" becomes the truth. As for "fame," its hollowness is emphasized as Merlin finally cedes his own to Vivien.[33]

The twelve great battles in which Arthur and his men defeated the "Godless hosts" ("heathen," "pagans") are not represented in Tennyson's narrative except in retrospective reporting. At the beginning of the narrative proper, they are already in the "glorious past," and the *Idylls* are rather concerned with the maintenance (or rather the failure to maintain) the Order of the Round Table. One very significant implication of the *Idylls* narrative is that ideals are sustainable only during a time of war. We are reminded of Hallam Tennyson's comment that "My father felt strongly that only under the inspiration of ideals, and with his 'sword bathed in heaven,' can a man combat the cynical indifference, the intellectual selfishness, the sloth of will, the utilitarian materialism of a transition age" (*Memoir*, 2:129). Even the apparently glorious legacy of righteous slaughter underwritten by Arthur's unquestioned idealism is not without its darker side, however, as suggested by its analogue in the massacre of the Red Knight and his followers and by the insidious function of the orphan Vivien, who tells Guinevere, "My father died in battle for thy King, / My mother on his corpse—in open field" (*Merlin and Vivien*, ll. 70–71). Arthur assumes that all of his professed values derive from or are at least consistent with Christianity and that his purpose writ large is to "uphold the Christ," that is, establish a Christian civilization, but it is unclear that either the worship of the King or woman-worship is entirely consistent with this assumption. At any rate, the operative principle of love in Camelot is eros rather than agape. Moreover, adultery had always been part of the heritage of chivalry.[34] In part, Tennyson's Arthur represents the masculine fear that masculine purity and goodness are not sexually attractive to women. But Tennyson also implies that even the greatest physical prowess and courage (displayed by Arthur on the battlefield and in his useful work as King) are inadequate unless performed (as in the tournament, where Lancelot excels). And yet if this generalization holds it would run counter to the values of bourgeois respectability. Seen in the context of Tennyson's structural problems of artistic representation, the chivalric plot of masculine initiation and quest does not mesh well with the marriage plot (associated with bourgeois respectability) that dominates Victorian fiction.[35]

In the final analysis, however, it is the failure of Arthur's order (based on his flawed ideal of manhood) to control the irrational force of male energy and the annihilating effects of male violence that leads to his downfall. As he marches with his men to the "last weird battle in the west" and the pathetic end of his reign, Arthur moans that God has forsaken him:

"I found Him in the shining of the stars,
I marked Him in the flowering of His fields,
But in His ways with men I find Him not.
I waged His wars, and now I pass and die."
                    (*The Passing of Arthur*, ll. 9–12)

To the disoriented and confused Arthur, it seems as though "some lesser god had made the world, / But, had not force to shape it as he would, / Till the High God behold it from beyond, / And enter it, and make it beautiful" (ll. 14–17). The "last, dim, weird battle of the west" (l. 94) itself is described in terms that remind us of the battle of Armageddon in Revelation as well as Matthew Arnold's "darkling plain / Swept with confused alarms of struggle and flight / Where ignorant armies clash by night" (ll. 35–37) in "Dover Beach":[36]

> A deathwhite mist slept over sand and sea:
> Whereof the chill, to him who breathed it, drew
> Down with his blood, till all his heart was cold
> With formless fear; and even on Arthur fell
> Confusion, since he saw not whom he fought.
> For friend slew friend not knowing whom he slew;
> . . . .
> And ever and anon with host to host
> Shocks, and the splintering spear, the hard mail hewn,
> Shield-breakings, and the clash of brands, the crash
> Of battleaxes on shattered helms, and shrieks
> After the Christ, of those who falling down
> Looked up for heaven, and only saw the mist;
> And shouts of heathen and the traitor knights,
> Oaths, insult, filth, and monstrous blasphemies,
> Sweat, writhings, anguish, labouring of the lungs
> In that close mist, and cryings for the light,
> Moans of the dying, and voices of the dead.   (ll. 95–117)

Before concluding the slaughter by killing Modred, Arthur tells Bedivere,

>   on my heart hath fallen
> Confusion, till I know not what I am,
> Nor whence I am, nor whether I be a King;
> Behold, I seem but King among the dead.   (ll. 143–146)

These passages, from the 1869 additions to the original 1842 version of *The Passing of Arthur*, reinforce the impression that the *Idylls* can be read as an exploration of dilemmas, uncertainties, contradictions.

5

I am convinced that Tennyson's doubts not only about social constructions of gender but about the foundations of Western civilization are increasingly reflected in his later revisions to his enormously suggestive masterwork.[37] However, in offering this reading of the *Idylls*, I am not arguing that it was the primary one intended by Tennyson, who continued to associate the "new-old" legend of Arthur with the Ideal and with meliorist hopes for future spiritual progress. Instead, I appeal to T. S. Eliot's insight that Tennyson, "the saddest of all English poets," was "the most instinctive rebel against the society in which he was the most perfect conformist" (*Essays*, p. 189).[38] McSweeney and other critics have continued to develop the idea that Tennyson's instinctive attraction to "naturalistic vision" is at odds with his conscious commitment to conventional Victorian moral codes,[39] but I believe that both Tennyson's intuitions about natural process (especially sexuality) and his commitment to Victorian social constructions are more complex than previously assumed.

In the course of defending Tennyson's *Idylls* against critics writing in the 1920s who found the poem "mawkishly insincere," Rosenberg observes that Harold Nicolson's dismissal of the *Idylls*

> makes perfect sense for the nervous system of 1923 once one recognizes that the system was in a state of shock from the First World War—a catastrophe of which the *Idylls* is in the profoundest sense a prophecy—and the seemingly rock solid values of the Victorians had proved as ephemeral as Camelot itself. (p. 6)

I think that Rosenberg is very perceptive here in describing the poem as a prophecy of the First World War; however, his analysis of the *Idylls*, although full of insights about Tennyson's method in developing the apocalyptic implications of the "last, dim, weird battle of the west," does not explore the profound associations of violence with "manhood" at every level in the poem and the implications they have for the dismal failure of Arthur's Round Table as a social order. These associations are particularly telling in the larger cultural context where the ideals of chivalry have often been linked to the origins of the Great War.[40]

An analysis of masculinity in the *Idylls* invites a further reevaluation of

Tennyson's great narrative poem, revealing structures of meaning in the work that have not yet been adequately discussed and implying a greater significance, a nightmarish prophetic quality that can be compared to that of Joseph Conrad's *Heart of Darkness*.

NOTES

1. Algernon Charles Swinburne, "A. C. Swinburne Replies to Taine" in *Tennyson: The Critical Heritage*, ed. John D. Jump (London: Routledge, 1967), p. 339; "A. C. Swinburne on the *Idylls*," in *Tennyson: The Critical Heritage*, p. 319; Henry Crabb Robinson, *Henry Crabb Robinson on Books and their Writers*, ed. E. J. Morley (London: J. M. Dent, 1938), 2:792; Henry James, "Tennyson's Drama," *Views and Reviews* (Boston: Ball, 1908), p. 177; T. S. Eliot quoted in Christopher Ricks, *Tennyson* (Berkeley: Univ. of California Press, 1989), p. 258.

2. Ricks's critique of the poem is of course primarily an aesthetic and formal one, and he places a generally low estimate on the Idylls, relative to Tennyson's work as a whole: "No other poem of Tennyson's was created with such a central uncertainty as to its shape, style, sequence, and size. Such uncertainty in composition is not in itself any evidence of ultimate uncertainty in achievement. Yet *Idylls of the King* must be judged strikingly uneven" (p. 250).

3 Elliot L. Gilbert's "The Female King: Tennyson's Arthurian Apocalypse" (*PMLA* 98 [1983]: 863–878) is probably the most influential study of its kind. Herbert Sussman, for example, refers to Gilbert's essay as "incisive and influential" (*Victorian Masculinities* [Cambridge Univ. Press, 1995], p. 208) and Marion Shaw incorporates Gilbert's main ideas into her feminist reading of the *Idylls* (*Alfred Lord Tennyson* [Atlantic Highlands: Humanities Press International, 1988], p. 92). Although I quarrel with some of Gilbert's principal ideas in the discussion below, I do not mean to suggest that previous studies of Arthur's gender or, more broadly, masculinity in the *Idylls*, have been without merit, and in this essay I refer to several of them that I have found useful and insightful. For example, Linda Shires' essay "Patriarchy, Dead Men, and Tennyson's *Idylls of the King* (*VP* 30 [1992]: 401–419) approaches the issues of masculinity in the *Idylls* with an appreciation for the complexities of Tennyson's attitudes toward gender—"Tennyson simultaneously collapses and retains a patriarchal order" (p. 401)—and recognizes the importance of "male irrational violence" (p. 415).

4. Walter Houghton, *The Victorian Frame of Mind, 1830–1870* (New Haven: Yale University Press, 1957), p. xiv; Jerome H. Buckley, *The Victorian Temper: A Study in Literary Culture* (New York: Vintage, 1951); John Holloway, *The Victorian Sage: Studies in Argument* (London: Macmillan, 1953); George Levine and William Madden, eds., *The Art of Victorian Prose* (New York: Oxford Univ. Press, 1968).

5. Antony H. Harrison and Beverly Taylor, eds., *Gender and Discourse in Victorian Literature and Art* (DeKalb: Northern Illinois Univ. Press, 1992), p. xii.

6 Herbert Sussman, *Victorian Masculinities* (Cambridge Univ. Press, 1995); Eve Kosofsky Sedgwick, *Between Men: English Literature and Male Homosocial Desire* (New York: Columbia Univ. Press, 1985); Michel Foucault, *The History of Sexuality*: Vol. 1, *An Introduction* (Harmondsworth: Penguin, 1984); Sussman, p. 8; James Eli Adams, *Dandies and Desert Saints: Styles of Victorian Masculinities* (Ithaca: Cornell Univ. Press, 1995), p. 11.

7. F. E. L. Priestley, "Tennyson's Idylls," in *Critical Essays on the Poetry of Tennyson*, ed. John Killham (New York: Barnes & Noble, 1960), p. 242. Tennyson is quoted in several places as identifying Arthur with the soul and the Round Table with the passions. His son Hallam Tennyson wrote, "To sum up: if Epic unity is looked for in the 'Idylls,' we find it

... in the unending war of humanities in all ages—the worldwide war of Sense and Soul, typified in individuals, with the subtle interaction of character upon character, the central dominant figure being the pure, generous, tender, brave, human-hearted Arthur—so that the links (with here and there symbolic accessories) which bind the 'Idylls' into an artistic whole, are perhaps somewhat intricate" (*Alfred Lord Tennyson: A Memoir by His Son* [London, 1897], 2:130; hereafter cited as *Memoir*).

8. In a review essay on recent books about war by Barbara Ehrenreich, Phillipe Delmas, and Chris Hables Gray, Michael Ignatieff comments: "In the developed regions of the world ... war is vanishing from our consciousness. The age of mass conscription is over for good, and with it ends the imprinting of military rituals and codes of masculinity throughout our schools, public institutions, and family life" ("The Gods of War," *The New York Review of Books* [October 9, 1997]: p.13). See Barbara Ehrenreich, *Blood Rites: Origins and History of the Passions of War* (New York: Metropolitan, 1997); Phillipe Delmas, *The Rosy Future of War* (New York: Free Press, 1997); Chris Hables Gray, *Postmodern War: The Politics of Conflict* (New York: Guilford Press, 1997).

9. As Joseph Carroll puts it, the view that gender differences "derive from an interaction of innate qualities and cultural concepts ... stands in clear contrast to radical theories of unipolar social causality: the idea that all gender designations are arbitrary impositions of an oppressive patriarchal social system" (*Evolution and Literary Theory* [Columbia: Univ. of Missouri Press, 1995), p. 270).

10. According to Jeffrey Weeks, the concept of "masculinity" for the Victorians was closely associated with male sexuality and "inextricably linked to concepts of male self-expression and power," while "manliness" had more to do with social behavior. See *Sex, Politics and Society: The Regulation of Sexuality since 1800* (London: Longmans, 1981), p. 39.

11. *Memoir*, 2:128; Roger Simpson, *Camelot Regained: The Arthurian Revival and Tennyson, 1800–1849* (Cambridge: D. S. Brewer, 1990), pp. 1–4.

12. References to Tennyson's poetry given in the text are based on *The Poems of Tennyson*, ed. Christopher Ricks (Berkeley: Univ. of California Press, 1987).

13. In *The Fall of Camelot: A Study of Tennyson's "Idylls of the King"* (Cambridge: Belknap-Harvard Univ. Press, 1973), John D. Rosenberg is particularly astute in interpreting Tennyson's dilemma in representing the paradoxical Christ-like duality of Arthur, who is both human and divine. For example, in "'Guinevere' ... for an excruciating instant we catch a glimpse of Christ with horns" (p. 127). As a "cuckolded husband he cannot speak like a surrogate god" but "it is worse still when he tries to speak like a 'real man'" (p. 130). Rosenberg also argues that "although the King is a Christ figure in origins, mission, and promise of his return, he is also a solar deity.... Arthur is so closely linked to the sun throughout the *Idylls* that his character never wholly detaches itself from the symbol, or the symbol from that ancient body of belief in which the gods, once housed in the heavens, descend to earth, are worshipped as heroes, and fructify the land" (p. 42). In discussing possible connections between Tennyson and the ideas about myth held by the Rev. George Stanley Faber, W. D. Paden similarly combines the concepts of Arthur as a warrior of God and his identification with a pagan sun deity (*Tennyson in Egypt: A Study of the Imagery in His Earlier Work* [New York: Octagon, 1971), pp. 79–88).

14. Hallam Tennyson quotes his father on "'the man-woman' in Christ, the 'union of tenderness and strength'" (*Memoir*, 1:326n).

15. Rosenberg, p. 13. Several critics have made persuasive cases for the structural or aesthetic unity of the *Idylls*, notably J. M. Gray in *Thro' the vision of the night: A Study of Source, Evolution, and Structure in Tennyson's "Idylls of the King"* (Montreal: McGill-Queen's Univ. Press, 1980), while others, like Kerry McSweeney in *Tennyson and Swinburne as Romantic Naturalists* (Univ. of Toronto Press, 1981) see profound differences in vision and artistry between, for example, the Guinevere group of idylls (the two Geraint poems,

Merlin and Vivien, Lancelot and Elaine, and *Guinevere*) and the Tristram group (*Balin and Balan, Pelleas and Ettarre,* and *The Last Tournament*). My own approach in this essay emphasizes the unity of the whole, although I acknowledge the usefulness of studying the extended compositional process of the Idylls in order to better understand individual poems and series of poems as well. The value of both methods is exemplified in the work of Herbert F. Tucker, who deals with issues that are related to my treatment of the *Idylls* here. In his essay "Tennyson and the Measure of Doom" (*PMLA* 98 [1983]: 8-20; see also *Tennyson and the Doom of Romanticism* [Harvard Univ. Press, 1988]), Tucker discusses the way Tennyson, with his characteristic sense of inevitable doom, "wrote *Idylls of the King* backward" and in later essays shows how Tennyson is responding to contemporary cultural pressures and the expectations of his novel-reading public as he composes his "epic" poem. See "The Epic Plight of Troth in *Idylls of the King*," *ELH* 58 (1991): 701–720, and "Trials of Fiction: Novel and Epic in the Geraint and Enid Episodes from *Idylls of the King*," *VP* 30 (1992): 441–461.

16. Gilbert quotes (p. 873) Gerhard Joseph on Tennyson's notion of woman as cosmic destructive principle. See Joseph, *Tennysonian Love: The Strange Diagonal* (Minneapolis: Univ. of Minnesota Press, 1969).

17. Sussman writes: "Entrepreneurial manhood with its emphasis on engagement in the male sphere of work, its valuing of strength and energy, and its criterion of commercial success measured by support of a domestic establishment generated particularly acute anxiety for the early Victorian male poet, for this definition of male identity conflicted with the ideal of the poet based on a romantic model in many ways constructed to oppose the new formation of bourgeois man" (p. 82).

18. An interesting late Victorian treatment of this theme is Walter Besant's novel *The Revolt of Man* (1882), set in a future when women are in control and men are subordinate. When the men stage a revolt and form a rebel army, the female authorities empty the prisons in order to build an opposing army of male soldiers. However, a group of women sympathetic to the men's movement frighten away the disorganized and ignoble conscripts before any fighting can take place.

19. Less obviously, but just as surely, it is absurd to imagine Victorian girls joining Robert Baden-Powell's (late Victorian) Boy Scouts, who are in effect being groomed to fight and possibly die in war. Scouts' rules were to a large measure derived from chivalric codes, and recommended reading-lists for Scouts were dominated by books on chivalry and King Arthur. See Mark Girouard, *The Return to Camelot* (New Haven: Yale Univ. Press, 1981), p. 255.

20. Girouard, p. 146. Among many obvious and well known examples of the association of specifically Arthurian "moral qualities" with conventional Victorian values in period art are the frescoes created by William Dyce for the Queen's Robing Room during the period 1847–64. See Girouard, p. 181.

21. See John Ruskin, *The Works of John Ruskin,* ed. E. T. Cook and Alexander Wedderburn, Vol. 17 (London: George Allen, 1909), pp. 36–37.

22. Girouard, p. 180. On chivalry and the royal family, see pp. 112–128.

23. See Rosenberg, p. 82. J. M. Gray has shown in some detail how Tennyson adapts Malory's version of the Balin and Balan story in order to explore and dramatize split and double personalities in this idyll. See *Tennyson's Doppelgänger "Balin and Balan"* (Lincoln: The Tennyson Society, monograph no. 3, 1971).

24. McSweeney, p. 106. Gray's richly suggestive reading, too detailed to be discussed adequately here, also has numerous implications for a study of masculinity in the *Idylls.* Particularly intriguing are his treatment of both Pellam and Garlon as aspects of Balin's personality and his discussion of the symbolic nature of the blood-stained spear (reputed to have pierced Christ's side) which Balin takes from Pellam's sanctuary in order to "kill

one whose identity is so close to his own that in the same act is murder, fratricide, suicide, genocide" (p. 45): In terms of male sexuality, U. C. Knoepflmacher's essay "Idling in Gardens of the Queen: Tennyson's Boys, Princes, and Kings" (*VP* 30 [1992]: 343–364) is also of interest, finding in Tennyson's last idylls—*Gareth and Lynette*, *The Last Tournament*, and *Balin and Balin*—evidence "to suggest that the entire poem is far more concerned with the maternal formation and deformation of an adolescent identity than even our best gender-critics have allowed" (p. 361).

25. John Updike, "Elusive Evil," *The New Yorker* (July 22, 1996), pp. 62, 70.

26. It is easy to speculate about underlying personal issues in Tennyson's handling of both male madness and the challenge to patrilineal authority that Gilbert believes makes Arthur a "female." Dr. George Clayton Tennyson, Tennyson's clergyman father (and boyhood tutor) was virtually disinherited by his own father (of the same name) in favor of the younger son Charles—a family tragedy that was always associated with Dr. Tennyson's subsequent alcoholism and suicidal madness. In 1820, when Alfred was ten, "relations between his father and grandfather became morbidly irreparable" and in the 1820s Dr. Tennyson "collapsed into drink and rage" (Ricks, p. 4). And "whether their father was fully responsible for it or not, the minds of most of the ... children were not to prove stable" (Ricks, p. 57). In *Maud* (1855), Tennyson's most explicit exploration of male madness (and his favorite poem for reading aloud), irrational and destructive male violence is closely associated with male sexuality, and the ending (disturbing to many modern readers and critics) suggests that the unstable protagonist (guilty of killing his lover's brother in a duel) will redeem himself by immersion in the righteous and patriotic cause of the Crimean War. Even to contemporary readers, "the speaker's bellicosity and actual fighting seemed ... hysterical and the war to reinstate 'The glory of manhood' ... seemed out of proportion to its grounding in the speaker's experience" (Alan Sinfield, *Alfred Tennyson* [Oxford: Blackwell, 1986], p. 176). Early in the narrative, the protagonist is increasingly smitten by Maud as he overhears her singing "A passionate ballad ... / A martial song ... / Singing of men that in battle array / ... / March with banner and bugle and fife / To the death, for their native land" (ll. 165–172).

27. For a representative feminist treatment of this issue, see Carol Christ's well-known essay "Victorian Masculinity and the Angel in the House," in *A Widening Sphere*, ed. Martha Vicinus (Bloomington: Indiana Univ. Press, 1977), pp. 146–162; John Ruskin, *Works*, 18:120.

28. Nancy F. Cott, "Passionlessness: An Interpretation of Victorian Sexual Ideology, 1790–1850," *Signs* 4 (1978): 221, 227.

29. See Clyde de L. Ryals, *From the Great Deep: Essays on "Idylls of the King"* (Athens: Ohio Univ. Press, 1967), pp. 89, 92. Rosenberg writes, "From [a] cyclic perspective, man's reeling back into the beast is both monstrous and *natural*. The Round Table is founded to arrest this process, and it succeeds only 'for a space'" (p. 37).

30. Sigmund Freud, "The Antithetical Sense of Primal Words," in *Character and Culture*, ed. Philip Rieff (New York: Collier, 1963), p. 44.

31. See Ryals, p. 89. In *The Duel in European History: Honour and the Reign of Aristocracy* (Oxford: Oxford Univ. Press, 1988) V. G. Kiernan explores the "fundamental irrationality" of the duel, a "remote ancestor" of "ritual tribal combat" which, persisting into the nineteenth century, helped "to illuminate the contradictions at the heart of European civilization" (pp. 328, 330). Kiernan's comments about increasing democratization in European nations and the reawakening of the "spirit of the tribe, where every man was born to be a warrior" (p. 331) are suggestive of the contradictions I that believe are implicit in Tennyson's use of medieval Arthurian legends in the cultural context of Victorian England.

32. Ian McGuire argues that "in Camelot, sexuality ... is sublimated into violence.

Violence is then controlled by reference back to an etherealized form of sexuality (chivalric/Christian love).... When, however, this form of control breaks down ... the force which maintains colonial and sexual law is revealed as itself demonic.... There is, in short, no alternative offered, on a political level at lest, between sublimation and chaos" ("Epistemology and Empire in *Idylls of the King*," *VP* 30 [1992]: 392).

33. It is clear that Vivien's principal motive in destroying Merlin is to steal his fame or glory: "'I have made his glory mine,' / ... 'O fool!'" she shrieks (ll. 969–970).

34. Extramarital game-playing among the upper classes in Victorian times was often associated with chivalric images and themes. See Girouard (pp. 178–218). As Girouard points out, "Purity as an element of modern chivalry," so important to Tennyson, only began to loom large in the 1850s," when it was grafted onto earlier concepts of chivalrous love, which included "devotion, tenderness, courtesy and protection" (p. 199). Kenelm Digby's novel *The Broad Stone of Honour* (1822), enormously influential in popularizing chivalry among young men, has little to say about purity.

35. Another problem for Tennyson in adapting chivalry to his purpose is the elitist tendency in chivalric traditions, but this is part of a very large and complex pattern of cultural assimilation that involves all Victorian uses of chivalry and the ideal of the gentleman. According to J. E. Adams, "The gentleman ... is the most pivotal and contested norm of mid-Victorian masculinity, because it served so effectively as a means of regulating social mobility and its attendant privileges" (p. 152).

36. Tennyson's "deathwhite mist" is an addition to Malory. Arnold's image of ignorant armies clashing by night is the best-known Victorian reference to the Battle of Epipolae as described by Thucydides.

37. J. M. Gray is among the scholars who have noticed the increasing prominence of dream, fantasy and the inward life in Tennyson's later-composed idylls, and in his analysis of *Balin and Balan* as Tennyson's "Doppelgänger," he speculates that the especially strong shift in this direction in the last-written idyll "may be the price the poet's creative unconscious exacted for so much epistemology previously. Here within Balin's seemingly irrational conduct there is psychological exploration, perhaps in compensation for the failure of so many conventional questions for morality" (p. 23). This observation is consistent with my suggestion that Tennyson's increasing emphasis on troubling issues of gender is related to his intuitions about fundamental contradictions inherent in the ideals he consciously espoused.

38. As I have implied earlier in this essay, Eliot was not especially perceptive about the *Idylls*; however, his insight concerning the apparently conformist Tennyson's instinctive rebelliousness helped to inspire studies like E. D. H. Johnson's *The Alien Vision of Victorian Poetry: Sources of the Poetic Imagination in Tennyson, Browning, and Arnold* (Princeton: Princeton Univ. Press, 1952), which argued that Tennyson had attempted to reconcile his need to maintain an aesthetic integrity with his need to satisfy a public whose demands were often at odds with his artistic vision. Terry Eagleton's more recent, politicized version of Tennyson's doubleness is that "Tennyson is ... at once a poet of the 'centre' and the 'margins': on the one hand poet laureate, spokesman for conservative values and Victorian patriarchy; on the other hand a radically alienated, deeply subjective refugee from the march of bourgeois progress, whose 'feminine' sensuousness finds its nourishment in the privatized and exotic" ("Editor's Preface," Sinfield, p. ix). Of course, in my analysis I am not primarily concerned with the ambivalences of an instinctively rebellious and aesthetic young Tennyson but rather with a mature sage figure brooding about the past and future of England and of humankind. Eliot writes, "I do not believe for a moment that Tennyson was a man of mild feelings or weak passions. There is no evidence in his poetry that he knew the experience of violent passion for a woman: but there is plenty of evidence of emotional intensity and violence—but of emotion so deeply suppressed, even from

himself, as to tend rather towards the blackest melancholia than towards dramatic action" ("*In Memoriam*," in *Essays Ancient and Modern* [London: Faber and Faber, 1936], p. 181). I would argue that Tennyson's melancholia is evident in both the narrative form and the expressive language of the *Idylls*.

39. McSweeney discusses this idea at length in his chapter "Sexuality and Vision in *Idylls of the King*," (*Tennyson and Swinburne*, pp. 98–122).

40. Rosenberg, p. 6. As Girouard puts it, "Opinions will always differ as to whether the Great War could or should have been prevented. But one conclusion is undeniable: the ideas of chivalry worked with one accord in favour of war" (p. 276). Michael C. C. Adams makes similar claims in *The Great Adventure: Male Desire and the Coming of World War I* (Bloomington: Indiana University Press, 1990): for example, "Chivalry obfuscated the inhuman quality of modern war and in so doing it not only failed to contain slaughter but helped to encourage it" (p. 72). Paul Fussell's discussion of the disjunction between the naive, chivalric language of Tennyson's Arthurian poems and other pre-war romances and the realities of modern warfare in *The Great War and Modern Memory* (London: Oxford Univ. Press, 1975) is especially provocative, but I am arguing that Tennyson himself is a prophet of the disillusionment Fussell describes.

ALAN LUPACK

The Once and Future King:
The Book That Grows Up

W orks that attempt the formidable task of telling the whole story of
Arthur must find a way to deal with the range of characters and themes and
the multiplicity of tales that constitute the Matter of Britain. The story of
Arthur is, after all, many stories even as it is one story. The history of Malory
criticism alone illustrates this point. And Malory, like his successors, felt the
need to tell many stories (actually many more than the eight that Vinaver
defined) in order to tell the one story of Arthur. Tennyson too found it
necessary to tell a variety of stories, each one so independent that it could be
read on its own—or even, as the Balin idyll was in 1885 and as various idylls
have been since, printed without the support of any of its fellows. Though
each idyll tells a different tale, the interactions among them reveal a theme
and a reinterpretation of the Arthurian world that, as with the various tales
in Malory's *Le Morte d'Arthur*, is more than the sum of its parts. Yet the
multiple idylls are necessary as a structural device that allows Tennyson to
treat the diversity of the Arthurian legend, which can overwhelm an author
or undermine a work of art. The attempt to tell the whole Arthurian story
despite the range of material it includes no doubt explains the fact that the
most common form for treating the Arthurian legend in the latter half of the
twentieth century was the trilogy (or in some cases the tetralogy or
pentalogy), as is demonstrated by the work of such novelists as Gillian
Bradshaw, Vera Chapman, Bernard Cornwell, Stephen Lawhead, Mary

From *Arthuriana* 11, no. 3 (Fall 2001). © 2001 by *Arthuriana*.

Stewart, Fay Sampson, Persia Woolley, and others. Since there are so many recent examples, it is easy to forget that one of the earliest and still most important sequences of novels to tell Arthur's story was that written by T.H. White.

Since most people now read the 1958 version of *The Once and Future King*, we tend to think of it as a single finished book, though a long one that is divided into four parts. Within each of those parts and within the book as a whole, there are some obvious structural devices employed to tie everything together. Evans Lansing Smith has commented on White's 'cunning use of the conventional devices of form that give extraordinary shape and significance to the novel's mythic materials' which involves a 'scheme of parallelism among the books' and a 'plot structure' in each of the books that 'oscillates between opposing settings in the progressive development of its plot, which culminates in a reconciliatory climax which recapitulates the entire action of the individual book.'[1] I do not intend to dispute or to discuss the specific parallelisms or reconciliations of the four parts of the novel. Instead, I want to focus on the shifting plans that White had for his Arthuriad and ultimately the structural experiment that is made clear by, but survives the excising of, *The Book of Merlyn*.

Much of the unity of the individual parts is due to the fact that each of the first three parts was published separately, as *The Sword in the Stone*, *The Witch in the Wood* (a title later changed to *The Queen of Air and Darkness*), and *The Ill-Made Knight*. Though initially White thought in terms of a tetralogy, he developed a five-part structure and actually submitted to his publisher a five-volume work, concluding with *The Candle in the Wind* and *The Book of Merlyn*. But his new plan required that he rewrite the first three books for thematic consistency with the concluding pair—and to be part of one book, not separate parts in a serial publication. In a letter to his publisher Collins (Dec. 8, 1941) accompanying what he thought of as a completed manuscript, White said: 'The last two books are like a hat made to fit on top of the first three *as re-written*. They would not fit on the first three as originally published. Anybody who bought the last two after having read the published volumes would be quite puzzled and annoyed. They have not got a unity of their own, suitable for separate publication.'[2] While it is not unusual for a multi-volume sequence to be published as an aggregate volume—as Mary Stewart's Merlin trilogy and Fay Sampson's Daughter of Tintagel pentalogy were—what is unusual about White's book is that his sequence ended with two volumes that were written as a capstone to the previous ones and not meant to be published by themselves.

In a 1939 journal entry, White talks of the parts of the Arthuriad as his 'quadruplets.'[3] White originally planned for a tetralogy that was to be the story of 'the Doom of Arthur' and even intended that the fourth volume would 'be in the form of a straightforward play or tragedy.'[4] But at some stage he decided to shift from a four-part to a five-part book. In a letter to his friend David Garnett (dated June 8, 1941), White outlines the five-part structure. He writes that 'the final epic, which will be called The Once & future King [*sic*], will have five books. (1) The Sword in the Stone, boyhood and animals. (2) The Witch in the Wood—that bloody bitch Morgause. (3) The Ill-Made Knight—Lancelot & the middle years. (4) The Candle in the Wind—final bust up with the sons of Morgause—none to blame except because of her—ending with the aged Arthur weeping and smashed on the eve of his last battle with Mordred. (5) The Book of Merlin.'[5]

At the same time that White was developing this five-part structure, his conception of the book was shifting from a classical tragedy to something more in line with what he says he 'suddenly discovered,' that is, that 'the central theme of Morte d'Arthur is to find an antidote to war.'[6] Nevertheless, his sense of the work as a tragedy is still evident. In the 1958 *Once and Future King*, at the end of 'The Queen of Air and Darkness,' White writes that though most of Malory's book—and by implication his own—deals with knights and quests, 'the narrative is a whole, and it deals with the reasons why the young man came to grief at the end. It is the tragedy, the Aristotelian and comprehensive tragedy, of sin coming home to roost.'[7] And White's book is better as tragedy than as treatise. Still, *The Book of Merlyn* remains important in understanding White's artistry in *The Once and Future King*, not so much because it is the most blatant exploration of the theme of war, which remains part of the point of the book in its ultimate revision, but mainly because it is the key to a brilliant experiment in artistic construction.

There is throughout White's sequence of books an awareness of time. The most obvious example of this is the fact that Merlin lives backwards in time. Because of this unusual quality, White is able to introduce any number of anachronisms into the book. As Marilyn K. Nellis has observed, 'Anachronism penetrates conversations, appearance, customs—constantly tying the modern world to the medieval for the incidental humor of the resemblance as well as for social comment.'[8] White's playing with time is not, however, just for purposes of humor and satire; it is part of the very fabric of the book.

Towards the end of *The Sword in the Stone*, Kay asks Merlin not to leave him and Wart. Merlin replies that he must go and adds, 'We have had a good time while we were young but it is in the nature of Time to fly' (199)—a strange statement for a character who is living backwards in time to make. Merlin is, after all, growing younger. Perhaps Merlin's departure is just another lesson about life that Merlin is teaching his young students, but it seems also to mark a passage, to be a sign that afterwards Kay will enter the adult world and Wart will become King Arthur and, time having flown, he will have responsibilities that will require him to apply his youthful education—perhaps without having as good a time as he has had as a youth. And since Merlin is getting younger but T.H. White was not, it may mark an authorial lament about the nature of the world and an authorial comment about the nature of his book. (More about the latter in a moment.)

In *The Sword in the Stone*, Arthur's nickname Wart marks him as a different figure from the hero of romance, a child who must learn to be king by learning about the world around him, the animals that live in that world, and from them and their political systems about man and his. In *The Queen of Air and Darkness*, Gawain and his brothers continue the childhood theme, sometimes with a darkness that it did not have in the earlier book. With a mother who is more of a figurative than a literal witch but who nonetheless casts a spell over her children, most of the brothers become psychopaths. Arthur, who is called 'the young king of England' (220), is beginning to mature. He arrives at the idea of Might for Right; and Merlin says 'the first few words of the Nunc Dimittis' (248) because his pupil has begun to think for himself and what he thinks is noble.

Early in *The Ill-Made Knight* when 'Guenever was twenty-two,' White introduces a long passage on the development of a seventh sense in middle age. This seventh sense is a sense of balance that is gained with experience of the world. It is the reason 'Middle-aged people can balance between believing in God and breaking all the commandments, without difficulty' (378). White speaks of this quality before Guenever or Lancelot has developed it because it is just this aging and balancing process that is the subject of the third and central book of his Arthuriad.[9] Midway through *The Ill-Made Knight*, Lancelot has fathered Galahad, lived with Elaine for a time, and returned to Camelot and resided there for fifteen more years. White calls attention to the new generation at court 'for whom Arthur was not the crusader of a future day, but the accepted conqueror of a past one—for whom Lancelot was the hero of a hundred victories, and Guenever the romantic mistress of a nation' (421). White emphasizes the passage of time with a deliberate cliché: 'Indeed, a lot of water had flowed under the bridges of Camelot in twenty-one years' (421). And when Lancelot returns from the quest for the Grail, Guenever gives him time to get over what she sees as his selfish holiness but is also aware that 'a woman could wait too long for victory—she could be too old to enjoy it' (475). Towards the end of this installment of his book, White writes that 'Now the maturest or the saddest phase [of Camelot] had come, in which enthusiasms had been used up for good, and only our famous seventh sense was left to be practised. The court had "knowledge of the world" now' (477). The characters have reached mature, worldly-wise, and a bit world-weary middle age. At the very end of the book, when Lancelot, after healing Sir Urry, weeps like a child who had been beaten, the force of the scene is different from that of its parallel in Malory. In the medieval author, the sense is that Lancelot is chastised by his own sinfulness in the face of the blessings God has bestowed on him. In White's tale, Lancelot's ability to work a miracle, a blessing that he thought had been taken from him when he lost his virginity by sleeping with Elaine and that he believed would never return because of his sinfulness with Guenever, has been granted to him once again; and the generosity of God brings him back momentarily to the ethic of his childhood, a time before he had developed his seventh sense.

In *The Candle in the Wind*, Arthur, prevented from reconciling with Lancelot by Gawain's anger and Mordred's innate iniquity, is referred to as 'the old man' (602); and when Mordred taunts Guenever before suggesting that they marry, the Queen tells him that she is 'old enough to be your mother' (602), a detail that Malory finds no need to mention. The pattern of aging characters continues into *The Book of Merlyn* where, on the first page, Arthur is said to have 'an old man's misery'[10] and is repeatedly described as old or referred to as 'the old man' or 'an old man' (cf. 69, 98, 105, 115, 130). Even Lancelot and Guenever are seen to have aged. When Lancelot goes to the convent for a last meeting with the Queen, he climbs 'the convent wall with Gallic, ageing gallantry' (132); and when she dies and Lancelot returns to claim her body, the hero of romance is depicted as an old man 'with his snow-white hair and wrinkled cheeks' (132).

It is perhaps not remarkable that characters in a novel, even a novel based on a romance, age or that the author so clearly calls our attention to their aging. But this awareness of aging does intensify the tragedy. As C.N. Manlove has observed, 'Time is at the centre of White's work as it is only at the end in Malory: we watch the Dark become the Middle Ages, and the Middle turn into the later Middle Ages; and we see the central characters aging. The story may have been given to White, but his peculiar emphasis on the fading of the dream and on the movement of time heightens the poignancy of the loss.'[11] What is remarkable is that White reflects this aging in the macro-structure of his book. In a rather brilliant structural experiment, at the same time that the characters age in the sequence, the book itself is growing up with them.

In the letter cited above in which White wrote to David Garnett of his book's five-part structure, he noted that *The Sword in the Stone* would be about 'boyhood and animals,' that the subject of *The Ill-Made Knight* was 'Lancelot & the middle years,' and that *The Candle in the Wind* would end 'with the aged Arthur weeping and smashed on the eve of his last battle with Mordred.'[12] This account of the structural divisions of the book is clearly tied to the aging of the characters. White's comment that 'The last two books are like a hat made to fit on top of the first three as *re-written*'[13] indicates that he saw these two books as a sort of diptych of Arthur's old age. What we have then is a pair of tales at the beginning depicting the youth of Arthur and of Gawain and his brothers, a central book depicting 'the middle years,' and another pair of tales focusing on an aged Arthur.

The Sword in the Stone is a children's book. As Elizabeth Brewer points out, 'The fact that White intended *The Sword in the Stone* to be a children's book in the manner of Masefield's *Midnight Folk* which he so much loved and admired differentiates it from the subsequent parts of *The Once and Future King*, and surely affects the way in which we should interpret it.'[14] The turning of Arthur into various animals, the adventure with Robin Hood, the talking owl Archimedes, Merlin's botched spells—all are the stuff of a tale for young readers. The distance from this book to the almost pessimistic philosophizing (some might say pseudo-philosophizing) of *The Book of Merlyn* seems great, but part of White's artistry is to make the process gradual, like aging itself. Looking from the first book to the fifth is like seeing an acquaintance from youth after many years and being surprised at how much the person has changed. But reading through the books in sequence makes the aging process less startling, like living with a person and seeing small changes day by day.

The other frame of the opening diptych, *The Queen of Air and Darkness*, also has elements of a children's book—though ultimately a darker and more ominous one than *The Sword in the Stone*. Arthur is the young king learning to think for himself; but much of the book is set in the Gaelic world of Lothian, and many of the adventures are those of a children's tale even though 'the snake is now in the garden.'[15] The killing of the griffin from *The Sword in the Stone* is paralleled by the hunting of the unicorn in *The Queen of Air and Darkness*. Both are adventures with a fabulous beast, but the latter— a revolting slaughter of a beautiful animal, an offense against the nature that Wart learns to love and respect in the first book and a double travesty because it is done to please an uncaring and unpleasant mother—is a sign of the deep dysfunctionality of the Lothian clan. This is then a step beyond the idyllic world of the first book but, despite ominous foreshadowing, the characters have not yet reached the world of adult trouble that later books depict. It seems as if White was trying in this second part of his pentalogy to write a *bildungsroman* in which Arthur comes of age and is no longer in need of his tutor but also to link it through both comic and disturbing elements to the part that comes before.

Similarly, the second installment of White's Arthuriad depicts love affairs, another step toward the adult world. But the love interest of Pellinore in the second book is much different from that of Lancelot in *The Ill-Made Knight*, and it has far less dire consequences. Pellinore's love-sickness because of his affection for the Queen of Flanders' daughter, called Piggy, remains largely comic; and the episode of the Questing Beast's falling in love with the artificial Beast created by Grummore and Palomides to distract the pining Pellinore is completely comic. In this book Lothian is at war with Camelot, a situation that would seem to provide a forum for treatment of the theme of finding an antidote to war. It does so to a certain extent in the scenes set in Camelot, but in Lothian the three knights from Arthur's court are not even aware of the war and no one bothers to tell them about it.

In this second part of the Arthuriad, White also demonstrates how Gawain and his brothers are shaped into the men they will become under the influence of their horrible mother and depicts Arthur's planting of the literal and figurative seed of the future tragedy. Perhaps even more importantly, the book portrays Arthur's maturation. In contrast to some of the arrested sons of Lot and Morgause, who are doomed not by fate but by the Freudian influence of their mother, Arthur learns to think for himself, and Merlin declares through the 'Nunc Dimittis' that his student is ready to face the world on his own. He proves that he is by arriving at the notion that Might is not Right but should be used for Right and by fighting in a new way, attacking the knights and thus providing a disincentive for the nobles to think of war as a lark. These demonstrations of Arthur's maturation make *The Queen of Air and Darkness* a *bildungsroman* that bridges the gap between his childhood and his maturity.

The Ill-Made Knight moves into the world of adult concerns and dangers. One marker of the change, for example, is seen in Morgan's Castle Chariot, to which Lancelot is brought by Morgan and her three sister queens/witches: it 'no longer had its fairy appearance as a castle of food [as it did in *The Sword in the Stone*], but its everyday aspect of an ordinary fortress' (343). The book was also conceived as belonging to a different genre. As Elisabeth Brewer points out, White repeatedly wrote in his letters to Potts and others that it was to be a 'Romance.'[16] With the adventures and quests and especially the love interest that that genre usually implies, the book concerns itself with love and religion and strife.

The sequence ages again in its fourth part, *The Candle in the Wind*, which White first wrote as a tragedy; and, as John K. Crane has observed, 'In changing it from its original form as drama to novel, White seems to have done little more than remove the stage directions and convert a few long speeches from spoken lines to narrative passages.'[17] The book not only

remains highly dramatic but maintains the tragic situation. Lancelot and
Arthur share a love for each other that is almost as strong as their love for
Guenever. Arthur is very much aware of the affair between his wife and his
champion; and yet he chooses to overlook it because he puts the good of his
kingdom and of his friend above his own pride. 'One of White's great
triumphs' Martin Kellman writes, 'is to make this attempt to avoid the truth,
indeed to be above jealousy, a sign neither of cowardice nor ignorance but an
indication of a profoundly noble nature.'[18] Arthur's nobility and Lancelot's
inability to yield totally to a seventh sense make the tragedy all the more
moving. But when the King is confronted with an accusation and his entire
system of law and justice depends on his condemning those he loves, he can
no longer look the other way. Mordred, like all true scoundrels, uses against
the one he would destroy that person's own goodness.

White intended to end his Arthuriad with *The Book of Merlyn*. When
White sent the five-part book to Collins, his publisher, Mr. Collins quoted
to White from a reader's report that said 'The Introduction of the animals in
the last book suggests *The Sword in the Stone*, but the purpose is sadly
different. White has changed into a political moralist. Fun and fancy have
abdicated in favour of a purpose. Nor do I see what can be done about it, if
the author feels that way.'[19] Of course, the philosophical tone of the last part
of the Arthuriad is not terribly inconsistent with the rest of it. As John K.
Crane has observed, in *The Sword in the Stone* 'the nature of man is either
directly or obliquely discussed continually.'[20] And the same can be said for
the other parts of the sequence. But *The Book of Merlyn* is different not only
from *The Sword in the Stone* but from all the books that precede it in White's
cycle. What the reviewer missed, however, is that it was intentionally a very
different sort of thing, a philosophical dialogue, not, to be sure, as profound
as Plato's but of the same genre. He also missed the fact that this change in
genre is a key to White's structural experimentation. It is the capstone in the
construction of the sequence, a speculative reflection on the nature of man
and on the problem of Might. And it is the last stage in the aging of White's
book, which mirrors the aging of the characters. Thus, in the five parts of
White's Arthuriad, the book grows up from a children's story to a
bildungsroman, to a romance, to a tragedy, to a philosophical treatise.

When White published the 1958 *Once and Future King*, he did not of
course include *The Book of Merlyn*. Most critics would agree with the
judgment of Sylvia Townsend Warner that 'It is difficult to read the fifth
Arthur [*The Book of Merlyn*] without exasperation. It could have been so good
and it is so bad. The fault is not in the choice of theme: abolition of war is an
interesting subject.... The fault lies in the book's schizophrenia. Giving the
impression of having been written by two different people it does not seem

sincere. Written by one man, it seems demented.'[21] Elisabeth Brewer offers a different criticism: 'Interesting as *The Book of Merlyn* is, it would have made a strange ending to the story of Arthur, had its author been able to carry out his original intention of concluding his epic with it as a fifth book. For what reader, after reaching the tragic end of the story, when Arthur, old and defeated, faces death at the hand of his own son, really wants to attend a Privy Council of animals, including the sentimental and sentimentalised hedgehog, for another dose of polemic and facetious humor at the end?'[22]

Brewer, however, also recognizes that 'the return to the animals at the end of Arthur's story [in *The Book of Merlyn*] is ingenious, too, in that it creates a circular pattern, somewhat similar to the older Arthurian tradition, in which the appearance of the Lady of the Lake with Excalibur marks the beginning of Arthur's career as king, while the return of the sword to her at the end signals its close.'[23] This circularity is only a part of the structural completion that *The Book of Merlyn* offers. For the dialogue about war not only occurs in Arthur's old age but it is also the 'old age' of the book, the final part and the culmination of the growing up of the Arthuriad. While the earlier genres are clearly related to stages in the lives of the characters, from youth to maturity, the philosophical dialogue of this final part is the culmination of the growing up of the book. It provides an opportunity for reflection on the experiences of Arthur's whole life and thus may be said to be the final stage in his growth and development. It is in one sense the maturest of genres because it looks back on the experiences of his life, from the youthful enthusiasm of a young boy learning about the world to the tragedy of an aging king forced to condemn his beloved wife and make war against his best friend. This is not to imply that themes as serious or as 'mature' may not be treated in the other genres that make up *The Once and Future King*, including a children's story. Indeed, the questions of education, maturation, love and friendship, and government and morality that the other books treat are serious and important. But White has structured his books in such away that this final part grows out of the others and depends on the experiences gained in them for its themes and insights. Therefore, it is important to recognize that, in spite of its clumsy execution, *The Book of Merlyn* strives for both aesthetic and philosophic fulfillment.

But the ending of the 1958 book is, as Brewer points out, 'a far more satisfying and elegant conclusion.'[24] White's final revision of his Arthuriad demonstrates that the artist has triumphed over the polemicist.[25] In fact, it is hard to imagine a better ending than that of the 1958 version—for several reasons. First of all, the omission of *The Book of Merlyn* forced White to move its chapters about the ants and the geese to *The Sword in the Stone*, where they are more suitable as part of Arthur's education about man's role as a political animal. The 1958 ending also seems appropriate to the concern with time throughout the sequence. In the end, time, so essential to the book, is part of its ultimate theme. There is not enough time to solve the great problems like war and human iniquity and the tragic consequences that result from them, and not enough time to teach the things that make it possible to solve these problems, not even enough time for someone like Merlin who lives many lifetimes. Thus art and culture, embodied in the young Tom Malory, become crucial so that one is not always starting anew, so that values and ideals can be preserved and absorbed even when Merlin or some Merlin figure like T.H. White is not around to teach. In addition, though the return to the animals of the first part was eliminated, another circular pattern is completed in the 1958 book. Given the emphasis on the aging of the characters throughout the sequence, it is only fitting that the ending introduce a child so that the cycle can begin again. His presence, accepted because of the pattern of anachronism and the muddled medieval time in which the story takes place, allows White to announce that the conclusion of his tale is not 'The End' but 'The Beginning.'

White's Merlin said that 'the best thing for being sad ... is to learn something' (183). The ending of the 1958 *Once and Future King* implies that the best answer to macrocosmic sorrows like war is indeed to learn something—from the examples of books like Malory's *Le Morte D'Arthur* and White's own sequence.[26] And White returns to a youth, not Wart but a young Tom Malory, who will learn and then inspire others to learn. In this ending, White suggests a different kind of return of Arthur from that hinted at in Malory, a return of the sort seen over and over again—in the literature and music and art created through the ages, a tradition to which White himself adds an innovative and experimental novel.

NOTES

1. Evans Lansing Smith, 'The Narrative Structure of T.H. White's *The Once and Future King*,' *Quondam et Futurus* 1.4 (Winter 1991), p. 39.

2. Cited in Sylvia Townsend Warner, *T.H. White: A Biography* (London: Jonathan Cape with Chatto & Windus, 1967), 187.

3. Cited by Elisabeth Brewer in *T.H. White's The Once and Future King* (Cambridge: D.S. Brewer, 1993), 17.

4. T.H. White, *Letters to a Friend: The Correspondence Between T.H. White and L.J. Potts*, ed. François Gallix (New York: G. P. Putnam's Sons, 1982), 109 and 111.

5. *The White/Garnett Letters*, ed. David Garnett (New York: Viking, 1968), 85–86.

6. Letter of Dec. 6, 1940, in *Letters to a Friend: The Correspondence Between T.H. White and L.J. Potts*, ed. François Gallix (New York: G. P Putnam's Sons, 1982), 120.

7. T.H. White, *The Once and Future King* (1958; rpt. New York: Berkeley Medallion, 1966), 312. All other citations to *The Once and Future King* will be to this easily available edition and will be given in the text by page number.

8. 'Anachronistic Humor in Two Arthurian Romances of Education: *To the Chapel Perilous* and *The Sword in the Stone,*' *Studies in Medievalism* 2.4 (Fall 1983), 73.

9. As Martin Kellman has observed, 'The tone [of *The Ill-Made Knight*], mostly somber, autumn and twilight, the season and time of transition, is appropriate because the lovers and the court are aging and maturing' (129).

10. T.H. White, *The Book of Merlyn: The Unpublished Conclusion to The Once and Future King*, Prologue by Sylvia Townsend Warner (Austin: University of Texas Press, 1988), 3. All other citations to *The Book of Merlyn* will be to this edition and will be given in the text by page number.

11. 'Flight to Aleppo: T.H. White's *The Once and Future King,*' *Mosaic* 10.2 (1977), 71.

12. *The White/Garnett Letters*, ed. David Garnett (New York: Viking, 1968), 86.

13. Cited in Sylvia Townsend Warner, *T.H. White: A Biography* (London: Jonathan Cape with Chatto & Windus, 1967), 187.

14. 'Some Comments on "T.H. White, Pacifism and Violence,"' *Connotations* 7.1 (1997/98), 129.

15. Martin Kellman, *T.H. White and the Matter of Britain* (Lewiston: Edwin Mellen Press, 1988), p. 103.

16. *T.H. White's The Once and Future King* (Cambridge: D.S. Brewer, 1993), 76.

17. *T.H. White* (New York: Twayne, 1974), 111–12.

18. *T.H. White and the Matter of Britain* (Lewiston: Edwin Mellen Press, 1988), 123.

19. Cited in Sylvia Townsend Warner, *T.H. White: A Biography* (London: Jonathan Cape with Chatto & Windus, 1967), 188.

20. *T.H. White* (New York: Twayne, 1974), 79.

21. *T.H. White: A Biography* (London: Jonathan Cape with Chatto & Windus, 1967), 182.

22. *T.H. White's The Once and Future King* (Cambridge: D.S. Brewer, 1993), 150. See also Martin Kellman, *T.H. White and the Matter of Britain* (Lewiston: Edwin Mellen Press, 1988), who observes that '... both volume one, *The Sword in the Stone*, and volume four would be weakened by the absence of material later donated to them from the abandoned book. Moreover, *Merlyn* is so different from them in style and tone and so uneven in quality that it would have been somewhat of a disruption, being too long for a coda.' Kellman adds: 'I believe White chose correctly when he did not include it in the 1958 edition of *The Once and Future King*' (131–32).

23. *T.H. White's The Once and Future King* (Cambridge: D.S. Brewer, 1993), 152.

24. *T.H. White's The Once and Future King* (Cambridge: D.S. Brewer, 1993), 164.

25. Elisabeth Brewer remarks that 'although *The Book of Merlyn* might seem to represent White's last word on the subject of Arthur, since it was not published until so long after the rest, his final revision of *The Candle in the Wind* before the tetralogy eventually appeared in 1958 enabled him to end it more judiciously and with more decorum. So, although it was not until November 1948 that White at last decided that he would have, in effect, to discard *The Book of Merlyn* and that he would insert the visits to the ants and to the geese into *The Sword in the Stone*, in doing so he surely made the right decision' (*T.H. White's The Once and Future King*, [Cambridge: D.S. Brewer, 1993], 150–51).

26. The 1958 ending also seems to resolve some of the 'schizophrenia' that Warner complained of. As John K. Crane observes, 'Though Arthur debates the improbability of perfection at great lengths in his tent in the final chapter, the fact that he seeks a boy to carry his message into the future seems to indicate that neither it nor the theme is one of fatalism and consequent resignation' (*T.H. White* [New York: Twayne, 1974], 115).

Character Profile

The legend of King Arthur is so pervasive in Western culture that it may be sketched out even by those who have read none of the relevant texts: this is the great archetypal leader of Britain; the king who proved his legitimacy by removing the sword from the stone; the founder of the Round Table, the greatest collection of knights ever assembled; the man betrayed by Queen Guinevere with the greatest of his knights, Sir Lancelot; the Once and Future King, mortally wounded but prophesied to return in the hour of England's need. The popular image of Arthur has been created by many writers over many centuries, and the story continues to be rewritten today.

Some argue that King Arthur has a historical source in a British general of the fifth or sixth century, while others have suggested that he is based on a Celtic sun god. While the origins of the character himself may remain somewhat murky, it is clear that the first major telling of the story of Arthur is to be found in Geoffrey of Monmouth's *History of the Kings of Britain*, completed circa 1136. In this highly fictionalized work of "history," the king is a larger than life character who once, in a single battle, killed 470 men. He is described as brave, generous, and religious, and is a great leader, galvanizing the British and conquering Europe. While he is fighting the Romans, Arthur's nephew Modred usurps the throne, leading to the battle in which Arthur receives a grievous wound. Taken to the Isle of Avalon to be healed—one day he will return, we are told—he is succeeded as king in Monmouth's telling by a series of less interesting men.

The influence of Geoffrey of Monmouth was both immediate and profound. In short order, many writers in England, France, and Germany were writing about King Arthur. Perhaps the most important of these early contributions to Arthurian literature is that of the French poet Chrétien de Troyes, whose romances—written in the second half of the twelfth century—give a detailed portrait of life at the court of Arthur. While Geoffrey of Monmouth describes the king's military conquests in great detail, he has almost nothing to say of his personal life. Adultery, which will tear apart his kingdom in future versions of the story, is not a major element in the story. (Geoffrey in fact briefly mentions that when Modred usurps the throne he begins an affair with Guinevere, but quickly adds that this is not the sort of topic about which he wants to write.) DeTroyes is the first writer—in *The Knight of the Cart*—to discuss Guinevere's affair with Lancelot, though in his story this does not lead to the destruction of the Round Table. He is also the first to associate Arthur's knights with the search for the Holy Grail. His stories of Guinevere's infidelity and the Grail quest are the primary sources for the *Lancelot-Graal*, the important prose compendium assembled sometime between 1225 and 1250. This work would in turn become the main source for the definitive telling of the story of King Arthur, that of Sir Thomas Malory.

Malory's *Le Morte d'Arthur* was published in 1485, and with it the popular story of King Arthur as we know it today was established. Malory's Arthur is, like Monmouth's, a great warrior, killing twenty and wounding another forty in one battle. In addition he is compassionate and honorable, and requires all his knights to swear the same oath: to fight only for just causes, to be merciful to the vanquished, and to always put the service of ladies first. Following *La Mort le Roi Artu*, the concluding work in the *Lancelot-Graal*, Malory gives the story of Arthur a tragic dimension, with the affair between Lancelot and Guinevere destroying the Round Table that the king has worked so hard to establish. Malory makes it clear that Arthur has known all along about Guinevere's infidelity—the wizard Merlin in fact had prophesied it even before their marriage—but has chosen to do nothing about it, partly because of the love he has for his wife and his favorite knight. It should be noted that Arthur's reasons for condoning the affair are also political: he astutely realizes that if the affair is made public, a crisis will ensue in which those knights loyal to the king will make war on those who choose to follow Lancelot, and that this confrontation will mean the end of his rule. When his treacherous nephews Modred and Aggravayne finally bring the affair out into the open, Arthur is forced to take action to preserve his dignity and authority, and this does indeed spell the doom of his kingdom. As in Geoffrey of Monmouth, the king is mortally wounded by Modred, and taken to Avalon. Malory mentions the legend of the king's survival, but says he does not believe it, and that in his opinion Arthur is indeed dead.

In denying the likelihood of Arthur's survival, Malory remarks that his own impulse is to let the king lie quietly in his grave, and in fact after the publication of *Le Morte d'Arthur* there is little Arthurian literature of note for well over three hundred years. This changes in the nineteenth century with the publication of Tennyson's immensely popular and influential *Idylls of the King*. The character of King Arthur—associated in some ways with the poet's fallen friend Arthur Hallam—had a lifelong fascination for Tennyson, and in the *Idylls* he uses the tragic dissolution of the Round Table as a metaphor for the spiritual malaise he sees dominating Victorian England. In his characterization of Arthur, Tennyson basically follows Malory, although some readers have been disappointed to find the Victorian king less "manly" and virile than in earlier versions of the story. Tennyson specifically mentions that Arthur has blond hair and blue eyes, physical details which are in contrast with other members of his family, and perhaps further the notion— implied several times by Tennyson—that the king has a supernatural origin.

The success of *Idylls of the King* touched off a new interest in the character of King Arthur, and led to a wave of Arthurian works that continues to this day. In the immediate wake of the *Idylls* Mark Twain published *A Connecticut Yankee in King Arthur's Court*, a fiercely American, "democratic" rewriting of the story in which Arthur mostly comes off as a well-meaning buffoon. More recently, twentieth-century readers have been fascinated by T.H. White's *The Once and Future King*, the Arthurian novels of Mary Stewart, the feminist reinterpretation of the story in Marion Zimmer Bradley's *The Mists of Avalon*, and even a well-received graphic novel, *Camelot 3000*, by Mike W. Barr and Brian Bolland. As early as Geoffrey of Monmouth the notion that Arthur will one day return had been a part of the legend; the rich history of writings on King Arthur—from Monmouth to the present, and undoubtedly on into the future—shows that this prophecy has not simply come true, but is continually coming true.

Works about King Arthur

Barr, Mike W. and Brian Bolland. *Camelot 3000*. New York: DC Comics, 1997.

Bradley, Marion Zimmer. *The Mists of Avalon*. New York: Knopf, 1983.

Chrétien de Troyes. *Arthurian Romances*. Trans. William W. Kibler and Carleton Carroll. London: Penguin, 1991.

Clemens, Samuel Langhorne. *A Connecticut Yankee in King Arthur's Court*. Ed. Allison Ensor. New York: Norton, 1982.

The Death of King Arthur (Mort le Roi Artu). Trans. James Cable. London: Penguin, 1971.

Geoffrey of Monmouth. *The History of the Kings of Britain*. Trans. Lewis Thorpe. London: Penguin, 1966.

Layamon. *Layamon's Arthur: The Arthurian Section of Layamon's Brut*. Trans. S. C. Weinberg and W. R. Barren. Exeter: University of Exeter Press, 2001.

Malory, Sir Thomas. *Le Morte d'Arthur*. Trans. Keith Baines. New York: Signet, 2001.

Marie de France. *The Lais of Marie de France*. Trans. Robert Hanning and Joan Ferrante. Durham: The Labyrinth Press, 1982.

Sir Gawain and the Green Knight. Trans. Brian Stone. London: Penguin, 1974.

Stewart, Mary. *Mary Stewart's Merlin Trilogy: The Crystal Cave, The Hollow Hills, The Last Enchantment.* New York: Morrow, 1980.

———. *The Wicked Day.* New York: Morrow, 1983.

Tennyson, Alfred, Lord. *Idylls of the King.* New York: Signet, 1961.

White, T.H. *The Once and Future King.* New York: Ace, 1987.

Contributors

HAROLD BLOOM is Sterling Professor of the Humanities at Yale University and Henry W. and Albert A. Berg Professor of English at the New York University Graduate School. He is the author of over 20 books, including *Shelley's Mythmaking* (1959), *The Visionary Company* (1961), *Blake's Apocalypse* (1963), *Yeats* (1970), *A Map of Misreading* (1975), *Kabbalah and Criticism* (1975), *Agon: Toward a Theory of Revisionism* (1982), *The American Religion* (1992), *The Western Canon* (1994), and *Omens of Millennium: The Gnosis of Angels, Dreams, and Resurrection* (1996). *The Anxiety of Influence* (1973) sets forth Professor Bloom's provocative theory of the literary relationships between the great writers and their predecessors. His most recent books include *Shakespeare: The Invention of the Human* (1998), a 1998 National Book Award finalist, *How to Read and Why* (2000), *Genius: A Mosaic of One Hundred Exemplary Creative Minds* (2002), and *Hamlet: Poem Unlimited* (2003). In 1999, Professor Bloom received the prestigious American Academy of Arts and Letters Gold Medal for Criticism, and in 2002 he received the Catalonia International Prize.

CELIA MORRIS is a writer of feminist non-fiction based in Washington, D.C. Her books include *Fanny Wright: Rebel in America* and her memoir, *Finding Celia's Place*.

STEPHEN F. LAPPERT received his PhD from the University of Pennsylvania. Before becoming a partner in the law firm of Carter Ledyard Milburn in New York City, he worked on the *Middle English Dictionary* published by the University of Michigan.

JOHN MICHAEL WALSH is Professor of English at St. Peter's College in Jersey City, New Jersey. He is author of *Cleanth Brooks: An Annotated Bibliography*.

ELLIOT L. GILBERT was Professor of English at the University of California-Davis with a specialization in Victorian literature. A leading expert on Kipling, he authored *The Good Kipling: Studies in the Short Story* and *Kipling and the Critics*, and edited *The World of Mystery Fiction*.

JOHN D. ROSENBERG is William Peterfield Trent Professor of English at Columbia University and has written on Alfred, Lord Tennyson, John Ruskin, Thomas Carlyle, and Walter Pater. He is author of *The Darkening Glass*, *The Fall of Camelot: A Study of Tennyson's "Idylls of the King,"* and editor of *Elegy for an Age: Essays in Victorian Literature*.

MARK ALLEN is Professor of English at the University of Texas-San Antonio. He is the co-author of *The Essential Chaucer: An Annotated Bibliography of Major Modern Studies* and author of *The Wife of Bath's Tale*.

E. KAY HARRIS is Associate Professor of English at the University of Southern Mississippi-Gulf Coast and author of "Lancelot's Vocation: Traitor Saint" and *Imagining Law and GenderDuring the Wards of the Roses: Treason and Retribution in Malory's* Morte Darthur *and Fortescue's* De Natura de Naturae Legis (forthcoming).

GEOFFREY ASHE is the leading expert in Arthurian studies and co-founder of the Camelot Research Committee. Among his many books are *The Discovery of King Arthur*, *King Arthur in Fact and Legend*, and *A Guidebook to Arthur in Britain*.

JOSEPH D. PARRY is Professor of Humanities, Classics, and Comparative Literature at Brigham Young University. His work has appeared in *Spenser Studies* and *Magistra* and includes "The Motion of the Soul and Spenser's *The Faerie Queene*, Book II" and "Margery Kempe's Inarticulate Narration."

CLINTON MACHANN teaches English at Texas A & M University and is the editor of *Kosmas*. He has edited books on Matthew Arnold and Katherine Anne Porter, and authored *Matthew Arnold: A Literary Life* and *The Genre of Autobiography in Victorian Literature*.

ALAN LUPACK is Adjunct Professor of English and Curator of the Rossell Hope Robbins Library and the Koller-Collins Graduate Center at University of Rochester. He has edited numerous editions of books on King Arthur and is the General Editor of the online Arthuriana/Camelot Project Bibliographies.

Bibliography

Alcock, Leslie. *Arthur's Britain*. New York: Penguin, 1971.

Adronik, Catherine M. *Quest for a King: Searching for the Real King Arthur*. New York: Atheneum, 1989.

Ashe, Geoffrey. *From Caesar to Chaucer*. London: Collins, 1960.

———. *King Arthur in Fact and Fiction*. New York: Nelson, 1971.

———. *Guidebook to Arthurian Britain*. London: Aquarian Press, 1981.

———. *The Discovery of King Arthur*. London: Guild, 1985.

———. "The Convergence of Arthurian Studies." In *The Arthurian Tradition*. Tuscaloosa: University of Alabama Press, 1988.

Ashton, Graham. *The Realm of King Arthur*. Newton, Isle of Wight: Dixon, 1974.

Atkinson, Stephen C. B. "'Now I Se and Undeirstonde': The Grail Quest and the Education of Malory's Reader." In *The Arthurian Tradition*. Tuscaloosa: University of Alabama Press, 1988.

Barber, Richard. *Arthur of Albion: An Introduction to the Arthurian Literature and Legends of England*. London: Boydell Press, 1961.

———. *The Figure of Arthur*. London: Longmans, 1972,

———. *King Arthur: In Legend and History*. Ipswitch, 1973.

Brengle, Richard L. *Arthur King of Britain: History, Chronicle, Romance, & Criticism (with Texts in Modern English, from Gildas to Malory)*. New Jersey: Prentice-Hall, Inc., 1964.

Bromwich, Rachel, ed. *The Arthur of the Welsh: the Arthurian Legend in Medieval Welsh Literature*. Wales: University of Wales Press, 1991.

Clancy, Joseph P. *Pendragon: Arthur and his Britain*. New York: Praeger, 1971.

Coghlan, Ronan. *The Encyclopedia of Arthurian Legends*. Rockport, MA: Element, Inc., 1991.

Donahue, Dennis P. "The Darkly Chronicled King: An Interpretation of the Negative Side of Arthur in Lawman's *Brut* and Geoffrey of Monmouth's *Historia regum Brittanie*." In *Arthuriana* 8, no. 4 (1998): 135–47.

Fife, Graeme. *Arthur the King: the Themes Behind the Legends*. New York: Sterling Publishing, 1991.

Goodrich, Norma L. *King Arthur*. New York: Harper & Row, 1986.

Jost, Jean E. *Ten Middle English Arthurian Romances: A Reference Guide*. Boston: G.K. Hall, 1986.

Kennedy, Beverly. *Knighthood in the Morte D'Arthur*. Cambridge: Boydell & Brewer, Ltd., 1985.

Knight, Stephen. *Arthurian Literature and Society*. New York: The Macmillan Press Ltd., 1983.

Lagorio, Valerie M. and Mildred Leake Day, eds. *King Arthur through the Ages*. New York: Garland Publishers, 1990.

Loomis, Roger Sherman. *Arthurian Tradition and Chretien de Troyes*. New York: Columbia University Press, 1949.

———. *Celtic Myth and Arthurian Romance*. New York: Columbia University Press, 1927.

———. *The Grail: From Celtic Myth to Christian Symbol*. Princeton: Princeton University Press, 1991.

———. "Oral Diffusion of the Arthurian Legend." In *Arthurian Literature in the Middle Ages*. Ed. Roger S. Loomis. Oxford: The Clarendon Press, 1959.

Mancoff, Debra N., ed. *The Arthurian Revival: Essays on Form, Tradition and Transformation*. New York: Garland, 1992.

———. *The Return of King Arthur: the Legend through Victorian Eyes*. New York: Abrams, 1995.

Merrill, Robert. *Sir Thomas Malory and the Cultural Crisis of the Late Middle Ages*. New York: Peter Lang Publishing, Inc., 1987.

Michel, Laurence. "The Possibility of a Christian Tragedy." In *Tragedy: Modern Essays in Criticism*, edited by Laurence Michel and Richard B. Sewell. Englewood Cliffs, NJ: Prentice-Hall, 1963.

Morris, Rosemary. *The Character of King Arthur in Medieval Literature*. Cambridge: D.S. Brewer, 1982.

Pickford, Cedric Edward, Rex Last and Christine R. Barker, eds. *The Arthurian Bibliography*. Totowa, NY: Biblio, 1983.

Pochoda, Elizabeth T. *Arthurian Propaganda: Le Morte Darthur as an Historical Ideal of Life*. Chapel Hill: the University of North Carolina Press, 1971.

Sheppeard, Sallye J. "Arthur and the Goddess: Cultural Crisis in the Mists of Avalon." In *The Arthurian Myth of Quest and Magic*, edited by William E. Tanner. Dallas: Caxton's Modern Arts, 1993.

Staines, David. *Tennyson's Camelot: "The Idylls of the King" and its Medieval Sources.*Waterloo, ON: Wilfred Laurier University Press, 1982.

Starr, Nathan Comfort. *King Arthur Today: The Arthurian Legend in English and American Literature 1901–1953*. Gainesville: University of Florida Press, 1954.

Taylor, Beverly and Elisabeth Brewer. *The Return of King Arthur: British and American Arthurian Literature Since 1800*. Cambridge: D.S. Brewer, 1983.

Thompson, Raymond H. *The Return from Avalon: A Study of the Arthurian Legend in Modern Fiction*. Westport, CT: Greenwood Press, 1985.

Vinaver, Eugene. "Sir Thomas Malory." In *Arthurian Literature in the Middle Ages*, edited by Roger S. Loomis. Oxford: The Clarendon Press, 1959.

Acknowledgments

"From Malory to Tennyson: Spiritual Triumph to Spiritual Defeat," by Celia Morris. From *Mosaic,* a Journal for the Comparative Study of Literature and Ideas 7, no. 3 (1974): 87–98. © 1974 by *Mosaic.* Reprinted by permission.

"Malory's Treatment of the Legend of Arthur's Survival," by Stephen F. Lappert. From *Modern Language Quarterly* 36, no. 4 (1975): 354–68. © 1976 University of Washington. All rights reserved. Reprinted by permission.

"Malory's Arthur and the Plot of Agravain," by John Michael Walsh. From *Texas Studies in Literature and Language* 23, no. 4 (Winter 1981): 517–34. Copyright © 1981 by the University of Texas Press. Reprinted by permission.

"The Female King: Tennyson's Arthurian Apocalypse," by Elliot L. Gilbert. From *PMLA* 98, no. 5 (1983): 863–78. © 1983 by the Modern Language Association of America. Reprinted by permission.

"Tennyson and the Passing of Arthur," by John D. Rosenberg. From *Victorian Poetry* 25, (1987): 141–50. © 1987 by Joseph D. Rosenberg. Reprinted by permission.

"The Image of Arthur and the Idea of King," by Mark Allen. From *Arthurian Interpretations* 2, no. 2 (Spring 1988): 1–16. © 1988 by *Arthuriana.* Reprinted by permission.

"Evidence Against Lancelot and Guinevere in Malory's *Morte Darthur*: Treason by Imagination," by E. Kay Harris. From *Exemplaria* 7, no. 1 (1995): 179–208. © 1995 Pegasus Press, New York. Reprinted by permission.

"The Origins of the Arthurian Legend," by Geoffrey Ashe. From *Arthuriana* 5, no. 3 (Fall 1995): 1–24. © 1995 by *Arthuriana*. Reprinted by permission.

"Following Malory Out of Arthur's World," by Joseph D. Parry. From *Modern Philology* 95, no. 2 (1997): 147–69. © 1997 by The University of Chicago. Reprinted by permission.

"Tennyson's King Arthur and the Violence of Manlines," by Clinton Machann. From *Victorian Poetry* 38, no. 2 (Summer 2000): 199–226. © 2000 by Clinton Machann. Reprinted by permission.

"The Once and Future King: The Book That Grows Up," by Alan Lupack. In *Arthuriana* 11, no. 3 (Fall 2001): 103–114. © 2001 by *Arthuriana*. Reprinted by permission.

Index